AFTER

A POST-APOCALYPTIC SURVIVOR SERIES

ORIGINAL STORIES BY

T.M. BROWN

DAVID GREEN

JAY SANDLIN

TIM MENDEES

CHRIS HEWITT

JOEL R. HUNT

HOLLEY CORNETTO

S.O. GREEN

EERIE RIVER PUBLISHING

HAMILTON ONTARIO

For those we have loved and lost and those still with us.
May we have the opportunity to do better tomorrow.

CONTENTS

Experience with us the terrifying possibility of a world rent asunder and the struggle to survive in a world AFTER.

An eight part mini-series:

Derelict
A Place Beyond the Storm
Quantum Rule
The Creeping Void
Heart of Thorns
Fading Echoes
Carry On
Sin Chaser

FOREWORD

"Our Earth is degenerate in these later days; there are signs that the world is speedily coming to an end; bribery and corruption are common; children no longer obey their parents; every man wants to write a book and the end of the world is evidently approaching."

These are the words carved into an Assyrian clay tablet dating back to 2800 B.C. Throughout human history, the end of the world has been prophesied and theorized hundreds, if not thousands of times. Monuments have been raised, books written, religions formed, and civilizations destroyed because of it. Every civilisation, every religion, every generation, believes it will see the end of the world. Call it Ragnarok, Armageddon, Maitreya or Al-Qiyamah or Kali Yuga. Everything that has a beginning must also have an end.

When faced with our own degenerate Earth—its natural disasters, its deteriorating climate, its zoonotic pathogens, its constant conflicts—and with future generations wondering what they will inherit, we did as the ancient Assyrians did. We wrote a book.

We wrote eight books.

We challenged eight Eerie River authors to imagine life AFTER the world we know is destroyed by a cataclysmic event, leaving our species on the brink and struggling to survive. In each of these stories you will find a new world, years after the old one was ravaged by war, disease, invasion, climate change or mythological event.

Remember, as you read: This is not our world. This is the world AFTER.

This is not a collection of stories about how the world ends.

These are stories of how humanity *survives.*

May you be forever entertained,
Michelle River

DERELICT

BY T.N. BROWN

CHAPTER 1
KINDLING

Mikaela sat on a precipice. Far below, humanity churned beneath a suffocating blanket of smoke and ash. Overhead, a sullen sky hung low and ominous. The city of Beacon sprawled before her, its overcrowded shanties clinging desperately to the face of a nameless mountain. In the heart of the city, a great chimney rose from a tangled assemblage of industrial structures and lesser smokestacks. The Hearth—as locals referred to the monolith—belched a black cloud into the slate-colored sky.

Beyond the gates of Beacon lay the lifeless, silty expanse of the Tidelands and, somewhere beyond that, the infinite horrors lurking beneath the waves of a dark and hostile sea. The grey sky met a grey wasteland on the horizon, muddling the distinction between the Earth and the heavens above. Even in a world forsaken by the gods, the Tidelands made for a singularly bleak vista.

"We should go back..." The words tumbled thoughtlessly from Mikaela's lips. They were directed at nobody in particular, but Donovan heard them and responded all the same.

"You know we can't." His voice was soft and measured—a characteristic common amongst members of House Repentance. "Not unless we have something for the Forge Masters."

"I know..." Mikaela sighed. Donovan wasn't telling her anything she didn't already understand. If Johanna and her Gatherers were not paid their due, there would be nothing to return home to. Tor—Johanna's chief enforcer—would make sure of that.

Long ago, Mikaela had visited the ruins of Walden before the smoke had settled and the charred bodies of its inhabitants could be laid to rest. The Gatherers had not bothered to hide their grisly work—quite the opposite. It was intended for all to see. Fire was the gift of the Forge Masters and it was fire they brought to Walden. Her home of Solstice was not so dissimilar from that ill-fated settlement. It would burn just as easily.

The elders whispered of a time before the Forge Masters, but Mikaela could imagine no such existence. For as long as she could remember, the residents of Solstice had harvested on behalf of their distant overlords and offered monthly tribute in the form of timber. Now, as Mikaela approached her twenty-fourth summer, the forests surrounding her home were all but gone. Johanna and the Forge Masters didn't care. The Hearth needed fuel and Solstice owed tribute.

The fates of Mikaela and her companions had been sealed the moment the Gatherers arrived to collect Beacon's tribute. At that moment, the six men and women from Solstice ceased being humans and became kindling—mere property of Forge Master Johanna and fuel for the Hearth. Whether or not the term was purely metaphorical was a matter of macabre debate amongst the settlement's residents.

"They'll be coming soon." Kira's eyes darted between Mikaela and her fellow travelers. "What are we going to tell them?"

She had always been high-strung—always eager to take things on but unlikely to see them through. In this scenario, however, Kira's nervousness could be forgiven. The most likely outcomes for Mikaela and her companions were not good.

In the best-case scenario, they would be permitted to live out the remainder of their lives toiling on behalf of the Forge Masters in the soot-choked streets of Beacon. If rumors were to be trusted, they were more likely to be pitted against one another, forced to spill the blood of lifelong friends in a desperate bid to ensure their own survival. Their only reward would be isolation, unrelenting pain, and—in the end—madness. The survivors would ultimately become what they had once feared and loathed: the soulless, mindless creatures known as Embers. The mere thought of such a fate left Mikaela sick to her stomach.

"We'll tell them nothing," Donovan replied in a reassuring tone. His features were weathered but his expression remained warm. "We'll tell Johanna the truth."

"And what exactly is that, Van?" Anders snapped. Overgrown, ruddy hair hid the young man's unwashed but otherwise handsome features. "We don't have a plan. We belong to Johanna now. She can do whatever the hell she wants with us and we can't do shit about it." He took a long drag from his cigarette and the group fell silent. "The sooner we all accept it, the better."

The truth in Anders's words did not sit well with Mikaela and she felt herself compelled to speak. "I know something they don't."

Anders scoffed. "Yeah?"

"Yeah." Mikaela extended her hand and gestured for Anders to hand over the cigarette. The young man rolled his eyes but complied. Mikaela inhaled and paused for a moment as she imagined the nicotine flowing through her arteries. "Yeah, I do."

"And did you plan on telling us?" Kira needled.

"Honestly…" Mikaela smiled and took another drag of the cigarette. The smoke she exhaled mingled with acrid, polluted air. "I didn't really plan on it."

"You…" Kira's mouth hung open in disgust. She struggled to find her words. "You're such a bitch, Mikaela. What's wrong with you?"

Anders smiled and removed another cigarette from the pocket of his faded leather duster. "I hope whatever you're holdin' on to is real good." He flicked his lighter open and conjured a tiny, wavering flame. "For all our sakes."

"Really, Mikaela?" Donovan flashed a look of disapproval in her direction. He took Kira by the shoulder and guided her back toward Stefan and Freja.

Of course, Mikaela was lying. She didn't know anything. The only thing she had up her sleeve was a single word whispered into her ear by Matthias Ekman, one of the settlement's elders, immediately prior to her departure from Solstice. While he was well-respected within the community and Mikaela had no reason to suspect he was lying, she had no idea what "Colossus" meant. For that matter, she had no idea if the word meant anything at all.

After decades as a prominent figure in Solstice, Matthias had grown frail and increasingly incoherent. His days apart from the Earth dwindled.

The thought of sharing the word with her companions had passed through Mikaela's mind on the journey to Beacon. Perhaps it would mean something to one of them? The desire to share such potentially valuable information, however, was fleeting. As devoted members of House Repentance, Freja and Donovan were trustworthy enough, but Kira was spineless and Anders had a rakish, untrustworthy reputation. Stefan was little more than a stranger. Better to retain every possible advantage than risk betrayal.

The odds, after all, are already stacked against me.

For the moment, Mikaela had no better plan than to simply blurt out "Colossus" if things got bad enough and try her best to bullshit from there. It wasn't a good plan—or a plan at all, really—but it was likely better than anything her fellow kindling had to offer.

Mikaela's cigarette dwindled and a bitter wind swept in from the abyssal wastes beyond. The summers in this forsaken land were fleeting and the nightly frost now lingered well into midday. The Tidelands' only bearable season dangled by a thread. Further up the mountainside, the eternal flames of Beacon's namesake tower twisted in the harbinger gale. Mikaela's reticence to share her single scrap of hope with her companions bought her a moment's solitude prior to the arrival of Johanna's enforcers. She inhaled a final dose of nicotine and raised her collar against the gathering cold.

"Mikaela!" Stefan called, from somewhere behind her.

The wrought iron gates surrounding Johanna's compound groaned and four figures wielding long rifles filed out from within. The kindling of Solstice rose nervously to their feet. Stefan's hard blue eyes met Mikaela's.

"It's time."

...

After being escorted through the compound's yawning entrance and a maze of ascending corridors, Mikaela and her companions entered a grand solarium. The air within was damp and warm. It smelled of freshly tilled soil and flowers. Every Forge Master possessed at least one such greenhouse, but few common folk ever had the opportunity to experience them first-hand. It was breath-taking and otherworldly, but not the sort of place anyone wished to find themselves.

The lives of vassals meant little to a Forge Master and, rumor had it, Johanna was particularly prone to violence. Even the most innocuous interaction could be deadly.

The solarium's glass-paned exterior soared three stories overhead and hanging plants draped from two tiers of balconies on either side of a central plaza. The vegetation was nothing like the scraggly, gnarled shrubs and conifers that eked out an existence in the rugged terrain of the Backveld. Their leaves were supple and delicate—likely to wither at the mildest frost or blow apart in the slightest breeze. Flashes of vibrance sprouted from amongst the verdant surroundings and tiny, colorful birds flitted from the branches of alien trees. Was this a reflection of the Earth that once was?

The contrast of the fantastic world contained within the Forge Master's glass bubble and the grim landscape outside was nearly impossible to reconcile. For a moment, the beauty of the solarium was sufficient to distract Mikaela from the dire reality of her situation. The reprieve was short-lived.

Shadowy figures lurked amongst the shade of the balconies and leafy canopy. At the plaza's terminus, several lounge chairs circled a babbling fountain. Only the most prominent of these chairs was occupied. Forge Master Johanna looked on as the small procession of enforcers and kindling approached. Several armed guards and various lounging courtiers occupying the surrounding balconies took casual note of the party's arrival.

A hulking mass of scarred flesh stood a few feet away from Johanna. Mikaela had only seen Tor once, but the freak was unmistakable. The image of it standing amidst the smoldering ruins of Walden had been burned into her mind since childhood. The monster pulled apart bodies and used them to festoon the burned-out husks of the settlement's few remaining structures. It had appeared so serene in the performance of its grisly task—so at peace. Tor had haunted her childhood dreams from that moment forward.

As years passed, Mikaela grew to suspect that her traumatized childhood imagination had somehow warped a mere human into a monster. To her horror, she now found Tor to be even less human than she recalled— too large and mutated to be real. Yet here it was, standing before her; a nightmare brought to life amidst a background befitting her most fantastic dreams. Its chest was branded with Johanna's all-too-familiar saw and axe insignia, as if the creature was some form of livestock. Pale, dead eyes stared unblinkingly at Mikaela and her companions as they approached.

The vaguely human monstrosity drew a stark contrast to the Forge Master herself. Johanna, while not exactly young, could not have been over forty and was strikingly beautiful. Her skin was deep ebony and her curly hair spilled out from a perfectly fitted, steel crown. Several jagged tines extended upwards on either side of the crown's pronounced central spike, topped with a brilliant orange gem. Mikaela had long been told that the Forge Masters' crowns represented the skyline of Beacon but had never actually seen one. Like the solarium itself, its composition was simultaneously beautiful and menacing.

"They say it's like stepping a hundred years into the past." Forge Master Johanna rose from an intricately-carved wooden chair. She scanned the kindling gathered before her. Tor mechanically shadowed each of her steps at a slight distance. When nobody responded to her comment, she continued. "Fragile though... Much too fragile for this world. Such a tenuous existence... It's no surprise that it didn't last."

Johanna summoned them forward with a wave of her hand and lifted a delicate crystal champagne flute from a nearby table. An odd assemblage of bracelets on either arm jangled with her every move. Mikaela and her six companions complied, forming a rough semicircle around the central fountain. Their escorts peeled away into the shade of the greenhouse perimeter.

"Speaking of tenuous existences..." The Forge Keeper took a sip of her drink. "Where is it you were from? Walden?"

"Solstice, Forge Master," Donovan responded, in reverent tone. "We're from Solstice."

"Ahhh... That's right. I suppose I'm getting ahead of myself. A woman in my position must be looking forward and the trajectory of your little wallows... Well... There are a lot of similarities." Johanna flashed a cruel smile. "I'm afraid your tragic tales tend to bleed together over time."

Mikaela felt anger welling up inside her. She tried to push the image of Tor effortlessly stripping limbs from charred bodies. She tried to forget the smell of burnt flesh and the helplessness of witnessing such atrocities as a small child. The past and the present were much the same. There was nothing she could do—neither then, nor now. She just needed to stay alive.

Mikaela unclenched her fists and held her tongue.

"So, when can I expect my kindling?" Johanna arched an eyebrow and awaited a response. Mikaela and several of her companions exchanged nervous glances. There was an extended period of silence before Donovan spoke for the group.

"We are this month's kindling, Forge Master."

Johanna nodded and took another drink. "The arrangement with your settlement is for fuel, not bodies. Does it look like Beacon needs more mouths to feed?" She gestured toward what Mikaela could only guess was the bulk of the city. The labyrinth of passages leading to the solarium had left her thoroughly disoriented and the overgrown garden blocked any view aside from the brooding clouds overhead. When Johanna failed to receive a response, her expression grew dark and she stomped a heeled boot against the ground. "Well? Does it?"

"No, Forge Master..." Mikaela and her companions mumbled in unison.

"No..." Johanna's face brightened as quickly as it had soured. "Fortunately for you, there was a recent accident in the ironworks and I've shouldered the burden of replacing a large share of the loss. You lot are a good start."

Mikaela felt an immediate sense of relief wash over her. While the prospect of a life in the ironworks would typically be something to despair, it was the best possible outcome given her predicament. Besides, the city of Beacon was tumultuous and teeming with humanity. It was an easy place to disappear—particularly if nobody cared to look. She could keep her head low and feed a furnace for a time. Whether in Beacon or in the Backveld, she could still forge her own destiny. Her relief was just as evident on the faces of her fellow kindling.

"Thank you, Forge Master." Kira spoke as if she had been holding her breath. "We'll work hard."

"I have no doubt." Johanna finished the contents of her glass and placed it back on the table. She raised a polished, antique revolver with a mother of pearl grip in its place. The Forge Master deftly snapped open the cylinder. Her cruel smile returned. "You do know why I always request six, don't you?"

None of the kindling responded but Johanna carried on with her task all the same. She selected a single upright cartridge from the table, loaded it into one of the revolver's six chambers and snapped the cylinder shut with a practiced flick of her wrist.

"As I said, your timing is fortunate... But I can't have the entire Backveld thinking they can skip out on their tribute and expect a job, now can I?"

Johanna spun the cylinder until it stilled, then let it rotate forward on her finger. She held the pistol away from her with a single finger in the trigger guard.

There was a certain, cold logic in the Forge Master's rationale that Mikaela understood and, at some level, could appreciate. One in six. Not the worst odds. The residents of Walden hadn't been offered such a courtesy.

Tor collected the pistol and approached the gathered kindling. It opened its palm and offered the revolver to Freja. Its massive hand made the weapon appear tiny.

"Take it," Johanna instructed in a playful tone. "The sooner we get this done, the sooner we can all move on with our lives. I'm sure there's a foreman somewhere eager to put you all to work."

Freja took the pistol with a trembling hand and Tor positioned itself behind her. The monster's figure dwarfed the waifish young girl and Mikaela could smell the stench of burnt flesh on it, even from that distance. Freja's expression remained resolute. She took a deep breath, placed the revolver's barrel to her head and pulled the trigger.

Click.

Johanna smiled. "See... Don't you feel better now that's over with?"

Freja only gave a faint nod in response and handed the pistol to Stefan without looking him in the eye. Tor followed the revolver along the line. Freja may have felt better but Mikaela certainly didn't. She liked the girl well enough, but her own odds of survival had just gotten worse. One in five.

Stefan took the pistol and examined it for a moment. His hands shook worse than Freja's.

"No peeking," Johanna cautioned. "There's no solace in knowing one's fate."

Stefan gulped then aimed the revolver at the Forge Master. Tor grabbed his arm and wrenched it violently back. Sinew tore, bone snapped, and Stefan screamed in pain. He pulled the trigger at empty air.

Click.

Johanna burst into laughter as Tor pressed her would-be-assassin into the ground with its immense weight. It took her a moment to regain her composure. "Yes! Yes! Oh, it's been a while since anyone had the balls to try something like that!" She gestured for another drink and a colorfully-garbed attendant fulfilled the request, slinking back into the shadows when his task was complete. "An Ember for certain!"

Shaken from their complacency, the guards on the surrounding balconies now took aim at Mikaela and her companions. The Forge Master took several steps forward and knelt to meet Stefan's wild gaze.

"You will know so much pain." The glee in Johanna's voice was gone, and her tone turned spiteful. The erratic ebb and flow of the Forge Master's temperament was dizzying. "Pain like you've never imagined. If you emerge on the other side, you will be reborn. You will come to see the order in this chaos—the truth in the purifying heat of the flame."

Johanna picked up the revolver and stood.

"Who knows, perhaps you may even become the new Tor. An Ember, after all, is a gift from the Hearth itself. Such a gift cannot be expected to burn forever."

The monster pressed Stefan into the polished floor one final time before turning its attention to Kira. The broken man did not stand. He merely curled into a ball. The Forge Master offered Kira the pistol.

Mikaela felt her stomach tightening. One in four.

"Your turn, my child."

Tears streamed down Kira's face. "Forge Master... I-I can't..."

"Of course you can, darling." Johanna pressed the pistol into her hand. "Let's get this finished up, shall we?"

"I..." Kira's lips quivered. "Mikaela," she sputtered. "Sh-she knows something. Something important."

That bitch. All she had to do was pull the damn trigger and take her chance. In a moment of weakness, Kira had accused Mikaela of withholding information she didn't even know.

The Forge Master's burnt copper eyes narrowed. "This information, your friend has... You don't know anything about it yourself?"

"No..." The weeping continued. "But Mikaela can tell you. It's something you would want to know. Sh-she told me herself!"

The Forge Master brushed back an errant lock of Kira's auburn hair. Her voice turned cold. "But it's not Mikaela's turn, now is it?"

Kira broke into uncontrollable sobbing and the pistol clattered to the floor. The Forge Master sighed and picked it up.

"How embarrassing." Johanna aimed the pistol at Kira's head and pulled the trigger.

A gunshot echoed through the solarium. Blood and grey matter erupted from the back of Kira's head, painting Tor's broad, scarred torso. The bullet had almost certainly passed through its target and struck the monster, but Tor didn't even flinch. Kira's body crumpled into a heap on the floor next to Stefan.

"Well, thank goodness that's done," Johanna said cheerily, wiping an errant fleck of blood from her cheek. "I could scarcely stand the tension."

That should have been it. Their debt paid, Mikaela and her three remaining companions should have been escorted out of the Forge Master's compound, down the mountainside, and on to the ironworks to begin the next miserable stage of their lives. Stefan's fate was unlikely to be as merciful but there was nothing she could do about that. Mikaela would have begun plotting her way out of the ironworks before she even arrived.

Instead, Kira had opted to roll the dice. She'd called all their lives into question. Except her own.

Johanna had already proven herself unstable and ruthless. Mikaela had no idea what to expect if she tried to speak. The Forge Master might have them killed to cover up the information, or just kill them in a fit of rage. Perhaps she would become frustrated with Mikaela's lies and kill them because of that. Maybe she'd have them executed for merely wasting her time.

If Mikaela tried to withhold the information or lie, the outcome would likely be even worse. What if Johanna decided to have them all transformed into creatures like Tor? Bile began to rise in the back of Mikaela's throat.

"So..." The Forge Master approached Mikaela with the spent revolver still in hand. Her expression teetered precariously between curiosity and annoyance. "You have something you'd like to tell me?"

"I do," Mikaela replied, in the calmest tone she could muster.

Heavy footsteps padded against the marble floor behind her. Charred, dry flesh scraped with each of Tor's steps. Mikaela didn't turn to look, but she could feel its malign presence and smell the pungency of death. Tor's body radiated an unwholesome warmth.

"A single word, Forge Master." Mikaela tried her best to ignore the stench of the monster's curdled breath. "For your ears only."

Johanna furrowed her brow and exchanged a sharp glance with Tor, granting the creature permission to tear her apart if she so much as flinched.

"Alright, dear. Let's hear it."

Johanna's bracelets rattled as she leaned forward and held a hand to her ear. There was no point in lying now. The die had been cast.

"Colossus," Mikaela whispered.

The Forge Master rose, expression confused. "Is that it? Should that mean something to me?"

Mikaela's throat tightened. "I-"

"You what?" Johanna's expression darkened. "Is it a person? A place? A codeword of some kind? " The copper in her eyes burned with intensity. "Are you *threatening* me?"

She pressed the barrel of the empty revolver against Mikaela's forehead and Tor's inhuman hand clamped around her shoulder.

"Speak, child!" she shrieked.

Whatever lies Mikaela had thought up seemed suddenly insufficient. Her expression hardened and she determined to tell the truth. She mouthed the words, *I don't know*, but her voice failed her. It was like her own body refused to let her speak.

Johanna withdrew the pistol and stepped back. The Forge Master threw up her hands and scanned the now-crowded balconies surrounding them.

"Colossus!" she yelled. "Do any of you useless parasites know who Colossus is?"

There was no response beyond the fervent shaking of heads and confused shrugs.

"*What is it!?*"

Johanna walked to the table and snapped open the revolver's cylinder. She plucked another two cartridges from the table and thumbed them into the waiting chambers. This time, she did not bother to give it a spin.

"Last call for Colossus?"

She paused a moment as she waited for a response from the crowd. No such response was forthcoming.

"And you?" She pointed the pistol at Mikaela and drew back the hammer. "Anything?"

Words stuck in her throat and the power of Tor's grip pressed into her shoulder. She was a child again, amidst the ruins of Walden. Far too little had changed since then. All Mikaela could do was keep a brave face. She wouldn't die blubbering like Kira. She glared defiantly at the Forge Master.

"Wait!" A voice cried out from somewhere on the second balcony. "I recall!"

A bent, old man tottered excitedly down one of the second-floor balcony's twin staircases. Courtiers and guards parted to let him pass as he approached the Forge Master. Johanna lowered the gun and redirected her icy gaze toward him.

"Shouldn't you be in the library bent over some scraps of paper?"

The old man seemed unflustered by the venom in her tone. "Perhaps if you spent a bit more time reading those scraps of paper and less time pulling the wings off butterflies, you would understand a bit more about the world, hmm?"

He let out a pained groan as he seated himself in one of the lounge chairs surrounding the fountain.

"So, what is it that you recall exactly?"

The old man seemed confused by the question, as if suddenly lost within his own mind. "Sorry, dear. Recall what now?"

Johanna exhaled slowly, closed her eyes, and rephrased the question. "Grandfather." She placed the pistol back on the table and took him by the hand. "What is it that you recall about Colossus?"

"Ah, yes!" The old man's eyes brightened. A smile formed amidst his wrinkles. "Before Beacon and the Parched and the ice... Before the skies were dark... Everything was different. The oceans were bigger then and men crossed them without fear. They built massive, floating machines as great as Hearth, itself."

"Grandfather, please." Johanna's voice remained warm, but it was clear her patience was wearing thin. "We can talk about history later. *Colossus*, remember? What is it? Why would it matter to us now?"

"I was getting there! Now listen!" He leaned forward in his chair, smiling proudly through rotted teeth. "Those sea machines had names. They're in my books. The largest of them carried the blood of the Earth itself—enough to power an entire city for years, maybe longer. Colossus was one such machine. I recall the name. It must have stuck with me for a reason! A blessing from the Earth itself and such timing-"

"You did well to remember, Grandfather." Johanna seemed eager to put an end to the rambling. "Anything else you can tell me about this machine?"

"A steel behemoth of monstrous proportions—an entire city capable of riding the waves." The old man's smile faded. "The sea claimed most such constructs long ago. Those that remained were consumed by Gatherers. Whether such a prize still exists, I cannot say..."

The old man's voice faded away. His expression became serene and then absent. Johanna squeezed his hand and turned her attention back toward Mikaela.

"This Colossus of yours... Where is it? If it remains intact, you may have done Beacon a great service."

"The Tidelands," Stefan groaned, before Mikaela could speak. He struggled to sit upright on the floor, cradling his shattered arm.

Johanna scoffed. "The Tidelands are vast. You'll have to do better than that."

"Several days travel to the North. I've seen it with my own eyes, Forge Master. The Colossus is just as your grandfather described."

Johanna considered Stefan's words. Before she could speak, a rail-thin courtier garbed in form-fitting attire approached from the shaded canopy. His arms were covered in geometrical tattoos, the fashion in Beacon's lower wards. His vest's high collar left his movements unusually rigid. He flashed Mikaela a knowing glance before turning his attention to Johanna.

"A word, Forge Master..." His voice was polished and smooth as the solarium's marble floors. "If you please..."

Johanna scowled but waved him over nonetheless. The courtier leaned in close and whispered into the Forge Master's ear. Mikaela couldn't make out his words, but he carried on for some time. Johanna's annoyance faded and, when the courtier finished speaking, she acknowledged him with a faint nod.

Unlike the guards and retainers, he did not withdraw into the shadows when his business concluded. Instead, he poured two glasses of effervescent liquid from a crystal decanter. He handed one to the Forge Master. The other he kept for himself.

Johanna turned to the group. "You're wasting my time with children's stories." She downed her drink in a single, unrefined gulp. The courtier refilled her glass. "I should have you all executed for impertinence, not to mention troubling the mind of a tired, old man."

Tor's grip on Mikaela tightened in anticipation of the command. At least a dozen assorted long guns trained their barrels on what remained of Solstice's kindling.

"But, as I said, your timing is fortunate and the need in the ironworks is great. They just can't seem to get enough bodies these days."

The pressure on Mikaela's shoulder relented and the monster behind her took a step back. A murmur spread amongst those gathered on the surrounding balconies and guards closed in from across the solarium. Tor grabbed Kira's corpse by an ankle and dragged it away, leaving a trail of blood in its wake. Stefan was escorted wordlessly into an adjacent antechamber, his expression fixed in hatred and defiance. What gruesome fate awaited him, one could only imagine.

Mikaela, Donovan, Anders, and Freja were ushered out the way they came. All the while, the Forge Master looked on and sipped her champagne.

Mikaela replayed the image of the bullet piercing Kira's forehead and the pressure of Tor's gnarled, inhuman hand against her flesh. For the first time in as long as she could remember, she had to blink back tears. Nobody seemed to notice but she felt ashamed. She could scarcely believe that she was still alive.

CHAPTER II
BEACON

The meandering journey to the Olander Ironworks felt like a bad dream. Mikaela and her fellow kindling were loaded onto one of several dozen cable cars condemned to climb and descend the mountainside in perpetuity. As they approached the city-proper, the sprawling compounds of the elites gave way to an unruly jumble of tumbledown structures, electrified billboards, and exposed ducting. The residents of Beacon streamed down narrow roadways below.

The ironworks complex was tucked away amongst an assemblage of virtually indistinguishable, soot-stained tenements and industrial structures near the very heart of Beacon. Smoke assaulted Mikaela's every breath and ash accumulated like fresh snow in the district's claustrophobic streets. Brick walls ornamented with tangles of rusty barbed wire separated the city's downtrodden residents from the less fortunate souls imprisoned within.

Upon their arrival at the compound, the party was greeted by a grizzled foreman who failed to introduce himself by name. His face remained obscured behind a singed beard and badly tarnished goggles. The Foreman recorded their names, ages, and places of origin in a greasy ledger. When the task was complete, the Forge Master's armed escort withdrew and the compound's heavy iron gate closed behind them.

The ironworks themselves were cauldrons of stifling heat, grating metal and the stink of sweat. Each of the compound's six sections centered on a towering blast furnace which devoured raw ore and shat pig iron. The other forges, holding furnaces, and molds refined the molten metal into pipes, beams, rivets, and rails that fueled the city's relentless growth. Anders and Donovan were assigned the role of pouring 3000-degree metal into molds. Mikaela and Freja were made to feed Blast Furnace 4 an endless stream of coke, ore, and flux.

Mikaela and her fellow kindling had arrived late in the day and their first shift ended with merciful swiftness. A whistle sounded from somewhere amidst the oppressive smoke and she followed the stream of exhausted workers as they shuffled into the cold night air. She stood in line to receive a ladleful of thin soup. She couldn't bring herself to eat and offered her meager rations to an emaciated coworker. The man looked confused by her generosity and slurped the food down without a word.

The allotted mealtime lasted only a few minutes, then the thralls of Blast Furnace 4 were ushered into a dreary barracks. It took Mikaela time to find an unoccupied bunk and her search ultimately led her to the draftiest corner of the room. The night air which had initially offered relief from the stifling heat of the furnace grew uncomfortably cold. A chill worked its way into her bones and she withdrew beneath a threadbare blanket. The events of the day and reality of her new existence weighed heavily upon her. Seeking relief from the cold and her thoughts, Mikaela closed her eyes and tried her best to sleep.

Had Stefan actually known the location of Colossus or had he lied, trying to save his own life? Mikaela's memories of the day were vivid but fragmented. She tried to recall the moment he'd spoken. She had grown adept at distinguishing truth from fabrication and Stefan's words struck her as genuine. He was a mysterious figure, having only arrived in Solstice a few months back. It made sense to assume he *might* possess information beyond that of most residents.

But why had Stefan volunteered as tribute in the first place and why had he been so eager to kill the Forge Master? Had assassinating Johanna been his plan all along? What had the thin, tattooed courtier told his master? Johanna had seemed quite interested in Colossus before the two had spoken. Had something changed?

Neither answers nor relief came to her. She drifted into a restless, nightmare-riddled sleep.

In her feverish dreams, Kira died time and time again. Stefan's bones cracked and Walden burned. Tor stripped limbs from freshly cooked bodies as if they were made of tissue paper. The loop replayed over and over until it was no longer Kira or Stefan that suffered—it was Mikaela. The bullet pierced her brain and Tor twisted her arm until there were no bones left to splinter. It was no longer Walden, but Solstice, that burned, and Mikaela was consumed right along with it. She tried to scream but found herself unable. She choked on her terror the same as she had choked on her own words earlier that day. She was powerless and bore the overwhelming pain in silence.

"Mikaela." A voice echoed in the flames. "Mikaela, wake up."

A cold hand shook her from her nightmare.

"Wake up," the delicate voice repeated.

Mikaela opened her eyes. Kira leaned over her, blood dripping from the bullet hole in her forehead. Mikaela screamed the scream that had been withheld through dozens of excruciating deaths. She shot up in her bunk and struck her head on the iron frame above.

"Mikaela, relax! It's me... Freja."

"What?" Mikaela struggled to regain her senses. "Kira... I thought you were Kira..."

"It's just me." Freja squeezed Mikaela's shoulder with an icy hand. "Are you alright?"

"Yeah... Yeah, I'm fine." Mikaela touched her head and felt blood trickling from where she'd struck the bedframe.

"We'll deal with that later. You need to come with me."

Rows of occupied bunks stretched into the gloom. Someone coughed further toward the barracks' entrance but nobody else stirred. Had her scream woken no one? Had she screamed at all?

"Freja... It's the middle of the-"

"We have a visitor." Freja's gentle voice turned stern and she crept toward a sliver of light filtering in through the barracks door.

Mikaela rose and followed, throwing the blanket around her shoulders for warmth. Four figures huddled together in a shadowy corner of the ironworks' central courtyard. The goggled Foreman paced several yards beyond them. The courtyard was otherwise empty. She approached and recognized Anders' hushed voice as she drew near. Freja and Donovan were also in attendance. She didn't recognize the fourth figure.

"About time..." the stranger whispered, shattered teeth glistening in the dim light. "Like I was tellin' your friends, there are still some keen on findin' Colossus. It's your lucky day."

Mikaela was in no mood for games. "And you're going to break us out of here to do it?"

"No need to break you out. You're the property of Forge Master Johanna. She can do as she likes with you. And she'd like for you to prove Colossus exists." The stranger spit a wad of phlegm on the hard-packed earth. He reached into a satchel and withdrew a small glass vial. "Here, take this... And don't even think about comin' back until it's full of the earth's blood or whatever it is the Forge Master expects to see."

"Such a task will not be quick." Anders accepted the vial on behalf of the party and brushed back his greasy hair.

"Take as long as y'need." The stranger shrugged. "But know that Solstice will burn if you're not back by the end of the week."

The party turned their eyes on Mikaela. Her head was throbbing, and she felt like she might pass out. Mikaela had no idea where to find this Colossus and one week left little time for aimless wandering. Besides, if this wrecked machine was indeed located in the Tidelands, the search was tantamount to a death sentence. The endless, shifting mire had been abandoned by all but the most desperate scavengers and delusional zealots. The Tidelands belonged to the Parched now.

"That's not enough time," Mikaela insisted, after a lengthy pause.

"That's not my problem," the stranger said. A revolting smile returned to his stubbled face. "Hell, maybe it's not even yours... Maybe none of you come back. The Forge Master clearly sees you as the respectable, community-minded sort. Tough to get a good night's sleep with that amount of blood on your hands I imagine."

Though Mikaela could not recall having been described as 'respectable' or 'community-minded' before, the residents of Solstice had been good to her. The thought of betraying them was not even a remote consideration.

"Fuck you," she hissed.

"Is that an offer?" The stranger let out a self-satisfied chuckle. "Everything you need for your little journey is waiting below Salvation Bridge. Just follow the canal downhill and look for the angels. You can't miss it."

Without Stefan, Mikaela knew she had no chance of finding Colossus in a week. She had been the one to mention the damn thing in the first place and the rest of the party expected her to lead the way. What they didn't know was that they needed Stefan if they were to have any hope of filling that vial. She could only hope the fool hadn't been lying when he'd claimed to know the wreck's location in the Tidelands.

"Fine," Mikaela said.

"Good." The stranger slapped Donovan on the back as if they were lifelong friends. "I figured you to be smart folks."

"But I need Stefan."

The stranger's good humor evaporated. "Fraid' that's not possible, miss. He's already begun the transformation."

"I don't care. We've listened to your terms. These are ours."

Donovan and Anders looked doubtful, but they said nothing. Freja remained obscured in shadow.

"I don't think you appreciate the gravity of your situation. Stayin' at the ironworks isn't an option." The stranger crossed his arms tightly and rested them atop his protruding gut. "Spose' ya find a knife in your back one o' these nights?

"Suppose you have to tell the Forge Master that you failed your task," Anders interjected. "I don't know her particularly well, but she didn't strike me as the sort who reacts well to bad news."

The stranger's eyes narrowed. "Your friend is beyond useless now... He's dangerous. Besides, his transformation was ordered by the Forge Master herself. He tried to kill her. She'll never approve his release."

Anders shot Mikaela a look. He didn't want to push Johanna's messenger any harder. Mikaela could only hope her companions viewed her increasing desperation as a selfless desire to free a friend.

"We wouldn't expect her to," Mikaela said. "I hear most don't survive the transformation and Stefan was already wounded. If he dies, he becomes an offering to the Hearth. Gone forever, without a trace..."

The stranger rubbed his stubbled chin in contemplation and nodded. His eyes fixed on Mikaela's. "Let me ask you... Do you really think you can find this Colossus? Do you really plan on comin' back?"

"We do," Donovan said, with the blind certainty only a devout

Penitent could conjure. Mikaela was happy not to answer that particular question.

The stranger shook his head. "You lot are dumber than I thought... Fine, I'll get your friend, but you've done a lot of talkin' and not much listenin'. Return to Beacon within the week with a filled vial and make sure your friend goes and gets himself lost somewhere—permanently. There's only one way this ends well for you and a whole lot of ways it don't."

He held up a crooked finger. "If you fail to come back, Solstice burns." A second finger went up. "If you return to Beacon with an empty vial, you all die and Solstice burns." A third finger. "If we get the slightest whiff that you've tipped off the folks back home as to what they've got comin', Solstice burns." A fourth finger went up, this one severed just above the middle phalanx. "If your friend ever steps foot in Beacon again-"

"I get it," Mikaela grunted. "Solstice burns and we all die. It's a pretty consistent theme."

"I spose' you're right. The stranger's shattered smile cut a swath through his stubbled cheeks. "It *is* a consistent theme, isn't it?"

He waved over the Foreman and pressed a small leather pouch into his hand when he arrived. The Foreman gave an understanding nod.

"Best get back to bed. You've got a long few days ahead of you. If you fools actually survive out there, you can find me at the Hoarfrost. Ask for Örjan." The stranger donned a worn workman's cap and swaggered toward the front gate. "Oh, and since you so rudely interrupted me before... If you try to go direct to the Forge Master about any of this? Well, that consistent theme you so rightly mentioned still applies."

He departed through the compound gates and the Foreman ushered the kindling back into the barracks.

Mikaela curled up under her blanket and closed her eyes. She did not sleep well.

...

"That has to be it..." Freja said, but she did not sound entirely convinced.

"The messenger said angels. Do those look like angels to you?"

Donovan pointed toward the nearest of four sculptures flanking the bridge. Each was stained black and crumbling. If they had once been angels, they had long since fallen from grace. The bridge was an old stone construction. Both its architectural flourishes and considerable wear suggested it predated Beacon's foundation.

The Bowery in which they found themselves was the lowest in elevation and therefore nearest to the Tidelands—a relic of a time when humanity valued proximity to the water. The retreat of the ocean and the arrival of the Parched had changed all that, however, and Bowery now found itself home to the least desirable of Beacon. Day-laborers, prostitutes, invalids and orphans huddled together amongst the crumbling cement and stone ruins of an old city being slowly digested by its successor.

In a time before Mikaela or her parents or even the Solstice elders were born, a star fell from the heavens. There was a great conflagration and the sky—once blue—turned forever grey. Ash fell like snow in the early days and the world grew cold. The seas withdrew and the Parched returned from beneath the waves. Life along the coast became untenable and what remained of humanity abandoned the towns and cities long-established along the shorelines, retreating inland toward the relative safety of higher elevations.

The forsaken, abyssal plain between the remaining waters and the ruin-strewn coast came to be known as the Tidelands. The stretch of abandoned civilization that had once defined the shore was now the Ghostlands and the highland interior became the Backveld. Hundreds of small communities like Solstice eked out a living in the Backveld, competing for dwindling resources. The city of Beacon stood alone, protected by its high walls, firearms, and Embers, at the intersection of the three regions. The coal mines in the surrounding hills proved too valuable to abandon and the shadow of the old world now loomed in the Bowery.

"I get it, Van. The angels have seen better days, but this has to be the bridge." Anders turned and scanned the street for signs of life. "We're getting close to the city walls and this is the only one we've seen that's even close."

Donovan shook his head. "I know you're right. I just..."

His voice trailed off as he gazed into the inky blackness beneath the bridge. The party did not possess a light source and there was an understandable reluctance to make the descent in search of the promised supplies. The city was generally secure but the Parched were rumored to gain access to the drainage canals during high tide. If any dwelled within Beacon's walls, this was exactly the sort of place they would be.

While there was considerable disagreement regarding the origins and motivations of the Parched, a few facts were widely agreed upon. First was the process by which they were created. Before a child was even old enough to leave the house, they had already been taught that the monsters began as humans who had been corrupted by the fallen star. The vector of the disease varied but it was typically the result of ash-tainted food or drinking water.

The infected initially demonstrated unsightly but otherwise mild symptoms. Their skin turned pale, their eyes developed a milky haze, and their vision blurred. They quickly developed an unquenchable thirst, and as they consumed an increasing amount of water, their bodies bloated, and their skin grew paper-thin. It was the thirst that gave the Parched their name.

The infected became fixated by water and lost interest in basic human functions including speech. Left to their own devices, they would ultimately submerge themselves in the nearest body of water. In those lakes, rivers, oceans, and swimming pools, the unfortunate souls drowned and extinguished the last flickering light of their humanity. Where a person died, a Parched was born.

The creature would stir to a cruel facsimile of life in a matter of hours. It would seek increasingly deeper, darker waters and disappear from the surface world for years—even decades. As time passed, they would be forgotten. Winters would come and go, and the lives of their loved ones would move on. Meanwhile, the Parched fed and underwent a slow metamorphosis beneath the waves. Every day, less human, more monstrous.

When they returned, the Parched were unrecognizable. Each was different, shaped by the disparate conditions of their rebirth, but all were horrible to behold. Some were covered in scales, others in a thick mucus membrane. Still others acquired the pseudo-transparent flesh of a maggot. Their eyes widened to inhuman proportions and their pupils morphed into narrow slits or runny-egg, amorphous blobs. Incisors, canines, and molars were replaced with rows of close, packed, needlelike teeth. Some retained a shambling, bipedal stride while others—perhaps more evolved—crawled about on disjointed, vestigial limbs.

A second widely agreed upon fact about the Parched was that the disease, once acquired, was irreversible. Any attempt to prevent the infected from reaching water led only to madness and death—either by self-inflicted wounds or internal trauma. The miserable souls would tear themselves apart to consume their own blood as a source of fluid and were not averse to killing anyone that intervened. Unfortunately, vestiges of humanity remained. Bereaved loved ones often remained convinced the victim could recover, until the moment their lungs ceased drawing breath.

A final, more fortunate, fact regarding the Parched was that they could only survive out of water for a limited time. This generally meant that, as people abandoned their homes near the water, the overall risk posed by the monsters decreased. The effort made to dredge the highland lakes of the Backveld had been bloody but productive and most of the region's inhabitants no longer lived in fear of the Parched. The best strategy for survival in this world was to avoid unnecessary risk and entering dark, ill-maintained drainage canals seemed like inviting trouble.

"Fine," Mikaela volunteered. "If none of you cowards will do it, I will."

"Mikaela, wait." Donovan appeared hurt by the accusation. "There's no need to put ourselves at risk. Morning won't be long. We can go together once we have light."

"We're running out of time," Mikaela said firmly. "I'm climbing down. You can join me or not. Your choice."

Donovan and Freja exchanged concerned looks. Anders put his hands in his pockets and shrugged.

"Good luck down there," he said. "If you run into any Parched just scream and I'll offer words of encouragement from up here."

Freja sighed. "Fine, I'll go. We're on this path for a reason, though I don't yet know why. Some help you men are."

She glared at Anders and Donovan. The latter, somewhat expectedly, caved. "Fine," he said plaintively. "I just think this is a bad idea."

Mikaela sighed as she lowered herself down a fissure in the sheer, stone embankment. "If you're uncomfortable with this..." She struggled momentarily to find a proper handhold. "Well, it's only going to get worse from here."

She had spent the last day peddling half-truths or outright lies. It felt comforting to tell her companions something in which she was reasonably confident.

Mikaela, Freja, and Donovan struggled down the embankment and gathered just outside the point where dim light faded to black beneath the bridge. The canal reeked of industrial runoff, rotten flesh, and shit. A shallow, contaminated stream coursed over algae the consistency of flowing hair. The low, unbroken gurgle of the water was the only sound. The surrounding streets were deathly quiet and devoid of life. Twenty feet above, Anders gave them an enthusiastic thumbs up.

Such an asshole.

Mikaela scooped up the most wieldable stone she could find as a primitive means of self-defense and stepped into the gloom. Donovan and Freja trailed close behind. In the absence of any other sound, the babbling of Beacon's sewage was maddening. After several minutes probing through the darkness with an outstretched foot, Mikaela's boot struck something with less give than stone. She recoiled instantly.

"Who's there?" she demanded, raising her stone overhead. "I've got a gun. I'll shoot if you don't speak up right now!"

Her grip on the damp stone was tenuous and if she didn't strike quickly, it would slip from her grasp.

"Wait," a voice, wavering but familiar, said from the darkness. "It's me... It's Stefan."

Mikaela's stone struck the ground. The sound of the impact echoed through the canal. "Stefan?" She couldn't remember ever being more relieved to hear another person's voice. "Are you alright?"

"I'm fine..." Stefan coughed, "or I will be. Our mutual friend left some goodie bags for ya."

The party pulled Stefan and four backpacks into the tenuous streetlight around the canal. The bags were filled with several days' worth of supplies: protein cakes, filled canteens, oil lamps, and several small pouches of coins emblazoned with a fiery beacon. Each also included an assortment of tools and, most importantly, a letter of free conduct stamped with Forge Master Johanna's saw-and-axe insignia. The letter would permit the party access into and out of the city but ended promptly in seven days' time.

Stefan was weak and in considerable pain. His right arm was broken in several places and his face was plastered with hastily prepared bandage, already saturated with blood. His wound seeped across his strained features. Singed flesh around his dressings suggested burns. Bad ones. The fact that he was coherent at all was surprising. Perhaps the Forge Master's messenger had been right about him being a dangerous liability.

"I don't know what you all did to get me out of there…" Stefan looked right through them as he spoke. "But thanks. I don't know if I… Just, thanks."

"Of course," Donovan smiled warmly. "Turning people into monsters is no way to atone for our ancestor's sins against Gia. I must confess though, your release was entirely Mikaela's doing. She's a truer friend than she lets on." He clapped a meaty hand against Mikaela's back. "I'm afraid I misjudged her."

If Donovan knew I only risked Stefan's release because I needed directions to Colossus, I'm not sure he would be so generous with his praise.

Whatever Mikaela's motivations, the outcome had been the same. Stefan was alive as a result of her actions. A good deed had been done and her credibility had increased. She took solace in that. The hard part would be getting a burn victim to lead them to the machine without revealing to her companions that she had no idea what she was doing.

Mikaela forced a smile. "I'm glad to have you back, Stefan. But Solstice's time is running out and we need to get moving."

A stone clattered to the base of the canal and splashed into a pool of sewage. Mikaela looked up to see Anders making his way down the embankment toward the rest of the party—no doubt eager to secure his share of the loot. She directed her attention back toward Stefan.

"Are you alright to walk? As far as Forge Master Johanna is concerned, you're dead and we need to get you out of Beacon as fast as possible."

Stefan rose to his feet unaided but winced in pain. Mikaela gave him a nod of approval and brushed what she assumed was ash from her sleeve, only to have it melt away. She looked up to see countless snowflakes drifting soundlessly to the earth. Summer dwindled and Mikaela could only hope Solstice's days were not similarly numbered. Best not to think too hard about it.

A sharp, briny wind whistled through the canal and sent a shiver creeping down Mikaela's spine. Somewhere, far beyond the walls of Beacon, amidst the lifeless Tidelands, the Colossus beckoned.

...

The land immediately outside of Beacon had been stripped of anything useful long ago and the party spent the better part of the day traveling through the wastes that remained. The coastal road would have been a more direct route, but the tide was in and the risk of running into roving bands of Parched was too great. Instead, the five travelers took a crumbling ancillary road which wound through the rugged hills of the Backveld. Ravens shadowed their journey and heckled them from perches amidst the barren, rust-colored hills. Whatever settlements had once existed here had long since been abandoned. Only brooding husks remained.

The party occasionally passed small groups of grim-faced merchants and armed patrols. A convoy of six Gatherer trucks rattled past early in the day. None paid the kindling much mind, and all carried on toward Beacon's increasingly distant flame without speaking a word in greeting. As the day drew on, the group strung out in a meandering procession. Mikaela seized the opportunity to speak with Stefan alone.

Given Stefan's poor physical state, he would no doubt be eager to leave the party at the nearest friendly settlement they encountered. Mikaela needed to convince him to continue leading the group, or at least give her detailed directions to the Colossus. It was not a conversation she was eager to have in the presence of others.

Despite being gravely injured, Stefan pressed forward with surprising vigor and Mikaela was out of breath by the time she caught up to him.

"Stefan..." Mikaela gasped. "How are you holding up?"

"Fine," Stefan responded flatly, continuing his steady pace.

She took a moment to regain her breath. "You seem to be doing better."

"I feel like shit."

"Well, you seem to be getting around well." Mikaela continued but Stefan said nothing. "Do you plan on continuing on with us? Into the Tidelands?"

"I appreciate everything you and the people of Solstice have done for me, but no... I feel like something is tearing me up from the inside out." He adjusted the bandage on his broken arm. "Astrid's Roadhouse shouldn't be more than an hour away. You can get a good night's sleep there and somethin' warm for your bellies. I'm afraid that's as far as I go."

"Stefan... We could really use your help. I'm sure you'll feel better-"

He stopped walking and turned to her. His uncovered eye was piercing. "You don't know where you're going do you?"

"I..." Mikaela was taken aback but saw no reason to maintain the lie any longer. She cast her gaze downward. "No."

Stefan nodded slowly. Pus ran down his exposed cheek. "I suppose that's why you got me out..."

"Stefan, I-"

"Makes sense," he interjected. "I was trying to figure it out."

"You don't have to keep going." Mikaela looked to see if anyone was close enough to overhear. Freja was approaching but still out of earshot. "I just need to know how to get there."

Stefan resumed walking along the disintegrating asphalt road and Mikaela followed. "You won't make it," he growled. "It's at the very edge of the Tidelands."

"Just tell me how to get there. I'm sorry but we don't have a choice."

"I'll go! That's what you wanted, isn't it?"

She wanted to object, but Stefan's outburst had already attracted the attention of the others. Their conversation hadn't gone the way she'd hoped, but she wouldn't refuse his help. And if he elected not to repeat what she'd said to the others, it was the best possible outcome for which she could have hoped. She'd lived long enough to know when to keep her mouth shut. She ignored Freja's curious gaze and continued the journey in silence.

The grey sky darkened, and the air turned cold. After cresting a steep ridge, several dozen low structures came into view. A small settlement nestled into the crease of a narrow mountain valley, as if seeking to hide from the outside world. Only a single building showed any sign of habitation. A dull glow emanated from inside. The others were dark and silent.

The corpse of a village straddled the roadway to Beacon and blackened windows kept ominous vigil over the southern approach. There was not a tree in sight and tangles of thorny shrubs were the only vegetation to grace the grim hollow. The single occupied building in the settlement squatted near the intersection of two main roads: one leading to Beacon and another trailing off to the East, deeper into the Backveld. The road-house—like all the surrounding buildings—was a relic of the old world. It was in a poor state and had been kept from total ruin only by cannibalizing its neighbors.

The Astrid's interior was pleasantly warm, illuminated by the soft, orange glow of firelight. Two small groups of haggard-looking travelers cloistered themselves at tables on opposite ends of a common room. One of the parties appeared to be freelancers. The other wore overcoats emblazoned with a faded cog-and-caliper emblem of a Forge Master that Mikaela didn't recognize. Individuals sat scattered but similarly hunched over a well-worn bar. The plump woman behind the counter wore a cheerful expression despite her tired features and the roadhouse's otherwise gloomy atmosphere.

The group ordered food and drinks then settled into a table near the warmth of the fireplace. Mikaela was relieved that none of the patrons seemed to pay them much mind. These were hard times and she was not interested in answering any unwanted questions.

As they waited for their food to arrive, Mikaela's attention was drawn to the severed, vaguely-human head glaring down at them from atop the mantle. Its gaping mouth was fixed in a primal scream and lined with hundreds of needle teeth. Several human molars remained toward the back of its mouth, displaced remnants of human anatomy. Its eyes were gone, leaving only grossly oversized, hollow pits of menacing black. Desiccated flesh clung tight to the skull.

Mikaela had never seen a Parched—even a dead one—quite so close before. It was grotesque and unsettling, yet she found her gaze drawn to it. Judging by the silence of the others, the remainder of the party felt the same.

"You like that, do ya?" a gruff voice asked from across the common room. Mikaela and her companions ignored the man, but he carried on anyway. "Yup, found that one crawlin' up the creek on its belly just up the road from here."

A barstool scraped against the floor and creaking floorboards indicated the man's approach.

"Just north of here, actually... Now which way were you folks headed?"

"North," Freja volunteered. "Good thing you've cleared the path."

Mikaela broke eye-contact with the ghoulish mantelpiece and shot Freja an irritated look.

The man chuckled. He was a big fellow with an unkempt beard and flushed cheeks. Judging by his slight sway, he was already well into his cups. "Not much north of here except the Tidelands..." His brow furrowed. "I think you're a bit turned around."

"Must be," Anders agreed, but it was too late. Freja spoke over him.

"That's exactly where we're going."

The disapproving looks from the rest of the party finally tipped Freja off that she'd said too much.

"We're salvagers..." she lied feebly.

The big man looked unconvinced. "Uh huh..."

He took another gulp from his dented steel flagon. One of the travelers seated nearby looked up from his companions and Mikaela felt compelled to redirect the conversation.

"The Parched," Mikaela gestured toward the severed head above the mantle. "You said you found it?"

The drunkard's eyes brightened. "Ah yes," he said proudly. "Killed it too."

Mikaela flashed a smile and used the most flirtatious voice she could conjure. "Well, it must not have been that tough then."

The big man responded with a lecherous, drunken smile of his own. "Tough enough to kill two men," he said, without a hint of pity. "Big fellas too. Tore their guts right out and started eatin' right there in front o' me!"

He took another swig of whatever it was he was drinking and wiped his beard with his shirtsleeve. He leaned across the table, ignoring everyone but Mikaela.

"Rumor has it the monsters are starvin'."

"Alright, Christer, that's enough of all that." The bartender approached with several steaming bowls on a serving tray. "I never should have let you put that disgusting thing up there."

Christer flashed Mikaela a smile and stepped back from the table.

"Don't worry," the bartender added pleasantly, as she placed the bowls on the table. "We've hired additional security. You're plenty safe here at Astrid's."

She withdrew to the bar but Christer lingered. "Now, what was it you all were planning on salvaging? I'm always in to make a bit-"

"Actually," Mikaela interrupted. "I'd be much more interested in hearing about how you killed the Parched. If you're willing to buy me a drink first."

Christer's self-satisfied grin returned. He chuckled to himself and departed toward the bar. Mikaela glared at Freja and the girl cast her gaze into her soup. Anders smiled knowingly as he watched the exchange. Donovan looked concerned and kept glancing at the ghoulish head watching over them. Only Stefan seemed unfazed by the whole ordeal, gulping at an overfull flagon and slurping his soup.

The boiled cabbage and unspecified protein were warm if not particularly tasty. The greasy, metallic tang of blur—a crude, distilled spirit common throughout the Backveld—was foul but familiar, and it helped ease Mikaela's nerves. The night wore on and Christer grew increasingly handsy. Fortunately for Mikaela, the hairy brute had not paced his drinking and ended up passing out on the dingy floorboards. By the time she retired upstairs, only Anders remained in the common room, drinking and carousing with the locals.

That fool better be ready to depart at first light.

As she closed her eyes to sleep, she couldn't help but suspect this ruined settlement had once been similar to Solstice. How long ago had Beacon bled it dry and left a husk in its wake?

She imagined the city as a great kraken, its tendrils—fueled by the Hearth—coiled around dozens of settlements. Once drained of life, the tentacles would stretch further, ensnaring yet another community in its vampiric embrace. How much longer would it go on for? How long *could* it?

The alcohol and exhaustion lulled her but the visions of violence returned. The feeling of powerlessness followed. For the seventh night in a row, Mikaela did not sleep well.

CHAPTER III
COLOSSUS

The descent from Astrid's into the Tidelands was relatively easy. Rugged mountains gave way to a thin strip of forsaken civilization, and beyond that, barren mudflats stretched for as far as the eye could see. Several small hillocks topped with the skeletal remains of trees broke the otherwise featureless horizon. The ocean no longer reached this far, even at high tide, but rainwater and runoff from the nearby mountains kept the plains damp throughout the fleeting months of summer. A wrong step and they'd be trapped in the sucking mire.

The freeze and thaw of the seasons left the ground they trod especially tenuous. Stefan's wounds were infected and his flesh grew sallow, yet he continued to guide the party through the treacherous wastes. He was clearly experienced in navigating the Tidelands and Mikaela quietly wondered what he was keeping from them. But she was hung over from a night of drinking and the last thing that sounded appealing was a drawn-out conversation. She pressed on in silence, the endless mire and relentless wind contesting her every step.

Grey faded to black. Stefan led the group up one of the lonely hillocks to shelter amongst the wind-worn stones and leafless corpses of long-dead trees. Upon finding a small depression sheltered from the wind, he dropped his bag and took a long drink from his canteen. Mikaela and the rest of the party followed suit.

"The tides don't make it quite this far," Stefan said wearily. "But the

Parched almost certainly will. Stay quiet and make sure your tarp covers you completely." He took another drink from his canteen and winced as his cracked lips contacted the rim. "They don't like to leave the moisture of the sands if they don't have to. Let's make sure we don't give em' a reason."

"Should we take turns on watch?" Donovan asked. "You know, to make sure we all get enough sleep."

Stefan shrugged. "If it makes you feel better..." He stowed his canteen and began rummaging through his bag. "Personally, I wouldn't bother. Stay out of sight and mask your heat as best you can. These Parched... They're different than the ones you're familiar with."

"Different how?" Mikaela asked.

Stefan produced a hammer and began driving stakes into the ground. "They come from deeper places... Darker places..." His uncovered eye met Mikaela's. "Just get your shelter up. High tide won't be long."

They did as Stefan instructed and spent the night in the shelter of the hillock. Despite her exhaustion, Mikaela couldn't sleep. A cold rain set in several hours after dark. As her consciousness alternated between dreams and reality, she swore she could make out a low, sonorous melody intermingled with the steady thrum against her tarp. It was a haunting, primal sound, unlike anything she had heard before, and it left her profoundly disturbed. She spent the rest of the night longing for a sleep that would never come.

By the time the muted daylight of the Tidelands finally arrived, Mikaela was packed and ready to depart. Stefan looked worse than ever and the entire party seemed like they'd joined her in lying awake all night. They gathered their supplies in the rain and departed the hillock without speaking a word. She did her best to ignore the hundreds of malformed footprints in the nearby sands.

Rain and sleet persisted throughout the day, and whipped at them on the scouring wind. The hills, with their stands of broken trees, dwindled as they progressed into the Tidelands, replaced only by endless, abyssal sands. Evidence of the ocean—tangled seaweed, rotten fish, and the husks of crustaceans—littered the ground before them. Near the day's end, Stefan led the party up a final, forlorn rise. Judging by the barnacle-riddled stones, it would scarcely break the surface of the water at hightide.

Stefan cautioned the party once more about the dangers the tide would bring and they did their best to shelter among the damp stones. The song of the Tidelands returned with the night and the Parched followed shortly after. The creatures were closer this time—much closer. It wasn't just their song Mikaela could make out. She could hear the scraping of claws against the stones now.

Long after nightfall, as the waves crashed against their tenuous shelter, one of the Parched oozed onto a rock only feet from Mikaela. Scaly flesh raked the stone and brushed against her tarp. She tightened her grip on the small knife that constituted her only defense and held her breath. The creature reeked of brine and rot. Through a narrow gap in her shelter, a dull bioluminescence glinted on teeth the length of human fingers. The primal song of the Parched was deafening. She could *feel* its hunger.

The creature continued along its path. The stench lingered for a time but even that receded. The tide withdrew hours later. The ghastly tune and the darkness followed but took longer than Mikaela would have liked. When she emerged from her shelter, she couldn't steady her shaking hands. The expressions on her companions' faces were not just weary. They were haunted.

Anders pressed that they return to the Ghostlands, but relented when no one was willing to accompany him. Stefan seemed to be wasting away. His features sagged and his flesh was ghostly white. Freja offered to change his bandages but he refused. With no medication to offer, there was nothing anyone could do but encourage him to keep drinking and try to keep his spirits up. For all the good that would do.

It was two hours into their day's journey when they first spotted the Colossus. At first, it was little more than a silhouette, obscured by swirling ice and snow. As they drew closer, however, the true enormity of the derelict became increasingly apparent. The Colossus was a giant amidst an otherwise featureless landscape. Only when the party gathered in the shadow of its immense bow, could Mikaela fully appreciate the machine for the wonder it was.

The Colossus was long-forsaken, stained with rust and painted white with the excrement of seabirds. Its enormous hull remained intact and soared what must have been at least a hundred feet above the surrounding wastes. Excluding Beacon's Hearth, it was larger than any building Mikaela had ever seen. She could scarcely imagine such a monstrosity moving under its own power. If this vessel still contained its original fuel, Johanna's eagerness for it was understandable. Any Forge Master would kill for such a prize.

There was no time to bask in the vessel's ruined glory. The tide would return shortly, and the Parched with it. Freja removed a grappling hook from her backpack and handed it to Donovan. After several failed attempts, the line cleared the vessel's hull and found purchase on the railing high above.

Donovan pulled at the rope and gave a nod. "One at a time. The last person can tie the bags on so we can pull them up."

Anders had a slender, muscular build and was an obvious choice to make the ascent first. He reached the railing without incident and called for the next of them to follow. As Freja prepared to make the climb, Anders leaned over the railing and yelled, pointing frantically at the horizon. Mikaela squinted to see what had gotten him so riled up.

There were dozens of figures shambling through the haze toward them.

Anders' frantic warning sent the rest of the party into a panic. They closed in on the rope all at once. Freja made the climb quickly. Mikaela tried to climb with her backpack, but the rope was slick and the weight was too great. She dropped her supplies in the sand.

The Parched were too close. There was no saving their packs. When Mikaela reached the deck of the Colossus, she could make out dozens of them converging. The low, haunting tune which had reverberated through her mind over the past two nights was replaced by a menacing, rapid pulse. The change in tempo left no doubt that their party had been spotted and the Parched were closing in for the kill.

After Donovan completed the climb, Stefan hurriedly tied the rope around himself and the party hauled him onto the deck. Once Stefan was safely onboard, Mikaela peered back over the railing and saw several Parched clawing at the hull. Unblinking eyes stared up at her with a hunger that would never be satiated. Their mouths opened and closed in ravenous anticipation of the meal to come. Hundreds more swarmed to join them.

The otherworldly drumbeat of their collective hunger was maddening.

Mikaela covered her ears, but it did no good. The song of the Parched originated from within.

After gaining their bearings, the party withdrew to the vessel's aft and climbed a staircase up a great tower. Stefan claimed that the soaring structure contained the crews' dwellings and 'bridge'—though he failed to explain what, exactly, a bridge was doing inside an enclosed tower. Snow scoured these upper decks and gulls screeched in protest as Stefan disturbed their long-established roosts.

Upon reaching the top of the stairway, Mikaela made her way to an overlook that offered a commanding view of the surrounding wastes. Innumerable Parched closed in around the Colossus like flies on a rotting corpse. The sea was not far behind.

"Mikaela..."

The falling snow grew thick and the song of the ocean lured her gaze toward the gathering horde.

"Mikaela!"

She turned to find Stefan leaning heavily against an open door. Donovan and Freja had already disappeared into the shadowy interior. Anders stood with his brow furrowed, his weathered duster whipping in the wind. Stefan's voice was strained, barely audible over the primal chorus that echoed through Mikaela's mind.

"Get your shit together!" He nodded toward the doorway. "Come on."

Mikaela complied and followed Anders into a large, window-lined room. Paint peeled from metal walls. The surfaces were crowded with hundreds of knobs, buttons, shattered screens, and dials, like the barnacles on the hull. Decades of accumulated salt and grime left the windows opaque. Those that were intact only emitted a sickly yellow glow. Wind howled through two that were shattered on the far side of the room.

Donovan sat on the floor, resting his considerable weight against the wall. Freja inspected a strange assemblage of buttons, clearing a thick layer of accumulated filth with her gloved hand. Stefan closed the door behind them and the air that had coursed through the chamber died away. Errant flecks of snow circled the area in momentary defiance before settling to the cold, steel floor.

"What is this place?" Anders asked.

"It's the ship's bridge," Stefan responded, in the tired but knowing voice of an elder. "The crew would control the machine from here."

"Imagine such a thing…" Donovan chuckled, his eyes closed. "The hubris of our ancestors…"

"It's an offense to Gia," Freja added. "If this machine is truly filled with Her blood…" Tears welled in her eyes. "We'll never be free of our curse as long as such desecration remains."

"I'm not sure what, exactly, you expected." Anders said. "Besides," he peeled a long strip of paint from the wall, "this pile of scrap won't last too much longer. The sea will get her back soon enough."

"I just didn't think it would be so…" Freja's voice trailed off.

"So what?" Anders plucked a pack of cigarettes from his pocket. "So big? It's kinda in the name isn't it? I mean, Colossus? Seriously? Do you think anyone would give a shit if we were talking about a couple buckets of the stuff?"

"I-I don't know what I thought…" Freja tightened her grip on one of the control panel's knobs. "This place is just…"

"We're on the edge of oblivion, Freja!" Anders struggled with his lighter. "This place belongs to the Parched now! You say Gia wants it back! Well, she already has it!"

He gave up on his attempt to light a cigarette and tossed it away in frustration.

"Nobody comes out here!"

"We did," Mikaela interjected. "And he did before us." She pointed accusingly at Stefan. "Why in the name of the gods would you ever come out to a place like this?"

Stefan suckled greedily at his canteen. Only when he'd drained it did he look at Mikaela. "Rumors," he said. "Rumors and desperation."

The light in his eye was fading. Dried puss accumulated at the periphery of his bandage.

"There have been people seeking the Colossus for a long time and it was winter." He stared blankly at one of the shattered windows. "The ice made things easier."

"Mikaela's right," Anders grunted. "You know something you're not telling us."

"I do. I know a lot of things I'm not telling a lot of people. Sometimes it's for the best."

Mikaela decided not to push further. Anders folded his arms, unconvinced.

"Listen…" Stefan lowered himself to the floor with a groan. "I got you here, didn't I? Your town took me in and I volunteered as kindling in return for their kindness. You saved my life and I will make sure you fill your vial with the blood the Forge Master wants so badly. There's no need to overcomplicate our relationship. I'm a man that pays his debts." His expression hardened. "I'm afraid I can't say the same for all of you…"

"Fine." Anders dismissed the conversation with a wave of his hand. "What now?"

"Get some rest. You're safe here and we won't be going anywhere until the tide goes out. Search the crew quarters for anything useful if you like, but we cleaned most of it out years ago."

"And the vial?" Mikaela asked. "Shouldn't we fill it now?"

Stefan shook his head. "You'll want the light of day for that and its already getting dark. Once we open the tank, you won't want any flames near your God's blood. There's a reason Beacon's so thirsty for the stuff."

An uncharacteristic smile graced the sharp contours of his face.

"It burns."

…

For the first time in over a week, sleep came easily for Mikaela. She was exhausted from the journey and the call of the Parched was softer at these heights. If anything, the song only served to lull her from consciousness.

But the nightmares returned and thrust her back into the bleak world from which she sought to escape. Awake, the cold and discomfort prevented her from finding sleep again. The faint smell of cigarette smoke wafting in through the windows lured her outside.

A shadowy figure leaned over the railing. A tiny orange ember was the only light in the darkness. Mikaela made her way to Anders and joined him at the railing. Far below, countless bioluminescent eyes fixed unblinkingly upon them. Cruel, malformed claws raked against the hull in a futile effort to ascend the Colossus. The glowing orbs shifted endlessly in the roiling sea. Anders placed a cigarette in Mikaela's hands without saying a word.

"You think your drunk friend back at the roadhouse was right?" Anders asked. The smoke he exhaled was carried away on a bitter wind.

"Right about what?" The nicotine and fleeting warmth of the smoke she inhaled offered momentary relief from the cold.

"About them starving..."

"Maybe." She took another drag of the cigarette and considered the question. She recalled the creatures gaping, mindlessly opening and closing jaws. "Maybe it's just the way they are."

Anders nodded slowly. "Maybe."

"I wonder what happened to the crew... You think they made it out of here?"

"Who knows?" Anders replied. He took another long drag of his cigarette and exhaled. "They might be down there right now. Kinda funny when you think about it. I imagine they were pretty desperate to get off this wreck. Now they're tryin' real hard to get back on board."

The hollow eyes bobbing in the waves parted unnaturally. The dark water glowed as if illuminated by some ethereal light. The disturbance snaked its way through the drifting Parched with the ease of something very much at home in the sea. Whatever lurked beneath those waves was massive and ancient. Its song was in tune with that of the Parched but also different. It was older, deeper, and tinged with sorrow.

The ocean belonged to such monsters now and neither Anders nor Mikaela said a word to acknowledge its presence. Eventually, the ghost light dissipated and Parched filled the gaps left in its wake. Anders finished his cigarette and tossed the remains to the waiting mouths of the creatures below.

"You can hear them too, right?" Anders finally broke the silence between them.

"Yeah."

"Good." Anders brushed greasy hair away from his eyes. "I was starting to think I was losing my shit."

"I didn't say you weren't." She half-forced a smile.

"You know..." Anders' face remained enveloped in darkness, but Mikaela could make out the characteristic smirk in his voice. "You don't have to go back... We don't have to go back."

Mikaela sighed. "Yes, we do. We can't just abandon our home...our families."

She took a final drag of her cigarette and flicked the butt overboard.

"And if they're lying?"

"We have to try." Mikaela was in no mood to argue with him. She turned and began making her way back to the bridge.

"Even if Johanna keeps her word for now..." Anders turned from the railing. "How long do you really think Solstice will last? They're already dead, Mikaela. They just don't know it yet."

Mikaela placed her hand on the door to the bridge and looked back. "Seems like there's a lot of that going around."

CHAPTER IV
THE BLOOD OF A DYING GOD

Mikaela woke to the sounds of metal clattering and hushed voices. Muted light filtered into the bridge through the grime-encrusted windows. Stefan and Donovan spread out items they had recovered in their search of the crew quarters: several well-made kitchen knives, a bright orange plastic pistol, and dozens of unlabeled aluminum cans one could only hope still contained something edible.

Anders picked up the orange gun and examined it. "Some kind of toy?" he asked.

Stefan snatched it away. "It's quite real—just different than a normal gun." He snapped open the breech, reached for one of several, large cartridges on the table and loaded it. "Shoots a flame. Just one shot per cartridge but it produces quite a bit of light. Could be useful. If nothing else, it'll certainly sell." He snapped the breech closed.

"Well in that case..." Anders reached for the pistol. "I don't mind holding onto it."

Stefan slapped Anders' hand away with surprising speed. "I think it's best if I keep a hold of it." He tucked the flare gun into his belt and made his way toward the door. "Access to the storage tanks is forward on the ship, back on the lower decks. The tide will be out before long, so we won't be coming back here. Grab whatever you think you can carry."

Outside, the Parched that had swarmed the base of the Colossus the night before were gone and the chill in the air had abated. Whatever snow had accumulated on the old vessel had already melted away. Summer still fought to retain its grasp on this dying land. Each winter seemed longer than the last and there were even those amongst the Penitent who claimed that one day ice would claim the forsaken remnants of humanity.

Today was not that day. For that much at least, Mikaela was thankful.

Stefan led the others back down the stairs and onto the sprawling deck of the Colossus. They gathered around a large hatch secured by a dozen badly corroded latches and a hand crank. Donovan bent over to try removing the latches and Stefan handed him a prybar he'd found. Decades of calcified salt and filth resisted his efforts but, eventually, the hand crank loosened and the hatch groaned open.

A shaft descended into darkness below. The bowels of the Colossus smelled sour and rotten. Mikaela recoiled and buried her nose in her sleeve. Freja threw up partially-digested protein wafers across the deck. Only Stefan seemed unaffected.

"This is what we're after?" Mikaela croaked.

Stefan gave a silent nod and seated himself on the hatch's rim. "The blood of the Earth, as promised." He took a long swig from his canteen and let the excess water run down his unshaven chin. He looked as if he'd aged a decade in only days. "My debt is paid."

Donovan, Anders and Mikaela exchanged uncertain glances while Freja tried to regain her composure. A narrow ladder descended into the gloom below.

"Ladies first?" Anders suggested, with a characteristic smirk.

"Fine," Mikaela said. "Hand over the vial. Let's fill this damn thing and get the hell out of this place."

Anders expression turned as sour as the air. "I was only joking..."

"I don't care, Anders. We don't have time for your shit." She gulped. "We can't waste another night here."

Anders gave her the vial. "You want to be the one to do it, fine, but I'm going with you."

Vial in hand, she began climbing down the service ladder into the tank below. A few feet down, her boots struck a solid surface. Mikaela groped through the darkness until she grasped a railing and made her way out onto a walkway. The grated steel on which she trod creaked in protest, threatening to collapse into the abyss.

Anders, true to his word, followed close behind and a shaft of light from the open hatch illuminated Donovan's bulky silhouette climbing down the ladder.

"You know we don't all need to come down here, right?" Mikaela grumbled.

"Just you and me, babe," Anders said.

Donovan lowered himself onto the walkway behind them. "Wait, were you talking to me?"

"I'm talking to anyone in this deathtrap! Seriously, Van, be careful. This thing feels like it might collapse."

Mikaela continued to follow the walkway's railing forward. After a few tentative steps, she reached a descending stairway. The stench of the chamber grew more nauseating. On the eleventh step, something squelched under her boot. She knelt down and ran her fingers through a viscous, black liquid—the blood of Gia Herself.

Mikaela felt both relieved and repulsed. It meant salvation for the people of Solstice, but the fluid was noxious and corrupt.

So, this is what the ancestors used to power their machines? No wonder they were able to accomplish such great things. No wonder we are damned.

"Well?" Donovan asked. His voice reverberated through the expansive chamber. "Did you find it?"

"Yes," Mikaela whispered, suddenly compelled to lower her voice.

She uncorked the glass vial and dipped it into the black lake. Her hands trembled as she lifted it.

"She found it!" Donovan yelled to the others.

A sucking sound emanated from the gloom and something disturbed the surface of the stagnant pool. Whatever it was came from deep within the tank. Mikaela struggled to reseal the vial. Neither Anders nor Donovan seemed to notice.

"Alright, we've got the vial." Anders took a couple steps back, toward the walkway. "Now let's get the-"

"Shut up!" Mikaela hissed. "There's something in here..."

Anders scoffed. "This place has been sealed for generations. The smell must be gettin' to you."

Before Mikaela could respond, a thud echoed around them. She turned toward the hatch. A second thud followed and then the sound of metal striking metal, coming from the deck.

"You alright up there?" Donovan asked.

There was no response. Several seconds later, Freja's thin silhouette began descending the ladder. When she reached the walkway, she stood in the beam of light from the open hatch without speaking.

Donovan cocked his head. "Everything alright?"

"No..." Freja muttered. "But it will be."

She withdrew the bright orange flare gun from her pocket. Mikaela's stomach sank.

"Freja..." Donovan raised his hands and took a step back. "What are you doing?"

"I see my purpose now." Freja said. "I'm so thankful to Stefan for showing me the way... So thankful to all of you."

"Freja..." Mikaela fought to still the tremble in her voice. "Where's Stefan?"

There was more gurgling in the black pool. Mikaela climbed away from the liquid's bubbling surface and slipped the vial into her inner coat pocket, as quickly as she dared.

"His suffering is over," Freja said serenely. "His soul has rejoined the Earth."

"Th-this can't be Gia's will." Donovan sputtered. "We need the blood to save our home—to save *hundreds* of people."

Freja shook her head. "This place is a blight, Donovan. A festering wound. We will only be free when we have removed the source of the infection. A true believer would see that."

Donovan took a step forward. "Put down the gun."

"I don't blame you, Donovan," she continued. "You have a kind heart. I love you all..."

Donovan lunged and grabbed Freja by the arm. He tried to wrest the gun away, but it was too late. Freja pulled the trigger and blinding flame arced toward the nearby wall. It ricocheted off the steel and plummeted toward the black lake beneath them.

Without a thought, Mikaela leapt to intercept the flame. She leaned over the railing and grabbed for the light. For a moment, the chamber went dark as her fingers wrapped around it. Then red light flared in her palm and illuminated the entirety of the expansive chamber. Ghoulish creatures, previously shrouded in darkness, rose from the thick, black pool beneath them. Outstretched hands groped at the stagnant air. Gaping mouths sucked at the corrupted fluid from which they emerged.

The walkway railing gave way under Donovan and Freja's combined weight. She fell toward the awaiting creatures. Donovan caught her overcoat, but his grip failed. Freja plummeted, striking the surface of the pool with a splash and a scream. Donovan, thrown off balance, nearly tumbled after her. Freja shrieked as bone-thin fingers pulled at her flesh and dragged her beneath the surface of her god's putrefied blood. Screams turned to wet gurgles as fluid filled her lungs. Her final expression was one of sheer horror.

Within seconds, Freja was gone.

The flare seared Mikaela's flesh. She pressed it against her overcoat, trying to smother the flame. The pain was excruciating, and the chamber once again went black. She struggled up the stairs and onto the walkway. Anders wasted no time in making his escape. He climbed the ladder with a speed Mikaela could not hope to match. She could hear the creatures clambering up the staircase behind her. Donovan stood where Freja had fallen, staring into the darkness in wide-eyed shock.

"Go!" Mikaela screamed, trying to push him forward.

He stared at her—through her—unmoving. She pushed past him and started climbing. Her left hand was ruined, and her right was slick with the black blood. Her grip faltered when she'd nearly reached the top. She braced herself for the fall. Then a hand from below pressed her upward. Donovan, climbing behind her.

Anders leaned down and pulled her onto the deck. As she struggled to regain her bearings, a pained howl echoed from below. Anders struggled to pull Donovan up. Mikaela stumbled to her feet and grabbed Donovan by the shoulder. She pulled with every ounce of strength she could summon but it wasn't Donovan's weight they were struggling against. The creatures had reached the ladder and were attempting to pull him back into the gloom. Hands reached up from the darkness below, flesh stained black and partially decayed.

Mikaela released Donovan and began frantically searching for a weapon. Stefan lay on the rusted steel deck. The left side of his skull was caved in and dark blood pooled around the prybar Freja had used to seal his fate. Without time to grieve, Mikaela hefted the blood-strained prybar and ran back to the hatch. She smashed the weapon down at the grasping hands, splintering bone and peeling back rotten flesh.

The creatures' grip relented and Anders hauled Donovan through the hatch. Mikaela threw the hatch closed but one of the creatures wedged itself into the gap. It pushed back against her with inhuman strength. Her burnt hand screamed in pain and she started to falter. She wouldn't be able to hold the ghoul for long.

"Anders!" she cried. "A little help!"

He picked up the prybar and rushed toward the creature. In the light, Mikaela could finally see it clearly. It had once been human but many of its features had long since rotted away. Its eyes were hollow pits and only an uneven hole remained where its nose should have been. Its lips and gums were gone, leaving its teeth exposed. Its mouth snapped open and closed in a manner similar to the Parched, but it showed no signs of having evolved. It was just an animated corpse.

Anders brought the prybar down on the monster's face, splitting its overripe flesh and leaving its jaw askew. On the second strike, its skull gave way. On the third, its neck snapped back at an unnatural angle. Additional hands pried their way from beneath the hatch. Mikaela's strength gave out and the creatures began pressing it open.

Anders joined Mikaela, trying to press the hatch closed, but even their combined strength proved insufficient. Donovan crawled to them, struggling to stand on mauled legs. A second creature began pulling itself through the opening, raw flesh sloughing away as it writhed against the steel. They were powerless to stop it.

If they abandoned the hatch, they might survive. There would be no saving Donovan but there was no other way. Mikaela glanced at Anders. He met her eyes and nodded, understanding.

Before they could move, Stefan's body shuddered and rose to its feet. Thick blood dripped from the mortal wound Freja had inflicted. His eyes were glassy but alert. Dead, yet very much alive.

He approached without saying a word. In her shock, Mikaela released the hatch and Anders did the same. Stefan brushed past them, seized the hatch and forced it down. Two ghouls caught in the gap let out guttural screeches as Stefan pressed the hatch closed. The steel lip cleaved them in two. Bones cracked and severed body parts struck the deck with a wet thud.

Stefan fastened the hatch's seals, leaving them writhing, then dispatched them beneath his boots.

Mikaela and Anders stood in stunned silence as Stefan went about his work. A trail of his own blood marked his every move. Those creatures had been unnaturally strong. There was no way Stefan should have been able to overpower them alone.

There was no way he should even be alive.

"How...?" Mikaela finally asked. "How did you do that?"

Stefan leaned wearily against a pipe the size of a small building and reached out his hand. "Water," he demanded.

Mikaela exchanged an uncertain glance with Anders before fetching the canteen she'd carried up around her neck. He took it from her and gulped down its contents until nothing remained. When he was done, he said, "The tides will be back soon. We need to go."

He turned and pulled Donovan to his feet. They made a grotesque pair, with Stefan's head partially collapsed and Donovan's pant legs saturated in blood. Donovan was in shock, staring blankly at the horizon. When it became clear that Stefan had no interest in answering any questions, they prepared to depart and climbed down the hull of the Colossus.

What remained of the party abandoned the derelict and returned into the blasted landscape of the Tidelands.

...

The further they travelled, the further Donovan and Stefan trailed behind. Anders and Mikaela carried on side-by-side, stopping intermittently to allow the wounded pair to catch up. It was not until midway through their day's travel that either spoke a word.

"What do you think those things were back there?" Mikaela asked.

Anders stopped and looked back. Stefan and Donovan had already fallen a hundred yards behind. The Colossus had begun to fade into the haze.

"I don't know..." he muttered. "The crew maybe. Or at least part of em'. I think they were supposed to be Parched, but..."

"And Stefan?"

Anders shook his head and kicked at the discarded exoskeleton of a crustacean. "Part ways to becoming an Ember, I guess." His eyes met Mikaela's. A briny wind disturbed the surface of a nearby tide pool and ruffled his matted hair. "We can't go on like this, you know? We'll never make it."

"I know."

Mikaela turned and watched the others as they approached. Donovan was lost within his own head but Stefan seemed to grasp his situation well enough. He gave Mikaela a knowing nod and knelt beside the tide pool. He unscrewed the cap of his canteen, filled it with brackish water, and guzzled the contents.

Mikaela felt a familiar lump building in her throat. Whatever Stefan was, he was no longer human—at least not entirely. "Stefan..."

"I know," he said. He refilled his canteen, screwed on the cap, and stood. "I can't go back. Not anymore." His good eye had turned milky white and it stared right through her. His lips had cracked to the point of bleeding. "I'll take care of Donovan. You two carry on."

Anders nodded. "Thanks, Stefan. We owe you big for this."

"We'll get you help," Mikaela insisted.

She doubted it was even possible to help Stefan at this point, but she would try her best to keep her word. No other person alive had done more for her or the people of Solstice. If there was a way to save him, or even ease his suffering, she owed it to him.

"Alright." Stefan managed a faint grin. It was the sort of smile a parent gave a disobedient child promising to behave—an acknowledgement of both good intent and inevitable failure.

Without saying another word, Mikaela turned and resumed her journey back toward Beacon. She could only hope Stefan and Donovan survived. The Tidelands were a cruel and unforgiving place.

Once her business with the Forge Master was complete, she hoped to never lay eyes on that bleak expanse again.

...

Mikaela and Anders returned to Beacon on the afternoon of the seventh day. Johanna's letter proved sufficient to get them past the enforcers at the city gates and the Hoarfrost was easy enough to find with a little asking around. The tavern was tucked into the winding alleys of the Green District, in the shadows of towering grain silos.

Despite being exhausted from the journey, Mikaela was unnerved by the sheer number of people coursing through the streets around her. Each coal-smeared miner or beleaguered mill worker was a potential threat to everything she had struggled for. How many passersby concealed knives beneath their coats? How many would be willing to kill for the vial she carried?

They stood outside the dingy, unassuming tavern. Somewhere inside, Johanna's lackey awaited their arrival. In a matter of minutes, this whole mess would finally be over. Mikaela took a step toward the Hoarfrost's front door, but Anders held her back. He tugged at her overcoat and led her into a nearby alley.

"What?" she sniffled. After several days in the windswept Tidelands, the polluted air in the city's lower wards was overwhelming. "Aren't you ready to get this damned thing over with?"

"Our friend, Örjan, is going to betray us."

"*What?*" Mikaela gaped at him. "You're telling me this *now?*"

"I can get us outta this. Just tell me you'll follow my lead."

"Not until you give me one good reason I should believe you."

"Think about it, Mikaela. Örjan insisted we meet him here rather than at Johanna's compound. Why would he do that?"

"I don't know! Maybe she's trying to keep everything quiet for as long as possible. Doesn't want word getting out to the other Forge Masters."

"Or, maybe Örjan realizes that getting us Stefan wouldn't exactly sit well with his boss and keeping us alive is a liability." Anders pointed back to the tavern. "I mean, look at this place. Kinda perfect to snuff out a couple nobodies without drawing too much attention, right?"

"Alright, fine. Let's go straight to Johanna."

"We will, but we need to tie things up with Örjan first."

"Tie things up?" Mikaela had spent the last several days just trying to survive and the people of Solstice were running out of time. She wasn't in the mood for Anders' scheming. "If we're going to go directly to Johanna, let's go. We don't have time for this."

"Do you really want a knife in your back? Because if we go to Johanna and leave Örjan in the dark, that's exactly what we're going to get."

"Fine. But whatever you're going to do, just do it fast."

She pushed past Anders and left the alley, walking directly to the front door of the Hoarfrost.

"Wait, Mikaela..."

Inside the tavern, a group of three men skulked in a shadowy corner booth. Only Örjan's flushed features were immediately recognizable. The place was otherwise empty, except for a cloaked figure seated at the bar Mikaela recognized as one of Johanna's goons, and a muscular barkeep whose bald head nearly scraped the low-hanging electric lamps.

Anders arrived through the front door shortly thereafter and shot Mikaela a concerned look. She didn't bother indulging him and marched directly to the booth where Örjan was seated.

"Well," she said. "You want it or not?"

Her demeanor seemed to make the gathered men uncomfortable. The man at the bar stood and reached into his overcoat.

Örjan forced a broken smile and waved his hand dismissively. "She's just who we've been expecting. Please," he gestured toward Mikaela, "have a seat."

"I'd rather not," she said firmly. "I *am* on a bit of a deadline, after all."

"To be sure, but... I insist you join us for a drink." He patted the empty seat next to him. "To celebrate your achievement."

Anders' voice filled the uncomfortable silence that followed. "Just one."

"Of course." Örjan made more room in the booth. Anders brushed past Mikaela and sat next to him. The goon scowled but said nothing. "I'm honestly surprised to see you again..."

Mikaela said nothing, but Anders seemed eager to keep the fool's jowls flapping. "It was quite the journey. I can confirm—firsthand—that the Tidelands are as infested with Parched as the rumors claim."

The bearded man in the corner scoffed but Örjan's expression turned serious.

"Is that what happened to your friends? I remember there being a pretty little thing... Big doe eyes."

Örjan looked at Mikaela as he spoke and slid the tip of his tongue between his stained, uneven teeth.

She rolled her eyes. "You want the vial or not?"

He extended a mutilated hand across the sticky tabletop. "I'll take whatever you've got for me, sweet cakes."

Only aboard the Colossus could Mikaela recall having a stronger urge to vomit. She removed the vial of Earth's blood and placed it on the table, refusing to put anything directly in the creep's hand. Örjan grabbed it and held it up to the light of the nearest overhead lamp. The other two men at the table leaned in to get a glimpse.

"Kinda nasty shit, isn't it?"

"Yeah..." Anders agreed.

Johanna's enforcer approached and placed a tray of five shot glasses on the table. Örjan eyed them with a thirst only the Parched could hope to emulate.

"I think that concludes our business." Mikaela said.

"A drink first," Örjan said, as he selected a smudged shot glass from the tray. The two men seated at the table and Anders followed suit.

"I'd prefer not to-" A stern glance from Anders stopped her midsentence. "Fine. One drink, as promised."

Örjan's broken teeth revealed themselves once more and he raised his glass. "To Gia—to Mother Earth!"

Anders smiled at Mikaela and raised his glass. "To Colossus."

Mikaela joined the others in choking down the blur. It was vile and familiar but somehow... different. There was an unusual metallic tang to the alcohol that made her wince. Örjan and the two other goons slammed their empty glasses back to the table. Anders, however, gingerly lowered his glass back to the table. Still full.

His smile evaporated.

He leaned across the table to Mikaela and whispered, "I'm sorry."

Mikaela's stomach sank. She felt as if her throat might close up. "I-I have to go to the bathroom."

She rose from her seat on unsteady legs and made it no more than five steps before the room spun and she collapsed to the tavern floor. Visions of the massacre at Walden returned. At that moment, she knew that Anders' betrayal meant the deaths of everyone in Solstice.

How could she have been so blind?

"Hey, you..." Örjan choked on his own words. "You son of...a bitch..."

The enforcer at the bar pulled a pistol from his coat just as a liquor bottle cracked off his head. He fell and the pistol slid across the uneven floor.

The hulking barkeep walked from behind the counter and crushed the enforcer's head with his heavy boot. He stomped until nothing remained of the man's face, every footfall punctuated by the sickening squelch of emulsified grey matter.

When the bartender was finally satisfied, he made his way to the booth and offered Anders the blood-spattered liquor bottle. Örjan and his fellow goons slouched over the table, motionless. Anders rose to his feet and accepted the offering without hesitation, handing the barkeep the vial in exchange.

Mikaela's vision blurred. She had managed to draw the knife from her belt, but her arms refused to obey. Her fingers might as well have belonged to somebody else. Even her voice failed her. Anders took a long swig of the liquor and sat down on the floor beside her. Tears welled in his eyes. The floorboards creaked as the bartender approached and placed a meaty hand on Anders' shoulder.

"I can't believe you actually pulled it off." There was a hint of laughter in the giant's gravelly voice. A faded tattoo of a cog and calipers peeked from beneath his sleeve. "You're sure you want to keep this one alive?"

"Yeah..." Anders said quietly, before taking another gulp of liquor.

The barkeep broke into a resounding laugh and picked Mikaela's knife off the floor. "I'd be careful if I were you... You've made some powerful friends, but you just killed this poor girl's entire family." His gore-slick boots squelched with each heavy footstep as he walked away. "She'll be comin' for you. I know I would..."

Anders look into Mikaela's eyes as her vision faded to black. "I didn't kill them," he corrected.

"They were already dead."

END.

Trevor Brown, who writes under the pen name T.M. Brown, serves as an officer in the U.S. Army. He currently lives in Colorado Springs, Colorado with his beautiful wife, Anna, and his two dogs, Fry and Zapp. Although Trevor has long held a passion for speculative fiction, he has only recently taken up writing for publication. His preferred genres include horror, strange fiction, and dark fantasy.

T.M. Brown's debut novella 'The Gloam' is currently available on Amazon in both paperback and Kindle formats. He also has a variety of dark fiction under contract with independent publishers including: Black Hare Press, Burial Day Books, Cosmic Horror Monthly, Eerie River Publishing, Kyanite Publishing, Nothing Ever Happens in Fox Hollow, Sinister Smile Press, and Terror Tract.

https://www.facebook.com/RavenousShadows
Twitter @TMBrown_Author

A PLACE BEYOND THE STORM

BY DAVID GREEN

Dedicated to all those doing their best,
we'll find our place beyond the storm.

PART ONE
EMERGENCE

"**P**anam? Wake up. It's time."

Rough hands shake me, ripping me from dreams of my parents. At least, I think it's them; they died before my brain formed lasting memories of them. I've heard some of the old-timers talk about 'pictures' but I've never seen one, don't think they exist anymore. When I sleep though, mother and father are always there, looking the same each time; olive-skinned like me—minus the constant dirt that covers me from head to toe most days—dark of hair and eye.

My first instinct is to roll over, to fall back into the dreams that call to me. Stavros puts an end to that.

"Up, girl," he grunts, sticking his hands under my armpits and lifting me to my feet. "Tradition won't wait for you to rub the sleep from your eyes."

The cold nips at me. Our fires have turned to embers, though those still sleeping, like old Davron and his wife Maas, haven't noticed. I glance at Mika, my sister, wrapped in her blankets beside where I lay. Just ten-years-old. A baby. Though I guess no-one's afforded much of a childhood these days, and me less than most. The adults used to say I never spoke much like a child anyway.

Today's the day I turn fourteen and become an adult.

In truth, I've felt like one for longer. I've acted as Mika's parent all her life. Our mother died in childbirth. Father died Topside.

I glance around the caves—my home, my entire world—gazing at all the people sleeping. There's fifty of us. I've never seen beyond these walls. Now, that changes.

"Ready?" Stavros asks. The embers glint in his eyes but other than that he's a shadow, his shaggy black hair and beard blending him into the gloom. He lays a thick hand on my shoulder, squeezes. A shocking sign of affection from him.

"Born that way." I grin at him and it could be a trick of the flickering light but I think he returns it. Stavros is a tough man; he must be as the Kin's leader, but he looked after me when mother died, and did his best to raise me right when he could have passed me and Mika on to any other family. One time, I asked why they didn't send us Topside, the way they did with anyone who burdened the Kin.

Banishment is a way of life, Panam, he said while teaching me to skin a rat, *but children don't deserve that fate. You're our future, and it's up to us to raise you well.*

He turns and walks away, picking his way through the sleeping bodies, careful not to disturb them. We sleep a set time from night to morning, when the sun rises Topside. It makes no difference inside the caves. One of the old-timers, Riklin, said his grandfather told stories of the Kin dropping roofs and sealing up tunnels Topside when they first settled here almost two-hundred years ago. The only light we get is from our fires, and that wood comes from the Scavengers—brave men and women who go Topside and scrounge for necessities the caves don't provide. They don't teach children why we can't go beyond the caves. Monsters, some say. Others say there isn't a 'Topside', just endless stalactites and rocks. I don't think that's true; the Kin *do* leave the caves. Something drove us down here.

Still, we possess the most valuable commodity. Fresh water. Something Stavros says others would kill for—*have* killed for—though he doesn't say why. I always assumed it only grows in caves.

Excitement builds in me. I've heard stories of the stars, moon and sun. We all have; Traak, the Kin's teacher, told me of them long ago. The sky, too. I picture them in my mind, and I still listen into Mika's lessons with the rest of the younger children when Mannom teaches me how to stitch rat pelts together to make clothing, a smile on my face, wondering just what they all look like. My stomach flips a little as I realise I'm about to find out.

I follow Stavros as he makes his way through the tunnels. He does it without light, knowing the system's twists and turns by instinct. I fare well at the start, but as we move further and higher than I've gone before, I stumble and trip. Refusing to call out and make him wait or, worse, hold my hand like a *child,* I grit my teeth then throw an arm out and feel the cave wall with my fingers. It slips away when an opening to another cavern or route takes its place, but I take a mental note of these and keep my stare trained on the shape of Stavros ahead of me. The air's changing. It tastes... fresh.

My stupid feet betray me. I fight to remain upright but I collide with something immovable.

"Steady on, girl," he says, catching me without looking around. "Suppose I should stop calling you that. You're a woman now. Come. We're close."

He places a hand on my back, urging me on, walking at my side. The caves grow light as we move up a gentle slope. The walls widen. Then I see it, though sudden tears threaten to spoil the view.

Topside.

"It's so... *massive.*"

I want to say beautiful, and it is, but I can't comprehend what I'm seeing. Everything is so far away. I can see land and trees stretching out ahead of me. My legs turn to stone, unwilling to move, and I feel my bladder weaken. Stavros draws me to the cave's mouth and sits, watching me as I gawp at my surroundings. At first, I gaze at eye-level, turning my head so I can take in the vista laid out before me, witnessing things I've only *heard* about like the gnarled trees and brown, rotted grass, wondering how long it would take me to walk to them, touch them. What they'd feel like.

A different kind of rock?

Then, I turn my stare upwards and the weight of the stars threatens to crush me.

I feel something in my chest, fingers like ice spreading as my heart hammers. My mouth runs dry, though I lick at the tears touching my lips, and I feel so small. I want to look away, to hide in my cave, to remain a child, but I can't... stop... *looking*. Everywhere I look up there, I see stars twinkling back. Traak says they're further away than I can imagine, that they're massive, larger than anything else in the night sky, but they seem so small, and, oh my, so many.

"There must be thousands of them," I whisper, sinking to the ground. My legs are telling me to run, but I tell them to shut up. I need to show Stavros I'm a woman. A child would flee.

"More," he says, glancing at them. "You know, before all this, we sent people up there in these things called space rockets."

I laugh, a shaky giggle. "You're trying to make me feel at ease."

"I'm serious," Stavros says. "My grandfather said his father could remember them doing it, and all other kinds of crazy things. Though he'd have been a child at the time, and you know what they're like."

He winks, and I goggle back at him. It's not just the gesture. That's the longest sentence I've ever heard him utter. And the first time he's mentioned his ancestors. He even takes my hand.

"I just... can't believe what I'm seeing. My entire life, Topside, all *this*, above me. I learned about it, but I could never see it. Now..."

"Now you're a woman, Panam. As you slept, you turned fourteen. Soon, you'll start your training, become a Scavenger, work to keep the Kin strong. But it takes time. Topside can overwhelm you. For the next few weeks, you'll come here with another of age and grow used to it. Never alone, Panam. It isn't safe."

Words I've heard so many times, whenever I asked why we're living in caves with the rats and bugs, why we're forbidden from leaving the tunnels. That's where the rumours of monsters come from. But now I'm a woman—Stavros said so himself—and I won't let *it isn't safe* stop me.

"What happened?"

He doesn't answer. Instead, Stavros looks away and studies the horizon. I follow his gaze. Behind the dead trees, the sky grows lighter.

"No-one knows," he replies at last, pausing as he weighs his words. "We used to live Topside until it all changed. The old world had this word for meddlers. 'Scientists', they called them. Well, these Scientists made Topside lethal, and to survive we had to hide underground."

"It doesn't look that dangerous to me," I mutter. My lips settle into a pout and I scowl at the ground. "Except for the massiveness of it all."

"Look."

Stavros points at the horizon. What I see sends me scrambling backward. A fire rises beyond the trees, the world growing brighter from its flames. "I can't."

He grabs my arm, pulls me beside him, forces me to watch. "Your first sunrise," he whispers. "You'll never forget it. It rises in the east, thereabouts, each morning, and sets in the west. Whenever you're Topside, use it to guide you."

I can't move—though my legs tremble out of control—so I avert my eyes and stare at the stars instead, though the thought of how many lie above my head makes vomit rise in my gullet. They grow faint as the sky brightens, and a grey vapour covers them. Taking a breath, I look to the sun. Its shine hurts my eyes. I glance at Stavros. He raises the flat of his hand to his brow while he watches the sunrise, so I copy him. Nice trick.

The sun continues to rise, bringing colour to the silent world. The sky is blue—vast, endless—except for the blotches of grey. I point at one, my hand shaking.

"What is that, in the sky?"

Stavros glances at me, his face grim. I realise it's the first time I've seen it in natural light. Lines eat into his washed-out olive skin, the daylight making him look older than his forty-five years.

"You want to know why Topside is death for us? Why we shrank back into the dark places of the world?"

I nod. What else can I do? Shake my head? No, even though I want to with the way Stavros says those words.

"Keep watching. Any moment now. Don't move forward, whatever you do."

I peer at Topside, wondering what I'm meant to watch for. It's a great open emptiness. If Stavros told me the Kin, in our cave, were the only ones who lived in the entire world, I'd believe him. Except... my father died up here, scavenging. And others have too.

At first, I think my eyes have gone fuzzy. I rub them, blink a few times, but I still see it and let out a cry.

"Water! Falling from the sky!"

Despite Stavros' warning, I surge forward. His grip stops me. I'd sooner make a stone wall budge. With a shake of his head, he reaches inside his tunic, pulls out a dead rat.

"Rain," he says, flicking his head at the cave's mouth. "It doesn't fall often, but when it does..."

The 'rain' cascades to the ground. Stavros tosses the rat into it. My eyes follow the carcass and the scream that tears from my throat takes the strength from me. The water strips the flesh from the rodent. When it touches the sodden floor, all that's left are bones.

Stavros grabs my shoulders, spins me so he can stare into my eyes.

"There's more," he shouts, so I hear his voice over the rainfall. "People live Topside, and they'd do *anything* to have what we possess: a natural source of water that doesn't kill. These people, Raiders we call them, are like a plague; rapists, murderers, and cannibals. No-one can ever know about us, Panam. When it's your time to scavenge, you *must* protect our secret, even if it means staying out here. Even if it means death. Nothing survives Topside for long. There are no animals and the water is poison. Some say the air is, too. This cave, the water and the people in it are our future. Mika is our future."

I turn back to Topside, the burning stench of the rain thick in my nose.

"Why wait till we're fourteen to tell us this?"

Stavros sighs, draws me close as I weep into his chest. He pats my head, like he did when I woke from nightmares as an infant, or when I couldn't get Mika to sleep and frustrated despair gripped me. "Because children must be innocent while they can, Panam. It's the only gift we can give them in this life. Now come, they prepare a celebration for your Age Day. Dry those tears."

Stavros pulls away, back into the caves. I gaze at the rat and watch as the ground swallows its bones.

PART TWO
SISTERS

"**W**ell, what happened *exactly*? Saying you 'just talked' isn't enough."

My sister's eyes are wide in her sweat-slick face. For days, she's pestered me with questions about my trip to Topside; I told her I'd bring her up to speed after the celebration but kept putting it off. But how can I tell her about what's out there?

Besides, Stavros made me swear I wouldn't, on my word as an *adult*. I dip my rat-pelt tunic into the steaming pool where we clean our patched clothes and scrub it. I think about the way it would have melted in the waters above.

"Mika, he just told me about my duties as an adult of the Kin."

She rolls her eyes. She's far too smart for her own good.

"To be honest, they're not much different from what I do now. Guess not everyone in the Kin had the benefit of being a mother at three-and-a-half years old."

"You're not my mother," Mika says, sure as an echo, a faint smile on her lips.

"No, but I'm the next best thing." She says it at the same time as me, her voice mock-stern, then she laughs. It turns into a scowl all too soon.

"It's not fair," she pouts. "You've never kept secrets from me before."

I reach out and tuck a stray hair behind her ear. "It's not like that, Mika. Your time to know will come soon enough."

Too soon, I almost say.

I glance at the Kin around us and smile. Some wash their garments as we do, others come here to pray. Water is our life. Traak says it blesses us, keeps us strong. We're born in it. We swim in the various pools too, except for those reserved for drinking. Sometimes, I find a body of water just to sit by and think. This cavern is my favourite; I love the way the stalactites hang low, almost touching the shimmering liquid with their tips. Some of those at prayer sing. I close my eyes, letting my thoughts drift.

Images of the sun rising over those dead trees flood my mind, and the words of Stavros fill my ears. I stare at the steaming pool and at the vapour rising to the stalactites, not seeing the water. Instead, I'm standing at the cave's mouth, Topside stretching out before me. It's all I've thought about since the morning of my Age Day and though I'm not due to start my 'acclimatisation', as Stavros calls it, for a day or so, I long to visit there again.

Alone, if I can.

Everything about Topside frightens me. No, it terrifies me. Not just the Raiders, and they're reason enough—the things Stavros told me of them—but the vast sky, the rotted trees, the rain that can melt the fur and meat from a rat in seconds and would do the same to me. My thoughts stray to father. I wonder what killed him; the Raiders, or the rain. I'm not sure I want to know.

The Kin needs strength. *Mika* needs my strength.

"Are you even listening to a word I'm saying?" Mika says, splashing warm water at me. I blink at her, confused.

"Sorry. Miles away."

"That's what I mean," Mika replies, and only now I notice she's holding back tears. "You've been acting weird since you saw Topside. Like all the other adults. You seem so... *sad.*"

I drop my still wet tunic onto the rocks and pull her close, cradling her head as I stroke her hair. *Mika needs my strength*, I repeat in my mind. Her body shakes with silent sobs.

"Hush now. It's okay. Trust me. Topside's just a lot to swallow. The sun, Mika. The stars! They're nothing like how Traak describes. You'll love it, so long as you're brave."

"Were you?"

"Let's say I did my best."

She giggles against my chest before sighing. A long, heavy one. "Promise the old Panam will come back soon?"

I push her from me, hold out my pinky finger. Stavros used to do the same to me, years ago. "Promise."

Mika wraps her little finger around mine and grins. Then yawns so wide I can see which new teeth are about to break through her gums. "You almost done, Panam? Time for sleep, I reckon."

I jump to my feet and wring out the wet tunic I've given a half-hearted scrubbing. I wrinkle my nose. Wet rat leaves a stink that won't wash out. "Come on. I reckon you're right, Little Miss Know-It-All."

We journey through the darkness, through the tunnels we know so well that lead back to the Kin and our sheets, Mika talking about this and that, her thoughts wandering. I half-listen. My thoughts are Topside once more.

PART THREE
HEADSTRONG

I keep myself awake by placing a large rock under my back. When sleep threatens to take me anyway, I pinch myself. It works. All's silent and still as I roll from my covers, careful not to disturb Mika. I stick my pillow where I lay. Her thin arms curl around it on instinct. For the last few nights I've done this, stole away in the night, and returned Topside.

Shivering, I pad towards the tunnel system in complete darkness, feeling my way against the walls as I recall the route Stavros took me on the morning of my Age Day. We only took a few turns, and always moved upwards on a gentle slope, but my memory tricks me as I map the route in my mind. I'm forced to turn back on two occasions when I hit dead-ends, but I make better progress than I've done before. The further I move into the darkness, the icy fingers that gripped my chest when I first saw Topside tighten, but I force them away. I'm an adult now and, each time I see it, the vastness of it gets a little easier to handle.

"Mika needs my strength," I whisper, waving a hand in front of my eyes. I see its faint outline. The tunnel is lightening. Before I could only see darkness.

I sniff the air. It smells different. Fresh. I'm getting close.

My steps quicken even though the slope becomes steep. I'm on the correct path and a grin splits my face as I pass an opening in the tunnel, one I recall from my earlier journeys. Before me, I see a faint glow.

Topside.

Determined, I keep my eyes forward, fixed on the patch of grey up ahead, telling myself that fear won't get the better of me this time. I break into a run before my body decides otherwise.

I stop at the line, and the weight of the endless, star-filled sky hanging above me, like stalactites threatening to fall at any moment, makes me lower my head. My heart jolts as I force myself to stare at a single spot above me but I refuse to give in. To turn and flee back underground.

"I'm not afraid of you," I snarl, baring my teeth and breathing slow, deep breaths.

The panic fades. As it does, I let my eyes fall to the knot of dead trees in the distance and frown. They're brighter than they were this morning. Silver, almost.

I look up and my hands move too slow to stop the scream that tears from my throat.

The moon hangs high in the sky, illuminating Topside. It's so clear. I've heard about it. Stavros even mentioned it on the way back through the tunnels on my Age Day, said those madmen in their rockets *landed* on it, but I never expected to see it with such clarity. Black pockmarks cover it, and a giant hole punches through it, off-center. It's so close I feel I can reach out and touch it. What keeps it there, floating in the sky?

"Who are you, little girl?"

This time, my hands stifle the scream. A stone's throw from me stands... a creature with a man's voice. Its eyes are wide and glassy, like an insect's, reflecting the moon's light, and it has a strange snout with dozens of nostrils. A white handprint—human—stands out stark against its shiny, black outer shell. It stands upright like me and it holds something in its arms—a long rectangular object with a small cylinder at its end, pointing at me. The creature's finger rests on a catch on the underside. I'm not sure what the thing it holds is, but a voice in my head yells at me to run.

"Can you talk?" it asks, taking a step forward. "I heard your scream."

I nod, but my tongue is frozen.

"Then I'll ask again: who are you?" The thing glances around and moves another step closer. "Do you live here? That tunnel, maybe? Are there more of you? How many?"

I stumble backwards, my hands balled into fists by my side, the nails digging into my palms so deep I feel blood. I've made a mistake, such a terrible mistake. I can't run. It will follow. But I can flee deeper into Topside. Maybe that will trick it, make it believe I just took shelter in the cave's mouth for the night.

Yes, that could work.

"I..." The words won't come. All I can manage is a strangled, weak noise.

The creature chuckles. It glances around again and I wonder why it's so nervous. It lays the object on the floor, splaying its fingers and showing them to me. Then it lifts them to the back of its head and pulls.

I gasp as the creature peels away its face. Underneath, it's human. Male. Younger than Stavros, I think, and hairless. He glances at the sky and takes a deep breath through his nose. The moonlight reveals the red, angry scars crisscrossing his bald head. He looks at me and grins. The man's teeth, the ones left, are sharp.

"See," he says, "I'm just like you, right? Nothing to fear. Now why don't you tell me where you're from? Dangerous, out here all alone."

He steps forward again, his head covering tucked under one arm, the object held in a loose grip in his other hand. He could touch me if he reached out with it.

"What's your name?" he whispers. A scar runs through one eye, robbing it of colour. The other blue, and I've never seen its like before. All the Kin have brown eyes.

"Panam," I murmur, my body urging me to run, but something makes me glance at the object in his hand. It's dangerous, though I don't know what makes me think that.

"Panam. Name's Klaus." He bares those fangs at me again. "Won't you answer my question?"

"Got separated from my family," I say, the lies tumbling out of me in a rush. "I sheltered here for the night. Screamed so they might hear me."

"Oh?" Klaus answers, glancing around again. He uses the end of the object to tap himself on the chest. "And what protection do you have in case it rains, Panam? The water would melt right through that tunic of yours. Then your skin."

He meets my eyes, then glances behind me, into the darkness of the cave. My home.

"Panam!"

Stavros' voice echoes from the gloom. Klaus smiles, backs away, the end of the object placed across his lips.

Rough hands grab me from behind and I almost collapse against Stavros' body. He pauses, scans the horizon, then pulls me back into the tunnels, almost throws me into the side-passage I avoided earlier. A fire burns at the back of the cave and, lined against the wall, are clothes like the ones Klaus wore, but yellow, not black.

"Why did you scream?" Stavros asks, eyes narrowed.

"The m-moon," I stammer. "It startled me. I didn't see it any of the times I came up here before."

"*Times?*"

I nod, the fury in his face stilling my tongue.

"Did you see anyone out there?"

I should tell him, but my head shakes of its own accord. The tightness in Stavros' face eases.

"Foolish girl," he says. "That scream... turned my blood cold."

My eyes return to the strange clothing, like the Raider's.

"What are they?" I ask, pointing at them with a shaking hand.

"Hazmat suits, passed down from the settlers. Scavengers wear them Topside, gives them some protection." Then he scowls. "Don't change the subject. Why did you come here alone? No, why do you *keep* coming here alone?"

I know I should tell him about Klaus, the way he looked, that he had a... hazmat... suit. But I can't. I've made a childish mistake when I'm meant to act like an adult. Meant to *be* an adult.

"I... wanted to show you I could handle Topside. Be brave, like you. So I could help the Kin and protect Mika. How did you know I came here, anyway?"

Stavros kneels before me, stares into my eyes. I force myself to meet his glare. "You passed a guard at their station and they came to me. Though it seems I need to speak with them, seeing as you've evaded their sight before tonight. Is that all you have to say, Panam?"

I want to tell him. Need to. The words are on my tongue. Instead, I shake my head again. A coward. A *child* unable to admit her failures.

"We forced you to behave like an adult too soon, Panam," Stavros says with a sigh, "that's where this curiosity is coming from. We'll let this slide, but promise me you won't do this again? Only go Topside when I say, no sooner."

My tongue is leaden and dry, but I whisper, "I promise."

"Let's go," Stavros says, leading the way back into the tunnels.

I look at the hazmat suits, the shadows cast by the fire turning the yellow plastic black. Klaus's hideous face hovers above each one, grinning at me with those sharp teeth.

PART FOUR
INNOCENCE LOST

Klaus' face haunts my dreams. Maggots crawl from that split, colourless eye as he stands beneath the moon. Grey clouds move in overhead, letting their rain spill. It eats his hazmat suit, melts the flesh beneath. Everything except his scarred, hairless face. He smiles at me, and crimson covers those jagged teeth.

I wake before Mika does and spend some time staring at her—my baby sister—as my tired eyes adjust to the low light of the caverns. She still sleeps, even as others are stirring. Stavros doesn't rest. He's sat by a fire at the cavern's mouth since returning with me, his silhouette stark against the flames, a staff in his hands. His turn on watch.

I bite my lip, realising what I must do. Mika grumbles as I slide from my blankets.

"Dawn already? No, it can't be. Whoever's on morning watch hasn't relit the fires yet. Where are you going?"

"Rest a while longer," I reply, pressing my lips to her cheek. "I need to talk to Stavros."

Mika sighs and rolls over, snuggling into her blankets. "More secrets."

I pick my way through the sleeping members of the Kin—lovers Daan and Jaap holding each other as they sleep, families with young children, like Ila and Marcos with little Pia and Jose huddled between them. Looking around, I realise now that everyone in the Kin over fourteen knows the truth about Topside; we all share that burden and none before me have let it crush them. They've just got on with life, for the good of the many.

"Panam," Stavros calls in a hushed tone as I approach. Orange firelight flicks his features as he studies me. "Hope you're not thinking of sneaking away again. Something on your mind?"

"Stavros, I must tell you. I—"

"You're sorry, I get it." He holds his hands up when I try to interrupt, balancing the staff across his knees. "Panam, Topside's a lot to take in, and I expected too much from you. I thought you'd take it in your stride, like you've done with everything else in your life. Want to know how I reacted on my Age Day? I cried for days. Refused to even go anywhere near Topside when my training began. My father had to carry me, and I kicked and screamed the whole way. Sneaking off to settle your nerves is a lot better than how I handled it. Alone, too. You're made of sterner stuff than I."

Tears well in my eyes. I could just laugh, return to my blankets for a while longer. But I *have* to tell him about Klaus. My lungs fill with air.

"No," I breathe, "it's not that, I—"

Stavros holds up a hand again, his head snapping towards the tunnels. "Hush."

"Please, I have to—"

"Wait."

He gets to his feet, creeps beyond the firelight. I follow, silent, straining to hear. Something moves, and my brain whispers one name to me: *Klaus.*

A faint bang echoes through the darkness.

"Stavros, a man spoke to me when I went Topside. He wore a hazmat suit, and he held something in his hands. He disappeared when he heard you shouting."

He doesn't look at me. His grip tightens on his staff. I can't tell if he even heard me.

Then he whispers, "This object. What did it look like?"

"Long, and it narrowed towards a small cylinder at the end."

Stavros turns to me. There's anger in his eyes, and something else. Fear.

"A rifle." Another bang, like a clap from powerful hands, and I think I hear someone scream. Then a laugh. "Raiders."

"No, no, Stavros." Tears slide down my cheeks. I want to sink to the floor and weep. "It's my fault."

"No time for that now," he snaps, striding past me and raising his voice. "Scavengers, wake! With me, right now!"

"What do you want me to do?" I ask, almost treading on his heels. The Kin move with startling speed, the Scavenger crew faster than the rest.

"Stay with Mika," Stavros replies, kneeling before me. "The Raiders are killers, Panam, and we don't know their numbers. But we have an advantage. This is *our* home. Stay in the dark places, keep quiet and wait until it's safe."

I glance around. Throughout the cavern, parents are talking to children, giving them instructions like Stavros gives me. Even though I'm not a child anymore, it comforts me, until I hear another yell from those black tunnels.

"And what if it never is?" I ask, tears stinging my eyes. "Safe, I mean."

"Then you take your sister, and anyone else you can, and you find somewhere that is. A place beyond the storm. An old saying, but one to remember Topside."

Stavros stands and signals for the Scavengers to follow him. The group, twelve of them, gather in the cavern's mouth, talking in hushed tones as I make my way to Mika. She kneels with her blankets wrapped around her, eyes wide and glowing from the fire's dying embers.

"What's happening?"

I take a deep breath. No more lies, no more weakness.

"Strangers are attacking us. We need to find somewhere to hide."

I expect tears but they don't come. Instead, Mika nods and takes my hand. She squeezes it tight.

"It'll all be okay, Panam."

I squeeze back.

Stavros jogs over. "Panam, when we leave, count to two-hundred. Then you and the other adults left behind lead the children deeper into the caves. Take anything you can carry that won't slow you down. Wait for a Scavenger to find you."

He turns away.

"Stavros?" I say, my voice catching in my throat. He looks at me, his face hidden in shadows. "Thank you."

I see his smile flash in the darkness. "You've always made me proud."

The Scavengers leave. I glance around at the others, struggling to make them out in the gloom. There's around twenty that aren't children but they are the youngest and the eldest of the adults. Word spreads and the remaining Kin roll up their bedding, wrap their bottles of fresh water from our springs. I assume that's what the Raiders want, but then I remember what Stavros said: *'Rapists, murderers and cannibals.'*

I count in my mind as I busy myself, feeling a swell of pride as I see Mika, already finished. She crouches beside me, watching the tunnel entrance.

"Stick by me, Mika," I say, reaching one hundred. "Stay silent and do as I say."

She nods in reply.

The shuffling noises in the cavern fall silent as the Kin finish their preparations. Another yell drifts in through the tunnels, another bang, a scream of pain. Close. Much closer than before.

One-hundred-and-twenty.

A sudden volley of noise; quick, powerful, claps.

One-hundred-and-thirty.

A howl of laughter.

One-hundred-and-forty.

A cry of anger.

One-hundred-and-fifty.

"We're coming for you all!"

Sound is funny in the tunnels; something minutes away can sound like it's on top of you. But that call—that taunting, cruel shout—sounds too close.

"Move!" I bark, the word racing from my mouth before I realise. The Kin rise, so quick they surprise me. Some lit by firelight, others in shadow, they run to the tunnel.

We head into the twisting passages and somehow I'm at the head of the party. Mika is by my side, our fingers locked.

A bang rips through the darkness, then a flash of light. Another pop sounds as we stand transfixed by the sudden strobe. Stavros wrestles with a Raider, both men with teeth bared, the rifle between them. It fires again, straight into the roof. Stavros slams his forehead into the attacker's face and it all goes dark. I hear grunts, harsh breathing, then a cry followed by the sound of a body hitting the rocks and sliding to the floor.

"Is Stavros alive?" Mika whispers. I feel the whole group press closer together as the silence stretches.

"Get moving," I hear Stavros hiss, his shape twisting in the darkness. He ducks into a nook and brings out two burning torches. He hands one to old Ivor who nods, leading people away. Stavros holds another out for me. "Here."

A blade tears through his chest. Warm blood spurts out, covers my face. I can taste it and I gag. Mika opens her mouth, ready to scream, but Stavros sweeps us aside, knocking us to the ground and towards the Kin who are watching, paralysed.

The blade is still inside him as he turns, throwing the torch at the Raider who impaled him. It strikes the hazmat suit but does nothing. Just bounces off. Another attacker steps into the light, rifle in hand, and strikes Stavros across the face, knocking him to the ground. We make eye contact, and he mouths one simple word: *'Run.'* Crimson fluid leaks from his lips.

I scramble to my feet as the Kin flee, like the unsaid word climbed into our minds and set our legs moving.

"After them!" a woman's fierce cry chases us as we flee into the darkness.

"Which way?" Ila asks, her voice taut. I can't see her, but I know she has her children close. My hand tightens around Mika's.

"Stay together, we head for the—" Traak, our ancient teacher, doesn't finish his instruction. A volley of gunfire rings out, and his words turn into a scream of agony. The children of the Kin, I hear their cries; Mika whimpers along with them.

"Keep moving," I hiss, knowing that to stand still means death. Or worse.

"What about Traak?" Jaap murmurs, but we're already moving through the darkness.

I glance behind me. We've moved around a bend in the cave, but I can see the Raiders torches in the gloom. And the shape on the ground. "He's dead."

Mika lets out a sob. I fight down the urge to silence her. She's a child. Why shouldn't she cry? I want to scream. The Raiders know we're here anyway. Stealth won't help us. They're just chasing us deeper into the tunnels and they're all dead ends. The only way to escape is to head Topside.

Gunfire explodes behind us. I throw myself to the ground, pulling Mika with me. She collapses on top of me, and I pull her into my chest and roll, clamping a hand over her mouth. I slam into a cave wall and press myself tighter against it, making us as small as possible, trying to avoid the Raiders' eyes.

"Leave some alive, won't you?" one says, his snarl more like a grin. "Want to have my fun. There's young ones down there, or so my ears tell me."

"Don't touch my children!"

My heart fills my mouth, and I all I can do is watch as Jaap hurtles towards the pack of Raiders, hands curled like claws.

He doesn't last long.

With a laugh, a Raider rushes him, her vicious, curved blade free, and slashes him across the throat. Jaap drops to his knees, gurgling as he tries to hold his blood into the gaping wound. The woman kneels before him.

"Too bad," she says, and licks the gore from her weapon. "Pretty one, this."

She kisses him as she drives the blade through his chest.

"More went that way," another Raider says. The one with the rifle. He moves away and others follow, chasing the younglings and elders of the Kin. They're going to die. They're *all* going to die.

Satisfied that Jaap is finished, the woman climbs to her feet and follows. "Find the water, once you've had your fun!"

Silence and darkness come, along with the knowledge of what I need to do next. I can't help the Kin, but I can save Mika.

"Listen to me," I whisper, stroking my sister's hair. "We retrace our steps, stay together and escape."

"But the Kin! We can't—"

"There's nothing we can do for them, Mika," I urge, keeping my voice strong though my heart wants to break. "We need to move. Now."

Her strength startles me. She pushes to her feet, hand still in mine and presses close to the wall. Shouts echo behind us, and we journey back the way we came, back to where I last saw Stavros. I want to believe he's alive, but how can he be? How can anyone?

Unwanted hope blooms in my chest as we pass through the dark. Only minutes have passed. Maybe all the Raiders are deeper in the caves. Maybe Stavros survived. I quicken my pace, and Mika matches my stride. Around another bend, I see light. Pressing a hand against Mika's chest, I creep forward, keeping low, eyes narrowed.

Stavros lies on his front near the mouth of our sleeping cavern, the blade still in his back. He coughs.

"Stavros…" I whisper, waving Mika forward. We run and kneel at his head. Blood slicks the ground beneath him, his skin white in the torchlight. He won't survive this.

"Told you to run," he manages, voice hoarse and cracked.

"We—"

"*Hide,*" Stavros snarls. It takes me a second to hear what he did. A whistle coming from the darkness.

Mika acts first, pulling me out of the light, into the mouth of the sleeping cavern. The Raider appears, scanning the ground, examining the man Stavros killed. A grin breaks out across his face when he notices that Stavros breathes.

He stamps on Stavros' back, bends and yanks the blade out, making him scream and growl. I glance at Mika. She's flat against the cave wall, sliding deeper into the shadows of the sleeping cavern. I know I should do the same, but I can't. Stavros' eyes plead with me. They tell me not to watch, but I can't look away.

The Raider kneels, blade held in a loose grip, his mouth close to Stavros' ear. "Killed one of us, eh? You had promise, but that's just too bad. Life's unfair."

He surges to his feet, the blade arcing above him, before he brings it down, severing Stavros' head from his neck.

My hands fly to my mouth. Bile rises in my throat. A scream builds, desperate for release. I've never seen someone murdered before today. Now, I have watched Traak and Jaap die before my eyes. My mind couldn't comprehend that. But *this*… Stavros taught me everything, protected me.

He's my family. Him and Mika.

The Raider bends, dips his gloved fingers into the gaping neck wound and licks the blood away, his wretched smile illuminated by the flickering light. He gets to his feet, blade dripping.

My body takes over, like I'm watching myself as my limbs seek to save themselves from the same fate or worse. I crawl into the shadows, flat against the cavern wall, following the curve into the sleeping area.

The Raider follows. I see him move into the cavern, unafraid, vigilant. Mika blends into the darkness, and I shrink down, my hands still covering my mouth, as he kicks at our discarded bundles of sheets.

He takes a step in my direction. I close my eyes in case the whites of them give me away.

More gunfire rings out, followed by high-pitched shrieks. The Raider laughs and sprints back into the tunnels. I drop to the ground, on my hands and knees, breath coming in quick, ragged gulps. More gunfire, more cries, more death.

"It's my fault," I whisper, fingernails clawing at the stone beneath me. "I brought them here. I killed Stavros. I killed them all."

"Panam?" I hear Mika whisper, and it snaps me to my senses. "Help me, please. I'm scared."

I wipe the tears from my eyes and crawl to our bundles, hefting them.

"Come on. Stick with me. The darkness is our friend. Just like hide and go seek, okay?"

"Where are we going?"

"Topside. We run until we find somewhere safe."

Mika nods, grabs my hands. We walk together. I swallow bile and regret as we step over Stavros' body. A rifle lies at his side. I take it.

His head is missing. A trail of gore leads into the darkness, where terror and death echo.

PART FOUR
TOPSIDE

We creep through the darkness, rats clinging to the shadows, as the Raiders rip our home away from us.

Mika moves with silent determination, resolute and following my lead whenever I pause, turn or hide. For years, as children, we played in the dark, without straying far from the Kin's main caverns. We became experts at blending with the shadows down here.

Or so we thought. This is our first real test.

They have infested our tunnels. Some carry devices that shine faint light through the gloom, while others brandish crude torches. They pass us, and each second drags like a year. I'm certain they'll discover us at any moment as we make our way Topside, but so far, we've gone unnoticed.

Blood covers the tunnel floor. The sound of gunfire has grown seldom, as have the cries from the Scavengers. I don't know what that means. I fear Mika and I are the only ones left.

We're moving uphill, and I notice that change in the air.

"How much further?" Mika whispers, her voice low and husky. The horrors she's seen today, the mutilated corpses of her family. Her Kin. Their screams echoing through her home.

"We're close," I mutter, seeing a light up ahead. But it isn't the cave mouth. It's a Raider. "Wait, there's a side room here, somewhere. We can hide in there until it's safe."

Their voices are indistinct, but I recognise one: Klaus.

I inch closer, Mika silent behind me.

"… found the water yet?" Klaus is saying. The firelight the other Raider holds makes his shadow dance against the wall. I see the opening, the one with the hazmat suits. I think we can make it there unseen.

"No," the other growls. "You sure there's water here? Only place in these parts I know of is that settlement built out of the caves east of here, and there's no chance we're getting in there. Too organised, too many weapons. Scouted it myself before you found this place. It ain't far, but I wouldn't rate our chances of taking it."

"There's water," Klaus replies, as we edge closer. I turn to Mika, a finger across my lips before pointing at the shadowy entrance. She nods. "So many people wouldn't survive down here without a large, clean source. Reckon these folks have lived down here since The Change. Seen the rat-pelts they wear? Still, they adapted in their own way, and they survived this long."

"Until us."

Klaus just laughs.

We duck into the tunnel and I let the breath I've held hiss out of me. Mika sinks to the floor, staring with unblinking eyes into the tunnel.

"Still," the other Raider says, his voice clear from our hiding place, "even if there ain't no water, plenty of meat, eh?"

Klaus grunts in agreement. "I can never get used to being underground. Men aren't meant to live like rodents. There's a girl I want you to look for. Dark hair cut like a boy's. Teenage, I reckon, but those eyes make her look older. I want to thank her."

The other Raider laughs as Mika looks at me. She knows they're talking about me.

"Plenty of girls down here, I reckon. Why her?"

A pause.

"You know how it is," Klaus drawls, "when you see something you fancy. Only that one will do. And you know me, I don't give up on a toy so easy."

Mika glares at me. A hard, accusing stare.

"I'm sorry," I whisper, reaching out for her. She stares at my fingers, like she's never seen a hand before. "I came here alone. They saw me. I had no idea what would happen."

She continues to stare. As I'm about to pull my hand away, she takes it.

Tears in her eyes match mine as she stares around the room at the hazmat suits.

"What are these things?"

"Protection for Topside. We'll need them."

I expect the other Raider to walk by our cavern, in search of water, but he doesn't. I try to forget about him for now, busying myself looking through the hazmat suits for ones small enough to fit myself and Mika.

"Protection from what?" she asks, reaching out to touch one helmet hanging above a suit. She taps at it, stopping as it echoes.

"Water from the sky," I answer, pulling one aside that will do for me. "It's why we all live underground. It burns through skin. I saw it turn a rat to mush. But the Raiders wear these suits, and so do the Scavengers. They must stop it."

"But these people," Mika asks, beginning to sob, "why did they *do* this to us?"

"It's what they do. They travel from place to place, taking what they want and moving on. Stavros called them Raiders." I select the smallest suit I can find. It's still too big, but it'll have to do. "Here, put this on. Helmet last."

I work on mine, pulling the suit over my clothes. It's hot, and I worry the bright yellow will stand out as we make our escape. But, when the alternative is hiding in the caves, waiting for the Raiders to find and butcher us, I'll take my chances.

When I'm finished, I help Mika into hers. It drowns her. I find some pieces of rope and tie them around her wrists and ankles, making sure the material doesn't sag so she can run.

"Listen to me," I say, placing my hands on her cheeks. "Topside's going to overwhelm you, but we've no time to wait. We *must* move. Know I'm with you, every step of the way."

"Where?" Mika asks, her bottom lip trembling. "This is our home, Panam. We don't *know* anywhere else."

I hesitate. Stavros said to move, to find a place beyond the storm. I hadn't given it any more thought than that, but something the Raider said...

"East. Those men, they mentioned a place in the east, one they wouldn't attack. We go there."

"East." Mika repeats. "Do you know what that is?"

"Stavros told me the sun rises in that direction. The attack came before dawn, so the sun should be on the horizon. We go that way. Ready?"

"Ready."

I fasten the helmet over her head, making sure it's secure before turning to my own. We need to run as soon as we emerge from the caves and, if it's raining, we won't have time to see to our helmets then. I stick my bundle of blankets under one arm and hold the rifle I took in the other as we move toward the tunnels.

The Raider's still there, back to us, gazing up the slope towards Topside.

I hold out my bundle to Mika and she takes it, wedging it under her other arm. Gripping the rifle in both hands, I creep towards the unmasked Raider. Before today, I'd never thought of hurting someone, let alone killing them, but this monster has the blood of my friends, my family, my Kin, on his hands and he's in our way. I must be strong for Mika.

I reverse the grip, holding the killing end, and run towards the Raider, jumping and swinging the rifle. It cracks him across the back of the head, knocking him to the ground in a heap.

"Come on," I say, pulling Mika with me.

She runs but, before I can follow, the Raider's hand snatches out, grabs my leg. I fall on top of him, his other hand smacking me across the helmet. It doesn't hurt—too much padding—but it disorientates me. He grabs me around the throat and flips me to the floor; I hear something tear against the rocks. Heat and pain on my arm. Then the Raider is throttling me and it slips from my mind.

Mika screams, but I can't even tell her to run. My vision fades as I stare at the Raider, blood running down his face from where I hit him, dripping onto my mask, his pointed teeth bared as he squeezes.

The rifle's between us. With numb fingers, I fumble for it, find the firing mechanism. I don't know who the bullet will strike—me or him—but it's that or death.

The rifle kicks when my gloved finger squeezes the trigger. The noise is deafening.

I feel no pain, but time slows. Hands still around my throat, the Raider glances down, then back at me, eyes wide with shock. He lets go, topples to the side, a smoking hole in his chest.

I scramble to my feet, grab the rifle and run to Mika, pulling her along with me. I've killed a man, but I had no choice.

I'd do it again.

"Brace yourself," I say to Mika as we pound towards Topside, the light growing brighter.

We emerge and come to a halt as I blink in the daylight. There's no sign of Klaus, save for his hazmat helmet with the white handprint. I grab it, toss it away into the darkness behind me. Perhaps the lack of protection will stop him from following us.

I glance around. It's a cloudless blue sky, the orange sun rising behind the dead trees.

"Let's go," I say, turning to her. She's rooted to the spot, taking in this strange, new world. I remember how it felt. "Mika?"

"I don't think I can…"

I want nothing more than to hold her, tell her everything will be okay. But I can't do that. Taking a bundle from her and sticking my rifle through it, I take her hand.

"Keep your head down, focus on your feet. I'm with you, but we *have* to run. Now."

I pull her, and she doesn't move. I try again, and she inches one foot forward, then another, and just like that, we're running together, down the slope, toward the rotten, twisted trees and the sun rising in the east.

PART FIVE
EAST

Sweat drips down my body and slicks my hazmat suit as we run through the barren trees. We haven't stopped since we emerged Topside. My breathing is laboured, and Mika stumbles beside me. My arm stings; blood drips to the dead ground. My suit must be ripped. Despite that, we move. We've run for an hour, maybe longer. The sun rose higher in the sky, but I've kept my feet trained in the direction I first saw it. East. Towards salvation.

I hope.

"Stop, Panam," Mika gasps. "Please. I can't go on like this."

I nod, coming to a stop. Mika collides with me, and we sink to the floor, holding each other.

"Five minutes," I say in between gulps of air. "Did you bring water?"

Mika nods and fishes inside her blankets, drawing out her canteen. I take off my mask and lift my own, though from its weight I can tell it's half-empty.

"Slow drinks, Mika," I say, taking a sip. "This has to last us."

"Your arm!"

I glance at it. The wound isn't deep, but it's long and angry-looking. "It's fine. Least of my worries right now. Look."

I point to the sky. Mika ducks her head, peeks at the stretch of blue from under her eyebrows. Grey clouds approach.

"What is it?" she asks, head sinking again as she stares at the ground.

"Means rain, and we've got to hope the suits hold up, or we find shelter before it starts. I saw what it does to flesh. It'll eat through my arm."

Mika's little body heaves as she lets out a sob. "How did all this happen? Why does the world want to kill us?"

Be strong for her, I tell myself.

"Nobody knows, Mika. From what Stavros told me, one day it all worked as it should. The next, this. We can't change that. All we *can* do is fight. Together."

A booming laugh rings out. I jump and so does she.

"I'm on your heels, cave rat," Klaus calls. He's still some distance away. His voice is thin, drifting, but he's used to Topside. We aren't. He can close the gap. "Why don't you come back to me? You don't want to get caught out here in the rain. You've got something of mine and I'm going to take it back. If you don't give it up now, I'm going to take a whole lot more."

"Move," I hiss at Mika.

"We can't outrun him."

"And he can't stay out here," I say, pointing upward. "I threw his mask into the caverns. Sounds like he thinks I've got it, but he'll turn back before the rain comes. Run."

She surges to her feet, jamming her mask back in place and stowing her canteen. I copy her, trying not to stumble as my arm aches and the grey wisps of cloud grow thicker and blot out the blue sky.

...

We run, hand-in-hand, drawing strength from each other. My breath comes in ragged gasps, and I hear Mika struggling. Inside the hazmat suit, my body cooks, the sweat steaming on my skin. We're moving east—at least, I think we are—but the going is slow; we stumble, weave and stagger as much as sprint. The sun rising in the sky, growing hotter with each passing moment, cooks us.

The rain hasn't come, though the occasional glance I throw upwards shows the dark clouds gathering. The landscape hasn't changed; Topside appears dead. Empty. A wasteland ravaged by disaster and picked clean by Raiders like Klaus.

He's getting closer. He shouts, calls for me, each time closer than before. Klaus' laughter as he tells me what he's going to do to me makes my step all the quicker, but it's no good. Unless we reach our destination—and they let us in—Klaus *will* catch us.

I can't let him take Mika.

"Please," she gasps, stumbling behind me. "My legs... My chest!"

I grab her arm, pull her along with me. My limbs scream in protest, the wound I took in the caves still bleeding. I think if I stop, I won't ever start again.

"Mika, we have to move. He'll kill us."

No. He'll do worse than that. But I can't speak the words.

She nods, masked head bobbing as she allows me to drag her. It's no use. Neither of us can run anymore; we're out on our feet, delaying the inevitable.

A gunshot rings out. Mika screams. I throw a glance over my shoulder, half-expecting to see Klaus just behind. Is he? There, in the distance... I squint.

Another shot, and a second later, sudden pain in my shoulder. I hear something slam into a tree just beyond me.

My hazmat suit's ripped where the pain is. Blood trickles out. It grazed me, but *it hurts*! Gritting my teeth, I test my arm. I can move it, barely.

Another shot. I throw myself to the ground, pulling Mika with me. We collapse in a heap, lying, gasping, gulping in air.

"What can we do?" Mika manages, voice shrill beneath her mask.

My rifle sticks into my side where I fell on it. I've already used it to kill a man. I can do it again.

Rolling over, I lie on my tummy, squinting back the way we came. I see Klaus, his black, helmetless suit stark against the brown horizon. He'll reach us in minutes. With care, I pull my rifle forward, aiming at him, my finger on the trigger. I tuck the end against my wounded shoulder, lay my cheek against its top so I can see where I'm pointing. Satisfied, I rise onto one knee and squeeze.

The rifle roars. It jolts, banging into my wounded shoulder, knocking me flat on my back. A scream rips out of my throat, but I force myself up again.

I missed. Klaus is still coming.

I brace myself, grit my teeth against the bloom of pain in my shoulder. I fire, rocking backwards, my feet sliding in the dead grass.

Another miss. Klaus laughs.

"Run, Mika!" I snarl, getting ready to fire again.

"No!"

I squeeze. Klaus runs, closer still.

"Do as I say, go!"

I take a deep breath. What am I doing wrong? I adjust my grip, pointing at where I think Klaus is *going* to be by the time the bullet reaches him. With a fierce smile, I squeeze.

Click.

I stare at the rifle, dumbstruck. I aim again, and fire.

Click.

"No."

Click, click, click.

"No, no, no! Mika, go, run! Now!"

Klaus is so close. The sunlight glints off his bald head. His laughter is triumphant.

"Life outside the cave isn't for you, girl," he cries, his voice ringing out through the rotten trees, "and you've brought a friend! My lucky day."

Fear fills me. I shake it off and move. Mika, too. She's ahead of me, running as fast as when we emerged Topside. The sunlight fades. I turn my face towards the sky to see the grey clouds smothering the sun.

"Keep going!" I yell. "It's going to rain! He can't chase us in the rain!"

"But your suit," Mika shouts back, "your arm, your shoulder."

I have to be strong for her—my sister, my baby—for as long as I can.

"Mika, save your breath. You keep going, whatever happens."

Another gunshot. Pain erupts in my calf.

"Run!" I scream, and then I fall. Blood gushes onto my gloved hands as I clutch my leg.

Mika stands there, frozen. But it isn't me she's looking at. Through a haze of pain, I glance behind me. A hundred paces away, Klaus raises his rifle again. He aims at Mika.

The *click* makes me sob with relief.

"Doesn't matter," Klaus calls, striding forward. He throws the rifle aside, draws a knife from the belt at his waist. "I want to feel her insides anyway."

I turn to Mika, gazing at her one last time. I wish I could see her face. "Go."

She hesitates.

"Go!" I scream, surging to my feet.

My weary limbs, the wounds in my leg, my arm, my shoulder cry out as one, but I stand. The sight of Mika, still heading east, gives me strength. I put myself between her and Klaus. I'd forgotten how large he is, and how I'm still just a child.

"Go back," I shout, pointing at him. "Look at the sky. When it rains, you'll die. Run while you can."

Klaus laughs, stopping so close I can see his suit swell and shrink as he breathes. The scars across his cruel face twist, his discoloured eye refusing to close.

"Why run when you've got a perfectly good mask right there?"

He takes another step.

"Wait!"

I throw my hand up. A raindrop pelts the back of my glove. A single bead of water. It sizzles as it trickles off the hazmat suit. I look at Klaus. He's not smiling now.

"Out of time, girl."

He lunges, blade swinging. I run to meet him, my rifle like a club, aiming for his exposed head.

My injured leg gives out. I slip. His blade misses my throat as I fall. My rifle batters his shins. Klaus grunts. I scream.

Because the knife passed through my hazmat suit and into my stomach, just below my ribs.

I try to move, but pain pins me. I grip the bloody handle and start to cry, fear and frustration swelling. My only relief is that Mika got away.

Klaus gathers himself, crawls over to me, grabs the knife.

"Might as well give up," he says, wrenching it free. I scream again, my vision blurring and blackening. I see him through a dark tunnel, leering at me with that scarred, evil face. "You're already dead."

The skin on his hairless head sizzles as a raindrop falls on it. Then another. He howls but I feel nothing. His body protects my exposed skin from the sparse drops. He throws the bloodied blade away and reaches for my throat.

No, not my throat. My neck, where the mask meets the suit. I grab his fingers, bending, squeezing, shrieking at him.

The rainfall turns into a deluge.

A splash hits my exposed arm. I feel it burn as it eats away at my skin. My scream is nothing compared to his.

The water melts his face.

His frantic fingers still fight with mine, his pointed teeth bared as he roars behind them, the rain carving bloody gouges in his skin. Steam rises from his head and chunks of flesh ooze from his skull.

The rain falls harder. Drops strike my shoulder, more on my arm, but still I fight.

Klaus spits a mouthful of blood onto my mask.

"I'll kill you," he slurs, lips disintegrating.

"No," I gasp, "you won't."

I kick out and hit him between the legs. He falls backwards, exposing me to the rain. My arm is numb. I see bone through the tear in my suit. I tuck it against my injured stomach, sliding backwards into the shelter of a tree's skeletal branches, hoping it will give me protection.

Klaus' screams become a gurgle.

He fights to stand as his good eye slides from its socket. He tries to grab it, like he thinks he'll save it. It's gone before it hits the ground.

Klaus follows it, falling onto his stomach, the rain still beating at his ruined head.

My back collides with the tree. I lean my head onto my shoulder, keeping the water from leaking into my suit.

It doesn't matter. I know I'm dead, but the rain's stopping and a strange calm fills me.

I turn my eyes to the sky, watching the clouds thin and disappear as the sun shines through them, like its rays chase them away. Resting my head against the scarred trunk, I close my eyes.

As darkness swallows me and I go numb, my thoughts turn to my sister. I whisper her name.

EPILOGUE

"**P**anam!"

Mika's voice breaks through my dreams of floating in water. Like I did in the caves. My body felt weightless as I stared at the rock ceiling.

"Go back to sleep, Mika," I mumble. "It isn't dawn yet."

No. That isn't right.

"Panam! Where are you?"

I crack my eyes open. The light hurts. Klaus' corpse lies nearby. My gloved hands cradle the wound in my stomach. The pain returns, and I whimper.

I try to call out. My voice is weak. But Mika's out there, searching for me, and I must be strong for her.

"Mika!" I bellow, my voice echoing through the wilderness.

"Over there!" I hear a man shout. My body goes cold. Am I dying? Or just afraid?

I hear the pounding of feet and turn my head towards it. It lolls from one shoulder to the other.

It's her. Mika. My sister. My life.

"They're coming to help, Panam. Hold on!"

Faces crowd me, eyes without masks. Men and women of all ages.

"She's lost a lot of blood," one says.

"Might lose the arm if she survives," says another.

Hands lift me, and it's like I'm floating again. I feel something squeeze my fingers. Mika. I gaze at her, looking at her face one more time. Maybe the last time. Someone lifts my helmet, and sunlight kisses my face.

I smile at Mika, and whisper: "It's okay, sister. It's all okay."

Darkness takes me again, as I'm carried away. But, even if I die, Mika lives. Our future lives.

She found it. The place beyond the storm.

END

David Green is a writer of dark fiction. Born in Manchester, UK and living in Galway, Ireland, David grew up with gloomy clouds above his head, and rain water at his feet, which has no doubt influenced his dark scribblings. David is the author of the Pushcart Prize nominated novelette Dead Man Walking, and is excited for his fantasy series, Empire of Ruin, debuting in June 2021 from Eerie River Publishing.

Newsletter: https://tinyurl.com/y6ah8brp
www.twitter.com/davidgreenwrite
www.davidgreenwriter.com
https://www.facebook.com/davidgreenwriter

QUANTUM RULE
BY JAY SANDLIN

CHAPTER ONE

Brooklyn Borough Outskirts: Scorchland Border

Fuel burned in Bruce Dempsey's nostrils as he opened his bike's throttle. The grinding engine of the salvage cycle carried him and his passenger dangerously close to the borough borderlands. Traveling this far out was taking a risk—hell, taking a damn sip of water was a risk—but he needed to get out of Brooklyn for a bit, away from the underground shelter, away from the crowds. Feel the wind on his face even if the stale air reeked of radioactive fallout. Besides, this might be his last chance for a long, long time.

Rebecca Stone's grip tightened around his waist. Her warm hands over his hips provided him no small measure of comfort. She spoke over the engine's growl, a tremor in her voice. "Haven't we've gone far enough?"

Bruce nodded without blinking. "This area was picked clean decades ago." He thought fast, inventing a story to justify carrying her so far out. "If we want a chance of finding somethin' worth trading, we've gotta go further."

Rebecca let out a low sigh, her sweet breath tickling his ear. "You're not a scavenger anymore, Bruce." She patted the quantum metal pendant over his heart. "You're our contender. You're too valuable to risk for trinkets."

Bruce applied pressure to the handbrake, and the worn tires kicked up rocks and cadmium dust as he skidded to a stop. He'd never been able to hide anything from Rebecca. She'd read him like a book since they were kids. "No wonder you're my repository. I'm just the lunkhead who likes hurtin' people."

"You're much more than that." Rebecca swung one of her long legs over the bike, sliding off the ripped vinyl seat to face Bruce. Leaning down, she planted a soft kiss on his lips. Her fingernails dug into his lean, muscular biceps. "You carry our future in those arms." Rubbing slowly down his forearms, she took his rough, weathered hands in hers. "You'll win by the strength of your heart and the power of your fists." Leaning forward, she whispered in his ear. "That's why they call you..."

"The Beast of Brooklyn," Bruce mumbled. Feeling a rush of emotions, he pulled her down on his lap. This was exactly why he needed to get away. Brooklyn might be their home, but the crowded borough offered as little privacy as it did canned goods and toilet paper. For several long moments, they sat kissing, enjoying the silence. His hands rubbed up and down her back, stroked her long braided hair between his fingers.

With a smack of her lips, she broke the kiss. Gazing down at him, her fingers gently patted the fresh tattoo beside his left eye. The design matched the one on the quantum pendant beneath his leather vest. "You became Brooklyn's contender when you won the contender trials, last fighter standing." She leaned closer, brushing back his greasy black hair. "Soon, the other boroughs will gather for the challenges, competing for supplies. You're the only one who can fight them for us."

Bruce snorted, eyes drifting down to the pendant around his neck. "I dunno about that. The Butcher almost got me in the finals." He swung his leg off the bike, rubbing his jaw. "Guy's got one hell of a right cross."

"Oh please, you beat him in less than three rounds." Rebecca scanned the area, bowing softly as she placed her hand against her chest. "You did good, Bruce. Face it, you're the best hope we've had in years. I'm lucky to be your repository."

Bruce let out a sigh, remembering Rebecca's studies. The burrough elders selected her as a repository for her brilliant mind, able to retain and remember facts almost as well as those old machines—computers, they'd called them. Bruce never cared much for histories or politics, but Rebecca and the other bookworm repositories spent hours memorizing facts about the world before the Scorch. He'd always been a bad influence on her studies, especially since he'd been so attracted to her in their younger days. The best day of his life was when she was chosen to be *his* repository, the one to match brains with his brawn. Now that she was his official repository, it made it so much easier to be together, though it wasn't always the case to have repositories and contenders as *close* as they were.

Letting out a frustrated sigh, she reached into the equipment pouch on her hip, fishing out a small syringe. "And as your repository, my role is to aid you in emerging victorious. Since you're determined to scavenge, let's not delay. The Q-Lords could summon you at any time." She bit her lip, shivering as she mentioned their overlords, far off in their shining tower of wealth and luxury. "Ready for your dose of quantum blood?"

"Yeah, sure," Bruce grunted, holding out his arm.

Rebecca injected the liquid quicksilver into his veins, then took a fresh needle for herself. At best, the dose provided a few hours of protection from exposure in the scorchlands. The red sun's placement above their heads told him it was about midday. Like his father and *his* father before him, Bruce spent a lifetime scavenging the ruins of what had once been New York City. Before the Scorch, people called it the greatest city on Earth. Today, the dead metropolis' bones had been picked so clean, they were hard-pressed to find anything of value to trade with other boroughs. That's why the contender challenges were so important. Brooklyn's supplies were dangerously low, and everyone counted on Bruce to win the Q-Lord's challenges and bring home food, medicine, and supplies. Everything revolved around the challenges, broadcast throughout all five boroughs on communal screens. No matter how rundown the boroughs got, the Q-Lords always made sure those kept running, even when the ancient plumbing didn't. This time, it was rumoured that even prizes of quantum would be on the line.

Bruce squeezed his forearm, feeling lightheaded. Quantum blood doses were carefully rationed, the borough possessed little to waste. Using some of their supply to come out here under false pretenses made him feel almost as guilty as lying to Rebecca did. He let out a deep groan, shaking his head. *Time to come clean.* "We're not here to scavenge. We came because I have to ask you a question."

Rebecca's hands went to her hips. He cringed as he saw the look forming on her face, he knew it well. "What on scorched earth did you bring me way out here to ask?"

Bruce's head dipped. He removed the quantum pendant from his neck, then placed it around Rebecca's. "This pendant is heavier than it looks." He motioned behind them. "To everyone back there it means hope. To me it means pain." He paused as he wet his cracked lips. "Loss."

Rebecca stopped and stared down at the thin disc. The Q-Lords' seal embossed on its face meant it was made of pure quantum, worth more than anything in their whole stinkin' borough. "That's the contenders' purpose, to fight for those who can't fight for themselves. Bear the pain they can't."

Bruce looked down, kicking at the leather straps on his boots. "What if I'm tired of fighting?"

Rebecca's eyes went wide, the pendant dropping from her hand and bouncing against her chest. "What? What are you talking about?"

Stepping forward, he held her cheeks in his hands. "Don't you see? It doesn't matter if I win or lose. The game's rigged against us!" He tapped the pendant around her neck with his fingernail, a dull metallic scrape. "When we were kids, you told me stories. Worldwide games played for thousands of years in the world before the Scorch. The prizes were pendants like these, but made of gold." He dropped her hands and sighed. "You taught me back then, the world lived under a Golden Rule."

Rebecca nodded, her eyes fluttering as she spoke softly. "Yes, whoever had the gold *made* the rules."

Turning on his heels, he stared off in the distance. "Look what that got us." He gestured to the endless wasteland of decaying metal structures before them, decomposing for over a century, set against the backdrop of black clouds in the scorched sky. "They raped the planet, turned it into this hellhole. Nothing's fucking changed!" He kicked a stone on the ground, red dirt caking on his boots as it bounced away.

He felt Rebecca's warm touch on his shoulder as she rubbed his bare arms. "You're right. Except the Golden Rule's been replaced by a quantum one."

Without another word, they both looked off at the horizon, their eyes drawn to the same spot. Stretching to the heavens, shining like a silver beacon, a single skyscraper remained unscathed. "Quantum Tower," he whispered. The Q-Lord's home. Shaking his head, he walked towards the leather satchel mounted on his bike. "This shit is more valuable than gold because it's unbreakable, the only substance that can survive the scorched earth." He spit out the side of his mouth. "Limitless applications, it could help us all. But what do the damn Q-Lords do with it? Build a damn tower out of it and hide inside, hoarding it for themselves like the fucking dragon in that book you used to read me."

Rebecca grinned sadly. "Smaug," she whispered. "From *The Hobbit*."

"Exactly!" Cheeks burning red, he reached inside the satchel, and retrieved the borough's greatest treasure, the prize from the fall of the Butcher: a pair of leather gauntlets, forged with protective quantum metal and ending in sharp spikes on his knuckles. "We beat the shit out of each other in the boroughs, then fight in the challenges. For what? Scraps!" He raised his fist aloft, the invincible metal reflecting red-orange sunlight over his face. "This is all the quantum Brooklyn's got and we use it so our contender can *punch* harder?" His voice cracked; he had kept so much of this inside for years. The dam burst suddenly, and tears fell from his eyes against the cracked red earth. "Rebecca, why should we keep playing their game?"

Rebecca moved close. "What else can we do, Bruce? The borough is dying, you're their only hope. I don't believe you'd abandon them. Please, what's the *real* reason you're saying all this?"

If only it were that easy. Taking her hand, he carefully placed her palm on the unsharpened backs of his claws, only prepared to share a kernel of the truth. "You said it yourself, the Q-Lords could summon me at any moment." He nodded to the quantum medal on her chest. "That pendant's tracker will flash and I'll have to report immediately." He swallowed hard. "Unless…"

Rebecca whispered. "Unless what?"

He studied her body, memorizing every detail of her face. "We take a journey of our own. Except we don't come back again like Dildo."

Rebecca's face scrunched up and she giggled. "*Bilbo.*"

Bruce grinned. "Whatever." He nodded off to the distant scorchland. "We walk away, take our chances in scorchland." Leaning close, he exhaled deeply, pressing his forehead against hers. "Leave this place, travel far from the Q-Lords, as far as we can." Stepping back, he stretched out his arms. "We can find out what's left out there. Start a new life together, just the two of us."

Rebecca's arms hung limply by her sides. Her expression remained stoic, but Bruce knew what she would say before she spoke. "What about Brooklyn? Can we abandon our home?"

Bruce sighed and shook his head. He felt like he was back in the ring at Barclay's arena, pressed against the sagging ropes. "We'll leave the pendant and quantum claws behind—leave everything behind."

As if on cue, the quantum pendant around Rebecca's neck lit up with a brilliant azure glow. Loud beeping, like an alarm, echoed across the wastelands. Rebecca looked down at the pendant, then back at Bruce, panic on her lips. "I-It's time. The challenges... they're calling you."

Springing forward, he raised up on the balls of his feet, like he was charging headfirst with a desperate combination of punches. "Don't listen to that, just look at me. Let another contender and repository carry the borough on their backs." Gripping her shoulders, he stared deeply into her eyes. "A life with you is the only prize I care about winning."

As the pendant alarm rang, Bruce felt Rebecca's shoulders shake in his grip. Her eyes avoided his gaze. "Assuming we could find a life together... I've spent my life training to be a repository, learning about the scorchlands and the survivors remaining." She shivered as a strong gust of wind that smelled of brimstone blew past. "Even if we had somewhere to go, we don't have enough quantum blood to attempt a trip like that, not even close."

"Damn the quantum blood, I'm a survivor!" He spoke above the ringing, thumping his chest. "We'll travel by night, avoid exposure. We'll find a way to survive the scorchlands together. I know we can!"

Rebecca shook her head, her voice drifting off as she stared in the distance. "There are *far* more dangers in scorchland than just exposure."

"Maybe so." Bruce sighed deeply, his voice dropping several octaves. "Before he died, my father told me something I'll never forget. He said he'd rather die a free man than live in quantum chains." Taking several steps back, he scraped the ground, drawing a line in the sand with his boot's metal toe. "There's the line. We cross it, there's no turning back." He nodded to Rebecca, his nerves on fire. "Moment of truth. What do you say?"

Rebecca's feet remained planted. "Bruce, I--"

The ground shook beneath them, cutting off her answer. Bruce stumbled, searching for signs of a groundquake. Instead, he heard the screeching of rusted metal. He watched as a series of hidden trap doors popped open within the red-sand scorchlands, surrounding them on all sides. Eyes forward, fists raised, he growled at Rebecca. "Get behind me!"

Burning gasoline filled the acrid air, heavy engines revving in all directions. Beams from cracked headlights pointed at Bruce and Rebecca. Thick tires kicked up the dust as cart-like vehicles with metal frames shot through the air, ramping up from their hidden pathways in the earth.

Bruce shoved Rebecca out of the way. "Move!" They rolled in the dirt as one of the carts landed where they'd been standing, front bumper covered in jagged metal spikes.

Rebecca rushed to her feet, shaking dust out of her braids. "What's happening? We're still on borough lands."

Smacking the side of his head, Bruce raised his claws. "Something tells me they don't give a shit." He counted three carts, outfitted with pikes, spears, and designed for death. The drivers had ashy, albino skin, and long tubes ran from metallic masks that covered their mouths and noses. Sun shade visors covered their eyes, making their expressions impossible to read. *Whoever these pale bastards are, they don't like the sun.*

The albinos whistled and shouted. "Our lucky day! Fresh meat this far out!"

"Yes, *God* will be pleased with us." The death cart driver flashed a series of hand signals with long, blackened nails. With another rev of the engines, the carts began to circle them.

Bruce spotted his cycle just beyond the carts. He knew the aging engine didn't possess the horsepower to outrun them—but if they remained on foot, they'd be roadkill. Grabbing her hand, Bruce shouted, "Go, go!" and led the way to the half-buried dirt bike.

They took off at full speed, but the drivers were ready. Bruce ran towards the bike in a zig-zag, tossing corroded metal scrap in his wake. He was so focused on clogging the path behind them he barely noticed a sunbaked rock jutting out of the dirt. Bruce's contender training kicked in, his body reacting before his mind had time to think. "Look out!" he shouted over his shoulder, but it was too late. With a loud grunt, Rebecca's boot hit the rock, sending her sprawling on the rough scorchland several meters behind Bruce. "Augh! Goddamn it!"

"Hang on!" Bruce tugged on the bike's handlebars, retrieving it from where the death cart's impromptu entrance nearly left it buried. Rushing sand fell from the wheels and seat as he threw his leg over. The bike sputtered as he kicked the clutch. "I'm coming!"

Bruce was right; his bike *didn't* possess the horsepower to keep up with these carts. By the time he'd kickstarted the small engine, one of the albinos reached out with their meaty hands, snatching Rebecca up by her braids. The albino tossed her, one-handed, into a back compartment, then honked the horn on the steering wheel. "We've got what we need, return below!"

"No!" The carts' roaring engines drowned out Bruce's screams. He kicked the bike into a higher gear, racing behind the contrails of dust as the carts sped towards the trapdoors. Bruce raced to keep up, arriving just as the doors were sliding shut. Rebecca's quantum pendant continued to flash its summons as the vanishing albinos carried her down into a dark underworld below.

CHAPTER TWO

Underground

Sending his bike into a deep skid, Bruce's cheek came so close to the ground it nearly tore his face off. The bike's back wheel spun out, showering his ankle in sparks as he cleared the closing trap door by centimetres. It clanged shut behind him with metallic finality.

Grunting, he twisted his hips and shoulders, righting the cycle. Blinking his eyes, he squinted to adjust to the near-total darkness while pressing forward down a steep metal ramp. He heard the death carts spiraling down in the darkness, beyond the scope of his limited vision. Bruce arched his back and pointed his head forward. The handlebars shook in his grip, metal clinking as at least half-a-dozen small engine parts threatened to break apart any moment. He wondered how much more punishment the old scavenger cycle could withstand. *No time to worry about that, they've got Rebecca!*

The tunnel was narrow and black, swallowing any light and everything that breathed. The longer it stretched, he wondered if the salvage cycle would stop before he reached the center of the Earth.

The answer came when he struck rocky gravel. Bruce's ass bounced up and down on the ripped cushion seat. Inhaling a mouthful of what smelled like death and feces, he struggled not to slide out of control or vomit.

His stomach maintained its contents, but his bike had enough. It collapsed as he rolled across a set of rubble-strewn railcar tracks, scattering loose plates of metal. Bruce went down hard in the ferrous gravel. Years of contender training kicked in; his body knew how to roll and fall to protect the most vital areas. Nevertheless, he felt sharp cuts forming on his arms and beneath his leather vest. Skidding to a stop, he let out a deep exhale. *Fuck...I'm gonna feel that tomorrow.* Rising to his feet, he spotted what was left of his scavenger cycle: a twisted metal frame with wrecked tires, smoldering in the darkness. "Shit, that is *not* good." The ramp which carried him down was so steep, it was almost vertical. However he planned to escape this place, it wasn't going to be riding *that.* He searched around, wiping the dust from his clothes. *What the fuck is this place anyway?*

Walls covered in graffiti stretched throughout a sunken city, long forgotten to time. *Damn.* If Bruce thought New York City's remains were rough on the surface, seeing what she hid below shook him. Checking over his shoulder, the steep ramp deposited him at the black mouth of what looked like a former train yard. The smell of this place was nearly unbearable. Countless rats scurried through hollowed out cars, rotting piles of garbage and hardened rubber tires.

The endless blackness unnerved Bruce most. The underground city's albino inhabitants wearing masks and sun shades made a lot of sense. If they lived down here full time, the sun must seem like a blowtorch in their face. Bruce dropped into a low stance, staying on high alert. *Living down here, they can move and see better than I can. They could be anywhere...*

Bruce spotted a body twitching in the darkness and took off in a full sprint towards it. He made his way down another row of abandoned cars, rats the size of small dogs snapping at his heels. Rebecca lay on her side, hands bound behind her back, illuminated by a pile of burning tires. The pendant remained around her neck, but the glowing and beeping had ceased. *Small favors, I guess.* She couldn't have been there long, but furry gray rats were already sniffing around, nipping at her long braids. Bruce choked on the flames as he slid like a runner on the baseball diamond, falling in next to her. "Hey, honey. Didn't anyone teach you about getting in cars with strange people?"

Rebecca groaned, shaking her head to ward off the hissing vermin. "Shut up and cut me free."

Bruce complied with a quick slice from his quantum claws. "What happened, why did they let you go?"

She rubbed her wrists, looking around. "When they made a sharp turn, I dove out the back of one of those kill wagons."

Bruce grunted. "I call them death carts. Did they see you fall out?"

Rebecca groaned as she rose to a sitting position. "Not sure, but they didn't slow down. Fuck, my back hurts."

Helping her to her feet, he squinted around the railcar graveyard. *Can't stay long. Too dark, too many places to hide.* "C'mon, we gotta move."

Rebecca took a couple of steps, then let out a sharp wince of pain. "Where's the bike?"

Bruce rolled his eyes, pointing back to the mouth of the ramp. "Most of the wheels are back there." He pointed a few other directions down the path he'd come. "Then there, there and a bit other there."

"Holy shit, Bruce. I'm so sorry." Rebecca tried walking again, but didn't make it far. "That was your father's cycle."

"Yeah, but he's dead and buried." Bruce slid his arm beneath her shoulder, carrying her weight. "We will be too if we don't find a way outta here. What is this place anyway?"

"The Subterranean—remains of an old city, even older than the Scorch." Rebecca let out a small yelp of pain, her feet dragging in the dirt and grime. The contender's pendant bounced against her chest. "Maybe they heard the pendant's signal. You know what this means. The Q-Lords are expecting you."

"Let those rich fuckers wait." Bruce guided Rebecca as they turned a corner, ducking behind another row of railcars. "Once we get out of here, we'll start again somewhere new."

A pair of headlights and a roaring engine drowned out Rebecca's response. One of the death carts waited at the end of the row, revving its engine. The driver waved, flashing a pair of milky red eyes which looked hungry for blood.

"Move, move move!" Bruce practically carried Rebecca as they ran, not that it would do any good—the narrow row didn't provide much in the way of cover. They were on foot, and Rebecca was hurt. It would only be a matter of seconds before their blood freshened the blades mounted on the death cart's grill.

The cart, however, maintained a steady crawl, but did not overtake them. Bruce wondered what it was waiting for. *A cat playing with its food?*

Another set of headlights and a second revving engine told him it was more than a single cat toying with them. Another death cart appeared, blocking their exit. This one was bigger than the rest, adorned with human skulls, and a collection of jagged spears sticking from its chassis.

Bruce kicked up the metallic gravel as he yanked Rebecca off her feet. With her over his shoulder, he looked back. The skull cart kept its distance, moving at almost a leisurely pace. The unseen driver stuck their head out the window, voice echoing in the darkness. "You see my flock, *God* provides!"

Lights flashed, followed by engines rising in a deafening chorus of RPM. Thick exhaust and the smell of burning petrol surrounded them as Bruce realized the terrible truth. "They weren't huntin' us, they *herded* us."

A parade of death carts circled Bruce and Rebecca, albino drivers shouting taunts and snapping their jaws. "Two for the price of one!"

Bruce put Rebecca down, giving her the nod. Unspoken signals passed between them as they got back to back. Rebecca reached into her utility pouch, slipping on a pair of brass knuckles she kept for safety. Casting a glance back at her, he grinned out the side of his mouth. "You know who these pale bastards are?"

"Let's find out." Rebecca's eyes rolled back in her head, her eyelashes fluttering rapidly.

Bruce recognized her expression. She'd told him how repositories trained to create something called the 'mental lockbox'. He didn't completely understand it, but it was a place in her mind where she stored the summation of all borough knowledge.

When her eyes popped back open, she looked like she'd seen a ghost. "Oh, shit."

Bruce wanted to ask more, but there wasn't time. Squealing brakes pulled their attention, one of the death carts breaking from the pack. Four albinos piled out, tugging off their masks as they approached. With the masks gone, Bruce could make out black, swirling tattoos covering the bottom half of their white faces.

"Oh, no, it's them." Rebecca pressed harder against his back. "The tattoos confirm it."

Bruce growled. "Confirm what?"

"They're morlox." Rebecca sucked air through her front teeth as she said the name. "They're like boogeymen, creatures in urban legends about people disappearing from boroughs, dragged to the Subterranean and never seen again."

Bruce thought about the number of skulls on the large cart. "Don't seem much like legends to *me*."

The albinos, morlox, wore little in the way of clothes and were armed with jagged, rusty blades, and closed in around them. Rebecca's tongue smacked her lips. "Yeah, we're fucked."

CHAPTER THREE

Quantum Tower

CPU: Fully functional. Subject: X...98% Online. X's CPU completed its reboot cycle, returning his cybernetic body to full charge. Cricking his neck servos, quantum plates implanted in his shoulder screeched as his HUD displayed that full functionality had returned since his last job. Optic and motion sensors registered optimal levels. Good thing too. He'd need to keep his optical implants open for his next appointment. It wasn't every day a pair of Q-Lords urgently summoned him to one of their precious Quantum Towers.

The elevator doors slid open and X groaned. Standing almost toe-to-toe with the collector, as though he'd been waiting for him, was Scott Tyson, a veteran collector with a pot belly and a prosthetic leg. The others in their circle unaffectionately called him Snott behind his back and to his face. The old codger smiled with yellow crooked teeth, let out a wet sniffle, and wiped fresh mucus on his coveralls. "Hello, X. Seems the Lightbringers are calling *anyone* for skipped call-ups these days."

X rolled his one good eye. "G'day, *Snott.*" He moved to step past him.

With a low growl, a waist-sized mountain of muscle and black fur blocked his path. X stopped cold. Snott raised his palm like a crossing guard nanny. "Not so fast, cyborg man. We need to chat."

X studied Snott from his replacement leg up to his bald head. The bloke had been a collector in the assassination and apprehension game since before X was wet behind the ears. What he lacked now in physicality, he made up for with his attack dog, Major. The genetically-enhanced pitbull snapped his jaws at X, saliva running from his teeth. X knew the bugger loved nothing more than chasing down skips and chewing on their asses like hamburger meat. "What the bloody hell you want, man? I'm here about a job."

Snott put his hands on his hips, his belly shaking as he chuckled. "Oh, you think you're such a big collector? The Lightbringers summon you all the way from Australia, *mate?*"

"I ain't your mate, bloke, and *no*. The Lightbringers were lucky I was in the area." X rubbed the back of his head, hoping to end the conversation as quickly as possible. "Unlike you, I don't need an attack dog to pick up my skips."

"Oh really?" Snott nodded slowly. "I heard you excel at letting your *bitches* die."

X remained silent; cool as the quantum metal armor grafted to his torso and half of his face. The old man wanted to get a rise out of him, but it wouldn't work. Memories of pale faces and countless white fingers reaching out in the darkness flashed in the CPU running in his brain. It was powerful, but it couldn't delete memories, no matter how painful. He'd let his emotions get the better of him before. It wouldn't happen again.

After a moment, Snott shook his head, making clicking noises behind his scraggly beard. "Seems we got a problem, Aussie. The Q-Lords called us for the same job. But I ain't keen on splitting the pot, ya dig?"

X kept still, hoping he'd stored enough solar energy for what came next. "That a fact?"

"Nothin' personal, times are tough." Snott shrugged. "There's only so much quantum to go around. You understand."

X trained his cybernetic eye on the slobbering dog, the mutt sunk down low on its muscular legs. Snott let out a shrill whistle as Major leapt up, slobbering jaws aimed for X's throat.

The solar-powered laser wailed in a high-pitched frequency as it fired from its hiding place in X's optic replacement eye. A scarlet beam of heat energy seared through the dog's neck, burning through flesh and fur.

Snott's jaw dropped as his mutt's severed head hit the floor seconds before its smoking body. X's sensors detected elevated levels of surprise and adrenaline running through the rival collector. Snott reached for the knife at his hip.

X unsheathed the machete from his back, and sliced Snott's throat in one stroke. *Too slow, old man.*

Snott's hand rushed for his neck, blood spewing between his fingers like a geyser. He stumbled backwards, tripping over his mutt's decapitated body, and landed arse first on the Lightbringer's fancy carpets as he choked on his blood.

"You understand." X spoke coldly as he stepped over the gurgling collector, tossing his machete from hand to hand. "There's only so much quantum to go around, but I earned *this* blade from a hit job in the Tokyo borough." Sheathing the unbreakable weapon, he continued down the footpath, ignoring Snott's final death gasps, and wondering what sort of job necessitated urgent summons and *two* collectors.

Cranking up his audio sensors, he caught sounds of chatter from down the hall. A male voice spoke, accented with a gentle refinement that could only belong to a fucking Q-Lord. "If he's not returned soon, our contender project will *fail.*"

"Yes, my dearest." A similar voice with a feminine, but equally nauseating tone responded, "But Dr. Nakamara insisted Dempsey be the one."

X let out a deep sigh as he stepped inside the foyer leading to the room where the two voices conversed. The high ceilings and grand, chrome furnishings told him everything he needed to know about the Lightbringers. *These blokes are Q-Lords, alright. So rich they probably wipe their arses with quantum toilet paper.*

An attendant next to the doorway nodded to him as he passed the threshold. "The collectors are here, milords." The pencil-necked geek looked around confused, then gazed down the hallway, mouth hanging open as he spotted the bloody scene left X behind. "F-Forgive me! *One* of the collectors is here, milords."

The Q-Lords let out a deep chuckle as X stepped inside the shining, pristine sitting room. He bit his bottom lip, metal hand stroking his beard. This job was unusual, to say the least. No clients as posh as the Q-Lords ever dealt with collectors directly. X cleared his throat, striving for his best diplomatic tone. "Greetings, Lightbringers…"

A shockwave of canary-yellow energy blasted him square in his chest. The blast sent him sailing into the foyer. X found himself on his back, staring up at the ceiling, breathing heavy, while sweat beads raced down his brow. Neural sensors registered pain levels off the scale.

"Pick him up," the male Q-Lord growled in annoyance. The attendant rushed to his side, but X waved him away. Rising shakily on his feet, he stared down two, almost identical, Q-Lords wearing matching white suits with platinum blonde haircuts. They pressed their palms together like they'd been welded by an acetylene torch. The male spoke again. "You made a mess of our hallway, *collector*."

The female spoke next. "Not so rude, Lucian. X is our guest. May I call you X?"

X's chin wagged, searching for words. Running a quick diagnostic on his torso, he found the blast contained a powerful concussive force, far beyond his solar eye laser's capabilities even on a full charge. If it hadn't been for his quantum armor plates surgically implanted into his chest, he would've been a goner for sure.

"Sit." The male, Lucian, commanded him like Snott's dog. X obeyed, choosing a chair wrapped in ornate quantum wire with a thick pearl pillow which looked ideal for his sore arse. Lucian and the woman returned to their couch. "If Eileen and I wanted you dead, you'd be *dead*."

The Q-Lords lounged on the sofa, sipping tea from fine china on saucers. Eileen spoke after a long sip. "Try to relax. We didn't summon you here to be executed. You're here for a job."

Shaking his head, he nodded at Eileen in an exhausted tone. "Of course, thanks." X studied their faces. *So creepy, nearly identical.* He'd heard whispers about these particular Q-Lords. Many wondered if the Lightbringers were siblings or spouses. They stared back at him blankly, unblinking. "What's the job?"

Lucian groaned while nodding to Eileen. She reached into the breast pocket of her silk suit, so white it appeared to be sewn with crystal threads. "One of our contenders failed to report during his designated call-up." She pulled out a tiny computer chip, holding it between two of her fingers. "You will return him to us." The chip slid across the coffee table.

X stopped it, picking it up with his finger. He studied it from behind his metal faceplate and performed a quick scan. "Bruce Dempsey, newest contender of the Brooklyn borough." He nodded slowly. "Also known as the Beast of Brooklyn." Once he finished uploading the chip's data on Bruce's description, medical history, fighting styles and known associates, he placed it back on the table. "Contender not answering a call is a simple skip job, snatch and grab." He gestured to the room's quantum trappings. "You have the means to handle that in-house. Why outsource this job to me? I don't come cheap."

Eileen tilted her head to the side, flashing her dead smile. "You're uniquely suited for this retrieval, considering your former line of work."

"Respectfully, I prefer to keep the past in the past." X crossed his arms in front of his chest. "What aren't you tellin' me?"

X's cybernetic eye detected Lucian's knees shaking, adrenaline spiking with anger. Eileen reached out, rubbing his knee in a soft, intimate circular motion. X felt a new surge of emotions from the Lightbringer which made him shut off his empathic sensors.

Eileen continued rubbing her partner's knee. "The job is not a simple call skip. The contender's pendant went out of range, even for our sensors." She let out a deep sigh, her pale eyes fluttering. "Based on his last known location, we believe he was *taken*."

"Taken? A *contender?*" X clicked his tongue, disappointed in how far standards had fallen. Accessing the pendant's last known whereabouts, he downloaded a set of underground schematics, information about underground ruins beneath New York. A place called the Subterranean. Scanning through information regarding its inhabitants, his mouth dangled open. "Oh, crikey..."

"Morlox, yes." Lucian completed his thought. "Our ancestors removed them from the surface ages ago."

"To keep our boroughs stable, of course." Eileen glanced to the side. "Pockets of survivors remain below. From time to time they abduct our borough citizens."

"I know all about damned morlox, those *pale faces*." X spat the slur. "Outback boroughs, our Q-lords found a whole slew of em livin' in the remains of an old mining town down South." X shuddered. "I tracked those savages for days. Found em eatin' folks from boroughs, they even ate..." Stopping suddenly, his eyes moved slowly from Eileen to Lucian, his tone changing to a deep rasp. "I hate those fuckers. You want me to wipe out the pale faces? I'll do it for free... *almost.*"

The Lightbringers stared at each other for a long moment. Then they did something far worse than blast X in the chest again. They tilted their heads back... and *laughed.* A chilling chorus of perverted amusement, tones joining together to create one of the most unsettling noises X's audio sensors had ever processed. Eileen slapped Lucian's knee, speaking to X between cackles. "Who said anything about wiping them out? We need them."

Lucian waved at X dismissively. "They keep the boroughs stable! Morlox snatching a handful every few months keeps the people on their toes, scary stories to tell their children at night." He spread his arms. "Of course, they turn to our tower for protection."

Eileen gripped Lucian's hand, nodding. "The contender and his repository are down below. It's imperative you return him alive."

X frowned. "His repository too?"

Lucian shrugged. "Expendable."

X held his tongue. His internal CPU quickly compiled a list of supplies, the bare minimum he'd need to travel down below, locate this Beast of Brooklyn and return him more or less in one piece before the morlox had their way. He quoted his fee, demanding more than triple his normal amount of quantum for a job like this.

The Q-lords downloaded his requisition form, nodding without betraying emotion. Eileen nodded. "You'll have all you need and more."

"With that old fool Snott dead, you won't even have to split the quantum." Lucian grew serious. "But you mustn't delay."

X cocked his head to the side. *They didn't balk at my price. Why?* "You seem eager to get this particular contender back." The servos in his joints wheezed as he stood. "Not my business, but it seems simpler to just replace him."

Eileen mimicked her partner's darkened tone. "We've chosen Dempsey to be a test subject of sorts." She spread her lips, flashing pearly teeth. "He's uniquely suited for a highly *experimental* procedure."

X studied his quantum implants, his body a patchwork of priceless metal. Cybernetics wired into his flesh and blood, making him more machine than man. *I know all about your experimental procedures.* Unlike the Q-Lords in their luxurious towers, he'd paid for his quantum in blood. Judging by the Lightbringers' body language, he sensed the meeting was over. "Job accepted. If he's alive, I'll bring 'em back." Heading for the door, he stopped and looked over his shoulder. "How long have they been gone?"

Eileen sipped tea for a moment. "He missed his call over an hour ago. That's why time is of the essence. You'll receive enhanced communications gear to boost your tracking abilities in the Subterranean. And you'll be traveling by the fastest means possible."

X nodded, but didn't object. He already knew that length of time was a death sentence. *If the palefaces had this Dempsey bloke that long, he's probably fucked.*

CHAPTER FOUR

The Subterranean

Bruce rubbed his quantum claws against one another. They grated together, surprising the approaching morlox and stopping them in their tracks. "Bad luck, punks. Today, you took the wrong people." Bruce puffed out his chest, showing off his weapons. "See these? Pure *quantum.*"

The morlox exchanged glances, gravely voices joining in deep chuckles. "Liar!" One stepped forward, a muscular body covered in scars. "Be thankful we didn't run you down like *dogs*, borough dwellers." He pointed a double-bladed machete almost the length of his forearm at Bruce. "Your kind drove us down here. Time to show you how the other half lives." He raced for Bruce, wild fury behind his eyes, blade raised high.

Bruce drove his claws straight through his pale chest, slicing through his torso like hot lead.

The remaining morlox staggered back, mouths gaping open as Bruce yanked his arm away from the monster's body. He kicked the body back to them like a game of borough ball. "I see how the other half *dies." He raised* his claw, still dripping in warm blood, and beckoned them forward. "Back home, they call me the Beast of Brooklyn. You're about to find out why."

The remaining morlox kept silent, but didn't back down. Two more raced forward, straight into low blows from Bruce. He stabbed one above the waist, quantum spikes shredded his outer stomach wall, which spilled out like a gutted fish. The other wasn't as lucky—Bruce sliced him a good bit lower. Wincing inside, he wondered where these freaks kept their genitalia. The castrated morlox rolled to the ground, and he barked at the others, their bare feet subtly backing out of reach of his claws. "C'mon you dickless punks. Let's see how you do against a contender."

The rest poured in like rats, two in the front approaching with spears. . . Flicking their wrists, the shafts telescoped forward to allow for more reach. The first jabbed forward with a vicious thrust.

Bruce batted the pole away, breaking the shoddy metal to pieces with a glancing blow from his quantum gauntlet. "What's wrong? Scared to get too close?"

The morlox didn't receive a chance to answer. Bruce pulled him forward, cutting the distance, then shoved his free hand down the morlox's throat. Blood and teeth leapt from his mouth; his skull shattered like a clay pot against Bruce's knuckles.

Two down, Bruce thought as he pivoted to the other lancer. To his credit, he didn't try the extending spear trick. Instead he drew a pair of twisted daggers from his breaches, and they whistled as they spun around his fingers.

The first strike went high for Bruce's temple, nearly slicing his fresh contender's tattoo. Bruce blocked it with the back of his hands, the inferior blade failing to leave as much as a scuff.

"Fool!" The morlox laughed, his second blade already in motion, whirling toward Bruce's unguarded stomach.

With a quick leap, Bruce jumped over the blade. It cut only the air as Bruce twisted his hips, driving a hard kick in the morlox's forehead. The warrior fell backwards, landing hard.

Bruce was on top of him before he had time to breath. "Arrrghhh!" Growling while raining blows tipped with unbreakable metal down on the albino's face. Scarlet tinted his vision, the haze of battle taking control. Rebecca wasn't kidding when she'd said the borough called him their beast. When he fought, sometimes he lost control.

"I think you got him." Rebecca's soft voice pulled him back to reality, as it often did.

Exhaling, he looked down to see the morlox's face beaten beyond recognition, body motionless. His outburst of rage hadn't lasted more than a few moments, but he'd delivered a frenzy of uncontrolled blows. Breathing heavily, he stared at his claws.

The sound of cracking bone spun him around to find Rebecca dispatching her morlox, a fresh set of brass knuckle impressions in his skull. She'd studied all her life to be a repository, but being a bookworm didn't stop her from having a hell of a punch. She smiled, yanking a sawed-off slugthrower from the morlox she'd beaten. Pulling the slide back, she cocked the weapon with a sharp click. "Save that for the contender challenges and we'll win for sure!"

Bruce returned the smile, but burned with fear inside. Fighting in the challenges almost certainly meant letting the beast within run free. Before they were interrupted, he'd asked her to run away with him. He'd given her a reason for leaving, but it was a partial truth at best. Since they were children, they'd shared everything together. But this was the thing he'd never told her, the one fear which kept him awake at night. *This is why we have to leave...so I never lose control.* He looked back at the morlox he'd beaten to death, the insects of the Subterranean already crawling over his still-warm corpse. *And* this *never happens to you.*

A piercing airhorn from one of the death carts caused them to look up. The largest vehicle, the one decorated in skulls, coasted forward before coming to a stop. The engine fell silent, as the biggest damn morlox they'd seen yet exited the driver's side. He peeled off his mask, and his entire face was covered in the swirling tattoos. The ink moved with his lips as he spoke. "Fortune smiles on my flock." His dirty cloak billowed as he gestured with long fingers. "We've found a contender to sacrifice!"

The surrounding carts honked their horns, flashing their lights as they hooted and hollered. Bruce sensed Rebecca's temper rising as she stepped forward, aiming the slugthrower. A deafening bang filled the Subterranean as fire sailed from her gun's short barrel, and a round of burning pellets struck the morlox square in the chest.

Bruce slapped Rebecca on the back, grinning like an idiot. "Nice shot, babe!"

The morlox didn't flinch. He shrugged, and his dirty cloak dropped to the ground. His fist clanged against the metal breastplate he wore beneath. "Pure quantum," he rasped.

Bruce's legs grew shaky. "H-How?" he stammered. "Who are you? How the hell did you get quantum down here?"

"I am Cabal." The morlox bowed his head slightly. "Warrior priest of the Subterranean church. To answer your question, I paid for my quantum in blood."

"What the fuck does that mean—"

Bruce wasn't finished speaking when Cabal covered the distance between them in the blink of an eye, striking him three times before Bruce raised a hand to defend himself. The priest drove back the contender with a strong headbutt to the nose.

Bruce went down, catching the blood as it poured like a faucet from his nostrils. *Definitely broken.*

Footsteps surrounded them as Cabal's minions left their vehicles, moving in with weapons drawn. Bruce covered Rebecca, backing away as Cabal raised a hand. The other morlox fell in behind him with silent obedience.

"My quantum comes from beaten contenders." Cabal towered over him, nodding towards Bruce's claws. He gestured for his minions to grab them both. "Bind them. God will be pleased with a double sacrifice." Stepping close, Cabal cupped Rebecca's chin. "Yes, you child will please Him very much."

Still feeling the whiplash, Bruce struggled against the morlox restraining his arms. "Leave her alone, you bastard!" A blunt strike from the butt of a rifle into Bruce's gut cut his resistance short, and the air rushed from his lungs. "Oof!" Pale, grubby fingers stripped off his quantum gauntlets and shackled his wrists.

Cabal slipped Bruce's claws over his white hands. Flexing his fingers, he laughed then turned to Bruce. "You, contender, you amuse me. You and your borough whore shall be God's *dessert.*"

"No!" Summoning his last reserves of energy, Bruce broke free of his captives' grips. Hands shackled behind his back, he aimed a headbutt square for the center of Cabal's nose.

Cabal easily sidestepped the clumsy attempt. The priest threw back his head and laughed darkly. "Fear not. Your sacrifices will not be in vain. You will give life to our people for another season."

Pivoting on his heels, Bruce gasped for breath. The Subterranean's stale, putrid air polluted his nostrils as he panted heavily through his mouth. "Y-You're insane."

Cabal cut off his panting, grabbing him by the throat. The quantum gauntlets creaked as the morlox crushed his windpipe, smiling with yellowed teeth. "Thank you, for your gift of life."

Bruce watched the morlox raise his arm high, quantum spikes poised to come down and finish him. "R-Rebecca..."

A strange accent echoed over his shoulder. "Close your eyes!" Bruce instinctively obeyed the commanding tone a moment before a blinding flash filled the undercity.

As he closed his eyes, bursts of purple, blue, and yellow flashes filled his inner vision. *What the hell?* Cabal wasn't fast enough to shut his eyes. The morlox priest let out an excruciating hiss, and the pressure around Bruce's neck receded. Gravel crunched as Bruce hit the ground, hands still cuffed behind his back. Lying on his side, he gulped the disgusting air like fresh water in a desert. He struggled to focus on the source of the incandescent rescue, and as the dots cleared, he barely believed what he saw.

A tall, heavily-built man wearing a metal suit shot through the railyard riding atop a flat metallic sled. Bruce watched in amazement. No signs of tires on the vehicle, but the flat transport kicked up serious speed, zooming above the ground like magic. The man leaned forward, guiding his flying sled to flank the morlox. Cabal and his warriors writhed on the gravel, still in pain from the first round of blinding light.

The stranger's deep voice rumbled through the Subterranean. "Don't like the light, palefaces?" Bruce realized the man wasn't *wearing* a metal suit so much as the metal was part of him. *Damn, heard stories about cyborgs but never thought I'd see one in the flesh... or what's left of it.* Half the man's face was covered with a slick metal plate, a red eye gleaming. Bruce heard humming, like a piece of old machinery powering up. The cyborg's glowing eye expanded as the hum grew louder. Then what looked like a needle made of fire shot from the metal faceplate, blazing with sweltering heat. The beam flew through the undercity, scorching the blinded morlox. Bruce heard the pale creatures' hissing cries; smelled their flesh burning as the beam cut them to pieces.

Bruce rolled over on his back, remaining flat as possible. "Rebecca, stay down!" He shouted, hoping she survived the chaos to hear him. Over the sound of the humming blasts, he heard metal singing as the stranger unsheathed a blade from a scabbard on his back, and began filleting any morlox unfortunate enough to be within reach. Bruce didn't know whose side the cyborg was on. All he knew was he'd never seen anyone like him, and dread filled Bruce's gut. Whoever he was, he'd warned them before he used his incredible arsenal on the morlox. *Only one place he could get that kinda power.*

The humming stopped as the red death beam ceased, and darkness returned to the undercity. Bruce heard the desperate turnover of death cart engines, Cabal shouting as they revved. "No time. Take the woman, flee!" Tires spinning out, the death carts made hasty exits. "Come, my children. God awaits."

As the death carts kicked up dust, Bruce caught sight of Rebecca being tossed roughly in the back of Cabal's skull-adorned vehicle. "No!" Bruce leapt to his knees, struggling to run. The carts sped off, vanishing in the distance in different directions throughout the undercity. He didn't make it more than a few steps before he tripped over his own boots, landing face first in the rough gravel.

A calloused palm lifted him up by the shoulder. "Easy, Dempsey." The stranger pulled him to his feet. "It's a miracle you survived down here *this* long."

Bruce balled up his fists within his bindings, shoving the man away. "Back off, punk!" Scarlet rage clouded his vision. This time, Rebecca wasn't here to tether his senses. *She's gone, they took her.* His blood pumped faster, the beast within threatening to take control.

"Name's X." The stranger sized him up, red eye glowing within his metal faceplate. "I'm a collector."

"Collector?" Bruce grunted, baring his teeth. "Must be how you know my name. Let me guess, the Q-Lords sent you for skipping my call?"

X pointed a finger to his nose. "Got it in one." Reaching into his belt, he pulled out a small device, a green blip flashing on a flat screen. "When you didn't answer the summons, they sent me. Been tracking the signal on your pendant. Seems you're quite the important contender."

He snapped at X. "I don't give a shit about the Q-Lords!" His body shook. White dots in his vision continued to dance the polka in his peripherals. "How'd you do that flashy trick?"

X extended his hand, showing Bruce a metal sphere, roughly the size of the oranges the burrough received once every few years. "Sun grenades." Flipping a switch atop the sphere, the ball charged with a growing hum. Bruce stepped back, hands lifting to his face. X stopped the sound by removing his thumb. "I designed them for hunting palefaces."

Bruce dropped his arms, studying the collector. "Look, I appreciate the help..." his voice trailed off as he stepped past the collector, searching the multiple paths the death carts used to escape. *Fuck! They could've taken her anywhere.* He exhaled. It didn't matter; *nothing* mattered except finding Rebecca. "But I can't leave. They've got Rebecca, I gotta go after em."

X sighed deeply. "I see why they call you the Beast of Brooklyn." The collector returned the tracking device to his belt. "Problem is, they ordered me to bring *you* back alive. Q-Lords made it clear your repository lady was expendable."

Bruce's knees shook, and red rage coloured his vision as he pictured Cabal. Along with absconding with Rebecca, the warrior priest had stripped him of his quantum gauntlets. He'd left him constrained, completely unarmed. After seeing the level of destruction X was capable of, Bruce knew there wasn't much he could do to stop the collector if he wanted to take him. Exhaling, he banished the warrior priest's ugly face from his mind. Focusing on Rebecca's voice in his memory to soothe the beast within, reminding him to fight with his head, not his fists. "You may just be doing your job, metal face," he looked X in the eye, unblinking. "But you'll have to kill me before I leave without Rebecca."

X nodded slowly, voice dropping low. "That your final answer?"

The red eye hummed to life. Bruce felt burning heat from the collector's metal faceplate. He swallowed, boots remaining entrenched as he faced the collector. It wasn't a hard question. "Fuck yes."

"Okay." X shot a fine crimson beam forward. Bruce's eyes squeezed shut from the light. Intense heat burned the skin around his arms. But instead of sending holes through his body, tension relieved around his wrists. The metal cuffs binding his wrists clattered to the ground.

Bruce looked down in confusion, rubbing his wrists. He shot a confused stare at X. "Why?"

X turned his back, walking away while speaking to Bruce. "Any contender who abandons his repository to pale-faced savages is lower than dirt." He stepped up on his sled, the vehicle hovering in place like a loyal dog. "If you'd left your repository to *that* fate just to save your own arse, I would've killed you where you stood."

Bruce tilted his head, taking a closer look at X. The collector's faceplate was only the beginning of his metallic implants. His muscular arms were a patchwork of metal. Not just *any* metal either. Bruce approached the floating sled. "Is that quantum?"

"Aye." X nodded, unbuttoning his padded vest. "When I became a collector, I lived by the quantum rule. For years, I've picked jobs by the size of the paycheque." X tugged open his vest, and Bruce's mouth fell open. The collector's pectorals were outfitted with quantum coverings, but what surprised him most were the wicked scars, signs of infection surrounding the unbreakable metal. X nodded slowly. "But unlike the Q-Lords in their towers, I paid for mine in blood."

"I understand." Bruce hopped on the back of the sled, his boots sliding into a pair of stirrups on the grated metal. They clicked to hold him in place. "I earned my quantum gauntlets in Brooklyn's contender trials." He slapped his palm in his fist. "That bastard, Cabal, took them when he ran off with Rebecca."

Pressing a set of buttons on a control pad, X revved the sled. The transport slid into gear, faster and smoother than Bruce's old salvage cycle on its best day. X used his shoulders to steer the controls, guiding them forward. "That isn't the only bad news, Dempsey." He tapped the side of his faceplate. "I spent the last of my laser's charge freeing you from those cuffs."

Bruce bit his lip. "Will it recharge?"

X shook his head. "Laser runs on *solar* energy." He pointed around the Subterranean. Hollowed-out buildings and ruins of old New York City zoomed past them as the sled carried them further into the undercity. "Not much of that down here."

"Damnit," Bruce swore. "You don't have your laser, they took my gauntlets." He scanned the dark buildings, barely able to keep up with where they traveled. "How are we going to find Rebecca, much less rescue her?"

X leaned into a wide turn, kicking up old newspapers from a tall stack of rubbish. "Luckily, your repository's still wearing your pendant. We can track her anywhere those *palefaces* take her."

Bruce detected the anger in X's voice. "You talk like you know them."

X remained silent for a moment, their speed building as the sled carried them to darker, lower levels of the undercity. "I know them a lot better than you, Dempsey. Don't be fooled by their appearance. They ain't people like you and me."

Bruce detected a slight cracking in X's frozen tone and wondered what sort of memories the morlox dredged up with him. He thought back to what Cabal had said. "They said the people in our borough drove them down here. And we were to be...fed to their god?"

"Fed to their *god?*" X exhaled deeply, shaking his head. "Living down here's made them crazier than usual." He looked over his shoulder, locking eyes with Bruce. "Only one thing to remember about palefaces: they'll kill *anything* to survive. You willing to do the same, Dempsey?"

Bruce contemplated X's words as the collector continued to navigate the Subterranean. The further they traveled, the larger the rats became. X guided the sled past the dilapidated structures and into an open sewer pipe. They squeezed through the circular entrance, so narrow they ducked their heads to enter. The world within turned black. Bruce held his breath, fighting the urge to vomit. If he thought the undercity smelled rank, it was a regular garden party compared to the smells in the deep sewer. Murky waters sloshed beneath the floating sled as they made their way into the deepest reaches of the morlox's domain.

Breathing through his mouth, he spoke in the darkness. "Once we find Rebecca, what hope do we have to bring her back?"

X adjusted the throttle, slowing the sled to a crawl. "Don't worry, Dempsey." Raising his metal hand, he contorted his mechanical fingers in impossible directions. "I didn't come down here empty-handed."

CHAPTER FIVE

God's Offering

Voices murmured from deep in the sewers. Morlox gathered in a cavernous chamber, deep enough to fit most of Brooklyn's starving population. The albino humanoids—palefaces, as X called them—sat in rows, hands raised to the unseen sky. The litanies they chanted told a tale of their banishment from the surface.

Bruce stifled his growl as he spotted Cabal at the head of the crowd, wearing *his* spiked gauntlets. The warrior priest stood on a high platform, framed by a sewer opening large enough to fit the Statue of Liberty's crumbling remains. The warrior priest paced before the crowd, flourishing long tattered robes. The morlox remained hypnotized by his words, breaking out in loud chants each time he hoisted a quantum staff nearly as long as he was. Dangling rings clinked from the ceremonial weapon's tip as he shook it in his pale grip. "In the days before the Scorch, we lived above. Children of the great yellow sun." He pointed the staff to the side, gesturing to a long table covered by roughspun cloth. "But when the Scorch burned the sun red, the world above rejected us!" Yanking the cloth from the table, he revealed Rebecca, held down by her ankles and wrists, cinched tight by leather straps. Cabal approached her, reaching out with his hand. She shouted at the morlox, words muted by a metal ball gag. The priest's bony finger stroked her chin. "Through blood and quantum, her *kind* drove us to the Subterranean's darkness, left to rot in the dead city we call home." Cabal removed his finger from Rebecca's chin, shaking it at the crowd.

"But my flock, we survive through servitude to God. Today, we offer Him a sacrifice!" Making a quick swipe with Bruce's gauntlet, he sliced Rebecca's shoulder with one of the spikes, and blood streamed from her wound.

X hooked Bruce by the arm, keeping him from leaping into the middle of the bizarre ritual. "Not yet, Dempsey." Reaching for his faceplate, the collector pressed a small button between the quantum metal lining and his scarred skin. The hover sled responded, silent repulsors maneuvering the flat transport into position. Nodding to Bruce, he handed off a pair of morlox sun shades they'd picked him up along the way. "Remember, put them on when you see the flash." He licked the corners of his cracked lips. "That's when we unleash *Hell* on the palefaces."

Bruce nodded, affixing the shades over his head. "We only found one pair, what about you?"

X turned and tapped the side of his metal face. "Don't need em, mate." Pressing another button, his faceplate extended. Bruce heard the sliding movement of invisible mechanical parts as the metal covered the rest of his head. X's single red eye flashed, his skull encased in a quantum helmet. "I brought my own."

Damn. Bruce rubbed the back of his unprotected head, feeling more vulnerable than ever. *I gotta get my claws back.* Studying the albinos, he didn't spy a single pair of sun shades among the wild worshippers. The morlox must've only kept them for their trips above to snatch up sacrifices for this god of theirs. Bruce shuddered to imagine the sort of unholy monstrosity Cabal might worship. "What about this God of theirs?" He whispered. "You sure it's just a buncha mumbo-jumbo?"

"There is *no* God," the collector groaned. "Get ready. Those red-eyed bastards will never expect the sun invadin' the heart of their stronghold."

Bruce wondered how X remained so calm. Beyond just a paying job, the metal-skinned man clearly possessed a deep hatred for the Subterranean dwellers. *They snatch people and eat them, I suppose that's enough reason to hate them. But is there something more to it?* He focused back on Cabal, presenting Rebecca to the cheering morlox like a side of rationed beef for solstice.

Rebecca screamed through her gag as Cabal used the spiked gauntlets to dig deeper into her fresh cut, and blood covered the quantum claws.

"Through blood and quantum, we take back from those who banished us below. O, Lord, hear our cries, smell the blood. We offer a sacrifice from Brooklyn borough!"

"Through blood and quantum!" The cavern shook as the morlox's chanting turned to cheers, pounding their chests, their raspy-throated chorus joining in a dark anthem. "Hear our cries, smell the blood. We offer a sacrifice from Brooklyn borough!"

"Now!" X whispered a shout, triggering the detonator in his palm. "Shades on!"

A charging hum rang throughout the chamber, undercutting the chanting. Bruce yanked down the visor, covering his eyes moments before X sent the sled flying into the middle of the morlox worshippers. The remaining sun grenades spilled from the back of an open footlocker affixed to the sled, detonating as one. Even through Bruce's shades, the blast burned like a supernova. He made out the frantic shapes of morlox worshippers, rushing to escape the chamber, their voices hissing, shouting upon meeting their long lost mother the sun once more.

Bruce detected Cabal's voice within the madness, shouting madly from his perch. "Guard the sacrifice, protect God's offering!"

X shoved him forward, shouting, "Go, Dempsey, go!"

Dank sewer air rushed through Bruce's hair as they leapt, dropping several metres from one of the stone alcoves. Shock vibrated in his knees as he landed on the pavement. While most of the morlox scurried for darker reaches of the Subterranean, a few of the warriors remained behind, forming ranks around Cabal and Rebecca.

X stepped forward, flexing his muscles. Quantum metal sang as he unsheathed the machete from the scabbard on his back. "I'll handle these palefaces, Dempsey. Save your repository!" The morlox raced blindly for X. He roared at them with blood-drunk rage, blood and albino fingers flying from his quantum blade.

Bruce charged ahead, focusing on Cabal. The warrior priest stood between him and Rebecca, leaning against his staff. "Hey!" Bruce shouted. "You have something that belongs to me."

Cabal hoisted one of his fists, Bruce's spiked gauntlet gleaming on his knuckles. "Come and take them, Contender!"

Racing forward, growling deep between his teeth, Bruce unleashed the Beast. An ever-present weight lifted from his shoulders. For once, he allowed his instincts to take control; releasing the fears of loss, of inflicting unintended pain. Right now, *all* he cared about was inflicting pain, on a single individual. Rushing towards Cabal, the red haze clouded his vision. He hit the big morlox low, connecting a shoulder tackle in his unprotected stomach.

He heard a deep "oomph" as Cabal toppled over, his quantum staff rolling out of his grip.

Bruce dove for the staff. Falling short, his chin smacked the concrete. He tasted blood, and looked down to find Cabal gripping him by the boot. Rearing back, he kicked him with his free leg, leaving grimy indentations on Cabal's white forehead.

Cabal maintained his bony grip. "You won't stop the sacrifice!" Raising his quantum gauntlet, Cabal brought down his fist like a hammer into Bruce's leg.

Bruce shrieked in agony as the claw punctured his lower calf. Calling on his contender training, he focused to block out the pain. *Pain is nothing to a contender, he fights through the pain, through death itself.* He crawled forward, setting his eyes on the staff. *Die to protect your borough.* Fingers extended, he was millimetres short of grasping the weapon.

Bruce's spine shrieked in protest as a heavy weight crushed his back. Cabal was recovering faster from the sun grenades than Bruce had hoped. He yanked Bruce by the hair, wrenching his head up towards the ceiling. His neck exposed, he felt the cool tips of quantum claws close enough to shave his beard stubble. Cabal's hot breath burned as he hissed in his ear. "I won't let your kind kill *more* of my people, borough dweller!"

Bruce wrestled with Cabal, shoving his elbow between his chin and avoiding the gauntlet. He pushed with all his might to keep the spikes from reaching his throat, but the Subterranean ruler was far larger and heavier, and the blood running from his punctured calf made him feel lightheaded enough to nod off. After the day he'd had, the idea of a good sleep felt as inviting as a warmed washtub...

Shouting from the side awoke him from his stupor. "Bruce!" Rebecca's voice rang in his head, stirring up the Beast within. Keeping his focus on her voice; the one who held his heart in the palm of her hand. His pain subsiding, he growled low, speaking to Cabal. "Ain't never touched one of your people, *priest*. But if your god's so damn hungry, tell him to eat this!" Dropping his chest to the ground, Bruce redirected his momentum. With a one-handed push up, his skull snapped back, smashing the morlox's face, crushing an eyeball like a soft egg.

Cabal howled in pain as he leapt off Bruce's back. Crawling backwards, he covered his swelling eye with his hands.

Shaking his head free of cobwebs, Bruce blocked the pain and dove forward. Gripping the staff, a memory flashed—scavenging some skinny metal sticks when he was a kid. His old man told him stories of men known as gophers carrying entire bags full of them to fight dogs before the Scorch. Seemed fitting for his current situation. *What'd they used to say before battle?* Winding up for a swing, Bruce shouted the gopher warrior's cry. "Fore!"

Torquing his hips, he swung the staff low. Sweeping up in a wide arc, the jingling rings connected squarely with the side of Cabal's cheek. Bruce smiled as the staff's quantum metal tone rang beautifully, the morlox skull cracking beneath the force of a swing. Shrugging, he smiled. "Guess that's what they called 'puttin' a hole in *someone*.'"

A deep pounding drew Bruce from his moment of victory. A tremor, like a groundquake, shook throughout the chamber. He shrugged it off. *They must get a lot of those down here.* Tossing the staff aside, Bruce slid down next to Cabal's motionless body, tugging the quantum gauntlets from the morlox's icy hands. Fastening Brooklyn's greatest weapons to his wrists, he stepped over the warrior priest's body, making his way to the table where Rebecca lay bound. A quick swipe of his quantum claws, *damn they felt good covering the knuckles again,* freed her arms and legs. Helping her sit up, he removed the ball gag from her mouth. "Miss me?"

Rebecca blinked rapidly. "B-Bruce?" Panic grew in her voice. "I can barely see."

"Yeah, sorry bout that." Bruce checked over his shoulder on X, the collector still having the time of his life eviscerating morlox with his blade. "My new friend and I blinded the morlox with a shitload of sun grenades. Don't worry, your eyesight will come back." He squeezed her shoulder reassuringly. "Just wait."

A stronger tremor rumbled beneath their feet, shaking the wooden table. Rebecca leapt up, grabbing Bruce around the chest. "We can't wait. We *must* get out of here. It's coming!"

Bruce held her hands; her fingers quivered with the groundquakes. "What's coming?"

"Weren't you listening?" Bruce watched Rebecca feeling for her hip satchel, retrieving her brass knuckles. "*God* is coming!"

Bruce opened his mouth to tell Rebecca their "god" was just a load of morlox superstition, but the groundquakes drowned him out. Something was off. The quakes seemed to be growing closer. Bruce turned to see the large spillway opening slowly filling behind them. Not with water or waste, but a creature from another age slogged unhurried in their direction. A walking wall of moss-green scales on four legs, smelling as rotten as a full landfill, with a massive tail whipping behind as it stalked into the chamber. Bruce froze, suddenly feeling very much like a small, juicy mammal in the monster's flashing yellow eyes. *Just like when Bilbo met Smaug.* Its long snout cracked open, revealing a mouth full of teeth taller than most well-fed borough children.

Bruce exchanged glances with his repository. "That thing…it's *GOD*?"

Rebecca shook her head. "Not in the literal sense. I heard Cabal talking before the ceremony." Pressing a finger to her temple, her eyes fluttered the way they did when she opened her mental lockbox. "I think I know what's going on!"

Short on time, Rebecca filled him in on the basics of what they were dealing with, and what to do. Bruce swallowed hard as she rushed to finish her spiel. "You really think *that* will work?"

Rebecca shrugged. "Hey, it makes sense…" She raised her wrists. "How else would a creature like that not just decimate the entire village. They're using it for something, but for what?"

Bruce chuckled. "I thought I'd lost you." Pausing for an instance, he pulled her close and planted a deep kiss on her lips. "I'll kill this thing," he whispered low. "Then we get the hell out of here. Just you and me, kay?"

Rebecca's lips fluttered but a boisterous voice behind them interrupted before she could speak. "Dempsey!" Bruce turned to see X yank his blood-soaked machete from a morlox carcass. "What the hell is that thing? A croc on steroids?"

Bruce filled X in on Rebecca's explanation, followed by her plan. X shook his head, pressing a button on the side of his helmet. The quantum coverings retracted, revealing a shocked look on his face. "You *really* think that's gonna work, repository?"

Rebecca's hands went to her hips. "Assuming you're as good as you *claim*."

Bruce steeled himself for X's retort, and was surprised when he heard him let out a small, choking laugh. "You remind me of someone." The collector's red eye drew a bead on the approaching monster. X scowled as digitized beeps processed invisible data. "Those scales ain't as hard as quantum. But thick as they are, they come damn close. Not sure how we're gonna pierce 'em."

Bruce raised his spikes. "I've got my claws, you've got your machete." He gazed into the darkness, studying the incoming croc, so close they could see saliva dripping from its big nasty tongue. His confidence took a sharp nosedive. "You're the hunter. Any ideas?"

"I'm from the Outback, mate. Doesn't matter the type of croc, softest parts are always his belly." X tapped the side of his head. "We make him show it to us, my laser can burn right through."

Bruce frowned. "I thought you used up your laser."

"My sun grenades ain't just for flash." X cocked his head to the side. "They'll recharge my beam in a pinch." He held up a single finger. "But only for one shot. That's all we get."

The croc's snout darted inside the chamber. Letting out a deep roar, the monster sent a gust of wind smelling of rotted meat, blowing his and Rebecca's hair back.

"Looks like one chance is all we're getting anyway." Bruce turned to face X. "Alright, Collector, any idea how to make it show its belly?"

"Yeah, I got one, Dempsey..." X slapped his machete hilt in Bruce's palms. "Hold it tight, point it straight." Stepping behind Bruce, he aimed his shoulders squarely at the croc's scaly face. "When you start to fly, whatever you do, don't let go."

"Fly? What the fu—" Bruce finished the remainder of his sentence as a scream.

With a burst of enhanced strength, X lifted him off the ground and chucked him through the air. Bruce flew like a javelin, headed straight for one of the croc's yellow eyeballs. Fear and adrenaline rushed through his body, survival instincts in the deepest level of his brain shouting for him to flee from the monster he was racing towards.

The croc licked its chops, mouth rising slowly like a castle gate, ready to swallow him whole.

Biting down, Bruce fought to obey X's final command. *Don't let go, don't let go!* The scaly tip of the croc's snout tore open the front of his shirt. He pointed the machete forward, blade cutting the wind as he sailed past its jaws. The quantum blade struck true, piercing the croc's wheel-sized pupil.

"Bullseye!" X shouted from below. "Now hang on!"

Bruce didn't see he had much of a choice. He wrapped his arms around the croc's snout, holding on as the morlox's god screamed in pain. Bruce felt his body rising higher as the croc tilted back on its hindlegs. Plunging his fist spikes deep in the beast's nose, he braced himself for the finale. "Do it!"

X responded with a charging burst of solar energy. Bruce felt the concentrated laser's heat; heard flesh searing from the croc's exposed neck as it bucked wildly beneath him. He dug his spikes deeper, fighting to keep hold as it thrashed under the pain.

After what felt like an eternity, the croc stopped thrashing, and its head collapsed to the ground. After several moments with no signs of movement, he pulled his claws from the dead croc's snout. Retrieving X's machete, he let the blade drop from his exhausted hands as he slid limply off the side. Landing ass first, he leaned back on the croc's body for support, gasping for breath. "I *never* want to do that again."

"Damn," X leaned over him, whistling low between his lips. "Never seen a bloke fly like that before. I didn't think it would work." The quantum-plated man knelt down, retrieving his fallen machete. "Let's cut into this croc and see if your repository was right about what's inside."

"Feel free." Bruce groaned as he stood up. Turning back to face X, his eyebrows shot up. "Wait... you didn't think it would *work*?" X ignored him, already knee-deep in the croc's guts. Shaking his head, he waved away the collector's words. *Best not to think about it.* He stepped around the monster's head. "Rebecca? Not sure how much of that you could see, but…"

Bruce stopped in his tracks. Cabal stood, holding Rebecca close to his broken body. Her brass knuckles lay by her boots, and the battered priest held a wicked double-bladed knife to her throat. The morlox studied the croc's body, his expression halfway between blind rage and tears. "W-What? What have you done? *God* is dead."

"Listen to me, Cabal." Bruce kept his feet planted, slowly raising his palms. "That thing was never a god." He nodded to Rebecca. "My friend you're holding a knife to there? She's a repository. She holds all knowledge from our borough *inside* her head."

"Repository?" Cabal shifted nervously, the knifepoint trembling by Rebecca's throat. "We've heard tales of such things from the sacrifices we take from the borough."

"Sacrifices you'll no longer have to make." Rebecca carefully tilted her head toward the croc's body. "Now that the Beast of Brooklyn slayed this genetically-enhanced food source."

Relief rushed through Bruce as Cabal pulled the knife away from Rebecca's throat. The morlox stumbled back, holding the side of his head where Bruce struck him. "Explain."

Rebecca's eyes rolled back in her head, eyelashes fluttering as she accessed her mental lockbox. "Years before the Scorch, the population grew larger than the world's food supply." She exhaled as her eyes returned to normal. "Scientists… uh, *priests* of those days fed special food to animals to make them grow far larger." She gestured to the morlox's fallen god. "Some grew too large to control, escaping into the Subterranean."

Cabal looked from Rebecca, then back to Bruce who nodded. "See? That ain't no god, just someone's overgrown pet."

"No…" Cabal's tone grew icy. "It exerted its will upon us." Cabal gestured to the creature. "It desired to eat those from the borough."

Rebecca's eyes grew wider. "How do you know?"

"B-Because…" Cabal stuttered, his face scrunching in pain. "For every season we failed to deliver even one sacrifice from above," he raised his arms to the ceiling, then dropped them below his waist. "It consumed scores of *us* below." His hands balled into fists. "Why?"

A metallic thunk answered Cabal's question. A metal box the size of a death cart engine slid across the floor, stopping just short of the priest's toe. "You can thank the Q-Lords for that, paleface." X stepped around the snout, covered in croc guts. "That right there's a quantum tracker." He pointed his machete at the pendant around Rebecca's neck. "A larger version of the one the lady's got here." X approached the gooey piece of machinery, nodding to Rebecca as he knelt down to inspect it. "Just like she thought. This one does a lot more than track the croc, it controls it too." He rose to his full height. "The Q-Lords used this monster to set you against the borough. They're the ones who drove you down here all those years ago. They told me themselves."

Cabal fell silent, his pale red eyes flicking between the dead croc and the quantum box. Bruce recognized his expression, it was one he knew well. "You've been played, Cabal." He gestured from X, to Rebecca then back to himself. "Whether it's in the Subterranean or in the boroughs, we all live under the quantum rule." Bruce pointed to the contender tattoo inked to the side of his face. "Whoever has the quantum..."

"Makes the rules..." Cabal finished his sentence with a hiss.

There was a long pause as tension filled the stale air. Bruce watched X, his fingers twitching as he squeezed his machete hilt. He knew it wouldn't take much for the collector to kill one last morlox. He'd begun to suspect why the half-man hated them so much in the first place.

Cabal let out a deep sigh and sheathed his knife. "Leave in peace." Retrieving his fallen staff, the priest limped on the quantum pole like a cane, waving over his shoulder.

"Wait." Rebecca stepped forward, blinking as she focused her returning sight on Cabal. "One thing was true. Before the Scorch, the morlox and borough dwellers *did* share the surface." She clasped her hands together. "We were one people."

"Once, perhaps, but no longer." Cabal limped on without looking back. "We have dwelled in darkness so long. This is our home." Cabal's lurching form joined with the shadows, his last words a hollow echo. "We will never plague the surface again."

Bruce stood in silence with Rebecca and X, the trio watching until Cabal's echoing footsteps fell quiet. X broke the stillness, pressing the small button on the side of his faceplate. The hover sled answered the summons, returning damaged, but still functional.

X mounted the sled, then looked down at Bruce, any trace of friendly disposition gone from his scarred face. "Alright, Dempsey. I've never failed to deliver on a job." He motioned to the sled. "I'd prefer you come willingly."

Fire burned in Bruce's belly. The Beast within growling as he puffed out his chest. "Why? Because you don't think you can take me by force, metal man?"

X steered the sled forward, coming almost nose to nose with Bruce. "Because if I take you by force, there won't be enough left of ya to return to the Q-Lords. They want *their* contender alive."

"Sure about that?" Bruce growled. "Your battery's drained, we both know it."

"Stop! Both of you!" Rebecca pulled Bruce from the collector, turning him around to face her. "You just got me back, I'm not ready to lose you again."

Bruce took Rebecca by the shoulders, a smile growing on his face. "This is it, Rebecca, don't you see?" He gestured around them. "This is our chance to get out. Escape their quantum rule, find a new life!" Kissing her on the forehead, he pulled back to find tears filling her eyes. *She's ready, she's happy to go!* A heavy weight lifted from his shoulders. He imagined trekking off into the sunset, just him and Rebecca. "No more Q-Lords! No more challenges..."

"No borough," Rebecca spoke softly, thicker tears dripping down her cheeks. "No more Brooklyn."

Bruce frowned. These didn't seem like joyful tears. "Rebecca, what—?"

Her voice cracked through her tears. "Do it."

"Do wha—?" A heavy weight fell on Bruce's shoulder. His body seized, his leather vest sizzling as shocking volts of electricity coursed through his body.

Bruce hit the ground, gazing up at X. Blue volts danced in his metal palm. The collector shook his head. "She was talkin' to me, mate." Speaking into his wrist, the collector spoke the last words Bruce heard before losing consciousness. "Target acquired, mission accomplished."

CHAPTER SIX

Rising Again

X sighed as he strapped Bruce Dempsey—the *Beast of Brooklyn*—to the back of his hover sled. Business never became personal for the collector; a job was a job. But this one came real damn close to crossing a line. *Shame, really. He wasn't a bad sort.*

His repository, Rebecca, tended to her wounded shoulder with the spray bottle of anagenesis which X provided. "I think I know your secret." She looked up from her wound, the flesh already scabbing over from the healing foam. "Why you hate the morlox so much."

X grunted. "I don't hate em." He buried his face, checking Bruce's straps one last time, confirming the contender was prepped for delivery. "Just business, Sheila."

"Bullshit," Rebecca shook her head slowly, taking her place on the sled behind him. "They took someone from you, someone important."

X said nothing. He knew repositories, they always spotted a lie. He passed her a syringe. "Here. There's enough quantum blood in that dose to see you safely back to the surface."

Rebecca took the dose, slightly cringing as the needle pierced her skin. "Bruce was right, you know. Whether it's food, medicine," she nodded at the empty syringe, "or just the right to live. We all live under quantum rule."

"Aye," X turned to face her. "If that's how you feel, why didn't you escape with him like he asked?"

"I wanted to, more than you know." Rebecca buried her face in her hands, her voice muted. "He may be the contender, but I'm a repository." Her long fingers brushed away her tears, wiping them into her cheeks. "I was trained from birth. The knowledge of the borough dwells within *me*. I can't walk away from that."

"Job's a job," X grunted. He flipped the sled on auto-pilot, letting it carry them out of the Subterranean. *Damn the quantum, I'm never taking a job like this again.* "You think Demp—*Bruce* will understand?"

"Yes," Rebecca nodded, still sniffling. "If we'd left, he would've hated himself. Maybe not right away but..." She sighed, burying her head. "The borough's lost so many challenges, they're starving. Without Bruce, they're doomed." Looking off to the side, she cracked a smile. "The Beast of Brooklyn's our only hope."

X squinted as the hover sled pierced the darkness and returned to the light. "Hello, beautiful." He never thought he'd be so glad to see the red sun, the cracked earth covering the scorchlands. He inhaled fresh air, remembering what it felt like to breathe with his old lungs. Finally, he spoke. "You're wrong about one thing," he looked Rebecca dead in the face. "He will need you. More than you know."

"He's the contender." Rebecca rolled her eyes. "I'm a repository, I'm expendable."

"That's what *my* repository used to say." X sighed deeply, shaking his head. "Before the palefaces killed her in front of me." X reached up and removed his metal faceplate for the first time in years. Rebecca tried muting her shocked gasp behind her hands, but it didn't offend him. Very little of his original flesh remained, except for this spot. Tilting his head, he showed her the traces of ink remaining on his temple.

Rebecca leaned closer, her voice shaky. "A contender's tattoo." She blinked in surprise. "Y-You were a *contender*?"

"In another life." He reset the faceplate back into place, covering up the dark reminder of what he'd lost, what he'd become. *More than a machine, but without her, less than a man.* He looked back at Bruce, mercifully unconscious in his straps. "Look, I overheard the Q-Lords talkin' about your boy. They've got plans for him. Shit I wouldn't wish on my worst enemy."

Rebecca recoiled, raising an eyebrow. "What are you saying?"

X guided the sled's controls towards Quantum Tower, sparkling on the horizon. "All I'm sayin' is, he'll need you. Because if he survives what they have in store, all he'll have to look forward to becoming... is me."

...

Bruce Dempsey will return for the contender challenges.

Jay Sandlin is a voice actor, podcaster and author of titles including: OVER THE ROPES, HELLFIGHTER QUIN, IT CALLS FROM THE SKY. GRIMM ToTQ: HH HOLMES. Neverland Annual: Dark Alliance, and more to come.

https://jaysandlin.com/
https://twitter.com/JaySandlin_
https://www.instagram.com/JaySandlin_/

THE CREEPING VOID
BY TIM MENDEES

*For Linda and everyone who reads the
madness the comes out of my head*

INTRODUCTION
STRETCHING NECKS

Present

"**S**ilence!"

A hush fell over the assembled crowd as a large man with cheeks like beetroots and a mighty white beard rose from his seat and addressed the two men on the scaffold. "William McTavish, Thomas Bell, ye two have been found guilty of a number of heinous crimes; chief among them being consorting with White Coats." His mouth puckered at the foul taste of those last two words.

Willie opened his mouth to protest as a disgruntled murmur spread through the crowd, but he was quickly silenced by a sharp tug on the cable looped around his neck.

The large man continued: "Those despised Sassenach invaders that want to corrupt our lands and feed our bodies to the ravenous void. Ye were once again caught in possession of outlawed items..." His piercing blue eyes fixed them with a hateful stare as he spat the next word like it was a disease. "Tech! ... This is despite being on yer final warning for such a crime. Ye pair are a disgrace to yer clan and to yer blood, and as Laird of the vale, I sentence ye to swing by yer scrawny wee necks until yer legs stop twitchin'!"

The crowd cheered. The clan of the Vale were a bloodthirsty bunch at the best of times, but especially when their nerves had been set jangling by recent events.

"What of the girl? ... I'm beggin' ye, let her go!" Tom struggled against the executioner's hands to plead for mercy.

The Laird firmly placed his black bonnet on his tangle of unruly hair and smirked almost sadistically. "She will be dealt with in accordance with the charter of 2146..." He paused and licked his lips, taking time to relish the moment. "She'll be tied to the dreaded monument and burned as a scientist... A fittin' end for one of those that have brought the world to ruin, don't ye think?"

"No!" Willie bellowed. "Ye don't know what yer doing... That girl could save us all. She knows how..."

Slap!

Watching the words being slapped from his friend's mouth by the brute in the black hood, Tom opened his mouth to speak but was silenced by a dagger pressed to his lips.

"Enough!" The Laird cried over the din of the enraged crowd. "Sound the drums!"

As the drums began to thump out a ponderous death march, Willie looked at Tom and sighed. "Well... that's the world fucked then."

"Aye, looks like... Och, well, at least we tried... Goodbye, Willie."

The pounding drums rose in tempo as they were joined by the mournful wail of a poorly-stitched bagpipe. As the executioner checked the cables one last time, positioning the knot behind the condemned men's left ears, the deafening crack of void thunder rent the air around them.

"Shite!" the Laird screamed. "Void storm! Inside, the lot of ye! ... To the shelter!"

Screaming villagers scurried like startled rats as vicious tendrils of oddly-hued lightning crackled and lashed the purple hills to the west of the settlement. The executioner launched himself off the scaffold and pelted across the muddy square to the shelter, blubbing like a little girl that had just dropped her favourite dolly in the outhouse. Tom and Willie were left standing on their gaffer-tape X's, with their necks wrapped tightly in electrical flex and their arms pinioned with bungee cords.

Tom looked at the creeping storm slowly spreading in their direction, then at his friend. "Great... now what?"

CHAPTER 1
GRIME & PUNISHMENT

Twelve Hours Earlier

"Ouch! ... Bastard thing!" Willie drew his hand back sharply from the football-sized thistle and blew on his pricked finger.

Tom chuckled. "I told ye to wear the gloves, ye daft bampot!"

"And I told you, that fake leather crap brings me oot in a rash." Wrapping a strip of cloth from his tatty shirt around his injured digit, Willie picked up the oddly glowing seeds that he'd managed to extract from the spiky triffid. "Fuckin' thistles... I hate the bastard things. How long 'ave we got to do this fer?"

Tom shrugged and dug a gloved finger into the heart of his own thistle. "You heard the Laird, we do this until our punishment is paid... whatever the hell that means."

"Aye, he does talk a load of shite, but we should probably count ourselves lucky. That poor sod Douglas is still mucking out the outhouses. Two months up to his elbows in shite, now there's a punishment!" Willie grinned and gave a thistle a hard jab with a rusty dirk fashioned from an old pair of meat shears. Seeds burst obscenely from the rupture in a grotesque parody of birth. "Jackpot!"

"It's a good job we only got caught with a couple of calculators. What was that contraption Douglas had?"

Willy thought for a moment. "A pizveeter."

"What the hell's that when it's at home?"

"Pizveeter," Willy stated flatly. "God alone knows what it does, but that's what was written on the front of it, just above this screen, a bunch of buttons with shapes on 'em and a couple of wiggly sticks. Pizveeter... Must be dangerous to warrant two months of crapper duty."

"He'd 'ave made a good bit of coin from the steam-wagoners if he'd got away with it," Tom sighed. "Come to think of it, so would we if we hadn't got collared by that bawbag provost."

"Still... he were lucky it was his first offence. People 'ave been hung for less," Willie sniffed. "He was lucky they didn't flog him raw, neither. You remember what happened to Shuggie Riley?"

"Aye," Tom shuddered. "Poor devil's back were stripped o' skin and rubbed with salt. I reckon I'd 'ave preferred the noose."

"Well, he got it the next time, didn't he? ... Poor sod." Willie finished stuffing the pile of thistle seeds into his satchel, then stood and peered up the heather-blanketed slope. More of the strange twisted weeds had sprouted overnight. They crept closer to the village every day. You couldn't destroy them; once they had sprouted, they were there to stay. If you lopped off their heads, they just grew back bigger, and the roots were lethal if you cut them. Strangely enough, though, the seeds were delicious. "The corruption's spreading... I swear we'll 'ave to move again soon."

"Aye," Tom muttered thoughtfully. "The void's getting closer... look." He pointed over to the south, where roiling clouds of blackness punctuated with splodges of indescribable colour blotted out the horizon. "It can't be more than a few miles away now... we're gonna need to go further north."

"There ain't much further north we can go, pal. Orkney and Shetland have been swallowed up and it's comin' in from the east now too... time's nearly up fer us. There's only this wee corner left." Willie sucked in the air and grimaced. "Even the air tastes shite. My great-granny told me that she used to come up here picking heather. Said the air was sweet and ye could see as far south as Inverness on a clear day. Look at it now... arse-end of the world."

Tutting and giving his thistle a slap, Tom stood and looked across the hillside. "Hey, what's that over there?"

"What?"

"Over there, next to that really big thistle, something glinted." Doing his best to avoid the savage weeds, Tom started towards a clump of fresh void-thistles a couple of hundred yards towards the boundary of the woods. "Come on, man... it might be worth a few bob!"

Willie sighed before chasing after his friend. "Aye, but if it's tech... we leave it, right? ... Right? ... I'm not scrubbin' the shitehouse, Tom... If we get rumbled, I'm blamin' ye!"

Tom wasn't listening, the young Scot was more magpie than man. Crashing through the sick-looking heather, he came to a stop next to the patch of shimmering thistles, dumped his satchel on the ground and started raking at the freshly split earth. "Come on, Willie... Pass me the trowel!"

Willie's apprehension diminished somewhat when he spotted that his compatriot was wrestling with a strip of gleaming metal and not some forbidden object. "Hell! Is that steel?"

Taking the proffered digging implement, Tom started to carve chunks of soil from around his find. "Aye... I think it's a car bumper... Gimme a hand wi' it will ye?"

Gripping the end of it firmly, Willie and Tom gave the strip of metal a good tug, tearing it from its grave. It was about a meter in length and ended abruptly where it appeared to have been dissolved by some kind of acid. "Hey, look at this, Tom... It must have been caught in the breach blast and buried under tons of shite."

"Aye, the thistles are always bringing stuff to the surface."

"I thought the scrappers had picked this hill clean?" Willie buffed the steel with the cuff of his jacket.

"Obviously not, useless numpties. This will make someone a nice wee sword," Tom beamed.

"Aye, and us some nice drinkin' money... Hey, look over yonder!" Willie's arm swept over towards the wood. "There's more metal over by the wood. I'll never be rude to a thistle ever again... This scrap will keep us in whiskey fer weeks; and not that pish they put in the generator neither... proper bloody whiskey!"

Tom stuck the steel bar under his arm and followed Willie towards the glittering points in the ground. The closer they got to the woods, the worse the smell became. An overpowering stench of rotting meat and animal musk drifted on the breeze.

The woods were strictly a no-go area. Known as the Dreaming Wood by the older locals, it had always been a place of dark legend. The difference was, since the void, the legends were one-hundred-per cent real. Not only did the woods teem with hostile life from somewhere beyond, but the trees and plants themselves had been warped by the kiss of the void. Nobody in their right mind went into the wood, and those that did never returned. Even the already grotesque thistles became larger and more menacing the closer they sprouted to the threshold of the trees. The tangled weeds grew in dense clumps and reached about five-foot-tall. Chin-scratchers, Willie called them.

"Hey, I've found one o' them pointless round things ye used to get on wheels!" Tom exclaimed as he plunged into the dirt.

"Hub-cap?"

"Aye, that's the very chap."

"Great, old Algie can make someone a nice shield to go wi' that sword... We're in the money, pal!"

Crack!

Willie's celebration was cut short by a snapping twig and a furtive rustle. "Hey, what were that?"

"Shite..." Tom cursed, reaching for the sword on his back. "I hope that weren't one of them furry beasties!"

"Nah, look!" Willie yelped as he pushed aside a thistle to reveal the face of a startled teenage girl. "It's a lassie!"

The girl sprang to her feet with eyes like a rabbit in lamplight and took off towards the trees.

"Hey, come back, lass! ... We won't hurt ye!" Tom cried after her.

"Don't go in there, ye flamin' bampot!" Willie added as he skirted the thistles and gave chase.

The raven-haired girl wasn't listening as she dashed into the safety of the woods.

"What in the hell is she playin' at?" Willie panted as they came to a stop at the edge of the wood. "She don't stand a chance in there wi' all them beasties."

Tom didn't reply. He was staring slack-jawed up the incline behind them.

"What shall we do, Tom? ... We can't just let her get eaten, can we?"

"Um... Willie?"

"Stupid girl... Did ye recognise her?"

"Willie?"

"What? Come on, man, help me find her..." Willie finally turned around. "What are ye gawkin' at?"

As Willie clapped his eyes upon the abomination creeping in their direction, the girl peered out from behind a tree and hissed: "Don't just stand there... run, you morons!"

Tom was the first to react, and grabbed Willie by his waistcoat before crashing through the low-hanging branches and into the gloom of the Dreaming Wood. The dark shape wasn't far away by the time they began to run but it was in no hurry to catch them. It moved slowly, flickering with the same nameless colours as the void on the horizon. It was roughly the same shape of a large bear, but its edges were blurred and pixelated, just swirling clouds of matter. It flickered as though it was out of phase with the rest of the world, shuddering with each step. The ground it touched instantly took on sickness, the heather twisted and died, the grass withered and drooped, the soil burned with acid. Whatever the creature was, it was clearly one with the void.

CHAPTER 2
THE DREAMING WOOD

Tom gagged as he got a lungful of the wood's sickly air. Entering the foul smell of decay and disease was like running into a brick wall. "Jesus, we shouldn't be in here. This is a deathly place"

As Willie grabbed his arm and dragged him further into the wood, he glanced around, looking for the girl. "Where'd she go... Hey, Lassie!" he bellowed, much to Tom's dismay.

"Shut yer gob, Willie!" Tom paused for a second, scanning the terrain. "Over there, quick!" Pushing his friend ahead of him, Tom directed them down a steep muddy bank and into a natural hollow under the wizened roots of a dead tree. "Keep silent, or we're dead, got it?"

Willie nodded emphatically as he took the weapon that hung next to his sword off his back. The home-spun rifle was a simple but deadly contraption that his father had knocked together in his workshop. A long, thin barrel was screwed into a basic trigger mechanism crafted from scrap metal and old bed springs. A cartridge, filled with rusty two-point-five-inch nails slid into the side of the housing and fed directly into a pneumatically-charged firing bolt. An old bicycle pump attached to a cylinder was used to build pressure to fire the projectiles, the more you pumped, the more powerful the shot. Once the cylinder was fully pressurised, you got about ten shots before the nails started flying with all the speed of an asthmatic snail.

Tapping Willie softly on the shoulder, Tom pointed to the tree-line where they had made their dramatic entrance and stifled a cry. The shimmering beast hovered on the threshold of the woods, questing tendrils of wispy matter tasting the leaves, sending an insidious rot creeping along the twigs and branches. Tears welled in Tom's eyes. He felt utterly empty in the entity's presence, a peculiar desolation seeping into his mind. The vile decay was spreading in his soul as surely as it travelled between the trees.

Pumping air silently into his rifle, Willie placed the heavy wooden stock to his shoulder and stared down the barrel. Preparing to fire, his trigger-finger shook violently, and his grip on the gun faltered. Dropping it silently to his knees, he hung his head and shook as he was overwhelmed by dark emotions.

Whispers cluttered his mind, a thousand tiny voices berating him with words like knives. He was an oaf and the son of an oaf, a product of a lifetime of mistakes, just as apt to die stepping in the wrong patch of thistles one day as to be hung for digging up forbidden junk. All of it, for what? All of his faults and neuroses were laid bare and exposed to scorn. Suddenly, embracing the nothingness of the void seemed like an attractive choice. He could barely comprehend as the creature withdrew its appendages and flooded the woods with a harsh buzzing sound that rattled the teeth and shook the bowels. The trees and ground trembled from the ferocity of the reverberation. Clutching their ears and curling into the foetal position, Tom and Willie prayed for the mercy of death.

Crack!

With a blinding flash of light, the void entity imploded, then burst outwards in a billion glittering particles that rose into the air in a spiralling column. As the weight of its influence lifted, Willie and Tom got up on their knees and dabbed at their eyes in complete bewilderment.

"Wha... What in hell just happened?" Tom managed to ask through ragged breaths.

Before Tom could answer, the mystery girl appeared on the ridge above them with tear-streaked cheeks. "Come on, follow me... We need to get to shelter."

"What?" Tom barked. "Who are you? ... What the bloody hell was that thing?"

"It's part o' the void somehow. Wherever it goes, the void goes... This is nae time fer explanations, there will be time fer that if we get out o' here alive. Come on, let's move!" Her voice was softer and more lyrical than theirs, a true Highland accent. Theirs was derived from their Glaswegian ancestors who fled north when the void hit. She held out her hand and helped Tom up the slope. Putting a finger to her lips and flashing her green eyes, she silenced his questions before gesturing that they should follow, and headed off into the trees. Once Willie had scrabbled up behind him, Tom raced after her.

As lightning flickered through the dense canopy, they reached a point in the wood where all the vegetation turned black. Tom paused briefly to snatch a leaf from one of the trees. It was still alive but as far removed from a healthy growth as was possible. The texture was oddly rubbery and clammy to the touch, more fungus than plant. Tom tore it in two, then gagged and tossed it aside as he doubled over, heaving and retching. It stank like festering game meat. Sickly iron, copper and burned sugar hung in the air.

"Tom, are ye alright, pal?" Willie panted as he stopped and patted him firmly on the back.

The girl suddenly stopped in her tracks, turned with a look of terror plastered across her face and hissed a sibilant "Shush!"

Willie stopped, eyes darting and mouthed, "What?"

"Listen," she mouthed in reply.

Sure enough, as they stood in silence, they could hear rustling undergrowth and an odd chittering. It was off to the west but quickly closing in on their position. The unnerving sounds on the forest floor were soon joined by crashing branches above.

"Shite!" Tom coughed, wiping his mouth and drawing his own pneumatic weapon, a pistol-sized contraption that worked like a crossbow and shot nine-inch-carpentry-nails at high velocity. "Here they come!"

"I knew this was going too well..." Willie sighed, taking aim at the tree-tops.

"Watch out!" the girl cried, and gestured to a large clump of black weeds as she drew two jagged daggers from the animal-hide sheaths strapped to her thighs.

Tom spun and fired as a ferocious ball of snarling umber fur burst from the bushes and hurtled towards his face. It was the size of a large cat, but was almost lemur-like in stature, with large pointed ears and an elongated tail. The nail hit the beast squarely in the breast, sending gouts of noxious purple ichor into the air.

Willie gibbered as he stared at the downed animal's hateful face. It was almost feline, except its whiskers had been replaced by worm-like tentacles with snapping clawed tips. The maw they circled snapped and snarled as it refused to die. Taking a breath, he lined up his shot and squeezed the trigger, ending the creature's pain. "Wha... What is it?"

Tom had heard about the furry horrors that called the woods home, though he had never seen one with his own eyes. The legends contained in his clan's old books said they came from a dimension of dream, and they poured out of the void like parasites. The books gave them a name... "Zoog! ... I think it's called a zoog."

"Aye, that's the buggers, there are colonies of the damn things further north... Watch out... here comes more!" the girl screamed as everywhere around them, the trees and bushes shook, then abruptly stopped.

As everything became unnaturally still, the girl held a finger to her lips and started to creep around the trunk of a tree to get a better look. She gulped audibly as she peered up into the trees and saw several zoogs prepared to pounce. "Shite...," she whispered. "We're in a bloody nest!" Carefully, she tried to back away from the trees, gesturing at Willie and Tom to follow her lead.

The preternatural stillness was finally shattered when another zoog leapt from the bushes, whooping and chittering. Tom fired again, but the nail went wide and embedded itself in the trunk of a large tree. Tom screamed as the tree convulsed, then ruptured in a torrent of oily black sap.

Willie started firing in bursts as several zoogs started to descend from the branches. Not one shot hit its target. "They're too damn fast!"

"Use your blades!" the girl ordered as she slashed and stabbed at two of the ferocious animals. They were almost preternaturally fast, seeming to phase in and out of space as they darted from side to side, hissing and thrashing their mouth feelers. Every three or four attacks would land, and she managed to take out two of the creatures before the boys even had time to ready themselves.

Tom unsheathed his rapier-like sword and flailed wildly at the incoming zoogs. Through some minor miracle, he managed to catch the closest one on the left flank and sent it spiralling into a pile of dead leaves, screeching in pain. Willie followed his example and unleashed his own blade.

His was of much rougher construction and was more like a cutlass, but it had the desired effect as he cleaved a zoog's head from its shoulders with a roundhouse swing.

The woods became a din of cracking branches, falling leaves and snarling zoogs. Despite their furious slashing, it was no good. For every zoog they despatched, another two took its place. They were up to their ankles in goo-soaked fur and shattered claws, but still, the zoogs just kept on coming.

"It's no good, Willie... there's no end to these beasties!" Tom wailed.

By now, they had been backed into a tight unit. Standing back to back to back, they struggled to keep the critters at bay. Growing weary from the exertion, the girl screamed loud enough to puncture Willie's ear-drum, "I have an idea... but it's a long shot... Close your eyes and think of Scotland!"

"What?" Tom asked in bewilderment as she took a tubular device out of her leather utility belt and pressed a button on its top.

"Down!" she yelled as she tossed it into the bushes, dragging both men by the arm.

The device exploded in a blue shockwave that crackled and fizzed in the atmosphere around them. Every hair on their bodies stood to attention as the electrical device rippled the air in a haze of static. The zoogs screeched as their bodies started to flicker, as if phasing in and out of reality.

"Quick, run!" The girl took off into the trees, dragging them with her.

"Where to? ... What did ye just do? ... What the hell was that contraption?"

"Och, stop asking damn fool questions, Tom. Just follow the lassie!"

Lightning flashed and flickered through the canopy as the void storm crawled in slowly from the hills. It was almost as though it too was stalking them. Their new acquaintance led them down a steep gulley to a festering burn that oozed sluggishly through the centre of the wood. By now, they could hear the zoogs snuffling and scrabbling after their scent, apparently having regained their footing in reality.

Tom stopped at the water and gazed in horror at the bloated and malformed toads that lined the banks. Eyeing them with the utmost suspicion, he edged along behind Willie.

"Over here, quick," the girl beckoned. She stood at a metal hatch built into the ground. With a screech of rusty hinges, the circular aperture opened, revealing a tunnel. "Quick... In here."

Stepping into the darkness, Tom helped the girl slam the door shut behind them and bar it with a rusty metal girder. "Come on, this way," the girl panted as she took a pre-void Zippo lighter from her belt, struck it, and used it to light a torch fashioned from an old metal bed-post and a bundle of tightly bound oily rags.

"Where the hell are we goin'?" asked Tom. "Come to think o' it, who the hell are ye?"

The girl sighed. Now they were out of imminent danger, she had no choice but to answer his incessant queries. "This drain leads to a small complex on the other side of the wood. I have friends there, we'll be safe." She stuck out her hand in greeting. "Mary's the name. Mary Ross."

Shaking her hand, Willie returned the greeting. "Pleased to meet ye, I'm Willie, this is Tom. What clan are ye from?"

"I have no clan..." Mary replied flatly. "Now, come on. If that storm carries on much longer, this place will flood, and ye may as well slit your wrists now, it'd be better than getting void-kissed."

Following Mary's lead, Tom resumed his questioning. "The thing that was following ye, what was it?"

"We call it the creeper... I'm not sure what it is exactly, but one of my friends is trying to work it out. I was after void samples for testing when it came. It's like the bugger knew what I was doing and brought the storm to stop me. We must be getting close to the truth."

"Truth? What truth? And, who's this we that you keep bangin' on about?"

"Jeez, Tom. Is all ye do ask blasted questions?" Mary sighed again. "The truth about the void, of course. What it is, where it came from... and how to stop it swallowing the rest of the world. I'm part of a group that is trying to halt the creep of the void..."

Tom gasped in horror. "White coat!" Drawing his sword once more, he pushed Willie behind him and pointed the sharp end at Mary. "You're a fuckin' white coat... Back you heathen!"

Mary snorted like a hungry pig. "A what?"

"White coat... one o' them that brought the void... a godless scientist!"

"Scientists didn't bring the void, ye numpty. That's just a bunch o' twaddle some o' the clans say to keep people in line and away from outsiders. We are trying to stop it. Now, put yer sword away before ye do yerself a mischief."

Tom held his position, his blade dancing in the air from the tremor in his hand. "My people say that you are responsible. That it started at some hellish place called CERN. The laird says that the void is hell and that you lot are its apostles! You want to cover the land in the void and take our souls!"

Mary erupted into laughter. "What? Do ye hear how ridiculous that sounds? What the hell would we want your soul fer? ... It had nothing to do with CERN or science... it was something else... Now, I'll ask ye again to put the sword away, or I'll introduce ye to my own blades." Her dainty hands started to drift down to the hilts of her twin daggers.

Tom gulped, his resolve wavering. For a moment, they stood in silence, their heavy breath echoing in the cramped brick tunnel. The sound of greasy water and muffled thunder added to the suspense.

After a moment Willie leaned into Tom's ear and whispered. "Maybe ye should put yer weapon away, Tom... I saw what the lass can do, she'll gut ye like a herring... and she did save our carcasses from those furry demons back there."

Tom suddenly remembered the device she had used to deal with the zoogs. "Yeah, what the hell were that thing ye used? It was tech wasn't it?"

"It was just an EMP grenade. We found a bunch of them in a police station in Wick. I didnae think it'd do anything, but Malcolm has this theory that anything kissed by the void is sorta out of phase with reality and an electro-magnetic pulse will disrupt their molecular structure..." She stopped talking and shook her head. "What's the point... you bumpkins don't have a clue what I'm talking about, do ye? ... Put the fuckin' sword away, I won't tell you again!""

Tom thought for a minute and looked at Willie, who was pleading with his eyes for him to stand down. Finally, he lowered his weapon. "There... now what?"

Mary smirked. "Good boy... Now? ... Well, ye can either come with me or wait until the storm passes and try yer luck with those creatures out there... your choice." She turned and started to hurry along the passage, her torch casting flickering shadows on the nitre and mould-stained masonry, before chuckling and calling back, "I promise, I won't steal your soul!"

"Come on, what choice do we have?" Willie gave Tom a playful nudge. "I like her..."

"Fine...," Tom replied with resignation. "Not a word to the clan, alright?"

"Deal," Willie smiled, following after Mary.

If they had thought that nothing could have smelled fouler than the woods above them, they were sadly mistaken. Stamping through two inches of stagnant water, rat urine and decaying matter, their senses were assaulted by unimaginable foulness. They had to maintain a quick pace to keep up with their nimble guide, sending droplets of filth up the legs of their leather trousers. Willie said a silent prayer of thanks that he wasn't wearing his kilt. Nobody on thistle duty is foolish enough to go unprotected in that department... vicious spikes in the sporran region is a nightmare best avoided.

Mary led them along the winding passage for about a mile before it opened onto a gantry with a rusty ladder reaching up to another hatch, and to the right a sheer drop down to a raging torrent. Willie paused and looked down. There were greasy black shapes in the water that sent chills down the back of his neck. They were too large and malformed to be rats or otters, and they seemed to be composed of a tar-like substance that rippled and shifted with the current.

"It's not far now, just pray that the storm hasn't caught up wi' us or we're stuck down here until it passes." Mary adjusted her satchel and headed towards the ladder.

Tom stood and gazed at the wall. Someone had painted the slogan '#everythingsucks' in lurid fluorescent paint about halfway up the shaft. Once Mary had checked the skies and flipped the hatch, he followed, leaving Willie staring into the abyss.

"There are some funny creatures down here, Tom," Willie muttered as he fished in his pockets. "They look like livin' oil or somethin'." Finally finding an old piece of flint used for fire-lighting, he took aim and lobbed it at the largest specimen. Instantly, hundreds of eyes snapped open on the creature's hide as it piped in fury:

'Tekeli-li!'

"Argh!" Willie screamed, and launched himself at the ladder. "Move yer arse, Tom... somethin's comin'!"

Tom climbed as quickly as he could, but was almost overtaken by his petrified pal. Willie was so terrified, it was a wonder his tangled ginger locks didn't turn alabaster. "What the hell's wrong wi' ye?" Tom spat as he dragged Willie out of the shaft and to his feet by his waistcoat. "Ye could have sent me flyin', ye daft bastard!"

"There... there was a thing down there... in the water," Willie babbled, his blue eyes swivelling wildly. "Bloody hellish, it was!"

Clang!

The sound of the slamming hatch nearly gave the startled Scotsman a coronary as Mary secured it with a metal bar. "I dunno what they are called, but those are mere bairns," she stated matter-of-factly. "Ye should see the size of the buggers in the loch."

Willie shuddered and took a couple of deep breaths before looking at his surroundings. They had come upon the edge of a deserted village. Once it could have been called picturesque, but now it was downright sinister. Darkened windows peered onto the weed-choked cobble street like the hollow sockets of weathered skulls. The sky had turned a bruised purple above the crumbling spire of a decrepit church, giving the graveyard an unnatural glow.

"Oh hell, Willie," Tom hissed. "I think this is the cursed village."

"Aye, I reckon so..."

"What are ye two talkin' about?" Mary asked.

"The clan calls this place the cursed village. When we first settled in the area, several of our men came here lookin' fer supplies... almost none o' them returned. We've never come near it since." Willie looked around furtively. "They said they saw demons here."

For the first time since they had met, Willie was hoping that Mary would cut him a withering look and tell him not to be so daft. Sadly, she didn't... "Come on, we don't want to linger by the church... this way." Mary nodded towards a narrow road between two twisted yew trees.

Willie started after her immediately, but Tom was distracted. The walls of the burned-out post office had been covered in more of the odd slogans: '#hopeends' and '#blackcloud.'

"Come on, Tom... quit yer dawdling," Willie hissed from behind a mangled red phone box.

Tom nodded brusquely and followed.

As the storm raged above the Dreaming Wood, the trio raced along the lane until they reached a rusty chain-link fence. Mary hurried over to the gate and pushed it slightly ajar. It made an awful grating noise that made Tom's teeth itch. Squeezing through the gap, he noted with some discomfort that the private property sign had been eclipsed with the slogan: '#projecttroll.'

"Mary?" Tom whispered as they jogged towards a large square glass-fronted building. "These signs everywhere, what do they mean?"

Mary shook her head ruefully. "I'll let Malcolm explain... I dunna ken it fully." She winked mischievously at Tom. "I'm a scout, not a white coat."

Tom cracked a smile for the first time in hours. "Point taken."

Willie looked up at the building at a large sign emblazoned with the word: APEPCORP. "What is this hellish place? Some kind of prison?"

This amused Mary greatly, her face creased in mirth. "Kind of... it's called a call-centre. People worked here before the void. Our historian, Samantha, said that they were evil places where people were forced to work all day and night fer a pittance... We have set up camp in one of the offices."

Twin doors emblazoned with the company logo, a three-lobed Egyptian eye ringed by a snake eating its own tail, hung at skewed angles from a rusty frame. Mary took out a small device and started to pump it rhythmically, a light flickering from the end.

"What's that?" Willie asked.

"Dynamo torch... it works on static electricity," Mary replied, sweeping the reception area floor. The light glittered off a carpet of broken glass and paper-clips.

Tom crossed himself as she picked her way over towards the desk. "Damned tech."

"Fer God's sake, Tom... Don't you have electricity in your village?" Mary snapped, finally losing her patience. They were all in danger of extinction, and he was worried about a blasted flashlight.

"Aye... but that comes from the old jenny... it runs on whiskey."

"Ingenious... quite ingenious, but it's still electricity. How is this any different?" she sneered, shaking the device in Tom's face.

"Um... I... I dunno, the Laird says..."

Willie cut him off, defusing the tension. "Can we save the arguments until later, this place gives me the heebie-jeebies... look at that!" He pointed to a six-by-six print of a grinning woman with a mobile phone clamped to her ear. Someone had blacked her eyes out and given her devil's horns. Under it was the slogan: 'Apepcorp, connecting the future.' Someone had scribbled it out and scrawled '#creepingfear' in its place.

Taking yet another device that made Tom extremely nervous, a walkie-talkie, from by the shattered computer terminal on the front desk, Mary motioned for them to follow her down a darkened corridor. More defaced pictures of air-brushed models pouting into their handsets lined the corridor as they headed towards a central staircase. Holding her hand up, Mary said quietly, "Hold up... Now, Tom, you've gotta promise me you won't have a heart attack, or shit yer kecks when I do this..."

"What?"

Pressing the switch on the side of the walkie-talkie unleashed a belch of static into the confined space. Tom jumped, and Willie pointed and laughed at him. "Sam, can ye hear me? ... It's Mary, and I have guests."

A second passed before the device barked again, followed by a female voice with a cut-glass English accent. "Right-o, my dear. I'll disable the traps, just a tick..." Mary smiled at the two lads sweetly and shrugged before the voice returned. "Okie-dokie, it's all safe. Up you come, I'll put the kettle on."

"Thanks, Sam." Clipping the walkie-talkie to her belt, Mary gestured to the stairs. "Malcolm has rigged up an old army turret he found at RAF Wick, it works on motion sensors... it would have torn ye to shreds." Smirking at their wide-eyed reaction, she carried on in an overtly-chipper voice. "Come along!"

CHAPTER 3
#PROJECTTROLL

Malcolm Tanner peered at the screen and frowned. He had successfully booted the system up but was now faced by a menu. Flicking open a ratty copy of 'Windows for Dummies' and flicking through the grimy pages, he searched for a solution. "What do you mean, you stupid machine?" Huffing with irritation, he slammed the book on the desk in front of him and swore under his breath.

"What's the matter?" a tall, fair man with a mighty blonde beard inquired.

"I dunno what to select, I don't want to lock myself out again. It took bloody ages to crack back into the blasted thing."

Before the other man could ask what the choices were, Sam's prim voice cut through the dusty atmosphere like a chainsaw. "Coo-ee, Malcolm, Viking... we have guests!"

"Guests?" Viking blurted in surprise. "Come on, Malcolm, there may be trouble!"

"No!" Malcolm snapped. "I don't have time for this nonsense, who knows how long that back-up generator will run for... it's already on the last of the fuel."

"Fine... Suit yourself." Viking picked up his M16, slung it over his shoulder and walked towards the hub of their camp, the canteen.

Willie and Tom stood in the centre of the room with one of the others, an Englishman named Dave, pointing a gun at them. "Hand your weapons over!"

"Not on yer life... damn thieving Sassenach!" Willie growled.

"It's procedure!"

"Aye," Willie snarled. "An it's procedure where I'm from to kill anyone who tries to steal yer stuff!"

"Boys, boys," Sam cooed. "Do knock it off with the testosterone, won't you. The air in here is ripe enough without you two polluting it with unchecked hormones... Now, put the bloody weapons away and sit the hell down!" Her sudden change in tone startled both men sufficiently that they did as they were told. Sam was a formidable woman who would have made a great headmistress back before the void. The steel in her eyes was matched only by the tight bun of hair on her head. "Now, who wants tea, hmm?"

Several hands were raised as Sam pushed a trolley with a tea-urn and a collection of chipped mugs into the canteen. "Now, where did you find these two gentlemen, Mary?"

"The other side of the wood, we got trapped by a void storm... they're alright." She pointed at Tom. "He's a bit wet, but they are good in a scrap. We had to fend off a pack of zoogs."

"Ah, useful allies, it seems." Sam arched an imperious eyebrow. "You must be from that small settlement at the foot of the hills?"

"Aye," Tom nodded, eyeing the brown liquid in the urn with suspicion. "That's right. Tom Bell and Willie MacTavish, Clan o' the Vale. Just tell this arse-face to keep his hands off our stuff, okay?" He jabbed a grimy finger in Dave's direction.

Dave rose to his feet again, spitting oaths and reaching for his gun. "Bastard!"

"Stop pissing about, Dave," Mary said flatly as she leapt over to Dave and held a sharp blade against his neck. "Put the pea shooter away or I'll fillet you."

Dave scowled at Mary, his grip on the gun faltering. Mary smirked, increasing the pressure of the blade against his skin. "You're a fucking psycho," Dave burbled as he returned the gun to his belt. Mary grinned.

"Enough!" Viking slammed his fist on a filthy plastic table, sending a stack of ancient Apepcorp flyers skidding across the floor. "We don't have time for this crap," he boomed in a strong Scandinavian accent. "Mary, did you get the samples?"

"Yeah... Yes." Startled by the big man's rage, Marystarted rummaging in her satchel, finally removing three Tupperware boxes filled with questionable matter. "Here... One of them is a mouse. The poor thing ran into the void and came out like this..." She opened the tub to reveal a black globular mass with a long wiry tail, pulsing with life..

"Bloody hell," Dave gulped. "Keep that thing away from me."

Thrusting the box under his nose, Mary giggled. "Say hello to the wee mouse, Dave!"

"Mary!" Sam snapped. "Do behave, there's a dear."

After blowing Dave a kiss, she placed the tub on the table and apologised. "Sorry, Sam... he just gets right on me tits is all."

Grumbling a series of foul slurs under his breath, Dave decided that discretion was the best part of valour at this point. "I'll take Malcolm some tea." As he skulked from the room, Mary fluttered her eyelashes at Sam and smiled innocently.

"Thank you, Dave." Sam turned to Willie once he was out of earshot. "You'll have to excuse Dave's manners... he can be a bit of a pain in the rear, but his heart's in the right place... sugar?"

Willie nodded then accepted a steaming Apepcorp mug. Taking a sip, he grimaced before setting it down on the table.

"Yes, it's not the best tea, I'm afraid," Sam shrugged, before plonking another sugar cube in his mug. "The tea bags are about a hundred years past their 'best before' date. The sugar will help."

Viking had missed most of the tomfoolery, engrossed as he was in poking a pile of sludge with an old Apepcorp pen. Straightening up, he spoke to Tom. "I assume you have questions, yes?"

"Oh, boy, does he have questions," Mary snickered. "He has nothin' but bloody questions."

Viking ignored her and continued. "Cutting to the chase, we are trying to halt the spread of the void. I come from Norway, across the North Sea. We took one of the old cruise liners and converted it into a mobile base. The radar and radio transmitters are great for tracking the spread of the void. Much of my country is still free of the void's kiss, but it covers more land each week. By my calculations, we have less than a year left. From what I can tell, only Norway and isolated pockets are safe. One such pocket is right here. When I came ashore at Wick, I found Mary and Sam hiding out in a library."

Sam interjected. "The library was my family's home... I'm a historian. Mary is my ward and bodyguard."

"I went there in search of anything that could shed light on what was happening," Viking continued. "They were under siege from a bandit caravan... bloodthirsty scum, the lot of them. We managed to get away with a bunch of plans, maps and schematics relating to Apepcorp, and those led us here. We found Dave and Malcolm in an old office complex, they are experts in ancient technology. There were others, but..."

"What's so special about this place?" Tom cocked a brow and stroked his bushy brown beard.

"This place is in the epicentre of the safe zone. From what I have gleaned from records, the reason this place is safe has something to do with whatever Apepcorp was doing here."

Before he could elucidate, Dave appeared in the doorway with a face like a wet Sunday. "Sorry, Viking... Malcolm says: 'get your hairy arse over here, pronto.'"

Viking sighed. "Fine. You lot may as well come with me. He can explain the science further."

As one, the group followed Dave back into an open-plan office and towards the desk at the rear. Malcolm sat in a cloud of cigarette smoke lit by the blueish glow of the screen. To Tom, he looked like the devil himself, embodying everything that Tom's clan had taught him to despise. He was the leader of their greatest enemy... and Tom was about to become his accomplice.

"Ah, there you are...," Malcolm sneered. "I've found a file related to this..." He pointed at the wall behind him where someone had scrawled '#projecttroll.'

"Really? What does it mean?" Viking replied, peering at the graffiti with distaste.

"I'm not sure. It says: 'Project Troll initiated. Black cloud almost at capacity. All satellites online.' Have you seen or heard anything about 'Black Cloud?'"

"It's painted on the walls in the village," Willie piped up.

"Yeah," Malcolm scowled at the newcomer. "I know. Not helpful, whoever you are."

"There used to be a thing called The Cloud," Sam began. "It was where everyone kept their precious data. Kind of like a digital bank. Try searching for The Cloud."

Malcolm tapped the keys frantically. "Wait... Oh, here we go..." His face went from one of elation to anguish in a heartbeat. "Oh, bollocks. I think this is it."

"What is?" Tom demanded. "Spit it out, man!"

"Well... The Black Cloud was set up to run alongside The Cloud. But instead of saving people's data, it collected their negativity. Look!" He pointed at the screen in horror. "It says Project Troll was designed to harvest hatred itself from the internet and build it to a critical mass."

"What?" Viking spat. "What in God's name for?"

"...To release the crawling chaos, Nyarlathotep, from his prison. This was all some nutty plan to bring an old god back to earth." Malcolm looked at him with a grim expression. "You know, you came here because you thought Apepcorp halted the spread?"

Viking nodded.

"Well, the only reason this area isn't covered by the void is because the signal in the area wasn't strong enough. They didn't slow it, they fucking caused it!"

"But, how... I mean, how could they bring the void with this Black Cloud?" Mary asked.

"It says here that they were about to 'roll out 13G,' whatever the hell that means, and that it was possible using something called a shining trapezohedron. This was some kind of ancient crystal that was somehow linked to another dimension, they thought. People experimented with it for years, thought it could somehow fix the energy crisis. It was only the boffins at Apepcorp who finally figured out how to use it. According to this the shining trapezohedron is somehow linked to this Nyarlathotep, and by using it, they could free him."

"Sounds like a load o' bollocks to me," Willie sniffed. "Why would they want te, that's the big question?"

Malcolm shrugged. "No idea. All it says here is: '#projecttroll will bring #crawlingchaos to earth.' It doesn't explain why."

"I do wish the pre-void people didn't use that god-awful 'twit-speak' all the time," Sam sighed ruefully. "I can't make head nor tail of it. It's just a bunch of gobbledygook!"

"This is all very interesting," Dave sneered from behind a white-board covered in Apepcorp jargon and team-building exercises. "But how does it help us stop the void-creep, and why are we safe from it?"

"Many of the Highland people complained about having no signal. You read it all the time in their emails and journals," Sam explained. "I read about it hundreds of times back at the library. Something to do with a 'black spot' or something."

"So, the only reason we're alive is because Apepcorp were shite?" Willie exclaimed in surprise.

"Well put, Master Willie. That about sums it up, yes."

Malcolm bit his lip and hammered at the keyboard. After a whirr of the processor fan and chatter from the CPU, the screen changed colour and showed a map of the United Kingdom. Most of it was purple, except for the North-Eastern corner of Scotland and a tiny speck in west Cornwall. The map was divided into squares, each with a green X in the centre. The X over the clear section was red.

"What I don't get is, how are all these green X things still functioning if they are in the void?" Viking mused. "I know that a lot of things ran on those ever-lasting nuclear-fusion batteries but I'd have thought that they would have been destroyed when the void seeped in?"

Malcolm thought for a second. "Maybe the void has joined with them somehow? ... Either that, or..."

"Or?"

"Or, something is keeping them going..."

Nobody wanted to elaborate on that particular theory.

"Malcolm, can you find out more about the red X?" Viking asked.

"Yeah... hold on, I'll zoom in." He tapped the keyboard again. The map zoomed in on their sector and showed a detailed topographical map of the area.

Tom squinted at the screen. "Hey, that's right by our village!"

Viking looked at him in astonishment. "Really? ... What's there, anything odd?"

Thinking for a second, "Nah, not really... there is a couple o' ruins... and the monument..." His eyes grew wide. "The monument!"

"Monument?" All eyes were now on Tom and Willie.

"Aye, a big metal tower sticking up in the air," Willie nodded. "Horrible rusty eyesore, it is!"

"A transmitter tower!" Viking exclaimed. "That's it! ... That must be the faulty part of the network." He looked down at the screen, where there was a countdown timer adjacent to the map. "What's that mean?"

Malcolm clicked a couple of keys. "Um... Not good. It says 'retry in...' I think there's an automatic process that tries to get the tower working again."

"The storms!" Sam shrieked. "Don't you see? I've always wondered why they happen so regularly... it's this damn process! Shut it down, Malcolm. Shut it down, now!"

"Ach... I can't. I need a password."

"Do something!" Sam was getting hysterical. "One of these days, that damn thing is going to actually work, and that's it for everything!"

"I'm doing my best, woman!" Malcolm yelled. "We will have to do it manually. If we can get..."

Clunk!

Malcolm's speeding train of thought was instantly derailed by the sudden failure of all power. The group was suddenly plunged into darkness.

"Damn," Viking huffed. "The generator must have run out of fuel."

Dave shook his head. "It shouldn't have. It was low, but not that low. It must be a fault... I'll go and check it out. Pass me a walkie-talkie, Sam."

"No... I'll come with you. You'll need someone to hold a torch while you play with your spanner, won't you? Mary, have you still got your walkie?"

"Aye."

"Good... Come along then, David, grab your tools and let's go."

As the two stalked off through the dusty rows of office desks littered with defunct office equipment, Viking handed out Apepcorp-branded dynamo torches to the rest of the group. Willie accepted his with a grin and started pumping the handle. Tom took his between a thumb and forefinger and let it dangle, much to Mary's amusement. Sweeping his light around,

Willie chuckled at the dust-bunnies and fungus spores that twisted in the beams, before scowling at a large painted slogan: #audientvoid... Willie shrugged, this 'twit-speak' was going to take some getting used to. He twisted his mouth into random shapes and made a scratchy noise with his throat, trying to articulate the hash-tag and making one hell of a din.

"Will you cut that out, I'm trying to think!" Malcolm banged his fists on the desk in frustration.

Willie jumped. "Okay, okay... dunna get yer sporran in a twist, big man."

Mary snorted and shook her head. "What were ye sayin' before the power went out, Malcolm?"

With a sigh and a shake of the head, Malcolm began. "All of the transmitter towers have a fail-safe system of their own. We can shut it down manually from there." He pointed at Tom and Willie. "You know where it is, yes?"

"Aye. It's right outside our village."

"Okay... Take me there."

Tom was about to explain how much manure they would be neck-deep in if they were caught, but the harsh belch of Mary's walkie-talkie stopped the words on his gums.

"Hello?" Mary replied, looking at the device in confusion and giving it a good shake. "Sam? ... You there?"

A moment of silence passed, before another bark followed by frantic screaming. "Get out... Get out now, it's a trap!"

"Sam? What the hell is going on? ... Sam?"

"Ghouls! ... Dave is dead, they lured us down here... Arghhh..." Sam's voice became a disgusting gurgle, and fell silent.

"Sam? ... Sam!" Mary's eyes welled with tears as she drew her blades. "Bastards! ... I'll kill 'em all!"

"No!" Viking growled as he grabbed her around her waist. "It's a trap, they want to take us one-by-one. They must have cut the power to kill the turret. We need to move... Now!"

"I can't leave her, Viking!" Mary struggled free and dashed away before coming to a halt and assuming a fighting stance when a furtive shadow caught her eye. "They're here... those dog-faced bastards are here!" Tears were streaming down her cheeks, and her body shook in fury.

Drawing his rifle, Willie took a knee and pointed it in the direction Mary was looking. Tom and Viking drew their weapons and moved towards Mary. Malcolm cowered behind his desk, shoving reams of Apep-corp documents into his satchel.

Breathing hard, Mary shone her flashlight into the corner of the room. Everything was still and quiet. She was about to relax when a shadow behind a filthy plastic plant caught her eye. Squinting to see, she suddenly went rigid. "There!"

As she spoke, the imitation tree was torn aside, and a slavering horror revealed itself. It was roughly the size and shape of a man but hunched forward, and its face was a foul hybrid betwixt man and canine. Its evil red eyes glared at Mary as it snarled and prepared to attack.

Thunk!

Before it could move, a large nail from Willie's rifle plunged through its eyeball and pinned its head to the stud-wall behind. Its clawed hands dangled limply, and its knees sagged, killed in an instant by a crack shot.

"Good shot, Willie!" Tom whooped before screaming in fright. "Oh, shite! ... Here they come!"

From the canteen came a barking horde of mottled-skinned creatures that Willie could only assume to be ghouls. They moved quickly, leaping over desks and swatting aside chairs. Willie fired a burst of nails, studding the largest of the group along the right flank. Tiny gouts of blood bubbled from the wounds, but the creature didn't stop. Tom fired again but went wide, cracking a computer screen down the centre.

Springing on a chair, Mary met an incoming ghoul with a vicious slice across its belly, the creature doubled over as its rank intestines slurped onto the carpet. Screaming like a belligerent banshee, Mary hopped over the desk and slammed one of her daggers into the cranium of the nearest creature. Its skull shattered like an egg and it crumpled, twisting to the ground stone dead.

"Mary! ... Down!" Viking ordered. She dropped flat as he unleashed hot lead in a deafening staccato from his well-maintained M16. The remaining ghouls were mowed down where they stood. Blood, brains and shards of bone showered the office in a red mist. "Quick! ... The fire escape!"

The corridor from the stairs was a din of slapping feet, scratching claws and howling screams. Even Mary realised that they stood no chance against a full horde of the corpse-eating abominations. Taking to her heels, she followed Viking's lead to the far corner of the room.

Slamming the escape with his broad shoulder, Viking opened the door and ushered Malcolm through, then the two boys and finally Mary. Slamming it behind him and barring it with a concrete rebar, Viking followed their flight down the rusty staircase. Their feet clanked on the creaking metal as they hurried to the ground.

"Through the trees, the front gate is crawling with them!" Malcolm bellowed, and took off at speed.

"What the hell were those things?" Tom panted as he raced after the fleeing tech expert.

"Ghouls..." Mary gasped as she sprinted. "Corpse-eating bastards that live under the graveyard... they must have got our scent earlier."

Viking overtook the three Scots and got level with Malcolm. Risking a look behind them, Mary was happy to see that the ghouls had yet to break through the door.

"Stop!" said Viking. "This is ghoul territory. We need to be quiet. This path lets out by the graveyard... there could be hundreds of them around."

"Then, why the fuck are we coming this way?" Willie asked.

"There's no other way. Malcolm said the road was compromised. There is only a river on the other side and that's full of shoggoths..."

"Eh?" Willie cocked a brow.

"Those jelly things ye saw in the drain," Mary explained.

"Did the ghouls come from the void?" Tom whispered to Mary.

"Who knows? ... Sam said that they were always here... Poor Sam."

"Shh!" Malcolm hissed with wild eyes before scampering off into the trees. Viking motioned that they should follow. Soon, they came to the chain-link fence and slipped through a hole festooned with tufts of wiry hair, this must have been the way the ghouls had gained entrance. Tom shuddered as his fingers brushed the bristles. Instinctively, he took his leather gloves from his pocket and slipped them on.

Keeping low amongst the trees, the group hastened towards the rear of the abandoned village...

CHAPTER 4
UNHALLOWED GROUND

Night had fallen by the time they reached the crumbling stone wall that surrounded the graveyard. The ghouls could not be far behind, and they had no choice but to go through the crumbling churchyard. Avoiding the sick-looking ivy that clung stubbornly to the masonry, Viking boosted Mary over the wall before clambering over. The other three were crouched behind an ancient table-top tomb, peering into the gloom.

"Any movement?" Viking asked as he wiped his hands on the yellowed grass.

"None... they must all be behind us," Tom answered, praying that he was correct in his assumption.

A low mist hung over the crooked gravestones and decrepit tombs. Above, a bloated yellow moon lurked behind the spire of the church, casting a menacing shadow. Visibility was poor as they crept from tomb to tomb in the direction of the ornate wrought-iron gates to the village.

Viking took the lead with a tight grip on his weapon. The others followed in his footsteps, with the bag of jangling nerves that was Malcolm bringing up the rear. His eyes darted back and forth as his lips trembled, and his breath came in ragged gasps. Mary eyed him with concern, he looked like he was about to scream and give away their position.

"Hey...," she said softly. "Take it easy... you'll give yerself a panic attack."

"I'm... fine... absolutely... fine," came his unconvincing reply.

Crack!

Before Mary could respond, there was a sudden noise from the bushes to their left. Malcolm leapt about six feet in the air, screaming like a void-kissed baby.

"Hush!" Mary pleaded, but it was no good, his brittle nerves had irreparably snapped.

"Fuck this!" Malcolm babbled and took off over the graves in the direction of the church, an ancient oak door hanging ajar.

Out of the doorway loped two wizened ghouls. These were obviously elders, too frail to join the hunt, but they had no trouble catching Malcolm. As Viking gave the order to run, they each grabbed an arm and pulled. Malcolm's arms were torn from their sockets with a disgusting slurp. Tom stifled the urge to vomit as they dived into his stomach cavity with slashing claws and snapping teeth. The feast had begun, but with the attention of the ghouls occupied, Mary pulled the rest of the group along, trying not to look.

Clattering through the gate, the remaining quartet took an overgrown path that skirted a village green thick with evil thistles and eerily glowing mushrooms. Behind them, one of the aged ghouls paused in his orgiastic feeding long enough to emit an ear-splitting howl.

The group stopped as one as the howl was answered by many more from the direction of the village. The empty-looking cottages suddenly became alive with the furtive eyes and movements of tens of ghouls.

"Oh, shite... This way!" Mary sprinted up the path and across a rubble-strewn patch of land that once housed the village pub. Scrambling up a bank, the group reached an old fence and mounted it. With a sudden crack, the weather-lashed timbers gave way, and the four of them tumbled head-first down a steep bank, landing hard on a road some ten-foot below the summit.

Winded, bruised and with blurred vision, Tom struggled to right himself and draw his weapon. The ghouls would be over the bank any minute. As his breathing returned and the hellish buzzing in his ears subsided, he became aware of a steady chug, chug, chug from behind a stout tree. Scrambling to his hands and knees, he moved towards the sound. His heart leapt as it came into view... the familiar shape of a steam-wagon, caught in the tree's mangled roots.

"Over... here...," he panted. "Quick."

Mary was the first by his side. "Where's the driver?"

Pointing to a sticky red smear down the side, he said grimly, "I think the ghouls have got the poor bugger."

Viking and Willie ran past them and started to back it out from the tree. "Mary... You drive, we'll keep it stoked and hold the ghouls off!" Viking grunted.

The Ford Transit chassis had been crudely adapted to house a steam-driven engine at the front. While Mary took the driver's seat, Tom opened the hatch on the top of the engine and shovelled in a heap of coal. The chimney belched smoke, and the improvised traction engine chugged louder and steadier.

Viking and Willie crouched behind pallets of overripe fruit and vegetables in a firing stance as Mary yanked a rusty leaver, sending the vehicle into a forward trajectory. The ancient suspension groaned as the heavy metal wheels struggled over the roots of the tree and onto the pavement. Pushing the lever forward even further, the pistons clanked and whirred as the vehicle began to gain traction and hurtle along the road.

The first of the ghouls slid down the bank just as they began to roll. Mary swerved and clipped the first one down with one of the repurposed wagon wheels, shattering its spine and flinging it into the air like a ragdoll. Whooping in triumph, she straightened up and pushed the lever to its fullest while Tom shovelled coal into the white-hot furnace.

As the ghouls gave chase, Willie pumped his rifle and loosed off rounds of

pointy death while Viking rattled off shot after shot. The ghouls went down in droves as the two hammered them with projectiles. After a few minutes, the ghouls stopped coming, and the group sped off around the fringe of the Dreaming Wood in the direction of Tom and Willie's home village.

CHAPTER 5
THE MONUMENT

Sprouting from a small concrete building, the monument stood on the top of a heather-covered tor and stretched over one hundred feet into the sky. Over a century of Scottish weather had stripped its blue and purple paintwork down to a thick layer of orange rust. It was bent and creaked in the wind, but still, it stood, a proud monument to Apepcorp engineering. It was a good thing that it didn't work.

They left the steam-wagon in a thick copse just a mile up the road. Tom explained that the area was patrolled by provosts and that, if caught, they would all be dangling on the end of a rope before sunrise. They had faced zoogs, ghouls and other horrors but they had yet to face the wrath of their Laird... that was an entirely different nightmare. Mary scoffed at this statement, but Willie's eyes told her that Tom was being deadly serious.

In the distance, the steady put-put-put of a diesel engine converted to run on quadruple-distilled grain spirit announced the presence of a provost. These tartan-clad terrors with plumes of white feathers sprouting from their bonnets roamed the borders of the clan lands on antique motorcycles searching for white coats to put to the sword. The Laird had whipped the terrified villagers to a peak of bloodlust. If they were caught, they would be killed.

Approaching the monument cautiously, Willie and Viking ascended the hill while Tom and Mary kept watch. Once at the concrete structure, Viking waved to the others to join him. Entrance to the control station was afforded by four steps leading down to a foreboding metal door. On it, in stark white letters, someone—the Laird presumably—had daubed: 'KEEP OUT ON PAIN OF DEATH. FORBIDDEN TERRITORY.' It was secured by a simple lock. Viking took a bent paperclip from his pocket and got to work.

"Can ye pick it?" Willie asked, stroking his beard and glancing around furtively.

"Easy..."

Click!

"Right," Viking said with some pride. "All done." Wrapping his large fist around the rusty handle, he gave it a sharp tug and yanked the door open. The air in the lightless chamber smelled like it hadn't been disturbed in over a hundred years. The inrush of fresh Highland air stirred up the dust into a miasma that clung to the skin and invaded the airways.

"Jeez, what a pong!" Willie choked and covered his mouth. "It smells like a dead rat's arse-hole in there."

"It's no' a rat, Willie," Tom said sombrely, gesturing to the back of the room. "Look."

The desiccated corpse of a man clad in a blue overall emblazoned with the Apepcorp logo sat slumped in the corner, with a red stain on the wall behind him. There was a large exit wound at the back of his head and a pistol in his hand. Clearly, this man had eaten a bullet.

"I think we have found the fault," Viking sighed, stepping into the control room.

"Ye can say that again... look." Mary pointed to the computer screen. "He's emptied a clip into the bloody screen."

"Poor sod musta figured out what was happening," Tom surmised. "Now what?"

Viking grumbled and poked around the displays He had learned enough about tech to know that the damage was only superficial. "It's just the screen. There's a generator over there... If we can get a new screen, I think I can patch it in with all these cables lying around. Malcolm may not have been good for much, but he knew his tech."

"Fine," Mary huffed. "That's all well and good, but where the buggery are we gonna find a screen?"

"Pizveeter!" Tom exclaimed. Mary's head snapped in his direction wearing an expression that could have curdled milk.

"Hey!" Willie punched him in the arm. "That's no way te talk to a lady."

"No, ye twat!" Tom grunted in reply. "The pizveeter! The thing that Douglas found. It'll be locked away in the vault wi' all the other tech."

"What in the hell is a pizveeter?" Mary asked with some bemusement.

"It's a plastic lump, about yay big." Willie held out his hands in a rough lozenge shape. "wi' a couple o' waggly sticks and some buttons with shapes on them... it has a wee screen in the middle."

"I know it," Mary nodded. "Sam showed me pictures of similar things. She reckoned that they were teaching machines. That our ancestors learned how to drive, make war and fall in love using 'em... sounds a wee bit sad, if ye ask me."

"Right," Viking affirmed. "You three go and get the pizveeter, I'll stay here and get the generator working... Mary, take this dead fellow's gun, there are some clips in that bag down there."

"I dunna like guns... blades are my thing." Mary pouted.

"Just take it, you might need it. There is another storm due in a couple of hours... Knowing our luck, it'll be the one that finally works. You might want a quick exit... oh, take this as well, it may come in handy." He tossed her the paper-clip which she caught and slipped into her belt.

"Fine." Wrinkling her nose, Mary prized the gun out of the corpse's grip. "Come on then, you two."

Leaving Viking to his work, the trio set out cautiously towards the village.

CHAPTER 6
HOMECOMING

The journey from the monument took less than twenty minutes along a muddy track that ran parallel to the road behind a low stone wall. Tom spent most of the journey ducking behind the wall, explaining in detail how foolish the plan was and how dead they were all soon to be. Willie told him on several occasions to put a sock in it and that the plan, such as it was, would work.

Willie had concocted the plan, which had a certain elegance of simplicity. He would run into the village, kicking up a fuss about the zoogs in the woods, and distract everyone so that Tom and Mary could slip into the Post Office vault and grab the device. Tom pointed out that it was the same plan they'd used when trying to liberate some decent Scotch from the clutches of the Laird, and it hadn't worked then—indeed, they'd both been horsewhipped—so why would it work now?

Mary liked the plan. If it went wrong, she would simply hack her way to freedom, so she won either way. Willie was convinced that his acting skills were up to the task, but Tom was less certain.

Mary and Tom approached the Post Office from the rear and vaulted the wall into what was once the loading area for a little red van. Once in position by the rear entrance, they waited for Willie's commotion to commence. Unfortunately, Willie's distraction never came. As soon as he set foot inside the village, he was punched in the mouth, thrown to the floor and clapped in irons. With confusion fogging his mind, he looked up to see the beetroot-red face of the Laird grinning down at him.

"Where are ye pals?" the Laird growled with some relish. The group hadn't been as cautious as they had thought. They had been spotted in the fleeing steam-wagon by a provost on an adjacent road. The eagle-eyed snoop happened to be in possession of a pair of old binoculars and had hastened back home to snitch on the infractors. The Laird had been stewing gently for hours in anticipation of their arrival.

Oblivious that the game was up, Mary quickly tired of waiting and ripped open the door.

Smack!

The gloved fist of a provost met her as she stepped inside. Her legs buckled, and she was dragged roughly inside and onto her face. Tom swiftly drew his sword but was immediately overpowered by two more of the brutes that had leapt over the fence behind him. Each one carried a rapier and a shield fashioned from a hub-cap surrounded by a ring of rusty circular-saw blades. One whack with one of those could easily sever a limb. He dropped his sword, raised his hands, and swore... the jig was up.

Mary found herself locked in a dingy stone outhouse with a harridan by the name of Morag standing watch over her. The Laird hadn't bothered with a trial and had decided to skip straight to the execution. The dynamo torches and presence of Mary were more than enough to convict Tom and Willie, and Mary was guilty by virtue of existing. She was a 'Sassenach,' a 'white coat', and was to be burned at the stake. The Laird believed in keeping things simple where possible.

Outside the ramshackle building, Mary could hear the jeers of the crowd and the booming voice of the Laird pronouncing his sentence. They had tried to explain what was happening but one mention of the word 'Apepcorp' got Willie another punch in the gob for his trouble. As Morag peered through a crack in the wooden door at the unfolding spectacle, Mary slipped the paper clip that Viking had given her into her palm and started work on the manacles.

"Aye... Kill the traitors!" Morag warbled as the drums started to pound. Her voice sounded like the croak of an angry crow. Mary had little time. She jiggled the length of metal around in the lock and finally, with a muffled click, managed to set herself free. Preparing to attack, she balled her fists and got herself into a crouched position.

Crack!

The deafening sound of void thunder and a bright flash sent Morag leaping back from the door in shock. Quick as a flash, Mary leapt on her, snatched a small dirk from the guard's belt and buried it in her kidneys. Clamping her hand firmly over the dying woman's mouth, Mary lowered her to the floor before removing the blade and embedding it in her throat. Muffled cries turned into a sickening gurgle as Mary took the cadaver's sword and a small pneumatic pistol. Moving silently, she edged to the door and pushed it open.

Before her eyes, the denizens of the village, provosts included, raced away from the scaffold as the terrifying sight of a void storm rolled in slowly from the hills. It was the most savage one that she had ever witnessed. The black and purple cloud was almost gelatinous as it rippled in their direction. She looked to the hills beneath, and a yelp of alarm escaped her lips. The storm was being ushered in by the void creeper. It blazed with living shadow and volatile matter, holding flickering arms out in a blasphemous cruciform as it approached.

Getting hold of her nerves, she looked away from the sanity-blasting sight and over to the scaffold. Tom and Willie were alive, but still trapped. Swearing and spitting, she raced out into the night and bolted across the square. "Hold on, I'm coming!"

Tom had never been happy to see someone in all of his days. As he and Willie had awaited the pull of the lever and the opening of the trap, he had said his goodbyes and made his peace with the situation. Now, an awesome sense of relief washed over him. "Mary, how?"

"Nay time!" She scrabbled up the ladder and swung her purloined blade in an arc, severing the noose. Tom dropped to his knees and kissed the wooden planks. He was soon joined by Willie, and in a few more seconds, their bonds had been cut. Helping Tom to his feet, Mary panted. "We need te get the pizveeter, we're almost out of time."

Tom looked in her eyes and smiled. "Thank you..."

Thunk!

"No!" Tom bellowed as she fell into his arms. A nail had hit her in the back of her left shoulder and stuck through obscenely, splattering his chest with her blood.

Willie snarled in fury as he looked down and saw the Laird holding the weapon. Grabbing Mary's sword, he launched himself off the six-foot scaffold and buried the blade to the hilt in the Laird's bulbous belly. "Tek that ye bastard!"

Mary grunted in pain. The wound wasn't mortal, but it hurt like hell, and she needed medical attention. "Viking had a medical kit... Let's get the pizveeter." As Tom supported her and steered her towards the ladder, Willie yelled up to them. "Go! Get te the monument... I'll get the pizveeter!"

Before Tom could argue, his friend charged off towards the Post Office with a frenzied look on his face. After lowering Mary to the ground and joining her, Tom looked out at the storm. Vicious spikes of lightning struck the earth, sending plumes of soil into the air. In the wake of each strike, a monstrous growth of thistles climbed towards the sky. The kiss of the void was spreading, and each rumble of thunder was like a hollow cackle from its shadowy herald... Tom knew it in his bones. Nyarlathotep was coming.

"We need te move... can ye run?"

"Aye," Mary nodded emphatically, holding her injured shoulder. "Come on."

Together, Tom and Mary raced into the countryside while Willie rummaged around in mountains of tech looking for the pizveeter. Time was running out. If the kiss of the void reached the tower, it was all over.

CHAPTER 7
THE VOID'S KISS

"Come on, you piece of junk!" Viking tugged on the rip-cord to the generator for what felt like the fiftieth time. Finally, it chugged into life. As soon as it did, a horrible thought crossed his mind. Now that the station was active, if the signal reached the transmitter, it would almost-certainly connect. By trying to stop the connection, he could have potentially caused it. His only hope now was Mary and the boys.

Using the wires and bits of broken tech he could find, he had managed to lash together a bypass to the screen and a means to power the pizveeter. The system's CPU chattered as it fired up fully. The ailing nuclear back-up batteries finally took a well-deserved rest. They had been ticking over for a century, occasionally firing the systems when it was time to retry the connection, and were on their last legs. Viking shook his head. His ancestors certainly knew a thing or two.

"Come on... where the hell are you?"

Poking his head out of the door, he took one look at the sky and gulped. He had been so engrossed in getting the piece of junk generator working that he hadn't heard the Sturm und Drang of the incoming storm. Nervously fingering the grip of his rifle, he moved outside and gazed down the hill.

To his surprise, he spotted two figures limping across the peat, one waving his arms frantically, the other soaked in blood and stumbling.

"Shit... what the hell happened?" Running inside, he grabbed his rucksack and retrieved a green plastic box stuffed with scavenged medical supplies. Racing back outside, he helped Mary up the gradient and lay her on the grass. "Did you get it?" he asked Tom as he began cleaning her wound.

"Willie went te get it, I had to get her outta there."

"Damn... We don't have much time."

"I know." Tom stood and peered into the distance. The storm had changed direction and was heading straight for them... and the tower. "Come on, Willie..." He pursed his lips and stared. "Look! ... There he is!"

Ahead of the storm, followed narrowly by the void creeper, was a frantic-looking speck.

Willie's legs pumped, and his heart felt like it was going to burst as he raced towards the tor. He dared not glance behind him; the void creeper was so close he could hear the molecules of the void crackle and fizz. Lightning nipped at his heels, and the roots of void-kissed vegetation coiled and burst from the ground, reaching for his tatty boots. The void was gathering speed, it knew the end was near.

There were whispers in Willie's mind, begging him to give in to the crawling chaos, to surrender to the creeping void. He felt as though his thoughts were being ripped from his head, pulled into the gravity of the void itself. It was all connected, all alive, thistles and creeper and storm, drawing Willie into its all-consuming purpose. Soon, he knew, it would be the whole world, and the only thing left to do was to stop running. Wasn't he tired of running?

Screaming his defiance, Willie took the pizveeter in his right hand and, once Tom was in range, paused and threw it at his friend. "Quick! ... Do it!"

As Tom passed the device to Viking, a bolt of purple lightning slammed into the ground between Willie's legs. Tom bellowed in horror as a monstrous thistle burst from the ground and surged six feet into the air, impaling his friend instantly. Willie screamed as the head of the thistle burst from his chest, showering the earth in his blood.

"No! ... Willie!" Tom went to rush to his friend's aid, but Mary grabbed his ankle and took him down just as several vicious needles shot from the gore-soaked head of the thistle and thudded into the ground closeby, spreading the void with their touch.

Viking slammed into the wall as he raced into the control centre. Tearing the back off the pizveeter, he commenced jamming wires into it. The device fizzed then flickered into life.

Outside, Willie's body turned purple, and his eyes started to glow with orange light as the void creeper touched his twitching body. Whatever new life had arisen in him, he was one with the void. "Ymg' goka soils l' Nyarlathotep. H' nafl'fhtagn!" The words spilling from his bloody maw belonged to the void itself, and Tom wept to hear them.

"Mary... the gun!"

She had forgotten about Morag's gun. Taking it from her belt, she tossed it to Tom. He didn't hesitate to put a nail through Willie's head. "I'm sorry, pal," he sobbed silently, and buried his face in the grass and waited for the void to claim him.

The void creeper howled in fury as a pulse of blue light surged from the base of the tower to its tip. The air crackled with static as the blue light met the lightning of the void storm above. Viking had done it. The pizveeter connected to the server and gave him a simple choice: 'Retry? Yes/No.' Using the left stick, he highlighted the negative response and hit the button marked with an X.

Mary and Tom shielded their eyes from the flash as the positive and negative forces collided and burst.. The void creeper's head elongated into a wispy tentacle that thrashed wildly as it bellowed in frustration. The tower sparked and fizzled with electricity that finally exploded in a shower of sparks. The creeper dissolved, shrieking, into particles, evaporating like the storm itself into the dawn sky above...

EPILOGUE
ACROSS THE WATER

"Ouch!" Mary winced as Viking finished bandaging her wound, he'd just accidentally jabbed a safety pin into her skin. "Dun ye think I have enough holes in me already?" She smiled and looked at his handiwork. He'd done a fine job. After removing the nail, he'd cauterised the wound, sterilized it and stitched her up.

"Sorry, Mary... My hand's still shaking. I can't believe we did it. This tiny portion of Scotland is safe... Well, safe from the void, at least." He looked over at Tom, he was still wiping his hands, after removing Willie's body from the thistle, he had buried him under scavenged rocks and said a prayer. He was pretty sure that there wasn't anyone listening, but it didn't hurt to hedge one's bets. "I'm sorry about Willie."

"Aye," Tom sniffed. "The silly sod saved us all... I'll miss him."

Mary moved over to him and took his hand in hers as they gazed out at the tainted countryside. "What will ye do now?"

Tom shrugged and pointed at the village, he could just make out a group of angry provosts marching in their direction. Their white feathers bobbed in the breeze. "Dunno... I can't stay here."

"Come with me... both of you," Viking smiled. "There must be more faulty towers in my homeland. I could use your help."

Tom looked at Mary and smiled. She turned and nodded at the tall Norseman. "We'd better get a move on... those boys look pissed."

Viking chuckled and tucked the pizveeter into his rucksack. "Come on then, best get started, it's a long way home."

--END--

Tim Mendees is a horror writer from Macclesfield in the North-West of England that specialises in cosmic horror and weird fiction. A lifelong fan of classic weird tales, Tim set out to bring the pulp horror of yesteryear into the 21st Century and give it a distinctly British flavour. His work has been described as the love-child of H.P. Lovecraft and P.G. Wodehouse and is often peppered with a wry sense of humour that acts as a counterpoint to the unnerving, and often disturbing, narratives.

Since breaking onto the scene in December 2019, Tim has had over seventy published stories in anthologies and magazines with publishers all over the world. His novellas, Burning Reflection and Spiffing are currently available on Amazon.

When he is not arguing with the spellchecker, Tim is a goth DJ, crustacean and cephalopod enthusiast, and the presenter of a popular web series of live video readings of his material and interviews with fellow authors. He currently lives in Brighton & Hove with his pet crab, Gerald, and an army of stuffed octopods.

https://timmendeeswriter.wordpress.com/
https://tinyurl.com/timmendeesyoutube

HEART OF THORNS
BY CHRIS HEWITT

PROLOGUE

As winter fell, an impenetrable shadow slid over the frozen Alpine peaks. A dark avalanche that devoured everything, swallowing the vibrant European stronghold that nestled at the foot of the Eiger. Only when Death retreated, driven back by the changing of the seasons, was the settlement's fate revealed.

Gone. Scoured from the face of the Earth. And with it, half of humanity.

Ava removed her glasses, the e-tablet falling from her trembling fingers as she realized she'd seen the fate of her people and all who remained. Maybe not this winter, or the next, but within her lifetime.

Once, the Cold War satellite relaying the images had watched dozens of outposts, clinging like limpets to mountain ranges across the northern hemisphere. But with each passing winter their lights blinked out, until only the Rox remained. She eased herself to her feet and walked stiffly to the window to soak in the spectacular Rockies sunrise, knowing she'd see few more if she didn't act.

These were desperate times, the end of days, and humanity's survival would require the most desperate of measures.

And an unimaginable sacrifice.

CHAPTER ONE

Adan looked up into an alien sky, the only sky he'd ever known. A generation had been born under these turbulent, indigo clouds. Three decades had passed since the alien invaders took control of the southern hemisphere, hijacking the planet's weather system. Now, purple lightning rippled across the darkening horizon, a filigree of fiery fingers exploring every pathway through the perpetual storm. Adan watched in wonder, raven hair whipping in the wind. He'd studied the ionizing effect all his life, but never so close. Mesmerized by the spectacular fireworks, he didn't see the signal for the squad to stop.

"You okay, Prof?" asked Private Coles, staring down at Adan's crumpled body.

Adan groaned. They'd started calling him Prof a few days out, and he wasn't sure it was altogether a term of endearment.

"Yeah, yeah. Thought I saw a flower."

The hulk of a private chuckled, holding out a calloused hand to yank the exhausted scientist to his feet. "Best not let Sarge catch you laying down on the job."

Adan rubbed his shoulder. There wasn't a part of him that didn't ache after the three-week march through the badlands. Thirty miles a day might be a breeze for crack marines, but he'd be lucky to do that distance in a year, pacing back and forth in the safety of his lab. The tall figure of Sergeant Harris approached, head bobbing, looking for the holdup.

Adan brushed himself down. "Are we there yet, Sergeant?"

"Twenty clicks out. Doable by nightfall if we don't keep stopping."

Adan couldn't hide his relief. "Great, I can't..."

The words died on his lips, gone with the wind. The squad and the world froze, as if the badlands held its breath. A spell only shattered by Sergeant Harris barking orders. Adan felt the gentlest of breezes whip across his dry, cracked lips. "Oh, crap! The wind's changing."

The strong northerly that had blown at their backs since they'd left the refuge of the Rox had vanished, replaced by a stiffening breeze from the south.

The sergeant wasted little time organizing his squad. "In pairs. Ten yards out. A hundred yards apart. Find cover and hunker down until we know what we're dealing with." He turned to the big private. "Coles, you're with Lee. Dig in behind that boulder fifty yards back."

Coles scanned the southern horizon, lost in thought.

"Private! Eyes on the prize."

The big marine snapped to attention. "Yes, sir."

As the squad scattered, Coles quick marched Adan Lee ahead, positioning himself between his ward and the now-gusting wind. Adan considered complaining about the rough handling, but one look at the private's stony face told him playtime was over.

Reaching the rock, Coles pushed Adan against the weathered stone before unfolding his entrenching tool. "Don't just stand there."

Adan jumped to, retrieving his shovel and matching the private stroke for stroke. Coles redoubled his efforts with every anxious glance up. Unable to contain his curiosity, Adan followed his gaze. A sinister tide of dark urchins rolled towards them, the largest of the monstrosities only yards away, an ebony heart surrounded by innumerable razor-sharp spines. The terrible tumbleweed had no eyes, no ears, no obvious senses, until you got too close, and the needles shot out like deadly harpoons.

Coles pushed the paralyzed scientist into the trench and threw his heavy backpack on top of him before gazing up, a look of resignation darkening his features.

Adan's world slowed as a thin black spine skewered the marine through the shoulder, ripping through flesh and bone before bursting from the private's hip. The marine screamed, droplets of blood splattering Adan's face, as the spiny ball descended in a crushing wave that blotted out the light. He wedged himself hard against the rock as the monstrosity pressed down, a deadly iron maiden. With death inches from his face and needles stabbing into the backpack clutched to his chest, Adan closed his eyes and prayed for a quick end.

When next he dared to peek, a jagged crack of light expanded from under the bed of needles. Coles still lived. The marine stared at him, lips trembling as he wheezed through perforated lungs. For a moment, Adan thought they might both survive. But a rivulet of blood trickled from the marine's nose, tracing his cheek until it dripped from his earlobe, and Adan realized the man no longer touched the floor. Rather, he floated, twisting in a sickening, slow rotation. The rolling urchin lofted its helpless victim skywards, until Coles' boots were higher than his head.

The urchin rolled on, ripping the rucksack from Adan's grip, leaving him shaking, heart pounding. He watched the big marine, a broken marionette, slide headfirst down the spines until his muted gurgling ceased with a sickening crack. Adan vomited as Coles rolled on, belongings tumbling from his pack onto the blood-soaked earth. More urchins followed. None as large as the horror that made for the horizon with its eviscerated spoils.

Sergeant Harris arrived in a flurry of dust. "You okay, son?"

Adan nodded, staring after Coles. The sergeant followed his gaze.

"Fuck! Okay. Let's get you out of here."

Adan clambered onto unsteady feet, leaning against the rock. "The device?"

"It's secure."

"I need to see it."

"Let's just get you—"

"Sergeant, I need to check the device. Now!"

Unimpressed, Harris ground his teeth, the whiplash scar along his jaw flexing as he watched his fallen, and yet still rising, comrade vanish. Adan feared the sergeant would call off the mission. Instead, he waved to one of his squad. "Prof needs to check the device."

A bearded, turban-clad marine sprinted over, and Adan unbuckled the straps of the backpack to reveal two metallic objects inside. Pushing the oxygen tank aside, he set to unscrewing the end cap of a large shiny container. Inside, four lights blinked green. Adan sighed. His life's work remained intact.

"Been treating it like my first born, Prof," said Private Yash Singh.

Adan replaced the cap and secured the straps. "Thank you, marine. Keep up the good work."

Yash nodded. "I'll get it there in one piece."

The sergeant patted Yash on the back as he fell into line. "Keep us standing about out in the open, son, and I can't give you the same assurance."

Adan nodded, remembering the promise he'd made to his mother. He might call the shots in his lab, but out here in the badlands he was a gust of wind away from becoming a shish kebab.

"Lead on, Sergeant."

...

Heart beating out of his chest, Adan collapsed into a ditch. They'd zigged and zagged across the badlands for two hours, avoiding the army of rolling urchins, and by his calculations they'd covered less than five kilometers. The only saving grace was that they'd found a road. Of all the things he'd expected to discover in the badlands, this tarmac relic of a fallen civilization had come as a surprise. The cratered, torn asphalt still bore road markings in places, and Adan would have given anything for a vehicle to whisk him away. Not that he'd ever seen a car outside of a movie or the rusted scrap littered about Larry's forge.

The largest urchin eclipsed the monstrosity that butchered Coles. A hundred yards across, it forced the squad to scramble clear as it sailed past, almost silent but for the dull rumble of spines tearing up the dirt. Such roaming monsters made the patch of torn tarmac even more remarkable.

Yash Singh slid down opposite, pulling out a flask and offering it to the exhausted scientist. "That was a close one. Did you see the size of that bugger? I'd love to know what they're doing out here, rolling about like they own the place."

"They're terraforming," said Adan, gulping down the water and wiping his stinging lips. "Turning this world into theirs and doing a pretty good job of it."

"If they're doing such a good job, why haven't they just wiped us out?"

"They are wiping us out. Look around. They're in no hurry. Why waste resources, when we offer no threat? No. They just go about their business. I doubt they even see us."

"You sound like you admire them."

Adan grinned. "Maybe. There's a lot to admire."

"Maybe you should tell that to Coles."

Adan handed back the flask, face flushing red. The marine changed the subject.

"So why purple, Prof?" asked Yash, pointing to the southern sky.

"The lightning?"

Yash nodded, adjusting his royal blue turban.

"It's the argon that glows purple."

"Argon?"

"Yeah, they need it to replicate."

"The urchins are made of argon?"

Adan shook his head. "No, they're made of a bio-alloy composite, but they require a neutral atmosphere to shape the material. Oxygen is too volatile, so the urchins replace the oxygen with argon, changing our atmosphere."

The marine rubbed his thick beard. Adan was no stranger to losing an audience. "The onyx-like material..."

Yash pulled a knife from his belt, the pitch-black blade glinting like glass.

"That's the stuff," said Adan, taking the blade and feeling its weight. "Not only is it incredibly light, strong and sharp, it's also a superconductor. A real miracle material, but a complete nightmare to work with."

"I've seen the smiths working it, in those tanks."

"That's it. They super-heat the stuff, reshape it, and then quench it in argon to adopt new forms. Otherwise..."

"Otherwise?"

Adan handed back the knife.

"Let's just say, it's a material with a memory and you don't want to be holding it when it remembers."

Yash looked at his blade suspiciously for a moment. "Good one, Prof. You got me."

Adan laughed as the marine sheathed his blade. "Yeah, I did. Didn't I?"

There were some details that people didn't need to know. Like Yash's knife being a heat-cycle from reverting to its original form. Like all the alien artifacts, the onyx blade once served a different purpose. A purpose Adan had only begun to understand, and the only reason he'd agreed to leave his lab.

"How's my baby doing?"

"Safe and secure," said Yash, patting the rucksack.

"Good. We've got a lot counting on that."

A dark shadow loomed over them, blotting out the hazy sun.

"You too, son," said Sergeant Harris, sliding on his sunglasses. "So, if you ladies are finished with your picnic, shall we?"

Adan groaned as Yash helped him to his feet.

...

Adan held a chunk of plaster, three embossed, white letters spelling out 'HEY' in big capital letters. The rest of the barely legible sign arched above the entrance tunnel to the C...enne Mountain Complex. He'd heard Hacket refer to the facility as NORAD. The old general had commanded the military base back in the day. Now it was a tomb.

They'd arrived before dusk and in the nick of time. Purple lightning danced in the thickening clouds to the south, and what it didn't illuminate filled the squad with dread. Shadows of immense urchins created an ever-shifting geometric tapestry of light and darkness, hinting at the unimaginable behemoths beyond.

The plaster crumbled in Adan's hands as Sergeant Harris approached.

"Right, son, we got you here. It's time to spill the beans."

Harris and his squad believed they were on a scavenging mission to retrieve vital components for Adan's device. Most assumed it to be a radio, one that might cut through the alien interference to allow the Rox to contact the other outposts. Adan hadn't dissuaded them of that, though he suspected Harris had seen through the ruse.

He reached into his jacket and handed over his mother's sealed orders. Only three people knew their contents—Adan, his mother and Hacket.

They'd not trusted Corvino or even Suzy with the full details. Harris tore open the envelope, eyes widening as he read Ava's orders.

The marine rubbed his scar, a flash of lightning illuminating his profile as he scrutinized Adan. "Can you do this?"

"I think so."

"You think so? This ain't your lab, son. Fuck this up and there won't be anyone to mark our graves. So, I'll ask you again. Can you do this?"

He spat the words, finger prodding the crumpled orders into Adan's chest.

Adan felt the hairs on the back of his neck bristle, a sensation that extended down his back and along his arms, each hair rising with static. "Oh, shit!"

The sergeant felt it too, and they looked up to see a black obelisk of a spine emerge from the storm. The onyx finger of God crackled with purple electricity along its length as it bore down on them.

Adan stood petrified, scientific interest replaced by animal fear as he stared, slack-jawed, at the monolith, a rabbit in the headlights. It took only a heartbeat to make a choice between fight or flight. Urine-soaked fatigues sticking to his skin, he sprinted for the tunnel entrance, the routed marines following.

CHAPTER TWO

Ava poured herself a glass of water and looked around the council chamber. One of the first caverns cut out of the mountain. She remembered when the space heaved with families, bunk beds reaching high into the ceiling. Now it housed a thirty-foot, onyx table flanked by twenty-six chairs.

Forged from a single alien spine, the long, black slab served as a reminder of their real enemy. The far wall commanded a spectacular view across the Rox, the sprawling outcrop of half-frozen, ragtag buildings enveloped in the billowing steam of the geothermal vents. Yellowstone Park had always been a popular tourist hotspot. Now, a quarter of a century later, it was humanity's last foothold on this forsaken world.

She'd taken her seat at the head of the table and kicked off the debacle at midday. Now, the setting sun bathed the room orange. Not that the two-dozen guild leaders noticed as they snarled and snapped at each other.

Ava longed for the days before guilds, those first few years before the Rox's numbers swelled with refugees from across the continent. Back when she ran the whole show and things got done with a wave of a hand and no hint of a dissenting voice. But hundreds became thousands, and the outpost grew, until the Rox boasted a hundred thousand souls. With so many people flocking to the outpost, some form of governance became necessary and the survivors demanded a democratic council made up of representatives from the emerging guilds.

Ava had originally opposed the idea, and she'd seen nothing in the subsequent decades to change her mind. She tapped her nails against the glass-like onyx table as the Council argued.

It was the same every year. She'd even given it a name. Spring Fever. The inevitable delirium of a hibernating populace cooped up together for six months. The first sniff of freedom and barely suppressed winter tensions boiled over. She knew better than to shout over her counselors, although she had to smile at Suzy's efforts.

Her protégé would take over the mantle of leader one day, but she had a little way to go yet. She'd yet to learn the limits of diplomacy. The guilds needed their moment in the sun, sparring like spring bucks, if only to remind them that yelling at each other achieved nothing.

Suzy slumped back in her seat, folding her arms and shaking her head as the accusations escalated. Ava gave her a reassuring smile. Maybe her daughter had learned to pick her battles after all? She'd always been a quick learner, from that first, terrible day she'd plucked Suzy from the wreckage of her parents' car, half a dead world away. That urchin strewn outback road remained seared into Ava's memory. The sight of Suzy's mother impaled in the passenger seat. Her desperate pleas and a promise.

She'd made so many more promises since and lost count of those she'd failed to keep.

Lost in reverie, Ava didn't notice the room fall quiet, the assembled council staring at her. She stood and brushed down her tunic. "Good. Are we done?"

A cacophony of voices washed over her, and she closed her eyes, raising a finger until the noise abated. On opening her eyes, the burly leader of the agriculture guild leapt to his feet.

"What about the quotas?" asked Dan Atkins.

"They stand."

"But... but..."

"But what? The Rox needs food. That's your job. Your only job. The most important job here. You miss your quota, and we starve. It's that simple, Dan."

The short, stocky figure of Groats shook his long, gray beard. "And tell me, oh great Oracle. What will you do when you need housing next winter?"

Ava grinned. "On that day, Arthur, we'll do what we've always done and spoon. But right now, you and your engineers work for Dan. Cause I'd rather share my bed than go hungry."

A wry smile played across Arthur Groats' face. It wouldn't be the first long winter she'd shared a bed with the wily old architect. Hell, as she scanned the ageing faces, she struggled to find one she'd not shared warmth with over the years.

Sabine 'Moses' Kennedy thrust a piece of paper into the air. "And what am I supposed to do with this demand for more rations?"

"How are we expected to plough fields with empty stomachs?" asked Dan.

Before the chaos resumed, Ava waved her hand. "Mo, I think I've made my position clear."

"Well, let me make *my* position clear, Ava. We have eight weeks of food in the stores. That's it. If I give it to Dan, the rest of the Rox starves."

Sabine had earned her nickname decades ago, miraculously feeding thousands during her exodus from the fallen Sierra Nevada outpost. But there were limits to even her miracles.

"Sacrifices need to be made," Ava said. "The Rox will go on half rations. Dan, you get your food. Use it well."

Dan nodded, acceptance rippling around the room. They'd had the afternoon to find another solution, and they'd failed, so it was down to Ava to tell them what they already knew.

"The crops need to be in the ground now, or this time next year we won't have the luxury of deciding who goes hungry." With her work done, Ava tried to lighten the mood. "I'm sure we can all get by on Mo's turnip soup for a few more weeks."

A collective groan echoed around the chamber, and Mo feigned hurt. It broke the tension and reminded them they were in this together. And although the turnip soup might not be manna from heaven, it wasn't bad.

As she left the council chambers, Ava suspected she'd be sleeping alone tonight. It looked like Mo had her work cut out.

...

Back in her office, Ava slumped into a tatty, leather chair and fished out a bottle and two shot glasses. She poured a good glug into each glass as Suzy burst through the door.

"Why do you let them get away with acting like that? They're like children."

Ava slid a glass across the table and Suzy collapsed into the seat opposite, reaching out and downing the fiery liquid.

She gasped and spluttered before finding her voice. "Oh man, that's got to be the '35. Smooth."

The moonshine burnt a path down Ava's throat, and she recalled the first still she'd found. They'd nearly starved that winter, and yet somehow, someone had created alcohol out of...

She shook her head, not wanting to think about it.

Few bottles of the '35 remained, although she suspected Mo had a stash. A surreptitious word with Corvino, the head of security, had failed to turn up any secret caches, which had become a source of frustration. She prided herself on knowing everything that went on in the Rox. Yet Kas, the proprietor of the Rox's only licensed bar, never had a problem getting his hands on a few bottles. Her unsuccessful hunt for the holy grain had become an unwelcome reminder that she'd lost touch as the outpost expanded. Ava waved the bottle, refilling Suzy's outstretched glass.

"Must I remind you we live in a democracy? That means everyone gets to have their say before I tell them what we're going to do."

Suzy laughed. "I'll drink to that. But you shouldn't. It can't be good for your heart."

"I'm sure it's just what the doctor ordered."

They downed the potent liquor, poisoning themselves a little more.

Ava turned to the e-tablets strewn across her desk. Reports from all around the Rox, but none contained the news she wanted. "Anything from Adan?"

Suzy shook her head. "His last update was yesterday. They were forty clicks north of the old NORAD site. Situation nominal. You know the military, never big on volunteering information."

"Good. So he's okay."

"I'm sure he's peachy. The enforced boot camp will do him wonders."

Ava smiled at her adopted daughter's efforts to comfort her. She knew Suzy would be just as anxious about her brother's fate. She hid it well, and Ava took solace in her subterfuge. It boded well for her future guild negotiations.

Suzy changed the subject. "There's nothing from Faye."

Ava rolled her eyes. "With Faye, no news is good news. At least I won't have to excuse her latest fuck up."

She'd feared for her son in the badlands, sent him off with an elite marine escort. She'd had no such concerns for her youngest daughter. Faye was feral; the badlands her playground. Winters were tough in the Rox, made worse by being caged with a prowling she-wolf. Come the first signs of spring, Ava and the outpost gave a collective sigh when Faye and her pack of rogues walked out the gates.

"I'm sure she'll be back when she's hungry."

Suzy looked as if she was going to say something. Instead, she slid her glass across the table. Ava obliged and Suzy held up her refilled glass. "To absent family."

Ava grinned. This daughter, the consummate diplomat, was ready for her role in the Rox. She raised her glass and gulped back the spirit, trying not to choke on the bitterness of her youngest's failures.

...

Mother and daughter finished the bottle, discussing the obvious lies in the guild reports, before the conversation descended into gossip from around the Rox. Exhausted and drunk, Suzy staggered off to bed, leaving Ava browsing agriculture preparedness reports.

Ava picked up an e-tablet and logged onto the Rox network. The network's installation had been the reason she'd found herself at the outpost when NORAD fell. The urchins had surged north. Only the Rocky Mountains had spared the Rox, though it could do little to stop the freezing storm the invaders rode upon. When the temperatures plummeted, the hot springs kept the survivors warm. A few years later, they'd got the first hydroelectric dam back online. Now they had enough electricity to run half the western seaboard, if there was anything left to power.

Ava had often wondered about the luck of their survival, the happenstance of geography that had given them a fighting chance. She muttered under her breath. "Right place. Right time."

"That I am," said General Hacket, rolling into her office.

Ava smiled. The old man must have called in some favors and found a can of WD-40 for his wheelchair.

"I come bearing gifts," said the grizzled old vet, holding up a bottle.

Ava ground her teeth. "'35?"

"That it is. Had two of 'em. Traded the other in for some lube for the old chariot."

Ava pushed aside the empty bottle on her desk and slid her glass over.

"Suzy looked the worse for wear. I guess you started early?"

Ava shrugged. "Yeah, I shouldn't but..."

The general took Suzy's glass, wiping it clean with a corner of his shirt before pouring two shots and sliding one to Ava. "To a good season in the sun."

They clinked glasses and gulped down the moonshine.

"How did you know?"

"That you'd need a stiff drink? After today's Council meeting, that ain't exactly a secret."

"No, when you sent me up here. How'd you know the Rox would be safe?"

Hacket refilled their glasses.

"I used to love hiking through Yellowstone as a kid. Not that I'll be hiking anymore. It always struck me that a savvy fella could live well in the valley. That and it doesn't take a rocket scientist to figure a two-mile-high wall of granite makes for a formidable barrier."

The general winked and downed his shot.

"But why me? Why not one of..."

Hacket held up his hand. "Remember that first day, back in Oz?"

"How could I forget," said Ava, knocking back her glass. The sight of the blood-soaked Darwin street, packed with disemboweled shoppers, was the first image she saw when she closed her eyes at night. If she hadn't sounded the alarm, they'd not have been standing in the street. Some might have stood a chance.

"And do you remember what I told you then?"

Ava's fingers gripped her glass tight. "Something like: 'You fucked up kid, get used to it'?"

Hacket shook his head. "I said: 'You made a call that didn't pan out and a lot more people are going to die.'"

"That's right, along with some bullshit about balancing the scales."

The general chuckled as he refilled their glasses.

Ava gulped her shot and gestured for another. "So, this is my penance? Christ, I've killed far more since then. There's not enough survivors left to balance my mistakes."

The general put the cork back in the bottle and placed it in his lap before taking his glass and tipping the liquor on the floor. "That's for the fallen." He placed the glass upside down on the desk. "That's all they get, Ava. That's all the mind you give them. Count the living, not the dead. You'll find it easier to sleep at night."

The general spun in his wheelchair and rolled towards the door.

"I chose you, because when everyone else was pissing their pants, you had a plan and made the hard choice. Never underestimate how rare that is."

Ava stared at the upturned glass. The old vet had been her mentor, her most trusted confidant, and the only one willing to stick a foot up her ass when she needed it. The irony was not lost on her as she picked up the e-tablet.

Real-time satellite imagery of the Cheyenne complex showed the perpetual storms of the south engulfing the mountain. Algorithms she'd designed a lifetime ago detected the edges of things unnatural in the tempest. How she longed for that lost life. No responsibility, no one relying on her.

Few knew of the Cold War satellite, half a century beyond its expiration date, hanging above the North Pole. Every day, it slipped a little deeper into the atmosphere. Another year and it would burn up, and she'd be blind, no longer the great and powerful Oracle.

But that was not the reason she kept her magic a secret. This Wizard from Oz hid the truth to keep hope alive. A burden that would soon be passed to her children. She prayed she'd prepared them.

CHAPTER THREE

Faye stood atop an icy ridge overlooking a kilometer long ravine, another scar on the flayed Dakota badlands.

The gouge hadn't been here last season. It wouldn't be here next. The alien urchins left nothing in their wake, scouring the land of every footprint. She wrapped her sleeping bag around her shoulders and picked up a handful of dirt, letting the grains slip through her fingers.

"Wind's gusting from the south today. We'll need to be careful."

She heard Carl scrabbling up the slope. He joined her, searching the horizon. "So much for the weather forecast."

"Ain't just the urchins on the move," said Faye, scanning the Rockies to the west, adjusting the binoculars until she found the distant vanguard of ragtag workers. "Maybe a hundred?"

Carl took the glasses and scrutinized the ranks of farmers and engineers, picking their way down the treacherous mountain pass. "A hundred today. A thousand next week. The whole damn outpost will be out here in a month."

"Fucking farmers."

"Christ, Roo," said Faye, spotting the girl camouflaged amongst the boulders. How long had she been there? Roo stared through her sniper rifle, finger caressing the trigger.

Carl handed back the binoculars. "People are going to get killed out here, Faye, but I guess the Council doesn't give a damn as long as they're well fed. What's a few farmers in the big scheme of things, eh?"

"What do you want me to do about it?"

"Well, you could talk to her. Tell her."

Faye shook her head, feeling a lifetime of bile twist in her stomach. She expected more from Carl. "Trust me, I'm the last person my mother is going to listen to."

Carl thrust the binoculars into Faye's hand. "You've got a lot in common with her, you know?"

She grimaced, tasting the bitterness tickle the back of her throat.

"You're both stubborn and you'll both have blood on your hands before this season's out," he said. "Mark my words."

She watched him leave as a deafening crack reverberated around the ravine. "Fuck's sake, Roo."

"Bunny!" yelled the girl, jumping up and sliding her sniper rifle into the leather holster on her back. The still-smoking barrel stood a foot above the fourteen-year-old's five-foot frame.

Another kid with a dangerous toy. But weren't they all? Ruby Pearson—Roo to her few friends—was another Sierra Nevada orphan, washed up at the Rox outpost. Another hungry mouth to feed, and what a mouth.

"Don't know about you, but I want to eat after you and fuck boy finish your domestic," said Roo, setting off in pursuit of Carl. "Get DJ Numb Nuts to pick up lunch. Oh, and there's a tangled-up urchin a click north."

Faye flipped a finger at the diminutive demon. The annoying little sister she'd never wanted, a sibling with a huge chip on her shoulder. She'd found Roo lying in her own filth in a Rox back alley, unconscious, deathly pale, surrounded by spent RoxNox canisters. Of course, she'd seen Roo running nefarious parcels around the Rox, a courier for people who didn't care if she took her payment in product. It was a dark path, one that Faye herself had traveled before her godfather had intervened and delivered an ultimatum. Hard labor in the mines or self-imposed banishment to the badlands working reconnaissance. A stark choice. The same choice Faye had offered Roo, after nursing her back to health, getting her clean. That had been two years ago.

Faye called out, "Ed!"

Silence. The silence you could only get in the vast emptiness of the badlands. The silence of a dead world. Faye stared back at the campsite, spotting the technician crouched behind a large boulder. She headed over.

Edward Chang sat, trousers around his ankles, back to her, fluorescent green headphones blasting out a brain-melting TechnoRox track. Faye placed a hand on his shoulder, and he shit a brick, ripping off his headset.

"Christ! Can't a guy take a crap around here?"

"Shit on your own time. We're out of here."

Faye retreated to the makeshift camp. The scratch of dirt had served as home for their twenty-eighth frigid night in the wilderness. One of four reconnaissance teams tasked with mapping the new lay of the land, Faye's team took care of anything that might impede or endanger the farmers, and with alien stragglers littering the badlands this year, they'd had their work cut out.

Faye's wolf pack harvested more than crops from the Nevada plains. Come winter, farmers set traps to snag the urchins. Most would be wrecked—little survived the alien migration—but every so often, they got lucky. Harvested spines fetched a good price back in the Rox, where skilled onyxsmiths fashioned the unique material into weapons, tools and even furniture.

She found Carl throwing his belongings into a rucksack before storming off, Roo his ever-present, dancing shadow. Faye rolled her eyes. Did he really expect her to go crawling to her mother? If he did then he didn't understand her at all. Packing up her kit, she threw the well-worn rucksack over her shoulder as Ed arrived.

"Right! What's the emergency?"

Faye pointed to the ridge. "Roo's got lunch, bottom of the ravine. And we've got a hooked straggler, north."

"Is that it?" said Ed, fingers dancing over the keypad strapped to his arm. Drones whizzed overhead. "The highlight of my day ruined by the trigger-happy orphan. Typical."

"How many birds got juice?"

"Three out of five. Maybe, two hours apiece."

Faye looked at her watch. Six, maybe seven hours of cover. Running around the badlands without recon drones was risky, but with civilians already flooding out onto the plain, they needed to cover a lot of territory. "Okay, get one on point, half a click upwind. We're going to put in a shift."

"Great. Another day strolling through the spinies' backyard half-blind."

"Get a message to the guilds. Tell them to stay above the 41st if they know what's good for them."

Ed's fingers tapped at his arm as he relayed Faye's warning.

...

The wolf pack stood a respectful fifty yards upwind of the twisting, snared urchin as Faye slipped her hand behind her back. "Three, two, one..."

"Rock," said Carl, revealing his fist.

Faye held out her flat palm.

"Fucking cheat."

"It's all about the reactions, baby," said Faye, letting her backpack fall to the floor. Her jacket and rifle followed as she removed layers of insulating clothing, anything that might restrict her movement.

"Look, why don't we just zap it?" said Carl. "Or I got a couple of acid grenades?"

"No point damaging the goods, and we need the juice for air cover," said Faye, tightening her bootlaces and tying back her jet-black hair. "I'm more worried about the ones we don't see than this baby." She nodded to Roo. "When I say, right?"

Roo deployed the tripod of her rifle and licked her trigger finger, a mischievous grin playing across her face. "Yeah, course."

Faye had heard that before. The kid's itchy finger was as much a liability as a blessing. Roo never missed what she aimed for, but the girl had the attention span of a gnat, as likely to pop a rabbit as the target.

One last glance to Ed for an urchin update, and Faye inched towards the flailing thing. This cleanup looked tricky. The specimen was twenty feet from tip to tip, bucking in the gusting wind. She understood Carl and Ed's concerns, but Faye lived for the excitement and adrenaline flooding her bloodstream. A potent and intoxicating drug.

Faye's earliest memories were of playing with onyx crystals. Her mother believed the urchins were interconnected, every fragment maintaining a link to the whole. Day after day, year after year, she advanced her research by exposing Faye's young mind to the material, teaching her daughter to sense the dark substance's subtle energies. Until, on her thirteenth birthday, Faye succeeded.

What she saw terrified her.

Faye prowled around the urchin, a caged tigress, waiting for the wind to drop, before launching herself towards the monstrosity, unsheathing a pair of long kukri knives. The shiny onyx blades were a memento of her first hunt, along with the six-inch scar along her thigh. Since then, she'd dispatched hundreds of urchins and buried that scar under a twisting dragon tattoo.

Inches from the urchin's spines, she kneeled and closed her eyes. Experienced hunters listened for the urchins' movement. A noise, like a scissor snip. The sound of a lunging spine. Faye needed no auditory cue. She felt it. Long before any movement, before any sound, the hairs bristled along her arms, the urchin's heartbeat an electrical impulse telegraphing death.

She rolled clear before the urchin moved, its rippling spines finding nothing but the edge of her kukri as she severed the onyx shafts. A process she repeated, dancing around the urchin, triggering layers of spines with well-practiced choreography, a breath from being impaled.

With an arcing somersault, she doubled back, triggering more spines, revealing the urchin's black heart. Faye lived for this moment, reveling in her mastery, born to dance on the razor's edge. It was the only time she felt alive, free from the Rox and her mother's disappointment.

But it was more than that. Faye was an addict, turning to Nox to dull her mind, allowing her to hide from her mother and herself, but she couldn't hide from *them*. They whispered to her with every touch of the dark material until Faye's curiosity outweighed her fears and she dived deep. The rush of alien thoughts eclipsed any RoxNox hit, igniting her brain and energizing her senses.

Hungry for her next fix, Faye reached out, mind craving the freedom that came with onyx.

Titanic urchins hid in the darkness, felt not seen, and something else. Conscious things that danced as she did along conduits of arcing purple lightning. The larger the urchin, the deeper she dived into their domain, learning the entity's complex ballet. There were patterns to their random movements, structure, and she learned their twists and turns as they traversed their alien plane.

In an explosion of light, a spark of consciousness stopped, turning as if it sensed her. Faye's heart froze, cleaved by an agony that tore her from the undulating conduits into a bottomless pit of darkness.

The bullet passed an inch from Faye's ear, and she felt a jolt of electricity as the life of the urchin ebbed. She landed on one knee, panting, blades buried in the dirt, and glanced across to see a three-inch hole in the urchin's heart. Electricity arced between the few remaining spines, the spasmodic death throes of the tortured horror. Faye shook her head, sweat burning her eyes, as a primal rage consumed her.

The sound of slow clapping grew louder. Ed held up an arm of flashing digits on his sleeve's LCD. "Whoa, one-forty. Never seen no one go toe-to-toe with an edgehog for longer than a minute-twenty. You're the boss, Flee."

Faye didn't hear him. Adrenaline coursing through her veins, she launched herself at Roo, slapping the girl and pushing her to the ground. "I told you to fucking wait."

Carl dragged her off. "I told her to take the shot. You think killing yourself is going to piss her off? Well fuck you, Faye. It won't be her heart you'll rip out. Get a fucking grip."

Panting hard, adrenaline and alien vision fading, Faye stared down in horror at her handiwork. Ed helped Roo to her feet, wiping the blood from the girl's angry split lip. She pushed him away before storming off into the wilderness. He knew better than to follow.

Carl shook his head and set to harvesting the urchin's onyx. When his eyes met Faye's, she saw concern, frustration and something else.

Pity.

...

Faye took her time retrieving her belongings and rejoining the crew. Remorse replaced rage. The same guilt an addict feels when they learn the cost of their latest fix on their loved ones. She found Carl and Ed burying their spoils. Left in the open, the wind would scatter the spines across the plain. Buried, they'd sell the GPS location to the highest bidder and, along with the other onyx stashes they'd secured, it was turning into a profitable season.

"Guys, I'm sorry."

Carl kept digging. "It's not us you need to apologize to."

Ed nodded to Roo, sat in a ditch fifty yards out, back to them. Guilt gnawed at Faye as she walked over.

"Roo, I'm sorry. I was out of—"

The girl turned, jaw dripping with blood, and Faye feared the worst.

"Oh, Roo. I—"

Roo held a knife in one hand, and in the other a half-skinned rabbit. She returned to skinning her prize, holding the ears of the rabbit in her teeth as she butchered it, tugging and slicing at its skin.

"I didn't mean to hit you."

Roo mumbled something between clenched teeth.

"What?"

She spat out the rabbit ears. "You hit like a little girl."

Faye kneeled beside her, brushing aside a lock of the girl's flame-red hair. She expected to see tears. There were none.

"I swear, I'll never—"

"No, you won't. Not twice. No one does."

Roo's words carried a glacial coldness that hit Faye harder than any slap and she searched the girl's face, finding no fear, no anger, only resolute conviction. The lock of red hair slipped through her fingers. Had she saved the girl from a life of abuse, only to become her abuser?

Roo's face transformed, the mask of a child falling back into place, jolting Faye from her regrets. The girl she thought she knew grinned at her through bloody teeth, and Faye flinched as Roo threw her arms around her, hugging her close. She felt the butt of the girl's knife in the small of her back, the wetness of the skinned rabbit sending a shiver up her spine.

"Sisters, right?"

Faye cradled the girl's head, stroking her hair as she stared across the scarred Dakota plains. "R-right. Sisters…"

Faye stood and offered Roo a hand.

She shook her head. "I'm gonna finish with Mr. Bunny first."

"Okay, but we're moving out in ten."

Roo nodded as she decapitated the rabbit with a flick of her wrist.

As she walked back, Faye struggled to shake the resolve she'd seen in Roo's eyes. She hadn't imagined it. There was a darkness there, a thing that masqueraded as a child.

CHAPTER FOUR

Adan's world came crashing down. Concrete slabs threatened to bury him and the marines in his wake. The collapsing tunnel kicked up a billowing dust cloud, stealing his breath as he stumbled on into the darkness. Exhausted, and with the rumble of rock dying behind him, he fumbled through his backpack, coughing and choking as he retrieved his flashlight.

"Anyone there?"

Only the sound of falling rocks answered his call. He shone his light back down the dusty tunnel, revealing the full extent of the cave-in.

"Anyone?"

A groan echoed along the tunnel, a hand scrabbling in the debris.

"Hang on! I've got you."

Adan pulled with all his might, freeing a body from the rubble before collapsing against the wall. He gasped as he stared at Yash, the marine's jet-black beard now gray and matted.

"Thank you, Prof. I thought I was a goner."

"The others?"

Yash shook his head, unleashing a dust storm as he rewound his disheveled turban. "I was right behind you, and they were a good few yards behind me."

Adan picked up a twisted rod of rebar, banging it against the wall. The noise reverberated, unanswered.

"Someone must have made it," said Yash, digging at the rubble. For each rock he moved, two more fell in their place. He picked up a large boulder. "Maybe they doubled back?"

Adan placed a hand on Yash's shoulder. Nothing could have survived the colossal urchin outside.

The marine threw the boulder against the wall. "Fuck!"

They were on their own.

Adan retrieved Yash's backpack, heart sinking as he removed the metal cylinder. To his amazement, the device still functioned, four lights blinking back at him.

"Is it okay?"

"Yeah, I think so," said Adan.

"Well, that's something."

The marine's words sounded hollow, defeated, and Adan felt a sickening sense of guilt. It was his fault, his mission, and four blinking lights were a poor exchange for Yash's squad.

Adan secured the device and picked up his flashlight. "Look, you need to know. I intend to see this mission through. We've come too far, lost too many."

When he turned, Private Singh held out his hand. "I got it, Prof."

Adan passed Yash the rucksack and the two men clasped hands.

"Before we get out of here, I need to find something to power this little baby, and I know just where to find it."

Yash nodded. "Well, ain't no way we're getting out this way. Let's go get your batteries."

...

"This place is incredible. It's more secure than the Rox," said Yash, adjusting the heavy backpack.

Adan's torch struggled to illuminate even twenty feet of the tunnel as they descended into the depths of the mountain. "Yeah, it's a fortress alright."

"So, why'd they abandon it?"

"Argon."

"Again?"

"Yeah. The thing about argon is that it's heavier than air."

"Oh man. So come the winter..."

"Yup, when the urchins pushed north, all that gas seeped down here. They planned for every eventuality, every toxin, biological, chemical or radioactive. But they didn't bank on no air. Not with so many down here."

"Shit, when did they realize?"

Adan shook his head. "Too late. Middle of winter, urchin party upstairs and no air down here. Talk about a rock and a hard place. Less than a hundred made it to the Rox."

"But it's safe now, right?"

"I doubt it, but that's why we lugged the O2 tanks down here. I'm just hoping it being spring means it's only the lower levels."

"How will we know?"

Adan pulled a device from his pocket. "This will give us a heads up. You won't smell it. Won't even know until hypoxia kicks in, and by then you won't care that you're dying. There are worse ways to go."

"Okay, on that cheery thought, what's that?" said Yash, pointing to a glimmer of light.

The tunnel stopped at a huge, metal door. Yash ran his hand over its surface.

"Whoa, how much would this be worth back in the Rox?"

"Good luck getting it back."

Adan walked over to a control panel embedded in the granite wall.

"Okay, Prof. More to the point, how are *we* going to get in?"

Adan's fingers tapped across a keypad and a low whirring sound preceded a deafening klaxon. Strobing red lights bathed the tunnel as twenty tons of steel swung open, stopping with a reverberating thud. The klaxons silenced.

"How?"

Adan winked and headed into the complex, leading them down a labyrinth of murky corridors, the air stagnant, heavy with the stench of decay.

"Looks like you know where you're going, Prof."

"Thank Hacket for that."

"The general?"

"The old man was the last out of here, back in '32. He spent hours drilling me on the layout. Reckon I could find my way around here blindfolded."

They arrived at the entrance to an unlit room, and Adan slunk off into the gloom to locate the fuse box. A moment later, the fluorescent lights flickered on, illuminating the large control room. Four rows of desks and a sea of consoles overlooked three, huge wall screens, the words 'No Feed' displayed on each.

"Will you look at this," said Yash, running a hand over the back of a leather chair. "It's an Aladdin's cave of treasure. We could live like kings back in the Rox."

The office chair spun around, and Yash's excitement turned to horror as a desiccated corpse toppled in a cloud of dust and bones. The marine jumped clear, blade at the ready.

"Put the knife away. He ain't up for a fight."

Yash slid the knife back into its scabbard and kneeled to retrieve a set of dog tags. Three more cadavers sat at their stations, maintaining their posts to the bitter end.

"I don't get it, Prof. Why'd they stay behind?"

"The way Hacket tells it, there's far more than these four down here."

"Oh man, that smell... I knew I'd smelled it before."

Adan nodded.

"How many?"

"Lots. Hacket described it as an underground city."

Yash rubbed his beard, intoning something under his breath.

"What was that?"

"Punjabi. Words my mother had too much cause to use in her life— whoever has come, shall depart; all shall have their turn."

"Ain't that the truth," said Adan, sitting down at a workstation. "How about before our turn is over, we see if we can get this mission finished?"

"And just what is that?"

Adan spun in the chair. He owed the marine an explanation but couldn't tell him the truth. Not yet. "We're going to send the urchins a message."

"The rumors were right then. It's a radio?"

Adan nodded. "Once I've juiced it up, we'll need to head south—"

"South? Are you mad? It's a meat grinder out there? How far south?"

"Until I get a signal."

The marine threw his arms in the air, shaking his head and laughing. "My squad got wiped so you could go wandering in the urchins' homeland? You're crazy."

Adan shot to his feet. "Look, I'm not ordering you to go with me, but I'm completing this mission."

Yash stopped laughing. "It's that important?"

"Yes."

"Important enough to die for?"

"Yes."

The marine kicked a trashcan across the control room on his way out. Adan might not have understood Punjabi curses, but he understood Yash's frustration.

It took him an hour to hack into the NORAD network. He'd rebooted several servers and routers before a ping packet echoed back from the Rox network. Yash returned, only to say he was going searching for supplies. Oxygen and water were still their highest priority, but Adan hoped the marine might find something to stop their stomachs rumbling.

The Rox network proved to be more secure than NORAD's antiquated systems. Adan could see his mother's handiwork, and she protected her secrets well. The council meeting room offered the only open connection, an old teleconferencing port. Adan glanced at his watch and hit connect. Where else would his mother be?

...

The daily council meeting had been running twenty minutes when Suzy slumped into her seat. Ava took a sip of her steaming coffee and winked at her hung-over daughter.

"By the end of the day, we'll have a thousand workers on the plains. The scouring this year is extensive. These two gouges, here and here, are slowing us down," said Dan, highlighting the long, urchin-ripped ravines on the projected map. "The engineers are saying it'll take a fortnight to bridge them. We don't—"

"Have any idea of what it takes to traverse sixty feet?" interjected Arthur Groats. "We've all got problems, Dan. Mine is the two hours extra getting anything in and out of the Rox, and that means—"

Ava waved her hand. "We all know what it means, Arthur. Can we get to the point?"

"You want it fixed quicker? You know what I need, Ava."

"How much?"

"If we're talking dynamite, maybe half a ton to fill these two holes."

"What about RDX?" asked General Hacket.

Colonel Corvino shot daggers at the old man, and Ava suppressed a smile. The ambitious colonel ran security and wasn't big on sharing. The young buck already had a low opinion of the wheelchair-bound general. Ava suspected their relationship might have reached a new low.

Groats raised a bushy eyebrow. "I didn't know we had any RDX."

"Seems we might have a couple of crates of anti-tank mines."

"Which are required to defend the Rox," said Corvino.

"From what? Last time I checked, Colonel, there aren't too many tanks rolling around. Sounds to me like Arthur might make better use of the explosives."

"That I might," grinned Groats. "It'll take us a couple of days if you can lend us some of your guys, Colonel."

Colonel Corvino looked like a man chewing a wasp, but under the eyes of the assembled council, he grudgingly nodded.

"Fantastic," said Ava. "That's that sorted, then. Next business."

"Hello?"

The familiar voice echoed around the chamber, and Ava's mug clattered onto the table. "Adan?"

"Mother."

Ava stared at General Hacket, trying to hide her joy at hearing her son's voice. "One moment, Adan. Anyone not on the Security Council, please leave the chamber."

A dozen faces stared at each other in stunned silence.

"Now, people," said General Hacket. "This is a security matter,"

The counselors filed out in a hubbub of speculation—all but Ava, Suzy, General Hacket and Colonel Corvino. The wall screen flicked on; Adan's dirt-covered face looked down on them.

Ava leapt to her feet, instinct taking over. "You made it!"

Adan gave a solemn nod and stared into the camera. *"Colonel, I regret to inform you that myself and Private Singh are all that remains of the squad."*

Silence descended over the council chamber. The general shook his head.

"An urchin collapsed the main entrance. We were lucky enough to escape the cave-in. I'm sorry. They were good men and I know they have families."

Ava slumped into her seat and said what they were all thinking. "The mission's a failure then?"

"No," said Adan.

"No? Even assuming you still have the device—"

"I do."

"And it's working—"

"It is."

Ava could tell her son was lying. In her mind, he was eight years old again, caught hiding food. She'd been furious until she discovered he'd hoarded it for Faye. That was her son. That was why he needed protecting.

"How are you going to deploy it without the marines?"

Adan had no answer. Ava removed her glasses, rubbing the bridge of her nose. The mission had been high-risk with a squad of elite marines. Now it was a suicide mission. She'd been willing to risk everything she loved for a chance of success, but this was hopeless.

"Ma'am, we'll find a way."

Ava slid her glasses on to stare up at the screen. Behind Adan stood a marine, and it took a moment for her to recall the face. Yash Singh. She'd shaken his hand.

"How?"

Adan nodded to Yash. *"We'll figure it out."*

Before Ava could respond, the screen went blank.

"What happened to the link?" asked Suzy.

Ava's finger rattled across the e-tablet, accessing the satellite imagery for the Cheyenne facility. She didn't need to zoom in to see the thing that sat atop the mountain like a thousand-legged, brooding spider. The mountain was under attack.

...

Adan dove for cover as the mountain shook, the bright lights of the control center replaced by red emergency lighting. Equipment danced from the desks, crashing onto the floor as ceiling tiles rained down in clouds of dust. He doubted tectonic plates would have anything to do with this quake.

"Move!" yelled Yash, grabbing the rucksacks and pushing Adan to the exit.

Purple stalactites descended from the ceiling, piercing through desks to bury themselves in the concrete floor. The needles widened, expanding as the spines pushed deeper into the heart of the mountain.

Adan chased Yash down an undulating corridor, spines sliding down all about them as the facility crumbled under the titanic urchin. Between the dust and argon, they struggled to breathe as they arrived at a cafeteria, the beeping of the oxygen meter drowned out by the roaring din of destruction.

Yash weaved through the tables before vaulting across the serving counter into the kitchen. "Move it!"

Adan fell over the counter, landing hard, gasping for air. The banshee wail of tortured, stainless steel cabinets promised a horrible death.

"Here!" said Yash, dragging Adan by his collar through a doorway and slamming shut the heavy metal door.

Once again Adan found himself in darkness, but for the insistent red flash and beep of the air quality meter.

CHAPTER FIVE

Workers poured down the gorge to their allotted plots. Families loaded up with their few belongings, everything they'd need to scratch out a living in the Dakota plains. Roo flitted around them, selling lucky rabbit's feet to anyone gullible enough to part with a few credits. She'd wasted no part of the dozen rabbits she'd bagged, the furs commanding the highest price to the right leather smith.

Faye moved aside as oxen lumbered past, laden with heavy machinery and irrigation pumps that would feed a vast network of pipes within the month.

"I don't have time for this, Jared," she said. "Right now, you're between me and the KasBar. The price is the price. Take it or leave it."

The foreman rubbed his chin and shook his head. "You've been out in the wilderness too long, Flee. A hundred credits? Food is scarcer than ever, and you can't eat onyx."

Faye spat at Jared's feet and left the foreman standing on the side of the mountain, staring at Carl in disbelief. She hated when they called her Flee. Granted, it was on her dog tags—F. Lee—but the only time anyone outside her squad called her Flee was when they were fucking her over.

"Let's go guys. I need a drink. We'll offload the co-ords back in the Rox. Screw these cheap ass dirt-eaters."

"Ninety!" Jared shouted after her. "That's my last offer."

Two burly workers blocked Faye's path, twin yetis, thick furs stinking of hibernation. She wrinkled her nose. A month out of the Rox and she'd only just got that stench out of her nostrils. It seemed like people had forgotten the pecking order.

"Look, I'm sure we can do a deal," said Carl, trying to deescalate.

It didn't work. Faye rolled up her sleeves as she marched back down the path. Jared saw her coming, not that it mattered as he flailed about in the mud. Faye's hands wrapped around his throat. The yetis' eyes glowed red, and they stayed perfectly still, Roo's flittering laser pointer the only warning they were going to get. The farmers streaming down the path scattered as Carl dragged Faye off the choking foreman.

"Crazy bitch," gasped Jared, spit and mud flying from his lips. "I'm going to report this."

Carl laughed. "Sure. Don't leave out the bit about the illegal onyx cache. Corvino will love that."

Faye set off up the mountain, brushing mud from her jacket. The workers gave her a wide berth. As well they should. She wasn't some snotty squaddie. She was an apex predator, and these were her hunting grounds. Even the yetis slid out of the way as she neared. Roo fell in behind, smiling and sticking her tongue out at the muscle as she danced past.

Carl and Ed caught up with Faye and Roo as they neared the top of the gorge.

"Too much?" grinned Faye. She'd gone hard on Jared. But he needed to understand the rules of the Rox didn't extend to the badlands.

Carl laughed. "Maybe. I just reminded him who your mother is and he rolled over on the hundred."

Faye ground her teeth, frustrated that the threat of her mother was more persuasive than her fists.

...

"I'm good," gasped Adan, refusing the oxygen mask.

They'd used half the tank hiding in the freezer, but after twenty minutes the shaking subsided, the deafening destruction fading as the titanic urchin rolled on. The only damage to the freezer was a fist-sized hole in the ceiling that offered a hint of fresh air.

"How big was that?" asked Yash, picking up his rucksack.

"I can only imagine. Bigger than anything I've ever seen."

The marine pushed open the metal door and they stepped out into a Swiss cheese kitchen, crushed and punctured steel cabinets strewn everywhere. The cafeteria beyond was illuminated by dozens of dusty beams of light from the polka-holed ceiling. They circumvented several tunnels to return to the command center, now a deep pit descending into the depths of the broken mountain. Split water pipes gushed a spectacular waterfall, the spray creating a rainbow that reached up into the purple-tinged sky high above.

Adan let the water run down his dirt-covered face as he stared up at the carnage. The secure bunker, exposed for the folly it was. For the first time, he realized that his home, the Rox, offered no protection from such monsters.

"Whatever we're doing here, Prof, you better get on with it. If that thing rolls back this way, we might not be so lucky."

Adan nodded, kicking a chunk of rubble into the depths. He didn't hear it land.

...

On any other day, the KasBar would be heaving, but with half the outpost busying to leave, only a dozen of the regular reprobates graced the Rox's only licensed drinking establishment. Faye sidled up to the bar, her thirsty pack in tow.

"Well, well, well. If it isn't the wolf pack, fresh from ravaging the wilderness," said Kas, arms wide. The portly proprietor poured four shots, and they snatched up the glasses.

"Nice try," said Faye, taking the glass from Roo.

"Oh, come on," said Kas, winking at the girl. "She's old enough."

"Yeah, Faye," said Carl. "Let the girl live a little."

Faye shook her head. "After last time?"

Roo sulked. Whether she was old enough was immaterial. She was a nasty drunk, and Faye didn't feel inclined to spend hard-earned credits bailing her out, especially only five minutes after they'd got back to civilization. Kas rummaged under the bar, pulling out a brown bottle and popping the cap off the ancient, fizzing artifact.

"Whoa, I'll have one of those," said Ed.

"Special customers only," said Kas, handing the Coke to Roo. The girl snatched it, gulping down the brown, sugary liquid in one, before unleashing a rasping belch.

Faye shrugged and held up her glass. "To another season in the sun."

They clinked glasses, Roo holding out her emptied bottle as the pack downed their shots. The house hooch lacked the benefit of ageing, and went down like industrial drain cleaner with slightly less taste.

Carl slammed his empty glass down on the bar. "Damn, Kas. You need a new bathtub. I can taste the rust in that one."

"I can't feel my lips," said Ed, pinching his face.

Faye downed her second shot as Kas refilled their glasses. "It'll pass. Or it won't. Either way, it's on the house. Welcome home, guys. And I thought things were about to get boring around here."

Faye turned to Carl, hand behind her back. "Winner checks in with the boss; loser takes care of business here."

Carl rolled his eyes and reciprocated. "Three, two, one. Rock!"

"Paper."

"Again?!"

Faye giggled, hand wrapping his fist as she nodded to Kas for a refill. She kissed Carl on the lips, lingering for a moment before pushing him away. "I'll catch you later. Enjoy the paperwork, and be sure to give Corvino all my best."

The head of security would want his cut. Carl would keep him sweet and declare four caches. A reasonable haul for most recon units. The official report would say three, Corvino pocketing the difference. Everyone had a sideline in the Rox. Even the head of security.

"Come on, you lot. Let's get checked in. Leave these two talking business."

The rest of the wolf pack followed Carl, Roo hugging the Coke bottle, her new favorite possession, and Ed staggering from table to table.

Kas refilled Faye's glass. "How is it this year?"

"Messy. A few big buggers tore up the place."

"That's a first."

"Yup. Lots of stragglers as well."

Kas' eyes lit up. "Not all bad then?"

Faye knocked back the shot. "We got six caches left. One of them is a twenty-footer, and I'm gonna want two hundred for that."

Kas nodded. "It's going to be fifteen percent."

"Since when?"

"Since things got so tough around here."

"They're always tough. Don't give me that bull."

"Not like this, Faye. Last two months, things have been pretty desperate around here and I ain't running no charity."

Faye had no reason to doubt the barkeep. Kas had always been fair, even had her back on occasion. Her mother believed she ran the Rox, feeding and sheltering the populace, but the KasBar kept them entertained, provided hope through the long winter nights. Without that outlet, humanity would have killed itself long ago. If the Council was the brains of the Rox, then Kas' bar was its heart.

Faye nodded. "Set up the buyers. I'll take a couple of bottles on account. The good stuff, mind you. I'll be needing my eyesight."

Kas returned with two bottles of '35. "Best enjoy it while you can. Ain't many of these left."

"I'd like to say they're both for me, but we all got our debts," said Faye, hiding a bottle in her rucksack. "You seen Adan?"

"Can't say I have, but it's been mad around here with everyone up and leaving. Seen Suzy. Looks like she pulled the short straw and she's coordinating this chaos."

"Probably my mother's idea of work experience. I'll catch up with her when the dust settles."

"Talking of your mother—"

Faye held up her hand. "Not interested."

"All right. Touched a nerve there. Look, give me an hour. I'll get the word out and we'll see if we can get the caches offloaded this afternoon. I'm sure we could both do with a quick turnaround."

"Good. I'll grab a pew," said Faye, and wandered off to a shady corner to drown her sorrows.

...

Adan shook the oxygen tank, watching the needle play from empty to full to empty.

Out of time and out of oxygen. He regretted his shopping trip to the lower levels of the mountain complex, the incessant beep of the oxygen meter his only company. He'd gotten lost several times in the labyrinth of storage rooms. The north side of the facility had fared better, the titanic urchin failing to crest the mountain's peak. The lights and lifts in this part of the complex still had power, but argon flooded into the lower levels, making breathing a pointless activity.

Adan shook his head, clearing his vision as he abandoned the spent tank. The beckoning elevator could only have been forty feet away, but it might as well have been a mile as he pushed the heavy trolley down the corridor. A dozen, well-preserved bodies littered the corridor, each one another obstacle in his increasingly desperate escape.

"Come on, Prof," crackled the radio. *"Your thirty minutes are up."*

Adan didn't have the breath to answer. His numb fingers gripped the cart tight. His vision had narrowed to a dark tunnel that stretched further with each step. He understood his predicament, but intellectualizing the effects of asphyxia did little to stop its progress. He stumbled, heavy limbs unwilling to do his bidding.

"Don't make me come down there, Prof."

The thought that Yash might recall the elevator terrified Adan, spurring him on. Vision gone, drenched in sweat, he closed the cage and fumbled at the controls as he lost consciousness.

"Prof? Prof! Fuck's sake."

CHAPTER SIX

Faye stared up at a familiar face, fogged brain trying to recall where she knew the mustached man from and, more importantly, how she'd ended up on the floor. A high-pitched ringing cut through her dull senses as the strange figure waved his fingers at her. She tried to stand, head swimming with the effort. Roo screamed at her from behind wire mesh, the girl's words lost amongst a cacophony of voices.

"Five!"

She remembered arriving at the Rox, the bite of the first shot, and spending the afternoon selling caches of onyx to various shady characters, each demanding a toast. Then the wolf pack returned from checking in and...

"Get the fuck up!"

There was no drowning out that voice. Faye mouthed two words back at the girl.

"No, not me!" yelled Roo, pointing. "Fuck *him*!"

Memories of a drunken evening in the KasBar percolated through her mind. Things had already been rowdy before the miners turned up. A push, a shove, something about mothers, and that had been it. She'd thrown the first punch, and the bar had descended into chaos. Only Kas unloading his shotgun into the ceiling had stopped the affray and, never one to miss out on an opportunity, he'd suggested an alternative resolution.

"Six!"

Now she remembered and, rolling over, stared up at a beast of a man, a mountain of muscle and tattoos. Mighty Mike McEvans. It said it across his chest, right under the shard of glinting onyx that hung around his neck.

The legendary trophy was a fragment of the only city-sized urchin humanity had ever defeated. Shame it was after it leveled San Francisco. Nevertheless, it served as a potent symbol for the Rox's cage-fighting champion.

Not that Faye needed to read his name or see his trophy. Everyone knew Mike the Miner, the very public face of the mining guild's strength. He'd gone easy on her until she kicked him in the nuts. That's how she found herself on the far side of the ring, wondering what day of the week it was and how many ribs she'd cracked.

"Seven!"

Mike stared down at her, pity in his eyes. The same pity she'd seen in Carl's and her mother's eyes. The thought enraged her, reigniting her fury as she dragged herself to her feet.

"Eight!"

Mike glanced over at his corner. His guild mates shrugged. "You don't need to do this, Flee. You ain't got nothing to prove here. We don't want any trouble from your mother."

Faye pushed the referee aside, stumbling to the center of the ring. She scanned the baying crowd, searching for Carl's face among the throng, but he was nowhere to be seen. With the referee and Mike scratching their heads, Faye kneeled, closing her eyes in well-practiced routine. The crowd grew quiet as she slowed her breathing. All except one.

"Oh fuck," said Ed, tapping at his sleeve.

"Shh!" hissed Roo.

Mike looked to the referee, uncertain if Faye had conceded. The referee shrugged, as confused as everyone else, and the big miner reached down to tap her on the shoulder. At the touch of his hand, she sprung like a jack-in-the-box, driving her head into Mike's jaw with sickening force and lifting all three hundred pounds of the man off his feet.

The crowd roared.

The headbutt would have floored a lesser man, but not Mighty Mike. He'd not have lasted long with a glass jaw. He stumbled back, visibly hurt, mostly by Faye's cheap shot. Faye didn't care as she circled him. He lunged, unleashing a flurry of kicks and punches, the kind that ground granite to dust in his day job. She danced, eyes closed, anticipating each move. Every time Mike thought he had her pinned, she'd slip through his legs or leap gazelle-like from his grasp. The crowd went wild, chants of 'Flee' echoing around the ring.

They wanted a fight, and they were getting one. Faye felt her opponent's growing frustration, the energy he spent with every swing. Her gnat-like punches and kicks chipped away at the mountain, a battle of will and stamina, a lifetime of hard labor in the mines vs. a childhood feral in the badlands. No rounds. No respite.

Faye's fist struck the onyx splinter hanging around Mike's neck, and for a moment she saw a glimmer in the darkness. On her next riposte, she tore the shard from his neck, burying it in her fist as she felt the familiar, exhilarating rush.

In her mind's eye, she followed a thread of connectivity, dancing along unfamiliar conduits, traveling further than ever on an intoxicating wave. The amulet, a shadow of its titanic form, focused her thoughts, allowing her unprecedented freedom. All pathways led her to a circle of glowing, semi-transparent spines, enormous tapering towers of thorns that funneled their energies down into a pulsing ball of plasma. The beating heart she sought. It called to her, and she found herself a moth to its flame, unable and unwilling to escape its mesmerizing draw.

The clock ticked on, the cheers and jeers of the crowd fading, excitement turning to awe. None had witnessed such a spectacle. Faye never tired. Mike never faltered. Minute after long, torturous minute; the bloody goliath, unwilling to throw in the towel; Faye, a whirlwind, lost in a dervish trance, her mind half in this world, half in another.

She didn't see the bottle arc across the ring to strike her on the head, shattering into a thousand shards. The impact threw Faye off-balance, sending her cartwheeling across the ring to land in a heap. The glowing onyx amulet slipped from her hand.

"Enough," screamed Roo, jumping into the ring and rushing to Faye's crumpled body.

The crowd looked on, disbelief turning to bedlam as Mike's team followed the girl over the ropes. Roo held Faye's head in her lap, ripping strips from her skirt to bandage the deep gash on her friend's forehead.

Faye struggled to catch her breath, but through gritted teeth, she howled. "Why?"

"I'm not going to let you kill yourself," said Roo, the girl's tears falling on Faye's flushed face.

Those were the words she'd whispered to Roo, the night she'd found her unconscious. She'd never imagined the girl might have heard her promise.

Ed arrived, waving a sleeve of flashing numbers. "You're crazy, Flee. Twenty-three minutes? Are you trying to kill yourself?"

"What?" said Faye, wincing as Roo dabbed at her forehead. Now Faye understood why Roo had stopped the fight. Twenty-three minutes. It had seemed like a heartbeat.

Mike pushed his team aside to stagger across the ring and recover his amulet. Faye clambered to her feet to face the miner, his 'Mighty' tattoo slick with blood. The referee slipped between them, taking their hands. "Ladies and gentlemen, winner by TKO after twenty-three minutes, the undefeated champion of the Rox, M—"

He tried to raise Mike's mallet of an arm, but the stoic miner remained a rock. The crowd settled under Mike's stern gaze, the referee stepping aside as the miner placed the amulet in Faye's hand.

"You earned that," he said, lifting her arm. "Ain't no winners here. It's a draw."

Pandemonium ensued, torn betting slips raining down into the ring. Amongst the confetti, Faye saw Kas grinning as he held up his betting slip and winked.

In a torrent of abuse, Faye scanned the angry crowd. Where was Carl when she needed him?

...

"Stand at ease," said Ava.

She sat behind her desk, shrouded in shadow, a solitary spotlight illuminating the imposing figure of Carl Jackson. The captain didn't move, arms by his sides, legs like drainpipes. Ava smiled. Her daughter's stubbornness had rubbed off on the handsome, young captain.

"Very well then. Report."

Carl remained silent and Ava sat in the darkness until he broke. They always did.

"Ma'am, you assigned me to protect your daughter. Not spy on her."

She liked this one. "That I did. How's that working out?"

The captain squirmed. Not much, but to Ava's keen eye, it spoke volumes. She spent so much time talking to professional liars, those that hid their heart. It was refreshing to see one that wore his on his sleeve.

"Faye is a headstrong, competent leader, and the most gifted hand-to-hand fighter I've ever seen."

"Tell me something I don't know," said Ava, standing and walking over to the captain. She scrutinized him. "Does she know?"

"No, ma'am. She has no idea you assigned me to her team."

"That's not what I meant."

"Ma'am?"

"Does she know you love her?"

Carl stiffened, his jaw rippling as he considered his response.

"Yes, ma'am. I tell her every day."

Ava nodded, easing her aching bones back into the leather seat. "Good."

She really liked this one. She'd chosen well. There was no doubt the captain would lay down his life to protect her daughter, and that was all she could ask.

"How can you be so sure she doesn't know I assigned you?"

"I'm here, aren't I, ma'am?"

She saw no hint of humor in the bodyguard's face and wondered how far Faye's retribution might go. Would she kill him, just to spite her? To send a message?

"I understand it's a risk to summon you here, but I've information you'll need to protect my daughter. Faye will leave the Rox tomorrow and it is critical that she does not go alone."

"She hasn't mentioned—"

"We haven't spoken yet. But trust me, when we do, she'll be heading south on an ill-conceived rescue mission to save her brother."

"Stop her!" said Carl, leaning across the table.

"At ease, Captain."

Carl recovered his composure, placing his arms behind his back and staring straight ahead.

"You, more than most, must realize I can no more stop my daughter than I can stop the wind. That's why you'll make sure you, and your so-called wolf pack, are ready to go with her. She'll try to slip away and that is something neither of us want."

Carl gave a curt nod. "Understood, ma'am."

Ava slid an e-tablet across the table. "Here's everything you need to know about the Cheyenne Mountain facility, and up-to-date satellite imagery. I would recommend that you use the northwest access tunnel."

Carl took the e-tablet, flicking through the hi-res images and detailed base schematics. When he looked up, it was with reverence. It seemed her reputation as Oracle was secure.

"Thank you, Captain."

Carl saluted and turned to leave.

"One piece of advice."

He paused at the door.

"Like her mother, my daughter is no fool. One day she'll find out about this arrangement and when she does, I hope you have an explanation for her."

Carl vanished through the door and Ava hoped she'd see the young man again. Ideally with her children, safe.

...

"Come on, Prof. You ain't checking out on me."

Adan's lungs inflated, a breath of life delivered on a long, hot exhalation that rattled down his dry throat as he stared up into an undulating sea of slick, black hair. It took his brain a moment to piece the sensations together. With the next breath, he convulsed back to life, waves of pins and needles—six-inch nails driven into his gray-blue flesh—rippling across his body.

"There you go," said Yash, helping Adan sit. "That's it, breathe. You had me worried there. What part of thirty minutes didn't you get?"

Adan cracked a wry grin. "I saw something you might like."

Yash glanced over at the laden trolley stacked with water and food, boxes of unopened rations. Best before July 2021.

"Nice haul. How many brain cells did that cost? Here, follow my finger."

Adan shook his head, gulping back a bottle of water, washing the sweat and saliva from his face.

"Did you get what you needed?" asked Yash.

Adan nodded, pins and needles receding to the tips of his fingers and toes, skin flushing pink.

"Good, cause that was the only shot we had," said Yash, digging through the trolley. Under the supplies, he found a bunch of components sat on top of a large, green crate. "Oh, you got me a present. You shouldn't have."

He slid aside the lid and peered into the box.

"No, I mean it. You shouldn't have. Is that a fucking nuke?"

"I needed a big battery."

"Bullshit. I've had it, Prof. You've buried a dozen of my mates under this mountain, and you won't be happy until we join them."

"Okay, okay, it's not a radio. But it's not a nuke either." Adan pointed at the crate. "Well, I mean, *that's* a nuke. But combined with the rest of the device, it's far more."

Yash stalked back and forth. "How much more?"

"Maybe enough to finish this. To finish *them*. For good."

"Bullshit. That little thing?"

"That 'little thing' is my life's work. If we can get it close enough, it'll generate a massive, electromagnetic pulse attuned to destroy the alien control network. Don't you see? We can end this. You have to believe me."

Yash shook his head. "What are we going to do, hand-deliver a nuke to downtown Urchinville? You're crazy."

Adan put his hand on Yash's shoulder. "Don't believe me? Then ask yourself this. Do you think my mother would let me risk my life for anything less?"

The marine chuckled and stroked his long beard, staring at the crate. "How long is it going to take you to jury-rig this weapon of mass destruction?"

"A couple of days, maybe. Wouldn't want to get any wires crossed."

"Yeah, Prof. I think we've had enough crossed wires."

...

Faye groaned, uncertain what hurt most, her ribs or the cut on her head. The amulet of champions hung around her neck, and she ran her finger over its smooth surface. Laid on the top bunk of her cell, she stared at the granite ceiling. A poor substitute for the majesty of the Milky Way. Eighty feet underground, the stars never seemed so far, her world never so small.

Roo sat cross-legged on the bottom bunk, counting and recounting her credits. Profits from selling every scrap of rabbit. The gentle tinkle of coins soothed Faye into a restless sleep.

She flowed through familiar conduits, pathways that interlinked the millions of urchins. She saw them now as neurons in a vast brain, as if her own mind stretched across half the globe. Each urchin, a fragment of a vast hive mind, and within the network, sparks of consciousness, the lightning, sentient beings that danced as she did through alien memories. Children, offspring of the thing that sat at the heart of this web, the Queen, that called to her even now.

"Faye," whispered a voice, as a hand like fire braised her arm. "Faye!"

She opened her eyes and looked out across the Rox. Early morning mist cloaked the outpost as the sun's first rays stretched across the valley, bringing the warmth of a new day. But for now, the Rox slept, streetlights illuminating the empty thoroughfares. The alien storm raged on far beyond the southern mountains. Faye stared at the onyx amulet in her hand, the black shard glowing with a fading, purple hue. She exhaled, cold hitting her like an avalanche.

"Faye?" said Roo, tugging at her arm.

"H-how d-d…?" said Faye through chattering teeth

"You were sleepwalking. I tried to wake you."

"S-sleep w…?"

"Yeah, right through the Rox. It was creepy. Your eyes were open, but there wasn't anyone at home. I thought you had brain damage from the fight." Roo hugged her close, fiery hands searing Faye's ice-cold skin. "You scared me."

She stroked the girl's hair, trying to hang on to her receding dream. But the more she tried to recall, the faster it slipped away, as if alien memories could find no home in her own synapses.

It faded, all but one memory. A monolithic spine reaching down from the heavens to skewer a mountain. She'd followed it down, through layers of sediment and rock, coming to a bunker, a room and…

"Adan!"

CHAPTER SEVEN

"Where is he?" yelled Faye.

She found Suzy at the Rox gates, talking with the guild officials overseeing the exodus. Her sister handed back an e-tablet and made her apologies before running over and embracing her irate sibling. Suzy had been many things to Faye—her adopted sister, her confidant and her mother, when Ava shirked childcare for the tribulations of the Rox.

"It's good to see you, Faye. I'm glad you're back. You're so cold. How was it out—"

Faye pushed her away. "Where's Adan?"

Suzy looked away, and Faye sensed her mother's hand, the bile bubbling in her stomach. Suzy had never betrayed her before. Why now?

"You let him go. When you should have protected him."

"He wanted to go, Faye."

"Don't give me that bullshit. He's never been beyond the Rox. He didn't want to go anywhere. She talked him into it."

"It wasn't like that."

"Where is she?"

"Faye, please. There's more at stake than you realize..."

The words died on Suzy's lips as her sister sprinted towards the council chambers.

...

Faye burst in. The onyx desk stretched like a petrified trunk across the cavern, oblivious to the sun's efforts to warm the room. She cursed the empty room and set off for her mother's office.

"I didn't order him to go."

Faye froze, the silhouette of her mother rising from a seat at the far end of the table. Anger threatening to overwhelm her, she tossed her rucksack aside and stalked the length of the chamber to join her, arms folded, overlooking the Rox. Faye had not seen her mother since the last harvest. No mean feat, given the size of the Rox.

She hadn't changed. A few more lines, a few more gray hairs, but behind the ageing facade, cool, unemotional calculation stared back at her.

"Is that how you keep your conscience clear?" said Faye, pushing her rage deep into the pit of her stomach. Emotion never worked with her mother. "I bet he volunteered. Jumped at the chance to do his duty. Anything to make his mother happy. Am I getting close?"

"He, at least, understands what duty is,"

"Does he? Duty is just a word you use to control your pawns, while you sit up here in your ivory tower. You've no clue what's going on out there."

Ava cocked her head. "And you do? The child who spends all her time hiding from her responsibilities in the badlands?"

Faye sighed. These were familiar battle lines, well-trodden trenches of resentment. "I don't have time for games, mother. Where is he?"

"NORAD."

"Cheyenne Mountain?" Faye gasped.

Ava nodded. "He made it. But there were casualties."

"How many?"

"Only Adan and one marine survived."

Faye stormed off. "You should never have let him out of his lab. What were you thinking? No, don't tell me. I've heard it before. Survival of the Rox. The altar you'll sacrifice everything on. Even your own children. Well, not this time, Mother."

"Faye! Corvino left yesterday with a squad of marines..."

"I don't care. I'm going to get Adan."

"You can't."

"Just watch me! That's what you do, isn't it?"

...

Ava slumped into her chair, hands fumbling for the pillbox in her pocket. A vise-like hand gripped her heart, as if Faye had reached into her chest and squeezed the life from her. Even when she expected her daughter's arrival, knew her reaction, Faye's words still tore at her.

The truth would do that.

"Are you okay?" asked Suzy, rushing across the council chamber to fuss about her.

"I will be."

Ava swallowed two pills with the offered glass of water. Suzy checked her racing pulse.

"I saw Faye. She didn't look happy. I assume you told her?"

"Is she ever happy? She's going after him."

"You have to stop her. It's too dangerous."

Ava wiped the sweat from her brow. "Even if I could, I wouldn't. I've made sure she won't be going alone."

"But—"

"But nothing. You think I'd leave something as important as this to Corvino? If anyone can bring Adan back alive, it's Faye."

"And what else, Mother?"

Ava smiled at her protégé, taking her hand and kissing her knuckles. When had she become so transparent? Suzy deserved the truth. "And, if anyone can convince Faye to complete the mission, it's Adan."

She hoped her youngest was as ready for her part in this most desperate of plans.

...

Faye blew into her quarters like a tornado, picking up and tossing anything not bolted down onto her bunk. Roo and the rest of the crew were nowhere to be found, which was fine by her. She'd no intention of explaining where she was going. This was personal.

Stuffing her belongings into her backpack, she heard a familiar *squeak, squeak, squeak.*

"Did she send you?" asked Faye.

The flap of fabric that masqueraded as a door slid aside as General Hacket rolled into the cramped cell. "Can't an old man talk to his god-daughter? The word is, you're riding your white horse south to save the day?"

"Don't try to stop me."

Faye fished the bottle of '35 out of her rucksack and tossed it to the general. He caught it with ease. Time hadn't slowed the old man's reactions.

"Now that's more like it. I traded a bottle for some WD-40. Think I might have got ripped off."

The general scanned the spartan cell for a glass and, realizing his folly, unscrewed the bottle and took a swig before holding it out to Faye. "It's a bit early, but..."

She shook her head, stuffing the last few items into her backpack.

The general took another gulp before tucking the bottle away. "So, I hear you beat Mike into early retirement, dissected a much-loved legend with an exhibition of savagery that would make an urchin wince, and pissed off half the Rox who had their wages on the big man to win. All within twelve hours of stepping back through the gates. That's a record, Faye. Even for you. So, no, I'm not here to stop you. Quite the opposite. You need to get the hell out of Dodge before the mining guild catches up with you."

"When you put it like that," Faye laughed, smarting at her bruised ribs as she sat on the bottom bunk, "I feel guilty about Mike."

"The old fool should have retired years ago."

"Like you?"

The general chuckled, and Faye realized how much she'd missed him. She'd had all winter to catch up with her godfather and always found another distraction. Things that seemed petty and pointless now.

The old man scrutinized her. "You, okay?"

"What, this? I've taken worse beatings."

"I ain't talking about your scratches, kid."

She stared at the general's ancient face, remembering when she used to stand on the plate of his wheelchair and he'd whizz them around the corridors of the Rox. It'd been a decade since she'd rode the Hacket Express, and yet a flame still burned in the old man's firebox, a warmth and wisdom that came with a lifetime of bitter experience.

"I understand why she did it. Why she kept pushing, even when it drove me away."

"She never..."

The old man stopped as a tear rolled down Faye's cheek. He rubbed his chin. They both knew the truth of it.

"It's okay. I know I was just another one of her experiments."

"Faye, that's unfair."

"Unfair? When most kids were playing games, I was in the lab playing with onyx. Do you know what that stuff can do to a developing brain? My mother did." Faye laughed, wiping away the tears. "She wanted me to be a weapon. Did you know that?"

The general shook his head. "It seemed crazy to me. Still does. But your mother was always convinced that the urchins communicated via some control network. She's spent years trying to hack into it with no success."

"Oh, she succeeded. I am what she wanted me to be. I am the interface and weapon she wanted."

"Faye!"

"It's the truth. I've seen it. Seen the network. Christ, I'm part of it now, whether I like it or not."

She stopped short of admitting what she feared most. That her connection worked both ways, that alien minds used her eyes to look upon all she held dear.

"My God! You're saying she was right? This could change everything. If we could communicate with them... Negotiate..."

Faye took the old man's hands. "I need you to give her a message."

"Tell her yourself."

"There's no time."

The old man sighed, and Faye stared deep into his gray eyes. "I know what awaits me in the south. I've seen them."

"Them? Who?"

"It doesn't matter. Just know Adan's device is only the prototype. A hint of my mother's grand experiment."

"Faye, come now. She—"

"Tell her I forgive her. For everything. Never being there, chasing me away, Adan, and even…Carl."

The general furrowed his brow. "I don't understand."

"She will," said Faye, picking up her rucksack. She leaned down and kissed the old man on the forehead. "If we see each other again, know all hell will follow. My mother believes she's prepared. She's not. Make sure you are. There won't be any second chances."

Faye vanished before the general could turn.

CHAPTER EIGHT

With all eyes on the Rox front gate, it was easy for Faye to sneak out the back. The sun arced high above the mountains, chasing the last shadows of night into the deepest recesses of the valley. She watched a golden eagle soar on the thermals, proof that there was still some wildlife left on this half-dead world.

The eagle wasn't alone. Faye ducked at the thrum of a drone. The sound grew louder until the whirling contraption hovered in front of her.

"Going somewhere?" asked Carl, leaning against the trunk of a pine tree.

Faye rolled her eyes, standing up and dusting herself down. "Look, it's a family matter. Nothing to do with you."

"And what the fuck are we?" asked Roo, dropping from a branch.

Ed appeared a moment later, recalling his drone. "Yeah, not cool, Faye. We're a pack. We ain't letting you go lone wolf."

"Guys, I get it. Thank you, but this time it's too dangerous."

Roo went to kick Faye in the shins, but Carl grabbed her by the arm. "Guys, give us a minute."

Ed wandered off down the path. Roo did not, crossing her arms and glaring at Faye. Only after Carl gestured for her to leave did she follow Ed, cursing under her breath.

"We're your family. Your *real* family," said Carl, pulling Ava's e-tablet from his rucksack and placing it in Faye's palm. "You need to know—"

Faye pressed a finger to his lips. "You're not the first my mother has manipulated to get close to me."

Carl stared at the floor, unable to meet her gaze.

"But you're the first to succeed," she said, kissing him on the lips. "I love you and I have my mother's twisted games to thank for that."

Carl hugged her close. "I'm sorry. I promise, no more secrets."

Faye bit her lip, unable to make the same promise. Not while she protected her mother's darkest secret. She hugged him close before they set off down the valley, finding Roo perched on a wooden fence, legs swinging back and forth.

"If you're done with the kissy-kissy, can we get this shit show on the road?" she asked, jumping down.

"Yeah, what's the gig?" said Ed.

"Rescue mission. We're going south to retrieve Faye's brother," said Carl.

"How far south?" asked Ed.

Faye wandered down the path, and the wolf pack fell in behind her, a distant rumble the only sound in the morning stillness. "Cheyenne Mountain."

"Right. Good one."

Ed looked to Carl, expecting to find himself the butt of a joke. The bodyguard raised an eyebrow.

"That's five hundred miles right into the big, bad basement of the urchins. You're joking, right?"

Faye picked up the pace. "We need to move fast. I want to be there in a week."

"That ain't possible. Even if we did fifty miles a day, there's no way to cover..."

The dull rumble grew louder as they descended, until its source blocked their path. The swollen river, fed by the thawing ice from Yellowstone Lake, raged down the valley—a swirling, foaming highway through the mountains.

"Shit!" said Ed, as Faye made for a weathered tarp covering a dozen kayaks. It would be another month before the lake ice melted enough for the fishermen to use their boats.

"This is crazy. It's going to be nothing but rapids."

"I'm banking on it," said Faye, dragging a battered, orange two-seater kayak free. "I said it was dangerous."

"There's dangerous and then there's drowning."

Roo threw Ed a paddle. "Grow a pair!"

"What about my kit?"

"Best keep it out of the water," said Carl, thrusting a life jacket into Ed's arms.

"I'll remind you of that when one of these stun units goes off."

"I'm with Faye," said Roo, slipping her rifle into the orange kayak and helping Faye drag the boat to the shore. Ed and Carl wrestled with a well-used, yellow canoe.

"Ed, get a bird up. We'll follow you. Any problems wave to the bank and we'll pull over," said Faye, twisting an arm to reposition the barrel of Roo's rifle.

Carl clambered into the yellow kayak. "You see anything. Tap me on the shoulder. Left or right. Got it?"

Ed launched a drone that shot off down the valley as he stowed his rucksack. "This is madness."

"Sure is," said Roo, whooping as Faye pushed away from the bank into the fast-flowing waters.

...

"I've not come five hundred miles to be stopped by...a...lump...of...fucking iron," yelled Faye, beating her fists against the rusted door of the northwest access tunnel.

The journey had taken them five days, the brutal rapids almost breaking them and the kayaks. The long climb through the Colorado hills sapped what strength remained, leaving them exhausted and out of rations. Ed's drone had discovered what was left of Cheyenne Mountain, torn apart like an almighty, erupting volcano. A mile-wide scar stretched from the storms in the south to the badlands in the north, the trail of destruction marking the passing of something unimaginable.

"Move!" yelled Roo, lying prone thirty feet out from the iron door.

"You can't—"

A deafening shot echoed around the valley and, hands over her ears,

Faye glared at the girl. "—put a hole in armor plate."

Roo tilted her head, reloading and taking aim again. Faye ducked as another ear-shattering shot rang out, followed by a third. With the gunshots still reverberating around the hillside, Faye glared at the girl.

"Happy now?"

Roo smiled and held up her hand. Between her index finger and thumb, she held a three-inch, shiny black shell. The girl nodded to the door. "Dum-dum."

Faye turned as the door fell with a crash, three fist-sized holes all that remained of the hinges and any securing bracket, the onyx dum-dum bullets tearing through the metal like butter.

"Damn, Roo. How'd you get your hands on onyx ammo? They're what? Eighty credits a pop. But what a fucking pop. Look at this," said Ed, dancing on the smoking door.

"Roo! Did you steal those?"

The girl shook her head, throwing her smoking rifle over her shoulder. "Me and the bunnies been saving up."

"That's a lot of rabbit bits," said Faye, unconvinced. Onyx bullets were next to impossible to manufacture, as likely to go off in assembly as the breach.

Carl bumped fists with the girl as the wolf pack peered into the gloom of the access tunnel.

"You know, you could have just knocked."

The words echoed from the tunnel as a tall figure emerged.

"Adan!" said Faye, hugging her brother.

"Hey, sis. You lost?"

She pushed him away. "Am *I* lost?"

"Gonna introduce me?" said Yash, stepping from the shadows.

"Hey, sure. This is my little sister, Flee," Adan said, ruffling Faye's hair. "And these reprobates are the notorious wolf pack. The big guy's Carl, grand wizard Ed, and this horror—" Roo threw herself at Adan, wrapping her arms around his neck. "Is Roo. Guys this is Yash. He's saved my life twice now."

Roo launched herself from the scientist and attached herself to the marine like an octopus. "Thank you."

"You're welcome," said Yash, smiling at the girl.

"I'm guessing you guys aren't here for the tour," said Adan.

Carl stepped forward. "We're here to rescue you."

Adan rubbed his neck. "Ah, about that."

...

"That's your plan?!" asked Faye.

Adan nodded. "Pretty much."

They sat in the holey canteen, water dripping from the perforated ceiling. Adan had set up a makeshift workshop, and the device sat on one of the few intact tables, the guts of the warhead duct-taped to his EMP contraption. The rest of the team had gone with Yash on one last supply sweep, the wolf pack eager to find anything not bolted down they might sell back in the Rox.

"Can you hear yourself?" Faye asked. "It's suicide. You won't get a kilometer."

Adan launched a can of nuts and bolts across the room. "What else am I supposed to do? I've dreamed of this all my life. The day we finally fight back, and if there's even a chance it might work then I have to try. If the price is my life, then so be it. We can't keep running and hiding, Faye. There's nowhere left to go."

Faye took her brother's hands. "There's another way. Let me help. I can bring them here, bring them to us."

"What?"

"You're not the only one who's spent their life working towards this. Don't you see? She's manipulated us both and if we want to survive, if the Rox is to survive, we'll need to work together."

"I don't understand."

"You don't need to. Just get that thing ready and I'll get it where it needs to be."

Faye clasped the amulet, the surface resonating like a tuning fork in her hand, as if the shard stirred, recalling the titanic urchin it had once been and might be again.

...

"When I say," said Faye, hugging Roo close. "Right, sister?"

The girl hugged her back, squeezing the breath from Faye's lungs. "Of course."

After a long moment, she pushed Roo away, the girl unwilling to let go. "Go on. Get ready. I'm counting on you."

It had taken them four hours to dig their way through the rubble and bodies blocking the east access tunnel. Not soldiers this time, but families, preserved as if they'd lay down to sleep only yesterday. More victims of the deadly argon gas from all those years ago. She'd taken some solace that their asphyxiation would have been less horrific than what awaited them outside. When they reached the end of the tunnel, Roo hadn't needed to blow the hinges. The iron door had opened with a hefty shove to reveal the familiar sight of the badlands.

"I still don't get it," said Carl. "Why aren't we going with you?"

Faye cradled his chin. "I'm going to be right there," she said, pointing out into the barren wilderness. "Don't get clingy on me now."

"I just don't like the idea of using you as bait."

"Me neither, but the alternative is we go to them, and we know how that ends. At least here there's half a mountain for cover."

"Will it work?"

"I trust Adan, and he's convinced. So, we have to try," said Faye, kissing Carl, her bodyguard, her love. She wished the moment could last forever and was slow to let him slip from her lips.

The tunnel buzzed, as if a thousand bees had taken flight and four of Ed's drones zipped off. The technical wiz's fingers danced across his sleeve as he wrangled the electronic birds into the sky. "I'll set up a perimeter around ground zero."

"Thanks, Ed," said Faye, giving him a hug before stepping from the tunnel.

It felt good to be home and she watched the drones vanish into the indigo sky, each flying off in a different direction. The alien storm front seemed closer, more violent, as if anticipating their plan. Waiting. Watching.

Just like her mother would be.

"Remember, you have three minutes," said Adan, sliding the backpack with the device over her shoulders.

She adjusted the straps to stop the weight digging into her bruised ribs. "Three minutes. Got it."

"Make sure you're back in the tunnel. If you're out there—"

"I'll be okay."

Faye leaned against her brother, head-to-head as they did when they were kids. With one last wave to her pack, she walked out across the churned-up earth towards ground zero.

CHAPTER NINE

*S*queak, *squeak, squeak.*

The noise echoed around the council chamber.

"I thought you got that thing fixed?" said Ava, laying down her e-tablet.

General Hacket rolled up beside her. "Seems to me like some things ain't meant to be fixed. You've been avoiding me, Ava. Why is that?"

Ava raised an eyebrow. "I have? I've been busy. Arthur has been showing me some of his engineering aspirations. Do you know they've almost got the Buffalo Bill dam operational? Thirty megawatts. More than enough to keep the lights on."

"You can bullshit everyone else," said the general, leaning across and swiping at the e-tablet. The satellite image transferred to the wall display, and he wheeled his way over for a closer look.

"Faye, and her team made it to the Cheyenne complex yesterday," said Ava, with just a little pride. In reality, her daughter's early arrival had caused her no end of problems, and a few sleepless nights.

"Yesterday? How? Corvino's team is days away."

Faye tapped on the e-tablet, overlaying her daughter's river route. Another line showed the progress of the marines, on foot, marching through the badlands.

"Oh, clever. But I guess that's why you sent her."

"I didn't send her. She wouldn't take no for an answer."

"Ava, this is me you're talking to, not one of your counselors. I'm not the only one who can see through your games. Faye knows everything."

Ava winced, heart skipping a beat.

"She's pieced it all together, including the bits that eluded you. She's accessed the alien network."

Ava's trembling, spasming hand reached into her pocket. Her pill box fell to the floor. She reached for the e-tablet, but her fingers cramped, arm jerking back to clutch her chest as if barbs pierced her heart.

The old man continued, oblivious to Ava's plight. "She even knows Carl's your man. Damn it, Ava. There's a lot I can condone and even more I can forgive. But spying on your own daughter? She loves the man. It's twisted."

Ava reached out, desperate to tell him the truth, to set the record straight, but she had no voice, her mouth a foaming mess that dribbled down her chin.

"You make no bones about Suzy being your heir, but the fact is you gave up on your own flesh and blood and she might just be the key to our survival."

The general spun around as Ava fell from the chair. She hit the floor hard, convulsing.

"Ava!"

...

Ground zero.

It sounded ominous, sounded planned, but it could have been anywhere in the badlands. Just another scrap of dirt marked by a smooth, black boulder. Faye placed the heavy rucksack down on the rock and stared back a kilometer at what remained of NORAD. The mountain had been ripped apart like one of Roo's rabbits.

There was no wind. The only sound, the distant whirring of Ed's ever watchful drones and the occasional muted rumble of thunder. Felt more than heard.

She saw the badlands for what they were now. The battleground between the world she knew and the aliens' new world.

Adan's EMP device flashed four green lights. Was that good? She couldn't remember. The kukri strapped to her legs provided more assurance she'd at least go out fighting. She felt for the radio Ed had duct-taped to her arm, flipping it to hands-free.

"*Ready?*" crackled Adan's voice.

Faye wasn't sure. In her mind, it had all made sense, but as she looked at the tiny, waving figure of her brother, she realized she didn't have a plan. She tugged the amulet from her neck. Even now, without trying, it connected her to that other world and she could feel it, feel them.

"I'm ready," she lied, gripping the amulet tight in her palm and feeling its vibrations.

She took a deep breath and kneeled, closing her eyes and letting memory take over. Hers and theirs. Destroying the network would never be enough, not if the alien entities survived. If they wanted to hurt them, she needed to snare one of the sparks of consciousness.

In her mind, she reached out into the alien neural network, searching, hunting. The entities were few, and they moved like lightning along their conduits. It took all her dexterity to follow, to reach out and...

The southern horizon erupted into fire, every lightning strike exploding at once to reveal the aliens' terra-formed world as a twisted urchin nightmare. A vista of thorns, urchins piled up into a city of sorts, a vision of their aspirations for the entire planet, illuminated for but a second. The sound that followed was not thunder, but the rending of worlds, a howl that spoke to the flesh and bones of things.

"*Faye!*" crackled the radio, as the wind hit her like a hurricane. She hunkered down, head bowed, mind elsewhere.

The entity flailed, twisting, turning, desperate to escape as she fought to bring it down. It tore at her, threatening to rip the fabric of its being and her mind. Faye hung on, knowing if she lost her grip there'd be no second chance.

Purple lightning rippled around Faye's fist, the amulet struggling to channel the unleashed energies. The howling gale carried an army from the south. A wall of urchins, small and large, rolled towards Faye.

"*Faye, it's not working. There's too many. Run!*"

She tried to stand, gritting her teeth as the wind threatened to carry her away.

As she'd feared, the amulet created a two-way street, and the flailing entity had turned on her, invading her mind. It searched for weakness, rifling through her thoughts, her memories. Pain, anger, loss. It found them and forced her to relive each emotion in a timeless nightmare. Faye reeled, grip slipping.

She looked up at the approaching wall of urchins and panicked, hand hovering over the priming switch. It was too soon. The entity, the master of these things, still hid in its network and her mind.

"Faye! Run! You can still make it back."

The entity seized on her brother's voice, perverting Faye's most treasured memories, moments from her childhood—her brother, her sister and, of course, her mother. The bile twisted in her stomach, the familiar thorn in her side marking where she'd buried a lifetime of anger. Decades of pain and rage that she unleashed upon the unsuspecting entity. The amulet seared into her palm, lightning racing up her arms to flow over her body as she screamed at the creature, scouring it from her mind even as the shadow of the urchin tsunami bore down on her.

"Faye!"

The first small urchins shot past like bullets, and she saw them, not with her eyes, but as living nodes within the alien network, each one home to an alien memory.

The radio crackled. *"Oh, Christ! Faye! No!"*

...

Adan fell to his knees as Faye vanished under the wave of urchins. Yash dragged the distraught scientist back into the tunnel, away from the meat grinder that flowed past the entrance.

"She's gone!" cried Adan.

He couldn't believe it. How could he have been so stupid? Why had he let her risk it? Risk everything?

Ed fought to keep the drones on point, his fingers a blur as low-battery warnings flashed along his sleeve. "I... I can't see her. It's just urchins. God, no!"

Roo lay in the shadows, staring through the scope of her rifle, unmoving, unblinking. "I see you..."

"What?" asked Adan, searching the flurry of onyx spines.

Ed shook his head. "Nothing could survive out there."

"She's there," implored Roo.

Ed kneeled beside the girl, placing his trembling hand on her shoulder. "She's gone, Roo."

"No! Watch!" hissed Roo, shrugging him off.

Yash inched closer to the exit. "They're...they're stopping."

Sure enough, the wind stopped. The urchins slowed and came to a complete stop, leaving the badlands eerily still, not a spine moving.

"What the hell?" cried Ed.

With the slightest of breezes, the urchins at the tunnel entrance retreated south. Those in the distance pushed on north. The wolf pack watched, spellbound, as a vortex formed, a rolling, anti-clockwise tornado of spines a kilometer wide. Urchins at the eye of the storm fled to its edge, revealing a figure. Faye, arms outstretched, as if conducting the surrounding chaos.

"Peek-a-boo," said Roo.

...

"Faye!" Adan's voice burst over the radio. *"Press it!"*

"Not yet."

She'd watched her alien adversary control the urchins, reaching out across its network to command countless spiny horrors to lower their body temperatures. The effect, amplified by the superconducting onyx and multiplied by sheer numbers, created a vast cold front that drove the urchin army towards her. Adan had theorized such a relationship, but could never prove it. She had, mimicking the alien entity to create the vortex that kept the urchin terrors at bay, whipping them high into the air.

Such power came at a cost as the glowing amulet, her conduit, seared into her flesh. An agony made bearable only by the knowledge that the alien entity suffered more as she dragged it, kicking and screaming, into her world.

Faye held her palm up to the sky, the smell of burning flesh turning her stomach as she offered the entity a way out from the tortures of her mind. The entity didn't hesitate, erupting through the amulet as a column of incandescent purple plasma that stabbed into the dark clouds, before exploding into a hissing, electrical demon. Long tendrils of chain lightning lashed out as the entity ripped urchins from the vortex and launched them at Faye. She rolled clear of the deadly projectiles and glared up at the enraged horror.

She'd done it. It was here. Now she had to stop it from escaping.

Digging her thumbnail into her palm, she ripped the red-hot shard free. The electrified fiend rushed to escape through the amulet as Faye threw it high into the air.

"Now, Roo!"

"*Bunny!*" crackled the radio.

The shard exploded with a deafening thunderclap as the onyx dumdum bullet obliterated it. The entity roared, recoiling as Faye flipped the switch on Adan's device and ran. Above, the demon raged, tearing the sky to shreds as it searched for another route, another oynx conduit powerful enough to allow it back into its own world.

Faye unsheathed her knives, preparing for one last dance to freedom as urchins fell from the sky all around. The winds did not change on a dime, not even for the furious alien tempest. Faye ran, dodging the urchins that the demon directed towards her.

"*Bunny!*"

An urchin exploded behind her, and Faye narrowly avoided the spine shrapnel.

"*I got this one,*" Ed's voice crackled.

Another large urchin exploded from her path as a drone sacrificed itself. Faye sprinted as Roo and Ed swatted away the worst of the urchins. What they couldn't dispatch, she ducked and sliced her way through until she was yards from the tunnel.

Carl peppered smaller urchins with machinegun fire. As she neared, he dropped his rifle and sprinted towards her. The hairs on Faye's neck bristled, an electrical charge that rippled down her arm. Out of options, she hoped the pack had her back.

Carl caught her in his arms and twisted, taking the full force of the urchin's impact. It happened so fast, and Faye looked from his terrified eyes to the bloody spines protruding from his shoulder.

"No!" she screamed, staring at the football-sized urchin and back to her love's eyes.

They both knew what came next. The urchin would flex, driving home its barbs and eviscerating the man she loved. It didn't stop him smiling.

Wide-eyed, Faye stared in horror. She couldn't lose him. He'd never been her bodyguard; he was her life. She rammed her fist deep into the urchin's core, needles skewering her flesh as she pushed on into its dark heart.

"I said, *no!*"

The urchin spasmed, and she feared it had finished the job, tearing her love apart. Instead, it disintegrated, spines falling like confetti as its black heart burst on the floor. She dragged Carl into the tunnel, a single spine still piercing his shoulder.

A moment later, the world vanished into a light brighter than the sun.

...

Faye looked out across the badlands and up into unfamiliar, blue skies. The shockwave had thrown them down the tunnel, and it had taken several minutes before they licked their wounds sufficiently to venture back to the entrance. The alien entity had vanished, its army of urchins shattered, dark cores exposed, stripped of their vicious spines.

"You did it, Sis."

"*We* did it," said Faye, turning to find the wolf pack standing behind her, watching.

No one had said anything, but they looked at her differently now. Even Carl, his shoulder bandaged, seemed distant. She looked down at her scorched palm and wondered if it was the only mark the aliens had left on her. As if to dismiss her fears, Roo wrapped her arms around Faye's waist.

"Is it over?" asked Ed.

Faye stroked Roo's hair, watching the hint of storms raging far beyond the southern horizon. Part of her wanted to believe they were the death throes of their vanquished enemy. But alien memories told her the fight was far from over. She slipped from Roo's grasp and headed back down the access tunnel into a new darkness.

Carl called after her. "Faye?"

It wasn't over. It wasn't gone. Some part of the alien consciousness still skulked in her synapses, and as she stumbled past the bodies of the dead, it morphed each mummified face into someone she knew. It's message clear, this would be the fate of the Rox. She tripped, an apparition of Roo's dead face leering at her from the gloom.

The remaining alien entities would rally, they'd come, and they wouldn't stop until they exterminated the Rox. She ran, seeing only the tunnels of her childhood stacked high with the ghosts of the ones she loved.

Roo's voice echoed behind her. "Looks like we're just getting started."

EPILOGUE

The council chamber was a riot of angry, scared voices. Suzy sat slumped in a chair, hands wrapped around a cold mug of coffee. General Hacket sat beside her, shaking his head. He'd assembled the Council to announce Ava's heart attack, but what had played out on the screen made Ava's plight the less pressing topic.

The satellite relayed high-definition images of ground zero that left nothing to the imagination. The destruction of the entity, the urchins and the clearing of the storm might have been hailed a victory but for what the satellite revealed now.

Deep in what had been the Gulf of Mexico, storms not of this world tore the world apart, and an endless, dark shadow slunk north.

Suzy's thoughts were with her mother, wired to a life-support machine, a ghost of the woman she knew. The doctors offered little hope; the next twenty-four hours would be critical. Sabine had offered to keep watch, and Suzy had been thankful for a break.

General Hacket leaned close, patting her arm. "She'll pull through. She's a fighter."

Suzy nodded, struggling to hold back the tears as her fingers tightened on the mug.

"So are you, and right now—"

"I know," hissed Suzy, springing to her feet.

She'd hoped this day would never come, but now it was here. Listening to the bickering counselors, anger took over. She smashed her mug down, shards of porcelain rattling across the onyx table. The room fell silent, all eyes turning to her.

She exhaled a long, quivering breath as she looked around the familiar faces.

"Death comes for my mother, and for us all. For all of us who remain," she said, walking to the window and studying the Rox. The people going about their desperate lives were her burden now and she felt it, a crown of thorns pressing at her temples. "Your friends, your family. We are it. All that remains. The last of humanity. So, I would suggest that the next words uttered in this chamber better improve our chances of survival, or we may as well go kiss them all goodbye."

She stared around the room, half-expecting the bickering to continue. Instead, she found people looking to her, nodding. And General Hacket, grinning.

Dan Atkins stood, and Suzy eyed him nervously. "I'll coordinate re-calling everyone from the badlands."

Groats stood next. "Well, if we're going to have visitors. I'll get to work on shoring up the Rox's defenses."

Suzy nodded at the old architect and smiled as the Council organized itself before her eyes. Maybe there was still hope yet.

Chris Hewitt lives in the beautiful garden of England and in the odd moment he's not walking the dog, he pursues his passion for writing fiction. With horror, fantasy, and science-fiction stories published in several anthologies from Eerie River amongst others.

Facebook: www.facebook.com/chris.hewitt.writer
Twitter: @i_mused_blog
Blog: http://mused.blog
Amazon: http://mused.blog/author

FADING ECHOES
BY JOEL R. HUNT

CHAPTER 1
WANT ANYTHING

Katie peered around the rusted car, training her binoculars on the strangers' hideout. Reclaimed by years of unchecked vegetation, it looked more like a cave than an underpass. Only the mould-splattered signs hanging from its ceiling and the rows of abandoned cars revealed its true origin. Deep inside, plunged into darkness by the oncoming night, four figures huddled around a burn barrel.

One had a rifle slung across his back.

Katie blew a sigh through her teeth and swept the binoculars around for any other weaponry. As she did, the man with the rifle leaned to one side, revealing a fifth figure who had been obscured by the others. Katie turned to her sister.

"They have a child with them," she whispered.

Bec hummed in acknowledgement. She reclined in the car's backseat, carefree smile at odds with the sharp focus of her eyes.

"Do you want anything from the shop?" she asked.

"They haven't yet," said Katie. "If they do see us, I'll let you know."

Bec's mouth tightened. It formed a series of little shapes without producing sound. When she finally spoke, it was with tension in her jaw, as though she were battling against her own words.

"Do you...want any... Do you want anything from the shop?"

Katie gave her sister's hand a squeeze.

"I'm scared too," she said. "But it's either this or we head out to find shelter in the dark. And I can't make a campfire with mud and wet sticks, so it'd be another cold, damp night. At least this lot have heat. And they've got a child, Bec. They're not a cleansing squad."

Bec stood up from the car seat, only avoiding striking her head on the frame due to Katie's guiding hand.

"Do you... Do you want..." Bec stammered, before swallowing back the echo and taking a deep breath. When she was ready, she continued in a chipper tone; "Yeah, I will, thanks."

"Atta girl," said Katie.

They wove their way between abandoned cars and crumbling concrete, approaching the underpass with relative ease. Katie didn't want to risk looking like an ambush party, so when they got within a few cars' distance of the entrance and the strangers still hadn't noticed them, she grabbed Bec's sleeve. They both stopped.

"Hello!" she called out. The strangers jolted, and the man with the rifle swung it around and thrust it in their direction.

"Who's out there?" he cried. "How many?"

"We're travellers," said Katie, "just passing through. There's two of us, me and my sister."

"Do you want... Do you want anything..." Bec said, struggling to supress the echo. Katie squeezed her hand, and the words settled back into Bec's chest. The man didn't seem to notice, or else ignored the question.

"Come into the light," he said. "Slowly."

Katie approached the flickering of the burn barrel, guiding Bec to join her. They halted at the light's edge, and now Katie could see the wary fear that creased the man's features. She lifted the sides of her coat to show her lack of weaponry.

"We're unarmed," she said. The stranger jerked his gun towards Bec. "And you?"

"Her too," said Katie. Bec plucked at her coat, and Katie opened it for the man to see. He huffed, nodded, then lowered his rifle.

"Can't be too careful," he said, gesturing for them to join the group.

"Don't worry, we understand," said Katie.

She led Bec toward the fire and found them a seat on a pile of old tires.

Haggard faces greeted them, with one hesitant smile to spare between the four. The man settled back near the barrel, placing the rifle aside and warming his hands.

"So, you got names?" he asked.

"I'm Katie, and my sister's Bec."

He grunted.

"Chris," he said, "my wife Susan, and our little Nathan."

Susan smiled and nodded, but there was a hollowness to the expression, like an old song with forgotten lyrics. Their son, perhaps seven or eight, didn't acknowledge them at all; he sat in his mother's lap, staring into space and chewing. Chris gestured across the fire to the other two figures, who sat as far away as they could while still getting the benefit of heat.

"And this is... ah..." Chris started.

"Fareed," said one of the strangers.

"I'm Asma," said the other. "We've not been travelling together long, things being as they are."

"Can't be too careful," Chris repeated.

After that, they settled into relative silence. Fareed and Asma shared a hushed conversation, and Susan whispered to Nathan as she fed him from a freshly-heated tin, but both sounds were masked by the steady crackle of the fire. It suited Katie. Their issues were none of her concern, just as Bec was none of theirs. Huddling together by the fire, Katie pulled out some rations and split them, passing half to Bec. She tucked the dried meat into Bec's fingers, helping her sister to grip the food in a hand that insisted on holding something larger. The struggle had become routine, and while Bec's grip never improved, it never deteriorated either, which was more than most could say. After a few minutes, the meat finally balanced between her fingers and Bec brought it to her mouth to chew. Katie watched until she was confident that Bec could handle the rest, and then bit into her own rations. The meat was tough and flavourless, but it would do until they were able to scavenge more food.

As she ate, Katie let her gaze drift around the underpass, eventually landing on Susan and Nathan opposite the fire. The boy was still staring into the distance, chewing constantly. Each time Susan fed him, she had to angle the spoon to tip food between his moving jaws. Then, after letting

Nathan chew for a while, she would whisper in his ear and massage his throat, helping him swallow. Katie watched this process repeat for minutes, until Chris leaned across and grunted.

"So, where are you heading?"

Katie jumped. She'd almost forgotten he was there. While she'd been watching Nathan, had he been watching her?

"We're heading east," Katie said. "We're looking for the Renshaw Institute."

Susan's spoon jerked, flicking food into Nathan's lap.

"You're trying to *find* it?" she gasped.

"Erm...yes. Why?"

Chris and his wife looked to one another. Susan nodded and gave Nathan's shoulder a gentle shake.

"Nathan. Do you want the toilet?"

He stared into the distance, unresponsive. She shook his shoulder again a little harder.

"Toilet, Nathan? Toilet?"

As she spoke, the boy's face twitched. His vacant stare transitioned into an alert expression almost without a middle step. It seemed to Katie that she was watching a film with several frames removed. The feeling was a familiar one, and confirmed what she had suspected since they sat down: Nathan was an Echo.

"Can I go to the toilet, Mum?" he asked, in a voice too young for his body.

"Of course. Let's go now."

Susan led her son to the other side of the underpass. Chris watched them go, and as they disappeared behind an abandoned lorry, he shuffled closer and spoke with a hushed voice.

"Where we've come from, the Institute are lurking all over. Saw them once or twice, out collecting folk, spreading their propaganda. But it's a trap. The Institute isn't trying to cure Echo Syndrome. They're just luring people in for sick experiments."

Bec squeezed Katie's hand. Behind her calm smile were cautious eyes.

"How do you know?" asked Katie.

"Met some captives who'd escaped," said Chris. "A pair of Echoes. One was too far gone, bless him, but the other was lucid enough. Kept telling us what they'd done, over and over. How long they'd been a prisoner, and the torture. The torture…"

Chris shivered, despite his proximity to the fire. Katie clutched her pocket, crumpling the paper that was folded inside.

"You're sure it was the Renshaw Institute they were talking about?" she asked.

"Who else would it have been? No one else is out gathering Echoes and taking them away."

"We've heard it too," said Asma, "haven't we, Far?"

Fareed gave a non-committal shrug.

"Well, we've heard rumours, at least," Asma continued. "I don't like it. If that's what they do to Echoes, I don't want to think what they'd do to normal people."

Chris grunted. He leaned in towards Katie, the fire playing in his eyes and emphasising his piercing stare.

"Tell me this," he said. "Why would they hide in some secret location if they want volunteers, hmm? How are people supposed to find them to help out?"

"They're hiding from people like Boss Clean," said Katie. "He'd never let a place like the Institute survive if they were out in the open."

Chris shook his head. "Open your eyes. They hide from us because they know what we'd do to them if we saw their experiments."

Katie bristled, and spoke sharper than she intended to; "You don't understand what Boss Clean is capable of! He runs this whole county with his fucking death squads!"

"Well we've heard there's nowhere safer," said Asma, with a shrug.

"Maybe if you're not an Echo," sneered Katie.

"We're not," said Asma, "and there's no reason we should be stuck out here scrabbling in the dirt if someone is actually rebuilding society. Run if you like. We want to start living again."

"Living again?" Katie scoffed. "He's a mass murderer and you're talking about living again?"

Asma turned her back and marched away, settling down at the edge of the light. Fareed opened his mouth, sighed, and then followed.

"Unbelievable," hissed Katie.

Chris grunted. "Don't take it personally," he said. "They just want their old lives back. All of us do."

Susan and Nathan returned to the fireside, and the rest of the evening passed in silence, aside from the occasional humming from Bec and Susan's whispered reassurances to Nathan as he sat, chewing. Asma and Fareed settled down to sleep first, and Nathan soon followed, led away to a nearby car which had been kitted out for sleeping. He had difficulty lying down, and Susan practically had to force him onto the bed roll. Katie could hear the woman's whispering, like she was addressing a toddler. She approached Chris and cleared her throat.

"I don't want to pry, but... Nathan is an Echo, isn't he?"

Chris narrowed his eyes and looked her up and down, as though her motive might be daubed on her shirt. He evidently sensed no danger, and nodded.

"My sister and I have seen what Boss Clean's people are capable of," said Katie. "They don't spare anyone, old or young. If the cleansing squads find you..." Katie pointed to his rifle. "You'll need that."

Chris barked a humourless laugh. "Ah, the damned thing isn't even loaded," he said. "Who has ammo these days?"

It was a fair question. Aside from Boss Clean's crew, Katie didn't remember the last person she'd seen with a working firearm. She looked over to Bec, then back to Chris.

"In that case, stay off the roads when you can," she said. "Don't trust strangers. And don't try to scare off the cleansing squads. They won't flinch from your rifle, loaded or not."

Chris fixed her with a hard stare. He grunted. "We've got this far."

Before Katie could reply, Susan called him over, and he slumped away to wish his son goodnight. Katie waited to see if he'd return to continue their conversation, but he didn't spare her another glance. Bec plucked at her shirt.

"No, I've had it for a while, actually," she said.

Katie nodded. "Well, we've warned them. It's up to them now."

The pair set up their bed rolls a few cars away from the others, and settled down close to keep one another warm. Despite the cold, it was a relief to have a roof over their heads, and there was something comforting in the crackling of the fire and the gentle snoring from Asma and Fareed. Katie almost felt safe. She stroked Bec's cheek as her sister's eyes drooped closed.

"Not long now," she whispered into her ear. Bec hummed in response, and Katie held her close. "Not long now."

CHAPTER 2
FOR A WHILE

Katie woke to the sound of footsteps. She jolted upright, casting a protective arm across Bec's sleeping body. Susan halted a few steps away, Nathan clinging to her side.

"We're setting off now," said Susan. "I just wanted to let you know. If you've changed your mind about running off to find the Institute, you'd be welcome to join us."

"Thank you, Susan, but we can't stay in Boss Clean's territory. I don't think you should either, for any longer than you need to."

Susan smiled her hollow smile. "Well, good luck then," she said.

"And to you," said Katie.

Bec stirred and sat up. "Hello, I'm Auntie Bec," she said, giving Nathan a kind smile.

Katie turned to the boy. "Look after yourself, Nathan," she said, as warmly as she could.

Nathan didn't respond. He stared into the distance, chewing on nothing.

"Thank you," said Susan. Chris called her over, and the five travellers made their way out of the underpass and into the morning light.

Katie and Bec had breakfast around the burn barrel, in no rush to leave the safety of their temporary shelter. They had another long day of walking ahead of them, and they needed the energy to see it through; who knew where their next shelter would come from? Katie couldn't stop thinking about the conversation she'd had the previous night.

After she finished her morning's rations, she took a folded poster from her pocket and flattened it out. Bec joined her and they read it together, as they had done a hundred times before.

'*The Renshaw Institute needs you!*

We are in urgent need of volunteers to aid in the study of Baccslau-Horvitz Syndrome, also known as BHS or Echo Syndrome. All volunteers are provided food, shelter and security indefinitely. Once a cure has been formulated, it will be provided to all volunteers immediately and at no cost.

Please help us to eradicate BHS.

Together we will heal the world.'

Notes were scrawled across the paper, clues to the location of the increasingly secretive organisation. On the back, a hand-drawn map represented the result of years of searching. The end of the map was less than a week's walk away.

"Is it true, do you think? Is the Institute just a trick?"

"Look how you've grown," said Bec, smiling at Katie's midriff. "How old are you now?"

Katie looked back to the poster, tracing the circle they'd drawn around the Institute's supposed location.

"I suppose it's worth a shot," she said. "Even if we find them, we don't have to go in. If we don't like what we see, we turn around and head someplace else. Does that sound alright?"

"Wow, you're nearly a grown-up!" Bec said, and she laughed the same laugh Katie had been listening to for five years.

Katie smiled. "Alright then."

They made good progress in the early part of the morning. The rain had passed for now, and sunlight made mirrors on the wet tarmac. Without the constant disruption of traffic, nature had retaken the roads. Birds wheeled overhead, rabbits chased one another along the grassy banks to either side, and a family of deer pranced ahead of them, almost oblivious to the presence of humans in their midst.

Then, far behind them, distant shots rang out, puncturing the air in quick succession. The deer scattered. Bec and Katie froze, turning to the underpass that had now disappeared from view. Katie didn't want to count the shots. She tried not to.

She couldn't help herself.

Five in total, followed by a painful, heavy silence. Bec reached for her hand, and Katie squeezed her fingers.

"Do you want anything from the shop?" Bec asked.

Katie swallowed back her sorrow. "We don't know it was them," she said. "Maybe the patrols are just out hunting."

She hoped that sounded more convincing than it felt. The two of them watched the horizon for what felt like an hour, but no further sounds emerged; no more shots, no screams or shouts, no patrol car engines. The weight of the silence had settled and refused to lift. There was nothing else to do but continue.

For the rest of the morning, no rabbits or deer returned to the road, and the patrolling of distant hawks kept the songbirds in hiding. A light drizzle chased away the sun, followed by dark clouds that threatened worse. In the gloom of the rain, the road seemed never-ending, a grey river clogged with rusting metal carcasses. Their silent march was unbroken for hours, until at last another underpass rose on the horizon. Katie picked up her pace, eager to get even temporary respite from the constant drizzle.

As they neared the structure, Bec gave a lilting hum. Katie imagined it had been part of a song, originally. Now Bec had remodelled it into a sign of disapproval. Katie soon saw what her sister was objecting to. By the entrance to the underpass, a familiar slogan was painted in broad letters.

TELL BOSS CLEAN WHO YOU'VE SEEN

Katie's face twisted into a grimace. How many Echoes had been betrayed and sold out because of that damned instruction? Boss Clean wanted people to believe he had eyes and ears everywhere, but if innocent survivors had just stopped reporting Echoes to the cleansing squads, Clean wouldn't have been able to hurt half as many as he had.

Evidently, Katie and Bec weren't the only ones to oppose Boss Clean's mission to 'purify' the world. Behind the slogan, an older version of the same phrase was just visible, layered over with an explosion of graffitied expletives.

It looked like the vandals had been caught. At the foot of the newly painted slogan lay two charred skeletons. The cleansing patrols usually buried their victims, but these had been propped against the wall in full view of the road. A warning.

Katie took a steadying breath as Bec's hum hit a loop. Taking shelter here no longer seemed a welcoming prospect. Though the corpses weren't fresh—having been exposed to the elements for a few days at least—they were a stark reminder of how far Clean's territory extended.

"Let's get off the road," said Katie.

"Yeah, I will, thanks."

Traversing the woodland was hard going. The rain had turned the ground to thick mud that sucked at their boots, and any footpath that once existed had long since overgrown. Brambles tore at their jeans and thick tree roots hooked around their feet, threatening to send them crashing into the wet dirt. Still, it was better than risking being caught by a patrol.

They struggled on for hours, only straying near the road every now and then to check they hadn't lost their way. When it was time to rest, they found what little shelter they could beneath a clump of thick trees. The rain grew heavier, showing no sign of letting up. Huddling close to Bec, Katie split the afternoon's rations between them. It left her bag almost empty.

"We'll need to restock soon," she said.

"Yeah, I will, thanks," said Bec.

When they had eaten, Katie helped her sister up and they continued, using Katie's backpack for shelter. It didn't make much difference. Despite the fabric, despite the canopy overhead, despite Katie's hunched form, the rain lashed her face as if it were the only reason it had left the sky. She didn't dare consult the map, knowing the constant downpour would turn the paper to pulp in moments. That, combined with her rain-blurred vision, left her leading on instinct alone, unsure if they were even vaguely heading in the right direction.

She supposed it didn't matter; any direction that wasn't back the way they came was good enough for now.

When the worst of the rain subsided, returning to the light drizzle of the morning, Katie slipped her sodden backpack over her shoulders and wiped Bec's eyes for her, smoothing back her hair so it didn't block her vision. Bec muttered some half-forgotten syllables in thanks. With that done, Katie turned her attention towards locating some form of landmark so that she could assess their progress. Ahead and to the left, the trees thinned out, so Katie set off in that direction.

She was rewarded with a complete change of scenery. The woodland fell away to a sloping hill, at the foot of which was a vast car park. Hundreds of vehicles dotted the asphalt, rusting and likely untouched since the fall of civilisation. Beyond those relics was a sprawling shopping centre. Katie pulled binoculars from her coat and inspected it closer. The shutters were closed over every entrance and window. That never stopped looters for long, but from what she could see, there were no breaches at all. The building looked secure.

"Strange," she said, holding out the binoculars for Bec. "No one mentioned a mall out this way. It must have all sorts of supplies. I'd have thought Boss Clean would have claimed it by now, or some other ganglord."

Bec hummed.

"Right," said Katie. "No sense risking it. I'll add it to the map when we're dry again though. Might come in handy."

Taking her binoculars back, Katie traced the road from the car park back to its source; a dual-carriageway that disappeared behind the woodland they had just left. She ran through the local roads in her head and nodded, confident they hadn't diverged too far from their intended route.

"Not far now, Bec. Are you up for another few miles?"

"Yeah, I will, thanks."

"Atta girl."

Now that the unrelenting downpour had ended, the next hour was significantly easier, though not without challenges. At parts of their journey, they were wading more than walking, and the chill of their wet clothes was beginning to sink in. More than ever, they needed a dry, warm shelter for the night. It was a relief when they came across signs of civilisation; a wall of junk blocking their path.

There was no doubt that this was a recent structure, one built after Echo Syndrome had ravaged the planet. Perhaps it had started as a simple composite or chainlink fence—certainly both were evident for stretches of the wall—but over time it had been reinforced with logs and sheets of metal, then further still with old cars and fridges and furniture. Along the top, strewn like tinsel on a Christmas tree, was layer after layer of barbed wire.

Katie consulted their map.

"This is Old Free Town," she said. "It's right on the edge of Boss Clean's patch. Another day's walk and we should be beyond the cleansing squads for good."

"Wow, you're nearly a grown up!" said Bec.

Katie allowed herself a rare smile. "Yeah, it'll be nice not having to worry about that bastard bearing down on us, won't it? Still, let's not count our chickens."

Bec laughed her familiar laugh. After double-checking the map, the pair followed the junk wall back towards the road, settling in amongst a mass of vegetation as the town's main entryway loomed into view. Brick and wooden towers flanked a heavy metal gate, practically ready for a siege. Katie edged closer, crouching beneath a bush and peering through her binoculars. The guard tower was manned by a single sentry, an old man with grey flecking his beard and bags beneath his sunken eyes. She couldn't see from her angle whether he was armed, but he didn't have the sharp zeal of a Boss Clean fanatic.

A quick conversation should be safe.

"Wait here," she said to Bec. "I'm going to ask him about that shopping mall. Might be a good place to shelter for the night and stock up for the next leg of our journey."

She crawled out from the bush, but Bec grabbed her leg. "The shop?"

"Yeah. You remember the mall we saw?"

"Do you want anything from the shop?" Bec repeated, pointing to the road.

Her face was as composed as always, but there was panic in her eyes. Katie followed her gesture, heard the patrol car's engine before it rumbled into view. She ducked back into the vegetation, easing Bec further out of sight and pressing a finger to her lips. Bec didn't need telling twice. Her smile twitched as she held back nervous echoes.

From the bushes, Katie watched the armoured truck approach. Few vehicles actually used the roads anymore, and most that did were part of Boss Clean's cleansing squads. Any Echo they found would be executed on the spot. Katie held her breath, as if that would help them go unnoticed as the truck drew closer. The windscreen was cloudy with dust, and mud caked the truck's lower half, which Clean would never have permitted; this team must have been patrolling away from their base for days. They might have even fired the shots that Katie and Bec heard that morning. Katie's binoculars dug into her skin as her hands clenched into fists. A single thought dominated her mind.

Murderers.

The truck pulled up a short distance from the town entrance, revealing four cleansers sat in its open bed, wearing the usual gas masks and armoured coveralls. Another clambered out of the passenger seat, rifle slung casually over his shoulder, and sauntered up to the gates.

He pulled off his mask and shouted up to the guard tower, "This is Old Free Town, right?"

"We paid our dues to the boss last week," the sentry called down.

"We're not here for that. We've heard some disturbing rumours about your settlement. Rumours that you've been giving sanctuary to Echoes. Boss Clean wanted us to eat tonight?"

The cleanser froze, seeming surprised by his own statement. He frowned and cleared his throat.

"The boss wanted us to check it out," he said, stressing each word. "You know the penalty for harbouring Echoes. We wouldn't want to have to burn this place down."

To emphasise the threat, another cleanser hopped off the truck, hefting a flamethrower with an air of lazy power.

The sentry threw up his hands. "We have no Echoes here," he said. "We wouldn't risk that kind of infection. In fact, we reported one to you a month ago, remember?"

"Ah yes, the Echo who ran away and was curiously never found," sneered the cleanser. "If it's all the same to you, we'll come in and check around anyway. After all, we wouldn't want to what are we having to eat tonight?"

The cleanser covered his mouth, and the sentry leaned in.

"Pardon?"

"What are we having to eat tonight?" spat the cleanser, from between his fingers. He shook with the effort of keeping the words inside, but they kept coming. "What are- What are we having-"

Behind him, his fellow cleansers muttered and gestured. He turned to appeal to them, staggering forwards. They took a collective step back.

"No, it's not... What are we having to eat tonight? ...it's not like that. I'm not an Echo. What are we-ah! I'm just, I don't know what... What are- What are we having to eat tonight? No! I'm not an Echo!"

As he rambled, his panicked face settled into a loop, his muscles twitching through the same few seconds of motion over and over.

"I'm not... I'm not an Echo. I'm not an Echo. I'm... I'm not...an Echo. I'm not an Echo."

In one fluid motion, the cleanser nearest to him drew her pistol, raised it level with his head and pulled the trigger. The sound of the shot tore through the treeline. Katie yelped as his body twitched and collapsed, the muscles of his blood-splattered face still looping that final denial as his brain leaked from his skull. The woman snapped her eyes to the trees, and Katie barely managed to duck out of sight in time.

"Did you hear that?" she asked.

"Some animal, I think."

Katie reached down instinctively to take Bec's hand in hers, but her sister's fingers slipped away. Katie turned to find Bec pacing back and forth, humming an identical loop that somehow seemed louder with each repetition. Her movements were calm, almost leisurely, but Katie recognised her sister's state of panic and knew that spoken echoes were soon to follow.

"Bec," she whispered, "I need you to stay calm, okay?"

"Parker," came the cleanser's voice, "burn his body. The rest of you, comb the forest."

Katie grasped Bec's shoulders, struggling to hold her still as her sister's legs repeated the same few steps over and over. Katie shushed her, but the humming continued. Bec opened her mouth, drew in a breath, swallowed hard. She was losing the battle.

"Come on," whispered Katie, pulling her deeper into the vegetation.

At the treeline near the road, branches rustled, sending Katie's heart into a wild pounding. The cleansers could cover ground faster than Bec could. Their only hope was getting a good head start before their trail was found. Forcing her sister to keep moving, Katie forged a path directly away from the road. The recent rain helped and hindered in equal measure; the damp silenced any leaves they trampled, but the mud grasped at their feet with every step.

From beyond the trees, a voice reached them, distressingly close.

"Do those look like footprints to you?"

Bec's lip quivered. Her eyes bulged. Her body tensed.

Like a crumbling dam, the words burst from her mouth.

"The shop? The shop? The – the shop?"

"Through there!" cried the cleanser.

"We've got an Echo!" another called back to the truck.

"Do you want – the shop?" Bec stammered, panic in her eyes. Now that the words were out, nothing could hold them back. "Anything from – Do you want anything from the shop? The shop? The shop?"

Katie heaved on her sister's arm, sending her stumbling through the mud. Escape was no longer about guiding Bec through the trees; Katie had to drag her, with Bec barely able to keep herself upright. Her face, caught in a constant loop, was as composed as always, but her eyes were locked in a silent scream. Katie clamped a hand over her mouth, muffling the words as they tumbled out on repeat. It wasn't enough.

"Over there! Two of them!"

A crack punctured the air. Over Katie's shoulder, wet bark exploded from a tree trunk.

"Idiot!" barked a voice from behind. "Wait 'til you've got a clear shot!"

The cleansers would catch up in moments. Staggering behind an overgrown bush and straining to build up momentum, Katie hurled her arms in an arc, swinging Bec to one side. The sudden change in motion dragged her with it, and she just managed to stay standing. Now they were running directly away from Old Free Town, back in the direction they had come. It wasn't much, but if the cleansers hadn't seen their sudden turn, it would buy them a few moments. In the panic of their escape, there was only one place Katie could think to go.

For the next few minutes, the two of them kept up their pace, getting as close to a sprint as possible with Bec's limited movement. Katie's legs burned, and her breath shot out in splinters, but she didn't allow herself to rest. At last, she was rewarded by the trees parting ahead. The shopping complex rose into view. In moments, they would reach the cluttered car park, and the endless hiding spots that those rusting wrecks would provide.

"Nearly there," Katie gasped, squeezing Bec's hand and beckoning her onwards.

Stumbling down the hill, they struggled to keep their footing. The grass beneath their feet had turned to a mud slide from days of continuous rain, and Katie had to clutch Bec tight to keep her upright. Her sense of balance had been lost to her Echo Syndrome years ago.

By some miracle, they reached the bottom without falling, but a new danger presented itself as the grass ended in a sheer drop onto the tarmac below. It would be an easy hop for Katie, but Bec could barely manage stairs. A jump like this was nearly impossible.

"We have to."

Bec didn't respond, but her eyes spoke for her, a bright mix of panic and understanding.

"I've got you, Bec."

Katie grasped her sister's arm tight and stood as close to the edge as she dared. She whispered a countdown into Bec's ear, and just as the cleansers shouted out from the treeline, they stepped off the hill.

Katie landed hard on her feet, but Bec's fumbled landing dragged both of them to the ground. Bec landed hard on her arm. As Katie hauled her upright, blood already bloomed from beneath her torn sleeve.

"Are you okay?" she asked.

Bec staggered on ahead. "Do you want anything - anything from the shop?"

Glancing around and seeing no cleansers, Katie closed the gap between them. At the far end of the road that linked the car park to the dual-carriageway, a barricade of junk had been erected. It had the same desperate quality as the walls of Old Free Town, but it put comforting distance between them and the patrol truck that would likely soon be dispatched to finish the job.

If the cleansers from the woodland didn't catch up first.

Katie staggered into the car park and pulled Bec behind the nearest vehicle that would hide them from view of the hill.

"Do you want – do you want anything – do you want..." Bec said, muscles moving through the same looping motions with every word.

Katie shushed her and pressed herself against the car door, heart thumping. She closed her eyes and took a deep, calming breath. "Okay, Bec," she whispered, "stay here and stay quiet."

She reached over to squeeze her sister's hand, but her fingers closed over nothing.

"Bec?"

"Do you want anything – do you want anything…"

Katie looked over to see Bec disappearing behind a van. As she bolted to her feet in pursuit, she caught movement among the trees. Two figures emerged and her heart spasmed. The cleansers. Katie lurched to a stop, dropping to her knees and using the car as cover. She edged along its frame and peered around the van, but Bec had already wandered further into the car park, rambling to herself in a terrified loop.

"Bec," Katie hissed, as loudly as she dared. "Bec!"

Whether Bec heard her or not, it was impossible to tell. She was no longer in control of her body, merely a conduit for the echoes of her past actions. She'd wander aimlessly between the cars until she calmed down enough to regain control of her body. Or until the cleansers found her.

Katie couldn't let that happen, but charging out now to grab her would be as good as lighting a flare for their pursuers. She needed to take their attention elsewhere. Katie scrabbled for something—anything—to use as a distraction. To her side, just within reach, was an old glass bottle. Footsteps squelched down the hill overhead.

"Shit, which way did they go?"

"Over there, by the red sedan."

"Hah, easy shot. I've got this one."

Katie reached for the bottle. As her fingers opened to grasp it, they brushed against a wire so thin she could barely see it. She jerked her hand back as if she'd been electrocuted.

"Wait," said one of the cleansers. "Don't waste your ammo. We lost a whole squad in this car park not long back. If the traps don't get them, the snipers will."

"Snipers?" asked the other.

"Yeah. If they haven't seen us yet, they will if we open fire. Let's get outta here. They'll be dead in a few minutes tops."

"If you say so."

Disappointment dripped from his voice. Katie could sense how eager he had been to get the killing shot. As they hauled themselves back up the hill, Katie looked again to the wire she'd touched. It was strung taut between the wheel of her car and the one opposite. If she had pushed the wire just a little further, what manner of deadly mechanism would she have set off?

The cleansers hadn't been lying; this place must be filled with traps to keep out intruders.

Bec!

Casting a quick glance at the hill and seeing no cleansers there, Katie shot up and scanned the car park. Bec was halfway towards the mall by now, lost in her own past and unable to respond to her surroundings. Katie took an exaggerated step over the wire next to her and scrambled in Bec's direction, all the while scanning the ground and the surrounding vehicles for traps and triggers.

Narrowly avoiding what might have been a pressure plate, Katie found her way forward blocked by an overturned van. She crept around it, careful for any further tripwires, and as she rounded the front of the van, a dozen ravens burst up and scattered into the air. Katie yelped, covering her face by instinct, but the birds disappeared, their raucous caws echoing through the car park like choking laughter.

She saw the feast that had brought them here. A body sat crumpled against the nearest car, a jagged length of iron protruding from their chest. Pale, shrivelled hands clung tight to the spear, as if trying to pull it free even in death. Bile rose in Katie's throat and she turned away.

The corpse's armour and mask were familiar. This person had worked for Boss Clean. They had probably killed for him. But in death, they had saved an Echo's life, triggering a trap that would otherwise have left Bec impaled and dying. For that, at least, Katie was grateful.

The thought of Bec pushed Katie onwards, and she marched past the corpse and towards her sister's echoing voice. She was getting close now. After another turn, Bec was directly ahead, strolling towards an expanse of cardboard that carpeted the floor.

"Bec, stop!"

Katie charged to close the gap between them. As she reached out,

Bec stepped onto the wet cardboard in front of her. Thin wood splintered beneath it and Bec's foot sank into a hidden pit. Unable to react, her body toppled forward as she continued to walk. Katie lunged, grasping Bec's arm and bracing against the nearest car. She screamed as Bec's full weight yanked her muscles, but she managed to hold on.

"The shop," said Bec, as she teetered over oblivion, "the shop – the shop."

Teeth clenched painfully, Katie heaved against the car. Her feet threatened to slip along the wet ground. Bec swung back and forth. Still Katie pulled.

Then, as if a string had been cut, Bec's weight shifted and she flung towards Katie. Their bodies collided, and it was everything Katie could do to stop them collapsing in the other direction. In moments, she whipped Bec away from the pit and embraced her tighter than she ever had before.

"God, you scared me," she panted.

Silent tears streamed down Bec's docile face. Her body relaxed as the behaviour loop finally eased away, and she squeezed Katie's hand, letting out a long, shaking breath.

"Oh wow," came a voice to their side, "that was a close one!"

Katie spun to face the newcomer, shielding Bec with her body. She scanned the car park, but there was no one in sight.

"I thought she was going in the pit for sure," the voice continued. There was a strange, tinny quality to it, one that Katie hadn't heard for a long time.

She edged closer to the nearest car and peered through the broken window. A walkie-talkie hung from the rear-view mirror like an oversized air freshener, green light blinking as it crackled in and out of life. Katie thought about grabbing it, but the jagged glass and the nearby pit warded her off; this was likely another trap.

"I can hear you, you know," said the voice. "Well, you're not talking right now, but I *could* hear you if you were. I have microphones and stuff set up."

Katie and Bec shared a glance. Now that she had overcome her echoes, Bec didn't seem inclined to break the silence, and Katie still hadn't shaken the oppressive weight of danger that had nearly befallen them for speaking out loud. She had to fight to find her voice.

"What do you want?" she asked the walkie-talkie.

"Are you players?" it asked.

"Are we what?"

"Players. I don't want any more NPCs, unless you've got a special skill. What skills do you have? I could do with a builder. Are either of you builders?"

Katie looked around the car park again. Nothing but vehicles and litter. She turned her attention to the mall itself, taking out her binoculars and inspecting the windows. She could barely make anything out through the shutters, but there was nobody watching her that she could see. She turned her attention higher, scanning the top of the mall.

Armed guards strolled back and forth, seeming oblivious to the walkie-talkie's attempted interrogation. As Katie ran her binoculars across the building, however, she caught a glint of reflected light. A rifle scope, pointed in her direction.

Her heart jolted.

"Is that you aiming at us?" she asked, struggling to keep her voice steady for Bec's sake.

"Oh, you *are* a player!" chirped the walkie-talkie. The rifle scope disappeared. "NPCs never notice me. Do you want to trade? I have loads of rare items."

"No," said Bec, "I've had it for a while, actually."

Katie squeezed her hand and nodded. "We'll be careful," she whispered, before replying to their mysterious observer, "Yes, we'd like to trade if you can let us past your traps."

"Sure! From where you are at the moment, you need to turn back and take the left before the motorbike, then another left, step over the tripwire between the two silver cars and climb through the red car, take a right and go for fifty feet, then left, cross the plank, climb over the bike shed and approach the main doors stepping only on the yellow tiles."

Bec and Katie looked to one another, and Katie swallowed heavily.

"Could you repeat that?"

CHAPTER 3
AUNTIE BEC

The mall shutters groaned open like the jaws of a mythical beast woken from slumber. Standing in the entryway was a teenager, almost a child, looking them up and down with a curious expression. Sparse hairs dotted his chin, and his face held the red bloom of acne scars. A rifle was slung across his back, and his overburdened belt held a walkie-talkie on one hip and numerous spray cans on the other.

"Thank you so much for letting us in," said Katie, pulling Bec close and making for the door. "We just need a place to stay for the night, and-"

The boy silenced her with a hand.

"Open your inventory," he said.

"Open our...what?"

"Your inventory," he repeated, patting his pockets for emphasis. "I want to see what you've got."

Eager not to upset their potential host, Katie unslung her backpack. It squelched as it hit the floor. She rifled through, pulling out her bedroll, some spare clothes—now soaking wet—and the last scraps of their rations. The boy viewed them with disinterest before eying her coat. Katie took the hint and emptied her pockets, revealing her binoculars, a half-empty water bottle and the Renshaw poster.

"What's that?" he asked.

Katie hesitated, holding the poster close. Bec shuffled uneasily by her side.

"It's...a map we've been making," said Katie.

The boy leaned in for a better view, and Katie flashed him her sketched directions before folding it back up. In that moment, his face lit up as if he was seeing a long-lost relative.

"Oh, this is your quest marker," the boy said. "You really are players. Cool! I thought most of us had quit!"

He grinned and thrust out his hand.

"I'm Player One."

Katie blinked. "I'm sorry, did you say..."

"Player One. It's my tag." He gestured to the shopping complex rearing above them. "And this is my base. You can stay here if you'd like."

Katie hugged Bec with one arm, relief flooding through her and washing away the ever-present chill of their sodden clothes.

"Yes, please," she said. "That's very kind of you."

She shook Player One's hand and they made for the door. This time, the boy didn't stop them. As they passed, he fiddled with some controls on the inside of the entrance, lowering the shutters behind them.

Even more than the cars outside, this place was a relic of the past. Katie found herself in a wide foyer, surrounded by shops and empty kiosks on all sides, with another level above their heads. In front of them, dead escalators had become stairs, giving access to the elevated shops where bodies milled back and forth. Voices drifted like dust through the air. There must have been two dozen people scattered throughout the building, maybe more.

Katie swore under her breath. "This place is incredible."

"Yeah, it's pretty cool," said Player One, scanning the shops half-heartedly before turning back to the sisters. "What are your tags?"

"Tags? Oh, right. I'm Katie, and this is-"

"Hello," Bec said, beaming and crouching down. "I'm Auntie Bec."

"Auntie?" asked Player One, frowning. Katie pulled Bec upright and was about to make some excuse when the boy nodded. "I had an auntie. Come on, let me show you around."

He bounded ahead, but a cold drip ran the length of Katie's back and she shivered. Now that they were indoors, it was harder to ignore the all-encompassing wetness.

"I don't suppose there's somewhere we can dry off first?" she asked.

"Hmm?"

The boy looked them up and down, seeming to notice the state of their dripping, mud-drenched clothes for the first time.

"Oh, sure," he said. "There's shops full of outfits. Just take some of those."

He directed them to one of the nearby stores. Sure enough, through the dusty windows with their faded display boards, Katie could see row after row of clothing. A man stood in the shop's doorway, staring into the distance and uninterested in their approach. Katie moved to squeeze past him, but there wasn't enough space, and Bec would have trouble getting through without barging into him.

"Excuse me," said Katie.

The man didn't move. He seemed frozen in thought, completely unaware of being in their path. Player One pushed him aside and beckoned them onwards.

"Don't take it personally," he said. "He's an NPC. They bug out sometimes."

Bec followed the boy inside, but Katie lingered for a moment to watch this 'NPC'. He hadn't responded at all to being shoved, not even turning his head. He was an Echo for sure. Katie wondered if he spent every day standing in this spot.

Perhaps he was just resting.

She joined the others and found Player One striding down one of the aisles, flicking each coat hanger as he passed.

"You can take any of this crap. It's all women's stuff, so I don't need it."

"Yeah, I will, thanks," said Bec.

Katie chuckled, then added, "Very kind of you".

Player One nodded. He rocked on his feet as the three stared at one another. Bec began to hum.

"Do you mind giving us a bit of privacy?" Katie prompted, nodding to the door.

"I've seen boobs and stuff before," said the boy, shrugging. "I change the NPC outfits all the time, and some of them are women too."

"All the same," said Katie, frowning, "we're not your NPCs. So we would appreciate some privacy."

Player One sighed. "Whatever."

He slumped past the two of them and disappeared around the corner of the aisle. Katie listened until his footsteps disappeared out of the shop, then turned to Bec. Her sister was plucking at some of the clothes.

"Do you want anything from the shop?" asked Bec.

Katie laughed, and her sister's face twitched into a grin. "You actually meant it that time, didn't you?" said Katie, hugging Bec's shoulder and helping her to pick out some new jeans.

After double-checking to make sure that Player One wasn't lurking around the corner, Katie stripped Bec and dumped the muddy clothes into a wet pile. She used one of the uglier shirts to dry her sister off, taking particular care around her injured arm, getting it as clean as she could without water and a towel. After binding the wound with a light scarf, Katie set about pulling on the rest of the fresh clothes.

Bec helped as much as she could, but it was as much of a struggle as always. Still, it was worth it. Afterwards, she looked like a new woman. Her hair was still bedraggled, but now it looked more 'fresh out of the shower' than 'Return of the Bog Monster 3'.

With her sister sorted, Katie cleaned herself in the same manner, picking out mostly sensible clothes that would hold up during the journey ahead, although one particularly nice top found its way into the mix. Too good to leave behind.

As they stepped out of the store, Katie gave an exaggerated catwalk twirl. "Much better, don't you think?"

Player One stared at her blankly. "Okay, are we going, then?"

He led them up the static escalators to what had once been the mall's food court. Katie let him go first so that he wouldn't see how much she had to aid Bec's climb. At the top, he was too busy surveying his kingdom to pay them any mind.

Katie looked around. A handful of seats were still occupied, the source of the voices Katie had heard as she entered the building, but the fast food outlets on all sides had long since been abandoned. Now the food on offer was a stash of canned goods on the far table, with some drink cans and—Katie noted with a grimace—a plump, skinned rat.

As they moved further into the food court, a heavy, artificial scent descended like fog, bringing with it a medley of other smells lingering beneath the surface. Katie didn't notice how she'd wrinkled her nose until Player One glanced over his shoulder and frowned.

"Sorry," she said. "I don't mean to be rude."

"No, it's cool," he said, with a shrug. "I've not done the bucket quest for a while. It's a shit one."

He chuckled, and Katie followed suit, though she wasn't sure of the joke. Player One plucked a can from his belt and sprayed towards the ceiling. It wasn't paint he was carrying, but air freshener. The sharp, chemical odour settled down, masking the less pleasant smells and worming into Katie's nostrils like an aggressive bouquet of sickly-sweet roses.

"So this 'bucket quest,'" prompted Katie, and Player One gestured to the food court.

Beneath every Echo was a bucket, and as some of the people shifted, Katie noticed trousers around their ankles and holes cut into every seat. She wrinkled her nose again as the purpose of the buckets became clear; toilets for a dozen humans who were no longer capable of controlling their bowels.

These people might not have left their seats in five years, destined to repeat their day in the mall until their final breath. Bec pressed in close and turned away. How long until she was reduced to this?

Katie squeezed her hand and turned to Player One to change the subject.

"You help take care of the Echoes here then?" she asked. When the boy gave her a quizzical look, she recalled his term for them. "The NPCs, I mean. You and the other players look after them?"

He laughed.

"No other players. Just me! Well, there's a party who load in every now and then, and we do quests together, but mostly I sort the base myself."

"What about the guards patrolling the roof?"

"They're NPCs too. They came with the base. I've given them guns, but…" He shrugged. "They're not very good at shooting people."

Katie took a moment to really assess the boy. "How long has it just been you?"

"I dunno. Forever, I guess."

"-you've grown," said Bec, concentrating hard beneath her smiling face to choose the words she wanted. "How old are you now?"

"I dunno," he said again. "I gave myself a few birthdays all in one go, but then the cakes started to go off, so I stopped. I got to about twenty-three, I think, but my last real one was...ten? So I might be ten?"

His sparse chin-hairs suggested otherwise, but Katie smiled and nodded. For a while, the three of them were silent. Player One seemed lost in thought and Bec grinned emptily at people no one else could see. Looped conversations drifted from the nearby Echoes, punctuated by the occasional splat of a bucket getting fuller.

"Come on," said Player One eventually, "I'll show you a basic quest. Maybe you can help me out while you're both here."

He consulted an old cleaning rota on the wall, covered in so many overlapping scribbles that it was more ink than paper, then marched off to the far end of the mall. The floors were cleaner here, free of the dust and debris that peppered the rest of the building. Before reaching the final row of shops, Player One took a left turn through a staff-only door and beckoned the others over.

"This is one of the staff rooms," he said. "An easy quest to get you started."

Inside, a pale employee slouched in a chair, long hair covering half his face. In front of him was an empty plate on a bare table, and beneath his seat lay another bucket, this one mercifully empty. If the man noticed them enter, he didn't react. In turn, Player One didn't so much as glance at him, instead walking straight to the countertop and rummaging through the cupboards.

"I'm telling you, man, I'm gone," the man said, shaking his head at an empty chair opposite. "Fuck this place."

He reached down to his empty plate, scooped up the distant memory of a meal and shovelled it into his mouth, chewing the air with a sullen expression. Katie made her way to Player One's side, finding him wrestling with the pull-ring of a dusty tin.

"Do you need any help?"

"Yeah, pass me his plate."

Katie waited until the man had grabbed another imaginary handful and then slid the plate away from him. As she did, Bec gave a discordant hum. Katie looked up to find her sister watching the man intently, sad eyes lingering on his face. Katie followed Bec's gaze. Now that she looked closer, she could see the pus blooming from piercings in his earlobes and nose, little specks of grey in a bubble of green-tinted skin.

"His piercings have got infected," said Katie, passing Player One the plate. "When's the last time you took them out and cleaned them for him?"

Player One glanced over from his tin of pineapple rings.

"They come out?" he asked.

"You've... never cleaned them?" asked Katie.

He shrugged, poured out the pineapples and handed Katie the plate. "We'll do it later," he said. "Refill his mop bucket."

When Katie tried the tap, she found it had been disconnected. Instead, a length of hosepipe had been installed over the sink. The water that flowed out wasn't exactly filthy, but it had a faint tinge to it, and a few motes of dirt settled into the bucket as it poured. Rainwater, Katie guessed.

"This is quite impressive," she said, as the turned off the tap and handed Player One the now-filled bucket. "Did you make this?"

He shrugged and returned the bucket to the corner, carefully lining up the mop against black marks drawn onto the wall.

"It's been like that for a while," he said. "Anyway, we're done here. Next quest!"

With that, he marched out of the room. Bec hummed and followed him, and since she didn't want to leave her sister alone, Katie joined them. As she passed through the doorway, the Echo at the table said, "I'm handing in my notice tomorrow. I'm not spending another day sweeping these fucking floors."

Katie froze. She turned back, half-expecting him to be looking right at her. Of course, he was speaking to a long-vanished colleague. She opened her mouth, unsure what she was about to say.

"Come on!" called Player One, from the end of the corridor.

Katie swallowed hard and let the door swing shut, moving to catch up with Bec and placing an arm around her shoulder.

"So, that was one of the easier quests," he said. "I do that one most days, 'cause it's quick, y'know? But some of the others are harder to feed, so we'll do those now. They have these tube-like things, and you have to-"

He was interrupted by his walkie-talkie crackling to life.

"Player One, are you there? This is Dr Nadar."

He bounced on the spot, pulled the walkie-talkie from his belt and answered it with a grin.

"Loud and clear, Doc! I'll come and unlock the gate. There's two new players who have joined as well!"

The walkie-talkie fell silent.

"I see," it said at last. *"I look forward to meeting them."*

Whoever this Dr Nadar was, she made a terrible liar. Player One didn't seem to notice. He beckoned Katie and Bec to follow him as he sprinted down the wide foyer, turning and encouraging them to hurry. Not wanting to expose Bec's inability to run, Katie made a point to move just as slow as her sister, gawking at their surroundings as if stunned by it all.

It was only half-faked; the mall really was an unusual sight, with fully stocked shelves and displays advertising long-forgotten sales. Between it all, wherever she looked, Echoes milled around, stuck in a loop of browsing the store windows or holding conversations with partners who were no longer present. It was a miracle these people had survived so long.

If Boss Clean found out about this place...

"Over here!" called Player One.

He stood next to a fire escape, gesturing for them to join him as he hauled off the layers of chains that bound the door closed. When they clattered to the floor, he pushed the lever and swung open the door.

Five figures waited on the other side. In their centre, sporting a frayed and grimy lab coat, was a diminutive woman with sharp features. The four guards flanking her were much larger, armed and armoured in a manner that would rival even Boss Clean's crew. As the woman—evidently Dr Nadar—stepped in, the four guards followed, but only she acknowledged Katie and Bec, giving them both a curt nod. Player One sealed the exit behind them before bouncing up to the doctor like an excited puppy.

"I found them myself," he said. "They're players, both of them! What do you think?"

Nadar didn't spare him a glance, analysing the two sisters as if they were specimens under a microscope. Katie shifted under her gaze, feeling compelled to break the silence.

"I'm Katie, and my sister's Bec."

Nadar nodded. "I was about to congratulate you for making it through Player One's defences," she said, "but it appears you didn't get through entirely unscathed."

Katie looked over to Bec's poorly bandaged arm.

"We were hoping you might be able to help with that, actually," she said.

Nadar's mouth tightened. She turned to Player One. "We need water and food. Two of my guards will accompany you. You can bring mine to me once I've finished with the patient."

"A lot of the traps have been used up," said the boy. "We need to go out and reset-"

"Water and food," repeated Nadar. "We'll secure your perimeter when we're ready to do so."

He lingered, pouting slightly, but when two of Nadar's guards peeled away from the group and began to walk toward the food court, Player One perked up and followed.

"So, have you scored any sweet kills lately?" he asked, as they disappeared around the corner.

Nadar sighed and gestured for the sisters to join her on a nearby bench. Her remaining two guards talked quietly nearby, but Katie could tell they were paying close enough attention to jump in if anything put the doctor in danger. What had they experienced out there to make them so cautious? Even if they'd encountered Boss Clean's patrols, none of them were Echoes.

Were they?

"Let's see the damage," said Nadar.

Bec lifted her arm towards Katie, who removed the bandages and angled her sister's wound for Nadar to inspect.

"Hmm, nothing serious," said the doctor. "It'll just need cleaning and closing up so it can heal properly."

She pulled a small pack from one of her pockets and unfurled it.

"I'm going to need you to restrain her while I apply the stitches."

"Yeah, I will, thanks," said Bec, holding out her arm and smiling at the doctor.

"She understands what's happening," said Katie. "She'll hold still while you help her. It's me you have to worry about. I've never been good with needles and people poking around wounds."

She grimaced at the thought. Years ago, Bec had made fun of her squeamishness. Now, she couldn't produce enough words to do so.

Nadar pulled a small torch from her pocket and shined it in Bec's eyes, observing the response of her pupils.

"Are you telling me that she—that you, Bec—are cognizant? You know where you are? *When* you are?"

"Yeah, I will, thanks," said Bec.

"How long have you been experiencing symptoms of BHS? Days? Weeks?"

Bec hummed, turning to Katie to act as her voice.

"She got it early," said Katie. "Not sure exactly when it first started, but it's been at least five years."

Nadar pulled away and covered her mouth with both hands. "Years?" she hissed.

"Yeah. Is that...unusual?"

The doctor didn't respond immediately. She rummaged through her bag, pulling out all manner of equipment before clipping a pulse monitor to Bec's finger and pressing a stethoscope to her chest. At last, she seemed to recall the question.

"It's more than unusual. It's unprecedented. Extraordinary. Most Echoes don't last a year without dedicated care, and to retain awareness of surroundings after the first few months... This is exciting. This is *very* exciting."

Katie and Bec stared at one another. They'd had no idea that Bec's progress with the syndrome was anything unusual. Perhaps they had Boss Clean to thank for that. With his murderous cleansers prowling the territory, other Echoes weren't common, especially not those who'd had the effects for as long as Bec.

Nadar was practically giddy, taking measurements and jotting down notes. In the excitement of it all, Bec's wound seemed to have been forgotten, and with the bandages removed, it had started to bleed again. Katie paled and turned away.

"Doctor," she prompted, "her arm?"

"Right, right," said Nadar, finishing her latest annotations and putting her notebook aside. "I don't suppose you have any water so I can clean it properly?"

Katie rifled through her pockets for the water bottle she'd been saving. As she pulled it out, her folded poster came out with it, drifting to the floor. Nadar picked it up, but as she caught sight of the map, she hesitated.

"You're looking for the Renshaw Institute?" she asked.

"...Yes," said Katie, leaning over and taking the map. She tucked it away in an inside pocket.

"Why?" asked Nadar.

"I've had it for a while, actually," said Bec. Katie was about to elaborate, but the doctor seemed to understand.

"I see. Of course. You're after the cure."

"Yes," said Katie. "What else is there to hope for?"

"The Institute doesn't have a cure yet," said Nadar. "You realise that?"

"The poster said they needed volunteers," said Katie. "We were hoping to help. Plus, you know, get the hell away from Boss Clean and anyone else who wants to murder my sister."

Nadar nodded, sitting back and peering at Bec. "We'll be leaving here in a few days," she said. "We'd be happy to have you join us as volunteers."

"We?" said Katie. She turned to Bec, and it was clear that her sister had the same thought. "Are you..."

Nadar extended her hand.

"Dr VG Shantha Nadar, researcher and lead field worker of the Renshaw Institute. Pleasure to formally meet you."

Katie's chest tightened. After all this time, she'd never expected to simply *meet* a member of the Institute like this. It felt unreal.

"Is something wrong?" asked Nadar.

Now, Katie realised, was not the time to bring up the rumours she'd heard about the Institute's practices. She shook her head and accepted Nadar's hand.

"We've just been searching for you for so long..."

"I understand. In any case, it's time for me to properly dress Bec's injury. If you're as averse to blood as you suggested, I'd recommend you sit away for a while."

"Right, of course," said Katie, head swimming as she came to terms with this new development. She moved to a nearby bench and watched some of the other Echoes. After a few minutes, she eased the poster back out of her pocket and read it again.

'The Renshaw Institute needs you!'

It seemed they certainly did, more than Katie or Bec had even anticipated. Only, now that it was in their grasp, the rumours they had been told felt far more potent. Could the Institute really be trusted?

She was still staring at the poster when Bec appeared by her side, brandishing a newly bandaged arm and a smile.

"Look how you've grown," she said.

Nadar joined them, tucking her supplies back into her bag. Katie slid the poster away before the doctor looked up.

"That should hold," said Nadar. "We'll keep an eye on it for infection, but I'm not expecting any issues."

"Thank you, doctor," said Katie. She paused, then added; "I think you should know, there's an Echo in the staff room who has some infected piercings. They're pretty bad. I think you should take a look as soon as you can."

Nadar sighed. "The mop kid," she said. "I've not got around to him in a while. Usually my time's taken up by the lower-functioning Echoes. A lot of them can't feed themselves anymore, so I've had to insert a number of PEG tubes. I presume Player One hasn't been maintaining those properly either..."

Katie nodded. And waited.

Nadar was silent for a moment before spotting her expression. "Yes, okay," she said, less than enthused. "I'll see what I can do."

"Thank you."

They rejoined Player One and the other guards and shared a meal. Player One offered them some rat, which Katie didn't even want to think about, but Bec tried some and seemed to enjoy it. Probably more so for knowing how much it made Katie grimace.

Afterwards, Katie helped Nadar feed the other Echoes, then the group settled down in the foyer to sleep. Player One fetched camp beds and sleeping bags, making it one of the more comfortable nights Katie had experienced in months, and after Nadar promised him that the guards would help him reset his traps in the morning, he settled down and fell to sleep. Nadar followed suit, and after passing around a flask, so did her guards.

That left Katie and Bec to settle in on their own bed. Under Katie's arm, Bec drifted off almost instantly. The rhythm of her gentle breathing always soothed Katie, lulling her into deeper and deeper rest.

A light tickle brushed Katie's skin. A creeping spider that vanished whenever she focused on it, only to return once she put it out of her mind. It might have woken her, or she might never have fully left the drowsy twilight of half-sleep, but when she could no longer ignore the sensation and opened her eyes, the mall was in darkness. She rubbed her arm. Nothing there.

Bec slept soundly, and Katie could make out the distant figures of Echoes sleepwalking through the moonlit food court. On her own floor, the forms of Player One, Nadar and the guards lay across from her, barely perceptible in the darkness. As Katie's eyes drifted past the doctor, the phantom tickle returned.

Nadar was staring right at them. Right at Bec.

At first, Katie wondered if it was a coincidence, if Nadar had opened her eyes just as she looked over, but there was no acknowledgement on Nadar's part. She lay perfectly still, as if sleeping. She didn't turn or look away, not for as long as Katie stared back.

Katie tightened her grip on Bec.

CHAPTER 4
FROM THE SHOP

When they woke the next morning, the first thing Katie did was hug Bec close. Her sister's warmth was reassuring. After the strangeness of the night, Katie had half-expected Nadar to have stolen Bec away, carting her off to the Institute once Katie was asleep. Now that she was awake and Bec was still there, sleeping soundly, it all seemed ridiculous.

Had she dreamt Nadar's stare?

The doctor was already up and active, inspecting the PEG tubes of some Echoes while Player One handed tins of food to the bleary-eyed guards. When he saw Katie and Bec waking up, he grabbed two more and headed over to them.

"I'm not used to having so many players here," he said while they ate.

"I hope we're not intruding," said Katie.

He shrugged. "It's just weird."

Once they were fed, Nadar strode to the centre of the group, clapping once for their collective attention.

"Phil, Aaron," she said, "head out with Player One and reset as many of the traps as you can."

"Yes, Doc."

"Gaz, Jack, sweep the stores and check on the barricades."

"Can do."

"Is there anything we can do?" asked Katie.

"Bucket quest?" suggested Player One. Aaron snorted a laugh.

"You seem invested in the welfare of the…NPCs," said Nadar, ignoring the others. "I want to check on your sister's arm, and since you don't like seeing blood, I suggest you explore a little, see if there are any other medical issues that might require my attention."

Katie nodded. The group split up as Nadar had directed. Katie was reluctant to leave Bec's side, but her sister was at ease in Nadar's company, chatting and humming away as though she expected the doctor to understand her. Katie peeled away from the pair once Nadar started to inspect the bandages, and she spent the morning checking in on a dozen Echoes dotted around the mall, some wandering the shelves, some sat in the food court, and one who was stuck in a loop of stuffing some item that no longer existed into her empty bag. They were gaunt overall, with ashen faces and heavy bags under their eyes, but Katie found nothing alarming to report back to the doctor.

Eventually, she found herself in the same store as the two guards who had been sent to check the barricades. She was about to greet them when she realised they were ignoring the barricade completely, and instead inspecting the shelves. The one Nadar had called Gaz picked up two cans, considered them both, then tucked them into his satchel and reached for another.

"What are you doing?" Katie asked.

He turned and peered over his shoulder. Seeing that she was alone, he grinned and gave a half-shrug.

"It's only a few cans," he said.

The other guard, Jack, stepped out from the next aisle, his satchel similarly full.

Katie grimaced at them. "You're seriously stealing from a child who's looking after dozens of vulnerable adults?"

Gaz's smile dropped. "You've not been here long, have you?" he asked, tucking the third can into his pocket without breaking eye-contact. "The only reason he cares for these Echoes is that he thinks he's in a fucking video game. He's delusional."

"So you're stealing from a *sick* child," Katie sneered.

"Ask him where the missing Echoes go," said Jack. "He takes real good care of those ones."

They both laughed.

"At least tell him," said Katie. "Don't just take it."

"She's right, Gaz," said Jack, gesturing to the nearly full shelves. "We need to tell him. Otherwise he'd never figure out it was missing."

They laughed again. Katie turned in disgust and marched away. Gaz stopped laughing. She felt his gaze drilling into her until she rounded the corner and left them to their theft. Part of her wanted to find Nadar right now and tell her what they were up to, but another part of her never wanted it to come up again. She didn't want to find out whether Nadar already knew. Perhaps that was the only reason they came here—to cart away supplies while Player One was distracted outside.

Lost in her thoughts, Katie found herself beneath the food court. The man from the staffroom was out today, mopping the floor with a sullen expression that matched her own. She softened as she approached him.

"The doctor's going to look at your piercings," said Katie, though she doubted he could hear. Then, without really knowing why, she added, "You're doing a great job with the cleaning. Thank you."

He sniffed and dunked his mop back into the bucket. Was that acknowledgement? Probably not. Nadar seemed convinced that only Bec was aware of her surroundings. Still, it was hard for her to believe that there wasn't a thinking, feeling human being inside there somewhere.

As she passed, she touched his arm and smiled, then made her way through the nearby doors. Player One hadn't shown her around this area yesterday, and with his oversight of the infected piercings, she could easily imagine that some poor, forgotten Echo was wandering around, waiting for assistance.

Rounding the corridor, Katie was met with a set of double doors. A dozen car air fresheners dangled from the doorframe, hung like garlic to ward off the undead. They filled the room with a pungent clash of odours.

There was something else. A smell that wasn't emanating from the paper trees and emojis. It put her in mind of the food court buckets, but the underlying smell was different here. Sharper. More unsettling. Katie checked she was still alone, then pushed through the door and stepped into the corridor beyond.

The stench hit her like a physical force. Spoiled food. Rotten meat. Stains smeared the floor and the air was thick with flies. She should have turned back, but as disgust fought with curiosity, curiosity won. She took a deep breath, covered her mouth and moved towards the end of the corridor, waving away the flies as she walked.

Where the corridor ended, a door marked 'DELIVERIES' stood ajar. Perhaps the stench was a shipment of meat that had never been unloaded, or freezers that had long since lost their chill. She steeled herself for the smell to get worse and pushed open the door, peering down the stairs into a large, concrete basement.

Nothing could have prepared her for what lay inside.

Bodies. Piles upon piles of decomposing bodies. The floor was covered with them, the stairs thick with old blood. Men. Women. Children. The heaps of limbs and torsos writhed as she watched, brought to ghoulish life by the carpet of flies that claimed every inch of their flesh. The hungry buzz of a thousand wings filled the air. Gaunt faces with glassy eyes appeared and vanished under the constant motion of the swarming insects.

Katie staggered back, reeling. Her eyes blurred and the sting of vomit bubbled up her throat. She heaved and staggered, shaking her head as though that might wipe the evil sight from her mind.

A hand grasped her shoulder.

She screamed.

"Katie, it's me!" said Dr Nadar, turning her away from the basement doors. The doctor looked her square in the eyes, re-establishing a link to the living world. Katie babbled and stammered, tears streaming down her cheeks. Nadar shushed her. "Come on, let's go."

Katie clung to the doctor and half-ran from the basement, retching and sobbing as she went. As they passed beneath the air fresheners, Katie staggered to a halt and gestured back down the corridor.

"They... They're dead!"

"Yes," said Nadar.

"Player One, he's been... He's..."

"Yes, I know."

"Did you see? Did you see down there?"

"The bodies, I know. I wish I hadn't, but yes, I've seen them."

Katie paused, wiping her face. She pulled out of Nadar's grip. "You knew about this?"

"We logged every patient when we first gained access to the building. Each subsequent visit, we found fewer patients. By the time we worked out what was happening to them, we'd already established a process that was reliant on Player One's compliance. We couldn't remove him from the system without putting everything at risk."

Katie fought back a retch. She wiped furious tears from her eyes with trembling hands. "So you just let him kill people? Because it's inconvenient to stop him?"

"Katie, please. I know it's horrible. We don't like it either. But we physically do not have the capacity to care for all of these Echoes in our facility. If we took them all, half would starve. They'd be sleeping in corridors. Infection would run rampant. Here, they're fed, they're protected. A few are lost, yes, but not as many as would die if we removed Player One from the picture."

"Then care for them *here*!"

Nadar threw up her hands. "With what force, Katie? What army of carers and nurses would come to our aid?"

The question hung in the air like the stench from below.

"You might think the Institute is powerful," Nadar said, "but in reality we're stretched to breaking point. This isn't the only location my team is attached to. If we stay here long enough to look after each and every Echo, then more will suffer from our lack of attention elsewhere. The best we can do is look after their immediate needs, help Player One to secure the perimeter, and take a few at a time back to our facility."

Katie leaned against the wall, sliding down until she sat on her heels. She shook her head, blinked tears from her eyes and turned again to the basement door.

"How many?" she breathed. "How many have died so you can take your time and save a few pennies?"

Nadar hissed out a sigh, and her mouth became a thin line. "Forty-seven," she said. "Don't think I haven't counted."

"I can't... I can't stay here..." said Katie. "I can't see him again. I can't let him near Bec. Oh god, where's Bec?"

"She's safe," said Nadar. "I left her in one of the clothes shops. I'm not going to let him hurt her, okay? Just put it from your mind as best you can, and tomorrow you'll leave with us and never have to see him again."

"I can't..."

"You can. You must. If you want to keep Bec safe, don't antagonise Player One. Leave him to us."

Katie laughed. It was the hollowest, bitterest laugh that had ever left her mouth. Nadar straightened, waited to see if Katie had anything else to say. When she didn't, Nadar left.

For a long time, Katie sat pressed against the wall, alternating between heaving and sobbing. She could have remained there forever, if not for Bec. She couldn't risk leaving her sister alone with that murderer for a second. She wouldn't leave Bec's side until they were far away from this wretched place. She staggered upright, wiped her face and marched out to the storefronts.

She passed the sullen cleaner on her way. She stopped to grasp his arm, squeezing tight and feeling his heartbeat. He was sick, but he was human. All of the Echoes were.

"I'm going to get you out of here," she whispered.

He didn't respond; not to her touch, not to her words. He simply kept mopping, as he must have done a thousand times before.

Parting from him, Katie jogged through the mall until she caught sight of Bec browsing in one of the stores. She almost knocked her sister over with her embrace, squeezing her tight and not wanting to let go.

"Wow, you're nearly a grown up!" said Bec, in surprise. Katie breathed in to hold back her tears, then cupped Bec's chin and looked directly into her sister's eyes.

"We're leaving tonight," she whispered. "And we're bringing as many of these Echoes as we can."

Bec's face shifted into an easy smile, but her eyes were hard and focused. She didn't need to know why. She knew Katie was serious, and that was enough for her. One day Katie would explain what she found in that basement, but there was no need to burden Bec with it now. Besides, she doubted she could put it into words if she tried.

They were interrupted by gunshots from outside.

By the time Katie reached the shop entrance, Gaz and Jack were by Nadar's side, weapons drawn. The doctor had her walkie-talkie at her lips.

"Player One?" she barked. "What's happening? Phil, Aaron, are you under fire? What's the situation?"

Another gunshot. The silence stretched, until finally Nadar got a reply.

"Open the front."

"Phil, what happened?"

"Open the front."

Nadar nodded to her guards, who rushed off to the mall entrance. They returned less than a minute later with Phil—the other guard was nowhere to be seen—and Player One, rifle in hand. Bile rose in Katie's throat at the sight of him. Knowing what the boy was capable of, he seemed older. Wilder. Even now, with tension thick in the air, his eyes were ablaze with excitement.

"What happened out there?" demanded Nadar.

"It was an ambush!" said Player One. "I wanted to stay and fight, but-"

"They got Aaron!" growled Phil, cutting the boy off. "The bastards were waiting for us. They split us up and they got him."

"*Who* got him?" asked Nadar.

"I don't know! Some gang, maybe? They had masks and an armoured truck."

"There's a lot of them," said Player One. "They've raided before."

"Boss Clean," Katie heard herself say. The others turned to her. She hadn't intended to speak at all, but with them all watching her, the words tumbled out. "He's the biggest ganglord in this territory. We're only here because his cleansers murder every Echo they find. They think it's a disease—contagious. Yesterday they nearly killed us both."

Phil turned white with fury, and Nadar's expression tightened. When she spoke, each word was crafted with precision. "Is the perimeter secure?"

"Fuck if I know," said Phil. "Listen, when we fell back, Aaron was still alive. They carted him off as a prisoner or something. If we go now maybe we can catch them!"

"Absolutely not," said Nadar.

"We can't just leave him!"

"Phil, I'm sorry, but there's nothing we can do. We can barely protect the Institute as it is. If we lost you three as well, thugs like this Boss Clean character could waltz in and destroy everything we've worked for. We need to cut our losses and evacuate."

"Aaron isn't a loss," Phil growled.

Nadar raised a hand. "We need to take as many supplies as we can, and any Echo who can walk," she said. "We leave within the hour."

"What about those that can't walk?" asked Katie.

Nadar turned to her, and for a fleeting moment, her face softened. "We'll see what we can do," she said. "Phil, Player One, rig the front with tripwires and explosives. We won't need that entrance again."

Player One perked up at the mention of explosives, but Phil glowered. He looked about to speak, but his lips never parted. Nadar watched him.

"Phil?" she said.

"Yes, doctor," he intoned, then turned on his heels and marched to the mall entrance. Player One skipped after him, pausing only to pick up some canisters of propane stashed near an abandoned kiosk.

The rest set to work immediately. Nadar focused on gathering Echoes, while Katie and the guards packed supplies for the journey. They met Katie's eyes while they worked, as if daring her to speak up about their earlier theft. She ignored them. This was no time to be creating more division.

Bec did what she could, bringing backpacks one at a time from a nearby camping shop. It was slow work, but it let the others focus on filling the packs with necessary supplies. Plus, it kept her mind on the task, preventing her from falling into an echo-riddled panic.

Before long, a pile of over a dozen packs lay in the foyer, and when Nadar returned, they were distributed. Each Echo capable of walking was given a backpack full of supplies, giving them the appearance of human camels. The sullen cleaner, Katie was pleased to see, was among them.

"It'll be hard work," said Nadar. "If this gang turns up while we're guiding them to the van, we might have to leave some behind. Do you all understand that?"

The guards nodded.

Nadar turned to Katie. "You understand that, Katie?"

Katie grit her teeth, and nodded. It felt dirty and cowardly, but it was true. Even though these Echoes could walk, they might choose to stop at any time, or try to sit in a chair that only they could see. With no time limit, they could be led across a car park easily enough, but with the threat of Boss Clean bearing down on them?

They just had to save as many as they could.

"We have company!" called Gaz.

They gathered by the shuttered entrance, peering through the gaps to the car park beyond. No sooner had Katie looked out than the barricade at the far end of the road exploded. An armoured truck rammed through, sending wood and barbed wire flying. The truck flagged for a moment under the wreckage, but it powered through. More vehicles followed, each one widening the hole. The convoy filled the road leading to the car park. Three trucks rode up front, with two more bringing up the rear, all flanking a lorry and an armoured car. Katie counted dozens of soldiers among them, with more drifting out of the forest beyond. This had to be every cleansing squad at Boss Clean's command.

"Fuck," said Jack. That one word captured Katie's sentiments perfectly.

Once the convoy had come to a halt, the door to the armoured car opened. A mountain of a man emerged and, with the help of several cleansers, clambered onto the nearest truck's roof. A clear visor covered his face, with a gas mask beneath it. The rest of his body was wrapped tight in a surgical gown and gloves that barely fit over his enormous form.

Bec paced back and forth, babbling to herself. "Want anything...anything from the...want anything..."

"What's her problem?" hissed Gaz.

"The shop...anything from the...anything from the shop...from the shop..."

Katie swallowed back her fear. "It's him," she said.

Boss Clean raised a megaphone, speaking through a receiver built into his mask. His booming voice tore across the car park, lashing against the shuttered door like a tidal wave.

"Greetings, doctor. We have learned much of you from our mutual friend. We know the purpose of this mausoleum to the old life. We know that you harbour the infected. I am a reasonable man. Perhaps you were unaware of the cleansing. I am willing to forgive your ignorance. But continued propagation of this disease cannot be tolerated. We have the numbers to overwhelm your defences, if it comes to that. I hope it will not. Needless bloodshed disappoints me. So I offer you this: Disable your defences, give up peacefully, and all uninfected among you may go free."

"He's lying!" said Katie. "He'll kill every Echo here and anyone who had contact with them!"

"But Baccslau-Horvitz Syndrome isn't contagious," said Nadar, as though her conviction alone could shield them from Boss Clean's wrath.

"He doesn't believe that!" said Katie, grasping Bec close and guiding her away. "He doesn't care! We need to get the Echoes and leave. Now!"

"You can't quit now," said Player One. "It's just getting good."

"My patience is limited," came Boss Clean's voice. *"Disable your defences. Emerge with your hands in the air. Or be cleansed."*

Nadar turned from Katie to her guards and back again. She clenched her fists. And nodded. The guards shouldered their backpacks, gathered the Echoes who had wandered away from the group, and began to herd them away.

"Open your doors, doctor," demanded Boss Clean. *"Perhaps you doubt the power of my cleansing? If you insist, we may begin."*

Nadar paused, glancing at the shutters. A gunshot punctured the air, followed by a dull thump from above. Katie shielded Bec with her body. A second shot rang out. A second thump.

"My sentries!" cried Player One.

He pulled the rifle from his back and darted to the stairwell. Nadar made to go after him, but Katie blocked her path.

"Let him go," she said. "We need to focus on getting the others out of here alive."

"Right..." said Nadar, and then, with more resolve, "Right."

They continued to shepherd the train of bodies through the mall. As they went, Katie spotted movement through the shuttered windows of the nearby stores. She slowed for a moment to work out what she was seeing, and her stomach turned. The cleansers had backed their lorry onto the trapped car park, and were unloading its contents towards the main entrance.

Sheep.

The animals flocked out, directed by the cleansers into the car park. They trotted in, and Katie thought back to the tripwires and pits that she and Bec had faced. Evidently, the cleansers didn't plan on stumbling into the traps themselves.

"Come on," said Jack, jostling Katie to continue.

They reached the doors as the first explosion shook the building. Katie grabbed onto Bec like a life raft, and a ripple ran through the group which even the other Echoes seemed to sense. Nadar hesitated, but the guards pushed on ahead.

"It's what the explosives are for," said Gaz. "Keep moving."

As they reached the side door, Gaz tore off the chains. He turned back to inspect the group, rifle at the ready.

"There's a path through the traps," he said. "We should be able to lead the Echoes through it."

"What if they're waiting for us out there?" asked Katie.

"I hope they are," said Phil. "I'll fucking kill 'em."

"Stick with me, Bec," said Nadar, standing just ahead. "Okay?"

Bec gave no cohesive reply, still stuck in her panicked echo loop. Another explosion rumbled out, this one followed by gunshots. They seemed to come from the roof. Player One was finally getting the battle he wanted.

"Now!" shouted Gaz.

He kicked open the door and swung out, firing three shots before he'd left the doorway. Phil followed, and then the herd of Echoes trickled out. Katie's heart thumped, hands slick with sweat. She didn't want to walk out into that battlefield, but there was no other way. Boss Clean was going to get inside sooner or later, and he wouldn't be taking prisoners.

Nadar, Bec and Katie approached the door.

"Run for the van," said Nadar. Then she was out.

Katie grasped Bec's hand and pulled her close. "I love you, Bec."

"The shop – the shop – the shop – the shop…"

A shove from behind pushed them both onwards, possibly Jack, possibly a bumbling Echo. Either way, there was nothing else for it. They had to go.

Katie ducked through the door, pulling Bec with her. The scene was hectic—Echoes milling between old cars as the Institute guards tried to herd them onwards, smoke drifting from the mall's entrance, shouts and animal cries filling the air—but it didn't take long for Katie to lock onto their target. Halfway through the car park, one van stood apart from the rest, lacking the rust and damage of the other vehicles. She just had to reach it.

Bec just had to reach it.

Seeing Nadar ahead, Katie pulled Bec close and pushed her onwards.

"Keep going," she told her sister. "Follow the doctor!"

Bullets whizzed overhead, some striking the nearby cars. Katie ducked and cried out, but she carried on moving. Ahead, one of the guards returned fire. A door to the van opened and someone clambered inside. A scream rang out. Boss Clean's voice boomed through his megaphone, but whether he was issuing threats or orders, Katie couldn't tell.

She stumbled and fell against a car door, pausing to catch her breath. She glanced behind, finding the remaining Echoes lagging and wandering away. One slowed to a casual stroll and looked in her direction. His mouth opened. *Bang.* Red mist burst from his chest. His face twitched as though it were about to crumple in pain, then it settled on a frown. He staggered. Turned to Katie.

"I've been waiting all day," he said. "I didn't think...all day...I didn't...I didn't think..."

Whatever he didn't think, Katie never found out. He teetered, lost balance and fell face-first, still muttering into the blood pooling from his punctured chest.

"He's been shot!" Katie cried out to the nearest guard.

The man turned, spotted the dying Echo and grunted. Ducking low, he scurried back to where the man had fallen and wrenched free his bulging backpack. Then he slung it over his own shoulder and continued his charge towards the van.

"No!" screamed Katie. "Help him!"

Her words were drowned out by shouted orders, followed by another explosion and the pained bleats of a dying sheep. Katie ducked behind the nearest car. It would only take her a few seconds to reach the man, but at the edge of the car park the first Echoes were being bundled into the van. Bec was close, almost within reach of the guard who had taken the backpack, ready to be driven to safety. But she stopped and turned. Her panicked eyes locked onto Katie.

"The shop..." she said, repeating words so engrained on each of their memories that Katie could hear them even over the deranged cacophony of battle. "The shop...the shop...the shop..."

In that moment, Katie remembered Nadar's warning. Some may be left behind. There was nothing else Katie could do for him. She needed to get Bec to safety. She charged over to her sister, and had nearly closed the gap when the first of the van's doors was yanked shut.

"Don't leave her!" cried Nadar from within. "Get the Echo! Get Bec!"

The two guards nearest the doors lurched into action, each grasping one of Bec's arms and hauling her up. The instant her feet left the ground, the van's engine rumbled and the vehicle began to drive away. Nadar was too busy tucking Bec away and strapping her in to notice that Katie wasn't yet on board.

"Wait!" Katie called.

The guards looked at her, offering no help as the van picked up speed. A shot rang out in the distance. One of Boss Clean's soldiers shouted, but the words were lost in the tumbling panic within Katie's head. They couldn't take Bec away from her!

"Doctor, please!" she cried.

Nadar turned. She marched between her guards, stood at the vehicle's edge, and reached out her hand. Katie pushed herself with every ounce of strength she had left, pounding the tarmac until her legs were ablaze with agony, until her heart was ready to burst through her chest. She tried to grasp Nadar's fingers, but the woman was slipping away.

Bec was slipping away.

With a final, desperate leap, Katie lunged for the doctor's outstretched hand. Their fingers brushed together. For the briefest moment, Nadar's expression flickered. She flinched back, as though Katie were filthy. Infectious. Dangerous.

Then, just as the void between them was becoming impassable, the doctor's face returned to firm resolve, and she leapt to grasp Katie as firmly as she could. The guards either side of her latched on, preventing Nadar from being pulled out of the van, and the three of them hauled Katie inside. She collapsed onto the cold, metal floor. For a moment, she lay panting, heart pounding in her throat, then she scrambled over to Bec and latched on as tightly as she could.

She was safe.

The van picked up speed, and the frenzied chorus of explosions and gunshots drifted into the distance. Soon, the only sound was the rumbling of the van's engine and the cyclical babbling of half a dozen Echoes.

It was nightfall when they finally stopped driving. The van pulled up along a country lane, and two of the guards hopped out to move aside a barricade of vegetation. The van slipped through and then waited for the barricade to be built back up, masking their path from anyone who might be following.

Another few minutes' travel led them to an old farmhouse. The years hadn't been kind, its walls choked with weeds and most of its windows shattered, but Katie and Bec had camped in worse. Gaz banged on the side of the van, waking up some of the passengers who had dozed off on the journey.

"Everyone out," he said, swinging open the doors.

Katie didn't have the energy to respond. She and Nadar helped Bec clamber out, then she slouched to the side and let the guards take over unloading the other Echoes.

Bec hummed for her attention.

"The shop?" she said, lifting an arm to the horizon. Beyond the trees, an orange bloom lit the night's sky; a sunrise without a sun. Katie's gut twisted. She was under no illusions about the source of the glow.

Boss Clean had won. The shopping centre was being cleansed.

"Come on," she whispered to Bec, guiding her away from the awful scene and following the others inside.

The interior of the farmhouse was as decrepit as the outside. In the centre of the building, however, locked away behind padlocks and boarded windows, was a single room that looked almost welcoming. The floor was clear of debris, two long sofas offered comfortable—if dusty—seating, and a stack of supplies lay beside a desk in the corner.

As the group milled inside, Katie realised that what she had first mistaken for rugs along the floor were in fact bed rolls.

"You set this place up?" asked Katie.

"That's right," said Nadar. "It's one of our outposts. It may be too dangerous now though. If this 'Boss Clean' has sent his people after us, we can't risk camping so close."

She blew out a long breath and rubbed her forehead. It was the frailest she had looked since Katie had met her.

"That's tomorrow's problem," she sighed. "For now we all need to rest. Another long journey begins in the morning."

The guards settled in with the ease of teenagers returning home, spreading themselves out on the sofas and unloading their baggage. The Echoes seemed content with their new surroundings, if indeed any of them were aware of the change. One sat next to a guard and had a one-sided conversation about which film to see that evening, while another browsed the wallpaper with the intensity of a keen shopper seeking a bargain. Only Katie and Bec were left hovering near the door, feeling out of place.

Beside them, Gaz fished a can from his backpack, then swore under his breath.

"No ring-pull," he grunted, displaying its smooth top as evidence before unsheathing his combat knife.

He made easy work of the lid, cutting and prying it open with his blade. Katie couldn't imagine a ring-pull would have been much quicker. When he was finished, he set his knife on the desk and dug into his meal with grimy fingers.

Following his lead, Katie fished out some food from her own backpack and helped Bec to eat, before tucking into some of the supplies herself. She hadn't realised how hungry she was until she began, finishing off two tins and splitting a third with Bec. The stress of the last few days had clearly taken its toll. As she placed the third empty tin to one side, she looked up to find Phil watching her with an expression she couldn't place.

"Oh, sorry," she said. "Did you want some?"

He shook his head.

For the next hour, Katie stayed with Bec at the desk, ensuring her sister was comfortable and her wound hadn't reopened in the madness of the car park escape. It was only after checking for spare bandages in her backpack that Katie noticed how quiet the room was. The four Institute members were huddled in the far corner, deep in a hushed discussion. Katie could only make out a few words, all coming from the guards.

"...mistake..."

"...seen too much..."

"...shouldn't have brought her here..."

For most of the conversation, Nadar didn't reply. She let the guards speak, then, once they had finished, she nodded just once.

Jack shared a look with the others, then strode across the room.

Towards Katie.

"Can you join me outside for a second?" he said.

"Erm...why?" Katie asked.

"I need your help with something."

Katie looked over to Nadar. The doctor was staring hard at the floor.

"Dr Nadar," said Katie, "what's this about?"

Nadar rubbed her forehead. "Just go outside with him," she said.

Bec moved to stand up, but Jack pushed her back down.

"Not you," he said.

"No, I've had it for a while, actually," said Bec, attempting to rise again. Jack gestured for Gaz to come over.

"If she wants to come with me, she can," said Katie. "I'm not leaving her."

"Yes, you are," Jack snapped. "We're not a fucking hotel. Now step outside while you still can."

Katie backed away, bumping into another of the Echoes. "No," she said. "I'm not going anywhere with you."

"It wasn't an offer," he said.

"No."

"I won't tell you again."

"I'm not going."

He reached for his pistol.

That was when Bec grabbed Gaz's knife from the desk. She moved in a sudden, jerking motion, one that was utterly unfamiliar to Katie. She must have cobbled together a dozen of her usual movements, twisting painfully to navigate her palm onto the blade's handle, then clenching tight. Gaz turned with his firearm drawn.

"Don't hurt her!" Katie and Nadar cried in unison.

The man hesitated. As he did, Bec turned the knife, razor tip angled straight at herself. This time, Katie recognised the motion. She saw it every time Bec ate. Her sister parted her teeth, moved her hand to her lips, and brought the blade to rest against the roof of her mouth. Then she froze.

Katie's heart raced. Her face burned. She slowly raised her hands and was about to speak, but Nadar beat her to it.

"Don't do anything stupid, Bec. I know you can hear me. I know you know what you're doing. Stop. Before you get hurt."

"Who cares if she -" started Gaz, but Nadar silenced him with a hiss.

"Bec," said Katie, taking a step towards her sister. The guards shifted, but under Nadar's glare they didn't dare move. "Don't do this. I'd do anything to keep you safe. If I have to go so you can get that safety, then I will. Don't worry about me."

"Listen to her, Bec," said Nadar. "The Institute can protect you. And you'll be helping so many people. You could be the one who finds us a cure! An end to Baccslau-Horvitz Syndrome. An end to your life as an Echo. Just put. Down. The knife."

A silent tear rolled down Bec's passive face. Her lip twitched, and Katie knew how hard her sister must be fighting to keep her echoes in check. If she couldn't use her voice, Katie had to speak for the both of them. She swallowed hard and found her words.

"Do you want us to go?" she breathed. Then, louder, "Do you want us to walk out of here and not come back?"

"You can't," said Nadar, but none of them moved. Even the other Echoes were silent, as if somewhere deep beneath the haze, they sensed the tension in the air.

Without moving any other part of her face, Bec turned her eyes to Katie. They screamed out her answer. Katie nodded.

"If you try to stop us," she said to Nadar, voice cracking as she held back a sob, "she'll push the knife in." The doctor opened her mouth, but Katie continued. "It's not a threat. I wouldn't use my sister's life as a threat. It's a fact. I don't want her to do it, but she will if any of you move a muscle. You said it yourself. She may be the hope for a cure. Don't let that hope die."

Nadar's mouth was a thin line of fury, and Gaz's eyes burned with hate, but they remained static as Katie stumbled back, opened the door and guided Bec through it. She didn't take her eyes off them until Bec was stepping out of the farmhouse, and then Katie eased the door closed, sensing the guards ready to pounce.

The door clicked shut.

Katie ran.

Bec dropped the knife as they passed the van, and the echoes she had been holding back burst out into the night. If Nadar's guards were following them, it wouldn't be hard to stay on their track, even in the darkness. That thought spurred Katie on, and she ran until her head was spinning, carrying Bec more than guiding her as they ploughed through the undergrowth.

The orange haze of the sky was dimmer now, but the fire still raged, and Katie used its light to guide them. The shopping mall was the last place she wanted to return to, but the glow was enough to reveal the outline of obstacles ahead. Once Katie had put the haze onto one side of her, it acted as a compass, guiding them, ensuring they didn't get muddled in the escape and start back towards the farmhouse.

There was no plan. No choice of camping spot. They ran until they couldn't run anymore, then collapsed into the nearest bush. Katie lay frozen for a long time, desperately trying to supress her gasping and listen for approaching footsteps.

Nothing. Only faint wind, hoots of night creatures, and—possibly—the slightest hint of crackling fire.

It must have been her imagination. The mall was miles away. The sound couldn't have reached her. Could it?

Impossible or not, the fire stayed with her, growing in her mind until it consumed her dreams.

Dreams of a basement, and Bec burning inside.

CHAPTER 5
I WILL

Katie woke to a pebble bouncing off her forehead. She jolted upright, blurry eyes focusing on a crouching figure several meters away.

The guards had found them!

Then the woman spoke, her voice muffled beneath her mask. Katie's mind whirred, and she realised it wasn't anyone from the Institute. It was one of Boss Clean's cleansers.

The one who had shot her colleague. Ordered the others to chase Katie and Bec through the woods.

"Are you listening?" she snapped, and Katie forced the fog of morning to clear from her mind. She shook Bec's arm and felt her sister shift. Bec was already awake.

"You're here to kill us," Katie said. It wasn't a question.

"Maybe, yeah," said the cleanser. "But it's not a done deal. I'm actually here to make an offer."

Katie hesitated. A bulky shape distorted the cleanser's coat along one side of her belt. Katie would bet good money it was a pistol. The same one she'd seen this woman use to blow a man's brains out just for being an Echo. Bile rose in her throat at the memory. She swallowed it back.

"If we're going to talk, can we at least stand up?" asked Katie.

The cleanser shrugged. "If you like," she said, "but try to run and I'll kill you both slow. Understand?"

Katie nodded. She eased herself upright, then helped Bec to her feet. The cleanser rose with them.

"So, here's the deal," she said. "The boss got a little carried away with interrogating your friend. He was supposed to give us the Institute's hideout, but his heart gave out too soon. Now we need to find it another way."

"What, and you think we know?" asked Katie, holding Bec close. "You can torture us if you like, but we couldn't tell you even if we wanted to."

The cleanser scoffed. "No, we didn't expect you'd have the location. But what you do know is where that damn doctor went. That's all Boss Clean wants from you. They left in a van; they were driving in this direction. What roads did they take? Where did they stop? When did you leave them?"

"My sister's an Echo," said Katie. "You'll kill us whatever we say. Why the hell should we help you?"

The cleanser's expression hardened.   Her scowl looked ready to crush stone. She reached into her jacket. Katie tensed, but it wasn't a weapon that emerged. It was a photograph. The woman tossed it towards them. It landed on a pile of leaves, and Katie craned her neck to see it.

A cottage. Flowers blooming in the garden, clean solid walls, fully furnished rooms inside that could have come straight from a pre-Echo world. It was the utter opposite of the Institute's farmhouse. It was the kind of place Katie had dreamed about finding after she finally got Bec out of Boss Clean's reach.

"The boss isn't heartless," said the cleanser. "I know it seems that way to people like you. You're too emotionally involved to understand his methods, but all he wants to do is help. Wipe out the disease, whatever it takes. Help us do that, and he'll agree to show you both mercy. You will live the rest of your lives in exile. Food will be provided, and you can remain together. So long as you don't leave the grounds of the cottage, you'll be left alone. It's a better life than the Institute would have offered you, probing your sister like some kind of lab rat until they emptied her out and tossed her away. Or worse, let her mutilated body wander out alive to infect more innocent people. Tell us where the van went, and anything else you learned about these monsters, and the cottage is yours."

The weight of the offer sank in, pulling down on Katie's chest as though she were being sucked into a vortex. Since the start of Boss Clean's reign, all she had wanted was a safe home for Bec. Now it was within her grasp.

But could she trust an offer from Boss Clean? And even if she could, was she prepared to betray the Institute for it? She owed Nadar and her guards no loyalty, but they had innocent Echoes in their company, and no doubt more at their facility. She swayed on the spot, mind reeling.

Then Bec squeezed her hand. In that instant, without looking, Katie knew her sister's decision. If that's what Bec wanted, so did she. She squeezed back and took a deep breath.

"We've never heard of any Institute," she said. "But we're tired of running. So do your worst."

The cleanser hissed beneath her mask. "Fucking Echoes," she said, and raised her pistol.

Katie clamped her eyes shut.

Bang.

Katie flinched. She waited for the pain. Worse, she waited for Bec to sag to the ground beside her. Neither happened. She opened her eyes to find the cleanser rocking back and forth, the anger on her face replaced with surprise. Then she collapsed.

"The shop?" asked Bec.

Katie held her close as one of the Institute guards emerged from the nearby trees. He probed the cleanser's body to make sure she was dead, then turned to Katie and Bec.

"Are you okay?" he asked.

Katie shielded Bec with an arm and stepped away.

"You followed us," she said.

"To protect you," said Phil. "Well...to protect her. I don't think you realise how important your sister is."

"She's the most important thing in the world to me," said Katie. "And she's a human being. You don't need to talk like she's not here."

"I've had it for a while," said Bec.

Phil shifted where he stood, apparently uncomfortable with talking to an Echo. He forced his eyes to meet hers. "Then I meant to say how important *you* are," he clarified. "You might be the key, Bec. To solving all of this."

"So, what, you'll wait until we fall asleep and then take her?" asked Katie.

"We're sorry for how things went down at the outpost," said Phil, raising his hands. "We're struggling for resources—have been for a long time—and we made a snap decision that you were one mouth too many to feed. But...we were wrong. We can't split you up. And if we take you, Bec, against your will, you're self-aware enough to try escaping or...worse. Maybe we could lock you up, have you on suicide watch 24/7, but fuck, I don't even think we have the people for that. So we need you to *want* to be there. We need you to want to help us. We just... We need you."

He walked towards them. Bec tensed up as he approached, but he stopped before he got in easy reach, pulling a map from his pocket and holding it out to Katie. The terrain was meticulously mapped, with paths and roads and settlements all annotated in tight, neat writing. It made her own map seem like a child's scrawl stuck on the fridge. Katie scanned it and held it open for Bec to see.

"The Institute is between the two rocky outcrops near the centre," said Phil, "north of Path 17, south-east of the stream. We've not added the location itself, for obvious reasons, but it'll let you find us. If you choose to."

"We'll...consider it," said Katie, folding up the map and tucking it away. "Are you going to leave us alone now?"

"I will. We'll be at the safe house for another few hours. After that, head to the outcrops. We'll look after you, Bec. We'll look after both of you. I promise."

Katie nodded and hugged Bec close, not moving until Phil had traipsed away and out of sight. She certainly didn't trust him—for all she knew, he'd still be following them, waiting in the shadows until they dropped their guard—but they would be dead without him. That was something, at least.

Perhaps half an hour passed before Bec eased herself out of Katie's grip, wandering towards the cleanser's corpse. Katie couldn't look. The pooling blood reminded her of that terrible basement in the mall, and of the Echo gunned down during their escape. Her heart hammered and she hissed out a shaking breath, trying to calm herself. Bec seemed to understand.

"Do you want anything from the shop?" she said.

From the corner of her eye, Katie saw her sister jerk and twist, combining a dozen memorised actions to bend down and lift the cleaner's dropped pistol. She straightened, holding the gun like a burger, and offered it to Katie.

"Thanks," Katie said.

She wasn't sure how good a shot she was, or whether she could touch the thing without thinking of death, but seeing it might ward off attackers, and she could always stick to firing warning shots. She checked the ammunition before tucking the gun into her belt.

"Well," she said, "plenty of places we could go. Or one in particular, if you wanted."

Bec hummed, and Katie curled their fingers together.

"Whatever you choose," she said, "I'll be right there with you."

Bec turned her familiar smile to the horizon. She squeezed Katie's hand.

"Yeah, I will, thanks."

Katie took a deep breath and nodded.

"Atta girl."

THE END.

Joel R Hunt is a writer, librarian, ex-teacher and part-time human currently residing in the UK. He has a passion for horror, science fiction and all things bizarre. Joel's short stories can be found in a range of anthologies by Eerie River Publishing, Black Hare Press and Scare Street, among others, and he posts daily microstories on Twitter.

Twitter: www.twitter.com/JoelRHunt1
Website: www.joelrhuntauthor.wordpress.com/
Reddit: www.reddit.com/r/JRHEvilInc/
Facebook: www.facebook.com/JoelRHunt

CARRY ON

BY HOLLEY CORNETTO

for Mom

PART ONE
THE JOURNEY

Diamond stood at the top of the hill, bicycle propped against her thigh, looking through a pair of military-grade binoculars. Fence posts jutted from dead lawns like crooked teeth, marking boundaries for gardens that grew nothing but sun-browned weeds. The houses stood empty against a desert landscape.

"Looks like a suburb. Several of the shells are still intact," she said, evaluating the rows of deserted houses along the cul-de-sac. Once, this place would have been crawling with SUVs, soccer moms, and kids. There were no visible cars, but cars had been one of the first things to go, after the food and water. "We should set up camp."

These families must have been among the lucky ones who'd evacuated during the Great Migration, before food and water became so scarce that the fighting began. Others, those who refused to leave their homes, were forcibly driven out by the Church of America Corps at the start of the Second Civil War.

Python snapped down the kickstand of his old mountain bike and walked toward her, taking the rag off his head to wipe his sweat-covered brow. With hands as coarse as old leather, he reached for the binoculars. "Any of 'em look promising?"

She shrugged, handing them over. She glanced at the sunburn on his arms, grateful for the protection of her dark skin. They hadn't had sunblock since they'd raided B3, the third bunker on their list, and everyone was suffering. "Scavengers have probably picked them clean. But walls will be better than sleeping out in the open. We're only a few miles out from B8."

She glanced over her shoulder. Hemingway, Sal, and Glitch were peddling their way up the hill. Hemingway had gotten off his bike to push. It was his turn to haul the supply trailer.

The desolate landscape had once been filled with young families and playing children. Once. How long had it been? Twenty years since the rivers started drying up in the west; fifteen since the Church of America Corps formed to keep the peace, or so they said. Looking back, the idea was laughable. The only peace they kept was for their wealthy backers.

It turned out the Corps was founded and funded by some of America's most powerful families, the Elite. As politicians, CEOs, and hedge fund managers, they'd made their fortunes bleeding the country dry financially—and in the process, bled it dry literally too. When the country ran low on food, water, gasoline, and all the necessities of life, they used the Corps to secure those resources for themselves.

War followed soon after.

"Want me to scout it?" Python asked.

"Why don't you take Hemingway with you?" she suggested. "I'll stay behind with the others and you can signal us the all-clear."

"Because," Python spat, "he's about as useful as a sack full o' shit."

Diamond took the binoculars and zipped them back into her rucksack, also military-grade. It was a relic from her time in the Church of America Corps. The name Johnson was patched on the side from the days when names still meant something. "He isn't useless, he just needs guidance. That's why I want him with you. You're a good example."

Python broke into a wide grin. "I'm a regular goddamned boy scout."

She glared at him side-eyed, and his grin faded.

"Fine. I'll take him, but you owe me one."

Diamond looked over her shoulder. The others were dragging, their shirts made of holes patched together with sweat stains. Sal was wheezing for breath. She was the oldest of their outfit, though no one knew how old exactly. Hell, she probably didn't even know herself, but based on the age spots on her face and the wrinkles extending from her face to her neck, they'd bet she was fifty-five if she were a day. She was wiry, with corded muscles that could've easily belonged to a man.

Glitch, more a child of the new world than the old, was the first to catch up. Damp, unruly curls fell across the dark skin of his forehead. As the youngest in their outfit, he'd been born just before the start of the war. He possessed few, if any, memories of the world before this one. "What's the plan, boss man?"

"Python and Hemingway are on recon. You, me, and Sal will join up with them after the area is cleared."

Diamond pulled her water bottle from the holder and drank deeply. They'd peddled for miles, and the back of her throat tasted like sand.

She pulled her 9mm semi-automatic from its holster and offered it to Hemingway. "Don't use it unless you have to."

Python scoffed, almost knocking it out of Hemingway's hand. "The gun's only useful if you know how to use it. Take the fucking baseball bat, and if that doesn't take care of the problem, yell for help."

Hemingway shrugged and lifted his bat. The paint was chipped and faded to hell, and only the '...ville' down the side was still legible. "He's right. I'd just be wasting ammo."

Diamond nodded; they didn't have bullets to spare for target practice.

They'd found Hemingway serving as a Domestic in B6. Ranchers, the legal name for slavers, were one of many post-war evils. They raided settlements and camps, kidnapping those they deemed able to work, like Hemingway, and selling them to the Elite as Domestics—modern day slaves.

Diamond nodded her approval and watched as the two set off down the hill.

Sal's gravelly voice filled her ears. "He'll be fine, Di."

Diamond didn't turn. "Today, yes. But, what happens when we get to B8?"

Her head throbbed from the pressure building behind her eyes. Somewhere along the way the others had begun to regard her as their leader, and now she felt responsible for them.

"We'll be fine too. We've cracked four bunkers since we left the compound at Sunnyvale. We've rode hundreds of miles. There's only one more stop before we make it to New Eden."

"You're right." Diamond turned and studied the crow's feet around the woman's eyes. "I know you're right."

"Damn right, I'm right. Now come on; let's go take a piss while the boys are gone."

"Hey!" Glitch protested.

Sal winked. "You don't count."

Glitch rolled his eyes and turned his back to them. "Guess I'll watch for the signal, then."

Diamond nodded, but couldn't shake the feeling that something terrible loomed over the horizon.

...

The shell's pantry had been picked mostly clean. The only things left behind were light bulbs and fabric softener—objects that belonged to the same world as names and years.

They dragged their bikes and trailer inside with them, having learned caution through experience. The trailer held spare supplies, food, water, batteries, matches, and a first aid kit. They travelled light, just enough to get them from one bunker to the next.

Diamond watched Sal take her broom—the one usually reserved for solar panels—and sweep the debris from what had been a cozy living room. Once, before the dust and stains of time, the yellow walls must have seemed sunny and happy.

Diamond helped Glitch clear the fireplace enough for a fire. They needed something to cook with, and nights in the desert were bitterly cold.

"You know," Glitch said, glancing at the family portraits on the mantle, "there's still a lot of junk left here."

Python cleared debris from the coffee table and spread their map across it. "Scavs probably haven't made it out this far yet is all."

"The cabinets were picked over," Hemingway offered.

"Different kind of scav. Everybody's got a use for food and water, idjit." Python nudged a broken chair in the firewood stack with his foot. "But stuff like this? Well, I reckon you've got to have a means to transport it and a place to put it."

Sal coughed, clearing a day's worth of dust and phlegm from her throat. "Python's right. Only communities or facilities have use for things like this. I don't think there are many of those left that aren't operated by the Corps, let alone out here in the middle of nowhere."

Hemingway glanced from Python to Sal. "I guess you know a lot about scavenging?"

"Yeah." Diamond tossed Sal a bottle of water. "Glitch, Sal, Python and me all worked a scav unit out of Sunnyvale for about five years. It's how we all met." She pulled out three tins of food. "Looks like canned chili, green beans... Oh, fancy! French cut and...peaches."

Glitch grinned. "I like peaches."

Hemingway removed the can opener from his pack and took the chili from Diamond. "You never told me why you left."

Python scowled. "What do you want, our whole life story? Jesus Fucking Christ."

Diamond sighed. Sunnyvale had been good while it lasted. She'd even come to think of it as home for a while, as much as any place could be home in this fucked up new world. "They were low on supplies. They used to ban Ranchers, but I guess they figured the fewer mouths to feed, the longer supplies would last. There were rumors about setting up a lottery, and we all knew what that meant. Winners leave with the Ranchers to get sold off as Domestics. Bastards."

"Oh." Hemingway's tone was flat.

Diamond gave a half-nod.

Sal propped her broom against the wall and walked over with two cook pots, holding them out toward Diamond. "Fill 'er up; the fire is ready!"

Python glanced back at the map. "Less than a day to B8, assuming we keep a good pace."

"How'd you find all those bunker locations anyway?" Hemingway asked.

"How in the hell have you survived so long without knowing shit about anything?" Python turned to Diamond. "This green fucker is gonna be the death of us."

Python had made it clear since they'd found Hemingway back at Bunker 6 that he didn't want to bring him along. He was untrained. Just another mouth to feed.

"That was Glitch," Sal said, ignoring Python and placing the pots on the fire. "Our crew was on a run, and he found an old laptop he was able to hook up to some doodad to get it running."

"Solar panel," Glitch corrected, looking over Python's shoulder at the map. "I thought, if I was lucky, it would have a game or porn on it. You know, something for fun. I didn't realize how lucky I was. The stuff I thought was garbage turned out to be installation and maintenance records."

"We grabbed coordinates off the old records and high-tailed it out of there on our next shift. Ain't that right, Diamond?"

Diamond nodded once.

Python wasn't much of a conversationalist, but he loved talking about their escape from the compound. "We figured we'd pop all the bunkers between there and New Eden. B8's the last stop. We'll stay there a bit and live large on the supplies."

"Put some fat on our bones!" Sal called from the fireplace.

Diamond gave Hemingway a skeptical once-over. He'd been with them only a few weeks, and he wasn't used to roughing it. Maybe he wasn't ready. Maybe he'd never be cut out for this life, but it didn't matter. After they'd found him back at B6, his options were to stay there and die, or join them on the road. The choice had been an easy one to make. For the sake of the group, she needed him to prove himself to Python, and there was only one way to do that.

"Hemingway, you're taking point when we get to B8."

...

Python took first watch while Diamond and the others settled in around the fire.

The room was warm and the fire cast shadows along the walls. The company sat, content to listen to the crackling of the fire. Diamond's eyes grew heavy.

In her dream, she was back at the reservoir, standing guard against a razor-wire fence in the time before. When she'd signed up to serve in the Church of America Corps, she'd been an idealist. The Corps had been billed as a relief effort after the scorched earth began to die. Diamond thought their mission had been a charitable one, to bring food and supplies to those in need and to help evacuate and relocate people living in areas that were suddenly uninhabitable. But after signing up, she quickly realized that the Corps were gathering supplies, not for humanitarian purposes, but to deliver to the Elite.

A plume of dust over the horizon was the only thing to announce their arrival. They were weak and emaciated, too hungry and exhausted to make much sound.

Diamond glanced out over the field at the approaching mob. They were women and children, boys and girls. Friends and neighbors, people so desperate for a drink of water they would break the law. They needed what was in the reservoir to survive.

The soldiers at her side held their guns at the ready. One look at their faces told her they were terrified. Their orders were simple: Let no one pass.

The crowd continued to press inward. A glass bottle flew past her head and crashed against the fence behind her.

The soldier to her left, a frightened kid with a hair-trigger rifle, opened fire. Then they all did. Bullets flew, blood sprayed, and bodies crumpled like dolls.

Diamond bolted upright, but the gunshots from her dream were just a log popping on the fire. It was only a nightmare; one she'd had almost every night for the last fifteen years. Shaking hands reached up to cradle her head; she wasn't that person anymore. She'd left the Corps after realizing they weren't fighting for God, but for the Elite, hoarding the resources of a dying planet and leaving the poor to die.

"Are you alright?" It was Hemingway who asked, his eyes the color of dead leaves in autumn.

She glanced around the room, taking in her surroundings. She was safe, or at least what passed for safe these days. The adrenaline drained from her overwrought nerves. "Yeah, sorry."

Hemingway unzipped his pack, pulling out a worn paperback and flipping to a dog-eared page. "Shall we continue our book?"

Sal shifted to toss another chair leg onto the fire. "So, this small fellow... It sounds like he had it pretty nice. What do you think made him pack up and leave his cozy, little hole in the ground?"

"There could be a lot of reasons, I suppose."

Sal settled back in against the wall. "I don't know. Getting someplace and settling down? That all sounds pretty good right now. He'd be a fool to leave it all behind."

"It's like you," Glitch said, looking at Hemingway. "You were all cozy at home in B6, but you left with us anyway."

Python scoffed. "He left with us because he'd have died otherwise. He's just a deadweight Domestic that don't know shit. Should have died back at B6 with the Elite that owned him. It would've been a mercy."

Hemingway glared at Python, then turned to answer Glitch. "I suppose it is sort of the same. That bunker was the only home I'd known for years."

"Best-treated Domestic I ever saw." Python grumbled and crossed his arms, staring out through the gaps in the front window.

To Diamond, Hemingway was a symbol of the before-times. But unlike her nightmares and military-grade gear—also remnants of the world before—he was a reminder of the good things, like art and music and stories. "Will you guys shut up so he can read?"

"We finished it last time, remember?" Sal asked.

"We can start it over again!" Glitch said.

"What's this, the third time he's read it?" Python groaned. "You ought to know it by heart."

"That's not the point," Glitch said.

"Okay, then. We'll start at the beginning again."

Hemingway turned to the book with barely concealed excitement and cleared his throat. He read late into the night, talking about holes in the ground, and the half-sized men that lived there.

...

Diamond's eyes flitted open. She sat up, suddenly alert. There had been a noise, a movement... Something had startled her awake. She scanned the room, silently watching.

The night was full dark. Although the fire had burned itself out, wisps of smoke still rose from the pile of ashes. She glanced to the window where Python had sat, keeping vigil when last she was awake. His seat was vacant.

Diamond held her breath and listened for the sounds between Sal's gentle snoring. She knew what to listen for: the scuffle of footsteps, the crunch of gravel beneath boots. The sound of danger approaching.

It had been a lifetime since she'd served in the Corps, but her instincts were still razor-sharp. Diamond leaned over and gently shook Glitch's shoulder. When his eye opened, she placed a finger to her lips and pointed towards the large window. *Get the others and hide,* she signaled.

She didn't wait to see if he understood. She pulled her gun from its holster and slunk against the wall to listen. Her heart pounded in her throat.

As the fear knotted and settled in her belly, she heard a scuffle—a furtive, uncertain step. Her shaking legs inched her along the wall, closer, soundless. Her mind had shut down, and that animal part of her—the part that knew only survival—opened its eyes.

There were three, maybe four of them. At least one by the front door. One on the far side of the window. She didn't have enough bullets to take them all down. If Python went out to check, he was likely already dead.

The door knob rattled and shook. Diamond glanced back into the living room. There was no sign of Glitch and the others. Good.

Broken glass crunched under a heavy step. Whoever they were, they weren't trying to be stealthy anymore.

It was the stranger's last mistake. Diamond stepped out from cover and fired a single shot in the direction of the sound. A groan and a thud told her she'd hit her mark.

A low whistle sounded from the direction of the door. "You'll pay for that one, bitch. Flesh for flesh. Blood for blood."

She'd killed one, at the cost of a precious bullet and the element of surprise. Her only leverage was the gun, and that they had no idea how many bullets she had left. "Leave now and I won't shoot the rest of you."

"You ain't gonna do that." The voice was like sandpaper against stone.

"Are you willing to bet your life on it?"

"You do anything stupid, and we're gonna gut your boyfriend here. We'll peel him like a piece of fruit."

Diamond peeked through the doorway. Python stood, trussed up like a pig waiting for slaughter. His eye was bruised and swollen and the left side of his face was a bloody pulp, but it looked like he'd given as good as he'd got. The man holding him had a busted nose, and favored his right leg.

She couldn't tell if the bruises running down his arms were fresh, but the fat lip definitely was.

Beads of sweat slid down her forehead. She needed a plan. She needed to stall. "How'd you find us?"

"Saw the smoke from your fire," replied the sandpaper voice. "If you come out and put the gun down, we'll let him live. Hell, we'll even let him watch."

Diamond's stomach fluttered. She didn't need to ask what they'd let him watch; the sharp edge of his laughter told her enough. The acidic taste of canned chili crept back up her throat.

Python gave them leverage, and they knew it. Or did they? If Python could fuck them up like that, they weren't Corps—just a bunch of thugs.

Diamond knew thugs; she'd worked with enough of them in her scav days. They were all tough when they had the upper hand, but useless as shit when things went sideways. She just had to deny them the upper hand.

"Gut him then. When the screaming starts, I'll know just where to shoot."

There was a moment of silence where she imagined the rusty gears of the man's brain turning. Was she really such a ruthless bitch? She never had the opportunity to find out just how far she'd let this go. A faded '...ville' swooped in low, arc cut short as it crunched into a kneecap. Hemingway lined up for another swing.

Diamond stepped out of cover and took aim, lodging a bullet in Sandpaper's shoulder a moment too late. Before he crumpled to the floor, the man's knife tore a gash in Python's side.

"Shit. Grab the first aid kit!"

Diamond knelt beside Python, ripping his tattered and bloody shirt to put pressure on the wound. The cut was deep, but it didn't look like the knife had hit an artery. If she could stop the bleeding, he might survive.

Glitch ran back across the room with the kit they'd found when they raided B6. It was more than just bandages and antiseptic wipes. This kit had the good stuff.

Hemingway knelt beside Python and offered him a hand. "Squeeze it."

Python grunted, taking the offered hand. Hemingway's face went pale as Python squeezed.

Diamond threaded the needle and knit her brow. "This is going to hurt," she warned, digging the stitch into Python's side.

Python grit his teeth and sucked in a breath.

"What should we do with this one?" Glitch asked, pointing a toe at the groaning figure writhing on the floor.

"He said it himself," Sal said, unsheathing her knife. "Flesh for flesh. Blood for blood. Ain't that right, boss?"

Diamond checked her stitchwork, then nodded. It was surprising to her how easy it had become to take another life without batting an eye.

Sal jerked the man's head back. With a flick of her wrist, the blade traced a red line across his neck.

...

The sun pressed down, and everything around them seemed to burn. Heat waves rose from the broken pieces of road. A hot breeze blasted them, covering them in dust. For miles they'd seen nothing but a few large cacti and the rusted-out carcass of a car baking in the sun.

Diamond thought about giving up—admitting that even she had limits. It was too much to ask to lead this group across a desolate wasteland to a place they weren't even sure existed anymore, if it ever really had. New Eden might just be a story parents told their children. It would have been a difficult task even if they'd all been in peak physical condition.

Python's injury was a major setback. He needed time for his wounds to knit, and even then, he couldn't ride. The risk of staying put was greater than the risk of moving forward. Python could heal when they got to B8, and they were almost there. They left the bikes behind and walked the rest of the way, bringing only what they could carry. The sooner they were inside the bunker, the better. They had to carry on.

"What's the first thing you're going to do when we get to New Eden?" Glitch asked, falling into step alongside Diamond.

"Eat something that isn't from a can or a package. Something fresh," she answered. "What about you, Sal?"

Sal was walking alongside Python, who held pressure on his bandaged side as he limped along. "When I get to New Eden? I'm gonna sit my ass down and rest is what. I'm tired."

Ahead, Hemingway stopped.

No one in the group had brought up the attack that night in the shell. No one mentioned the nonchalant way she'd told those men to gut Python, or the fact that Hemingway had been the one to save all their asses. Quiet, soft Hemingway with his books and his stories.

The area had once been a major highway, but was now reduced to rubble. Hemingway waved them into the lot of what had been a service station. The doors were removed, and two of the walls had either crumbled or been knocked down. The two remaining walls cast enough shade for them to rest and regroup. The gas pumps had long since been dismantled, and any fuel that remained taken for vehicles or generators.

Glitch unfolded the map and smoothed it out against the crumbled pavement. "We need to turn off the main road soon."

Sal sighed and wiped sweat from her forehead. "We know the drill."

"Not all of us know," Diamond said, casting a meaningful look at Hemingway. "It's his first time. We need to make sure we get it right. There's no room for fuck-ups."

Hemingway nodded. "What do I need to do?"

Diamond felt that same sense of creeping unease she'd first felt a lifetime ago, when her commanding officer ordered her unit to fire on civilians. The epiphany she'd had back then had been accompanied by a pit opening in her stomach. She couldn't breathe; she couldn't think. Once, it might have been called anxiety, and she might have gone to a therapist or a psychiatrist.

Now, it was just the way things were.

...

The landscape grew bleak as they closed in around B8. The bunker's location was no doubt chosen for the advantage of the plateau and surrounding forest. The trees were long-dead, charcoal corpses sticking out of the sandy soil where raging wildfires had taken their toll. Some shrubs and cacti had managed to fill in the underbrush in the valley below.

As they ascended the hill where the bunker stood, skeletons with sun-bleached bones hung from trees along the ridgeline like flags waving on poles. An amateur mistake, Diamond thought. A concentration of bodies like this clearly pointed to the presence of something.

A half-rotted corpse hung from a scorched tree limb. Fresher than the others.

"Keep your eyes open," Diamond ordered. "They aren't even trying to hide, which means they aren't afraid of being found."

Diamond and Hemingway each stood under one of Python's shoulders. Hemingway had practically dragged him to the top of the plateau. His blood-stained bandages needed to be changed and the wound cleaned. He needed stronger pain killers. Diamond wasn't sure how he'd done it, but he'd traveled the entire distance without complaint. Doing his duty. She respected that.

They lowered him against the dead tree.

Sal and Glitch set out to search the perimeter for guards or traps or security cameras. The Elite—the only ones who could afford these bunkers—had a virtually unlimited pool of resources at their disposal, and they were willing to use them. Anything to keep out the rabble.

"Just give me a few minutes to catch my breath, and I'll be good to go." Python's voice was faint, his face pale.

"You aren't going anywhere. You stay here while we clear the bunker. When it's safe, we'll come back for you."

Python winced and spat, "Like hell you will. You need me."

"Yes, we do, which is why you're going to sit this one out."

He didn't look her in the eyes. He ran his fingers through the sandy soil beneath him, blood still caked around his nails.

"Whatever you say, boss."

Had her reply to those men hurt him more than he'd let on? She shook her head to clear those thoughts. She'd deal with it after they were inside, after he had time to heal.

The whole trip she'd worried about having to rely on Hemingway, but with Python down, she had no other choice.

Sal and Glitch made their way back from the charred remains of forest surrounding the bunker. Glitch rubbed his hand over the blackened bark of a nearby tree and smudged dark lines across his face. "We found the entrance, but no signs of people."

"No guards or anything?" Diamond asked, skeptically. Someone was responsible for all the bodies.

"Weird, right?" Glitch shrugged. "There were a lot of security cameras though. A couple lining the path up, and a few more closer to the door. Definitely more than we've seen at the other bunkers. But that might be because this one's three times bigger than those, at least according to the schematics. They're all offline now, at any rate."

He blew imaginary smoke from the tip of his needle nose pliers, then twirled them in his hand like they did in the old Westerns.

"Alright then. We proceed as planned. Is everyone ready?"

All eyes were on Hemingway. He nodded nervously.

Python held out his gun. "You're going to need this."

...

Diamond's feet vibrated beneath her. She glanced across the ridge. Closer to the bunker's entrance were the remains of a garden. Dried up hedges and shrubs grew beyond the dead forest surrounding the area. She waved her gun forward, signaling the others.

Glitch had cut the power to the security cameras; it was only a matter of time before someone came out to check. That would provide the opening they needed.

Diamond stood on her mark, waiting. This part was always the worst. It could take minutes for the people inside to notice a disturbance with the cameras, or it could take hours. Either way, eventually, someone would come.

Her thoughts were interrupted by a whirring noise like a mosquito by her ear—the unmistakable sound of the bunker doors opening.

A head popped out. Male, wearing tactical gear. He took a cursory glance around and climbed out of the hatch. Diamond prayed he was just hired security, and alone. If this was a military installation, they were all about to be very dead.

It was already too late to call off the attack.

Diamond held her breath and counted. *One step. Two. Three.*

A boot scuffed the ground, louder than a gunshot. Hemingway had moved too soon.

Diamond leapt from her cover and fired at the man from the bunker. His gun was already drawn, aimed at Hemingway's advancing form. A spray of red cut the stillness of the landscape, and Hemingway fell.

Diamond charged, screaming with rage. She fired off her last two rounds. One missed, but the other struck the soldier in the chest. He staggered, but didn't go down.

The tactical vest. It had stopped the bullet. He retreated back to the cover of the doorway.

Diamond squeezed the trigger, willing bullets from an empty gun, but it clicked uselessly. She'd gotten Hemingway killed, and now it was her turn.

Seeing her standing there, helpless and unarmed, the soldier's panicked expression gave way to a predatory grin. Cautiously, he moved from the doorway.

In the edge of her vision, Glitch crept behind the soldier, spear in hand.

She let the empty pistol drop from limp fingers. Glitch sprang up from behind the soldier, sinking his spear deep in the man's side, straight through the unprotected armpit. The soldier crumpled with a groan. His body twitched as he bled out into the sandy earth.

Diamond had known this was a bad idea, and that Hemingway wasn't ready. She'd hoped he would prove her wrong, and that something soft and beautiful could survive in this fucked up world. She'd been a fool.

Diamond knelt beside Hemingway, wadding his shirt against the bullet wound. Blood pulsed under her hand, weaker with every beat, then nothing. Now she had two men down, and no one to blame but herself.

From the corner of her vision, she saw Sal lean down and pick something up off the ground. She held it out to Diamond--Hemingway's battered paperback, the one he'd read from every night. His favorite book. She hugged it against her chest and swallowed down the bile rising in her throat.

Sal crouched and placed her hands on Diamond's shoulders. "We don't have time for this now. Whoever's in there knows we're here."

Diamond sniffed and wiped her nose on her arm. She'd fucked up, but the mission wasn't over. She tucked the book into her waistband and picked up Hemingway's pistol. "Let's go."

PART TWO
US AND THEM

Sal and Glitch led the way down into the bunker. The first room was little more than an entryway, lined with polished metal cabinets secured with keypads. Diamond nodded toward one of the lockers. "Can you open it?"

Glitch inspected the keypad, making quiet hmms and huhs under his breath. He stared at the panel, like he expected it to tell him its secrets. Eventually, he popped it off and started fiddling with the wires beneath.

The red light on the panel turned green and the door swung open. Inside the cabinet glittered a store of firearms large enough to outfit a small company of soldiers.

"Holy shit..." Sal said, but if there was any more to her statement, it was cut short by the shrill blast of an alarm.

Diamond clicked a magazine into one of the assault rifles. "We've been made. Arm up and shoot anything that moves."

She knew she should urge caution, but blood demanded blood.

The alarm's wail rang through the passageways as Glitch led them through the interior. Most of the other bunkers had been in roughly the same proportions as a house from the before times, built to accommodate one or more families, but B8 was different. Glitch had taken the time to painstakingly memorize the blueprints for each, sketching out rough maps and labeling any rooms he could. He knew the layout better than any of the others.

Glitch called something over his shoulder, but Diamond could only make out the words "door" and "security" between the blasts of the alarm. At the end of the hall, he stopped and nodded to a door on the eastern wall. To anyone else, it would've looked like a closet.

Diamond returned the nod and took up position on the opposite side of the doorway. She took a breath and let loose with her rifle, sending her whole clip into the wood surrounding the doorknob. She tossed the empty rifle aside, drew Hemingway's pistol, and kicked in the ruined door.

A bullet whizzed past Diamond's ear, and she dove forward, taking cover behind a large table. Two men in Corps uniforms had been sitting beyond it—one already dead, slumped over in a pool of his own blood, and the other trying to kill her. The far wall glowed with black and white monitors, some freshly riddled with holes.

Sal sprayed a burst of suppressing fire, and it was the soldier's turn to duck behind the table for cover. Diamond signaled to Glitch, and the two of them fanned out to flank him.

"Drop it," Sal growled.

The man made no move to comply, though whether out of stubbornness or fear, Diamond couldn't guess. "Better do it. She's a mean, old bitch."

Sal smirked as the man slid his gun from behind the table.

Glitch moved closer to the wall of monitors. "How many of you are in the bunker?" he asked, eyes flitting from screen to screen.

The soldier glanced at his dead comrade sprawled across the controls. "Three."

"Awfully big place for three people," Sal said, taking a step towards him. "What do the cameras say, Glitch?"

Diamond didn't wait for Glitch to answer; she was done fucking around. She drew her knife and pressed seven inches of carbon steel to the man's throat. "What's your name, soldier?"

He stiffened. "Howell, ma'am."

"Howell, I've had a bad fucking day. My bullshit tolerance is zero. Tell us what we need to know, and I'll make it quick. If you fuck with me, I'll give you to her."

Diamond nodded in Sal's direction. She flexed a bulging bicep in reply.

Howell swallowed hard. The sour stink of urine filled Diamond's nostrils. She might have laughed if she hadn't felt so raw inside, like salt scraped over a deep hurt.

"You said there were only three of you," Glitch said, pointing to a group of figures huddled together on one of the monitor screens. "Who are they?"

"Them? They're just Domestics."

"Why are they hiding?"

Howell's gaze shifted from Diamond's knife to Sal. "They're not hiding. That's just their cell."

"Cell?" Sal asked.

"Yes, ma'am."

Diamond pressed the knife hard against his Adam's apple. "Howell, you're starting to piss me off. You're going to tell us where everyone is, why there are cells, and what in the holy fuck is happening here, or so help me I'm going to start cutting at your balls and work my way up."

"This bunker was a Corps outpost during the war."

Diamond took a deep breath, but it didn't stop her hand from trembling. The knife pressed harder and a tiny red pearl formed against the blade. "If this is an outpost, why are there so few soldiers?"

"Former outpost, ma'am. The others are out driving herds to their buyers."

Herds?

Diamond felt the heat of shame on her face. How could she have ever considered herself one of them? How could she have ever worn the uniform? In a fit of disgust—at herself, the soldier, and the whole damned world—she plunged the knife into the man's throat.

A shower of crimson arced across the room. The look of surprise slipped from his face as he slumped to the floor

"So, what do we do now, boss man?" Sal asked.

"We go get Python, bury Hemingway, and then decide what to do with the people in the cells."

...

The bunker had a well-stocked infirmary on the lower floor, wedged between the mess hall and the cells. The room was stark white with buzzing fluorescent lights. Diamond wondered how many wounded Corps soldiers had been treated here, given the best available medical care, while ordinary people on the outside died from preventable diseases. Hygiene, sterilization, antibiotics... Things once taken for granted turned out to be privileges, not rights, once the Elite started hoarding resources.

They loaded Python onto a gurney. When they'd gone out to retrieve him, they'd found him unconscious. Diamond had checked the wound. He'd lost more blood than he let on, and that combined with dehydration was taking its toll.

Glitch rifled through the cabinets until he found bottles of amoxicillin and Oxy. "Holy shit, this place has everything," he said, holding up a bottle of Pedialyte he'd pulled from yet another cabinet. "We should try and get some of this down his gullet."

Sal cradled Python's head gently in her arms and tilted his chin back while Glitch funneled the liquid into his mouth. In another life, it might have been the image of a mother caring for a sick child.

"Sal, you stay with him until he wakes up," Diamond said. "Glitch, go around and make an inventory of supplies. See how much and what kinds of food, medicine and firepower we've got. I'm going to find out who these prisoners are, and how long they've been here."

"Any ideas on what we're going to do with them?" Sal asked.

Diamond sighed and ran a hand through her hair. "I guess that depends on how much food and supplies are here. And don't forget, the men trafficking those Domestics will be back. We'll need to get those security cameras back online."

"Can do," Glitch replied, with a sloppy salute.

Diamond took a long look at Python and then cleared her throat, turning back to the others. They'd lost so much, all under her command.

"But before we do any of that, we're going to give Hemingway a proper burial."

...

Diamond washed Hemingway's body and wrapped him in a thin, white blanket from the infirmary. Glitch had started to say something about wasting supplies on the dead, but one look from Diamond killed the protest on his lips.

Diamond hugged Hemingway to her chest while Glitch and Sal finished digging a grave under the burnt-out husk of a large tree with shovels from a supply closet. In the world before, Diamond thought, shovels were used for more than digging graves. That was the world Hemingway belonged in. A world with art and music and books.

"Diamond?" Sal crouched beside her.

Diamond rubbed her face with the back of her arm. "Yeah?"

"I'm sorry about Hemingway, but I know you, and I know what you're thinking. This wasn't your fault."

Diamond's face twisted into a sneer. "Then whose fault is it? You tell me, so I can make it right."

"I know you cared about him, but he wasn't your responsibility. In the end, we're all responsible for ourselves."

"He had faith in me, and I couldn't keep him safe." Diamond buried her head against Hemingway's body. "What is the point of any of this if I can't keep anyone safe?"

Glitch climbed out of the hole and stood beside her. "It's time," he said solemnly.

Diamond nodded as the two lifted Hemingway from her lap. She stood at the edge of his grave and watched as Glitch and Sal lowered him in.

She pulled Hemingway's paperback from her waistband and turned it over in her hands. The book, a relic from the world before, belonged in the grave with him. There was no room for it in this new world; she'd been fooling herself to pretend they could make it to New Eden, that there'd be a place for Hemingway and his stories.

Diamond held the book over the grave. Hemingway's ending had come too soon. Her vision blurred as tears collected in the corner of her eyes, but didn't fall. She was a commander, goddamn it, and she would not show weakness.

Before she could drop the book, Sal caught her arm. She shook her head. "He'd want you to keep it."

Diamond hesitated. Tears blurred the edge of her vision, and she swallowed down the lump in her throat. In the end, though she couldn't say why, she nodded. "Alright."

Sal stood and stepped forward, looking down at the hole in the ground. After staring for a few moments, she finally spoke. "Python was wrong. You weren't soft. You saved our asses."

Glitch nodded. "All because you were brave enough to come with us."

Diamond tucked the book back into her waistband and scooped a handful of sandy soil, dropping it on Hemingway below. She cleared her throat as Sal and Glitch lifted their shovels and began filling the grave.

"At ease, soldier."

...

The room was heavy with the stench of body odor. The drab gray linoleum floor looked as though it hadn't been washed in years. The old-fashioned iron bar doors could've been taken straight out of a prison block from the before-times. For all Diamond knew, they might have been.

"Come 'ere," Diamond said, waving to a dark-haired, timid-looking woman.

The woman approached hesitantly, keeping enough distance that Diamond couldn't reach her through the bars.

"I've never seen a woman guard before. Are you new?"

Diamond shook her head. "They're all dead."

The woman's eyes went wide with a flicker of hope. Diamond had seen that look, back when people still thought the Church of America Corps was going to help them, before they'd started pointing guns at the desperate and hungry. What was it their commander had said? It was God's will, because God helped those who helped themselves.

She never bothered to tell him those had been Benjamin Franklin's words, not God's.

"How many of you are there?" Diamond asked.

"About thirty."

"What's your name?"

"Tracey. What are you planning on doing with us?"

There was no point lying. "I don't know yet. We didn't know what this place was when we took it. Are you all Domestics?"

Tracey nodded. "Some of us have injuries, or are sick, and others they keep around to do work here."

Other Domestics started to crowd the cell doors, watching Diamond curiously. Diamond studied the faces in the group—old and emaciated, dirty and unkempt. Each one was a reminder of the civilians she'd turned her back on all those years ago. In the blur of Domestics, Diamond made out the shape of a little girl who might have been eight or nine. She wore the face of a ghost.

"Johnson!"

"Sir?"

"Any trouble on last night's rounds?"

"No, sir!"

"Wilkes said there was an intruder snooping around the supply tent."

"Yes, sir. A child, sir. I gave her a warning and escorted her away from camp."

"Follow me, Johnson."

She nodded and fell into step behind her commander. He led her out back and through the perimeter gate. She thought he was going to show her something, a weakness in the razor wire fence or a place that needed patching to prevent others from sneaking inside.

Instead, she saw the tall oak with the tiny figure swinging from a low branch. Her stomach turned, and she pitched, spewing vomit all over her boots. The girl couldn't have been more than nine years old, but it was hard to tell for sure from the blur of purple and black around her face.

"...prevent others from doing the same..."

"...discourage this sort of behavior..."

"...unpleasant, but necessary..."

"Miss?"

Diamond shook her head, banishing the memories. "Sorry." She crouched down to the little girl's height. "What's your name?"

The girl smiled. Despite being captured and locked in a cage, despite whatever horrific things had happened to her, she smiled. "My name is Hannah. What's yours?"

Diamond stared at the girl, trying to think how to answer. Before she was Diamond, before she'd been Corps Officer Johnson, who had she been?

After she'd deserted from the Corps, she'd spent a few years wandering alone, living like a wild thing. In those years, she'd become something different, something hard. Her old name, Lily, so gentle and delicate, didn't fit anymore.

"Call me Diamond," she finally answered.

"Is that your real name?" the girl asked, eyes wide.

Diamond shrugged. "Real as any other."

"Why do they call you that if it isn't your name?" Hannah asked.

She gave the girl a small smile and said, "Why don't we get you out of this cell, Hannah?"

...

Glitch paced back and forth. "Python ain't gonna like this."

He'd claimed the room with the security monitors for his base of operations. "The better to see them with, my dear," he'd joked, pointing toward the screens that lined the walls.

Diamond huffed and crossed her arms over her chest. "What was I supposed to do, leave them locked up? They're innocents."

"We could give them food and supplies and send them on their way." Glitch suggested.

"They'd probably wind up captured by Ranchers again if we did that," Sal said.

"I have the security cameras back up and running, but we can't stay here for long," Glitch said. "Those men will be back in a matter of days, likely heavily armed."

Diamond chewed her lower lip, studying the map spread across the expansive oak table. "Do you think any of them might know where New Eden is? Maybe they've been there, or heard of it, or know someone who has."

Sal shrugged. "Maybe, but even if they do, what will we do with them? Leave them behind? Take them with us? Both options are fucked."

Diamond looked up from the map. "What if we ambush the returning soldiers? We've got the advantage of the high ground, and we can give the Domestics guns. There's enough firepower in this bunker to arm every man, woman and child, and then some. I thought I saw some grenades too. We could rig up some traps..."

Sal and Glitch exchanged glances. "These people don't know how to shoot," Sal protested. "Hell, most of them have probably never held a gun."

Glitch glanced at the map, then at Diamond. "It's better than taking them with us. It'd be a logistical nightmare, managing a supply train for so many. There's no way we could carry enough supplies, especially if we don't know how far New Eden is. But, if we help them secure the outpost, then we don't have to take them with us. They can stay on here..."

"... and if we needed an emergency place to hide out, it would be good to have allies that owed us a favor," Diamond finished.

Glitch pointed out the road they'd come in on. "We can't outman or outgun Corps soldiers, but when they come back, they'll be returning from the main road. That gives us a strategic advantage because they'll have to climb the hill to get to the bunker. There are only two paths up large enough for a convoy of soldiers. One to the east, here," he slid his finger across the map, "and one to the west, here. There are a shit-ton of explosives in the lockers. We could rig up each location and catch them off guard when they come back. Easy-peasy lemon-squeezy."

"Do you have what you need to make it happen?" Diamond asked.

Glitch nodded. "Yes, sir."

"Good. Get it done."

...

Diamond sat, staring at Hemingway's paperback. She'd made a habit of keeping her mind too busy to leave space for memories and regrets to creep in. But now that the immediate business was done, she had nothing to distract her from thoughts of Hemingway and the world that was gone.

"What's that?" Hannah asked.

She'd been too preoccupied to notice the little girl's approach. "It's a book. It belonged to a friend. He didn't make it." What more was there to say? "Can you read?"

The girl flushed. "A little. My mom taught me. I haven't practiced in a long time, though. Not since the Ranchers took us."

Diamond placed a hand on the girl's shoulder. "Why don't you take this and go read to Python? You know, the scary-looking man in the infirmary? He can't really do much while he heals except sleep a lot. I bet he'd appreciate the company."

Hannah hugged the book to her chest and skipped off toward the infirmary.

...

Tracey sat in the command room with several other Domestics. "So, you're just going to leave us here to fend for ourselves?" Tracey rubbed her temple with her fingertips. "We can't hold this place. Those men are trained soldiers, and less than half of us are strong enough to fight."

Diamond paced back and forth in front of the wall of monitors, back online thanks to Glitch. "We'll help you defend the bunker when the Ranchers come back. After we've taken care of them, it'll be yours. The only thing we want in return is enough supplies to get us to New Eden."

Tracey looked to David, a middle-aged man with a long, gray-streaked beard. He worked maintenance on B8, and was a surprisingly good brawler. David shook his head. "What if others come? People like you?"

Glitch waved his hand in the direction of the monitors. "You'll be prepared. You aren't helpless. We won't be leaving you without a means of protecting yourself."

"I think we should all stick together," Tracey said, drumming her fingers on the tabletop. "We could all go to New Eden."

Diamond stopped pacing and turned. "Absolutely not! We can't move that many people safely, and there is no guarantee that New Eden would even let us in. All of that is assuming we can *find* New Eden in the first place."

"There is no guarantee it's even there," David said. "You'd all be better off staying here with us."

Tracey scowled and slammed her fist on the table. "You're going to leave us here to die. You're just as bad as the Corps men!"

Diamond felt an ache in her chest.

"Lily?"

"What is it, Derek?"

"Don't do it. Deserting is punishable by death. You'll be marked for the rest of your life. No place will ever be safe for you."

Tears slid down Lily's cheek. "You didn't see her, just hanging there, like someone's dirty laundry. He wouldn't even let me cut her down and bury her.

He wanted her to stay there so everyone could see. How is that God's will? What have we become?"

"You can't save the world by yourself, Lil. His methods are harsh, but it's for the greater good. Now stop crying. We're soldiers; we can't show weakness."

"I can't do it anymore."

"Please reconsider. You know what happens to women out there. You'd be better off staying here with us..."

"I..." Diamond sighed. "I'll have to talk with the others, see how everyone wants to move forward. This isn't a small thing you're asking of us."

Tracey stared at her hands, not meeting Diamond's gaze. "You know all those bodies you found outside when you approached?"

Diamond nodded.

"Some of them were our friends. Our family. You want to know what happened to them? If the Ranchers thought they were too old or sick to work, they used them for target practice. They starved them, they stabbed them, and they did other things too. We'll all end up the same if we stay here. Even Hannah."

...

Diamond put down the tray of chicken soup and saltine crackers and sat next to Python's bed. She lifted the edge of his blanket and pulled it down to reveal the gash in his side. The skin around was no longer swollen or inflamed. The stitches weren't expert, but they'd held him together well enough.

The infirmary was kept a few degrees cooler than the rest of the bunker. Diamond closed her eyes and listened to the low hum of cold air being pushed through the vents, a reminder of gentle spring breezes that no longer existed.

As she pressed a fresh bandage onto the wound, Python's eyes flitted open. "How long have I been out?"

She pushed the tray closer and ladled soup from the bowl. "Days. You need food. Here."

He grunted in pain as he leaned forward to eat, his face a sickly shade of white. "The others?"

Diamond scooped more soup into the spoon. "You know I didn't mean it when I told those men to gut you, right? I was trying to call their bluff."

She hadn't planned on bringing it up, not if he didn't, but she needed to confess. The guilt she felt over him and Hemingway was a burden she couldn't shoulder all the way to New Eden.

He nodded almost imperceptibly, swallowing another mouthful.

Diamond looked down at the pale-yellow broth with tiny, pink flecks of meat. She couldn't meet his eye, not with what came next. She could feel the lump rising in her throat even before the words came.

"Hemingway didn't make it."

Python placed a hand on top of hers. "I never thought he would. We shouldn't have brought him with us in the first place." A shadow passed over his face. "It isn't our job to save the world."

"Then whose job is it?" she asked, her voice barely a whisper.

"Diamond-"

"Do you know why I deserted?" she asked.

He winced as he raised his arm to rub the back of his head. "Irreconcilable differences?"

She smirked. "Yeah, the difference being that they were killing indiscriminately. Guilty or innocent, adult or child, none of it mattered. Everything was fine so long as you knew your place and behaved like a good sheep. The Corps guarded stores of food and water, enough that they could ration and provide relief for everyone, but they didn't. The Elite wanted it all for themselves, and left the rest to starve."

Python opened his mouth, but before he could respond, the door swung open. Hannah stepped in, hugging the old, battered paperback.

Her eyes lit when she saw Python sitting up in bed. "You're awake!"

Python looked side-eyed at Diamond. "Who the hell is this?"

Hannah climbed the stool on the opposite side of his bed. "I'm Hannah, Mr. Snakes. I've been taking care of you. I'm here to continue our story." She flipped open the book and cleared her throat. "Chapter Six."

Diamond stood and pushed the tray table against the bed. She glanced at Hannah. "Make sure he eats something, okay?"

Hannah nodded without pausing in her story.

Diamond smiled at the look of sheer confusion on Python's face. The door swung shut behind her.

...

In the days that followed, the bunker's inhabitants fell into a rhythm. Diamond led firearms training and Sal took small groups to train CQC. Glitch scouted and set up explosive traps to ambush the returning convoy.

The remains of burnt-out trees and shrubs along the top of the ridge offered several defensible positions for B8's crew. Long, thick rows of hedge—planted before water became too scarce to sustain them—looked down over the valley below. They had long-since wilted, but even dead they provided cover. The group dug a series of trenches near the bunker's entrance in case they needed to fall back. The trenches would provide room for them to retreat in stages, with the bunker itself as their last line of defense.

Sal leaned against her shovel. They'd taken a break from training to dig a mass grave for the bodies outside the bunker. They weren't just corpses; they were people, and deserved the same care and respect the company had afforded Hemingway.

At least Hemingway won't be alone in his rest, Diamond thought.

"Ya know," Sal began, "we have enough firepower to blow those bastards to hell."

Glitch wiped the sweat from his forehead with the back of his arm. "And we also have the element of surprise."

Diamond looked over her shoulder at Tracey, who, along with David, was cutting a corpse down from a tree. Tracey lowered the body gently, and David took it in his arms as he might've held a newborn babe, laying it on a tarp.

"When they come back and see the bodies gone, and this place cleaned up, they'll know something is wrong."

"Then why'd you do it?" Glitch asked.

"Because I think they need it." She tilted her head towards Tracey and David. "It's about time someone treated them like people, don't you think?"

Lily Johnson stood with a knife in her hand, sawing at the dead girl's noose.

"Johnson!"

"Sir?"

"What do you think you're doing?"

"I am going to bury the body, sir."

"Wrong, Johnson. You're going to leave the body there, and that is an order."

"She's a person. She deserves a proper burial."

"No, Johnson. She's not a person. She's a criminal. She's the reason we need the Corps to protect America's resources in the first place. 'Thou shalt not steal' is one of the Church's commandments. When she broke it, she sinned against the Church and against God, damn it."

"What about forgiveness?"

"Forgiveness is not ours to give."

"What about 'Thou shalt not kill'? Isn't that, too, one of the Church's commandments?"

"Do you think God gives a damn when you swat a fly? When you weed your damned garden? She will remain here as a warning to others of her kind. You are not to touch this body, Johnson, and that's an order. Do you understand?"

"Yes, sir."

"Diamond?" Sal's voice snapped her back to the present.

"Sorry."

She shook away the memories. They'd all happened a lifetime ago. She wished she'd known the little girl's name.

Glitch tossed another shovel of dirt over his shoulder. "I'm all for helping out, but how are you going to convince Python? You know he isn't going to want to help these people."

"He sounds like a real asshole to me." Tracey stood at the edge of the half-dug grave, surveying their progress.

Sal glanced up, squinting against the sun. "An asshole? Maybe. But even if he's a right bastard, he's the kind you want watching your back."

"What do you mean?" Tracey asked.

"Back in Sunnyvale, there was a man—a complete shit, full of piss and vinegar. Didn't like Diamond, 'cause he thought she was too butch. He figured himself to be the one to remind her she was a woman. I tried to stand up to him, but he slung me aside like a ragdoll. I started screaming bloody murder, and in came Python, every bit the hero. He jerked that asswipe right off her and broke every bone in both his hands."

"*Every* bone?" Tracey asked, eyebrows raised.

Sal smirked. "Yep. He's loyal to the people he cares about. He ain't bad. He's just...an acquired taste."

"Either way," Glitch added, tossing another shovelful of dirt over his shoulder, "he's someone you want on your side in a fight."

...

Python sat on the edge of the bed, shirtless, pointing out a jagged scar on his right forearm. "I got this one in a bar fight, back when I was a bouncer."

Hannah's eyes were wide. "What's a bar?"

"Oh, it's a place where people would go and drink before."

Diamond stood by the door silently, listening to the unlikely pair.

"Like a restaurant?" Hannah asked.

"Sort of, but one where people get drunk and fight a lot."

"Did you fight a lot, Mr. Snakes?"

"Only when I had to."

"You weren't a soldier, were you?" There was an edge of fear in the girl's voice.

"Oh, hell no. Nothing like that. I hated those Corps bastards from the start."

Diamond cleared her throat. "I see you're feeling better."

Python scooted away from Hannah. "Yeah. The meds have really done the trick. When are we getting out of here?"

Diamond sat on the stool beside his bed. "I don't know yet. We've promised to help the Domestics defend this place against the Ranchers before we go anywhere."

"Defend...?" He threw himself back onto the bed and closed his eyes. "Are you out of your mind?"

"Maybe I am, but it was my call to make, and I made it."

"How long are you going to keep putting our lives in danger so that you can have fucking pets?" Python asked. "You already got Hemingway killed. How many more corpses will it take?"

Diamond bristled. "Fuck you. Hemingway saved your ass back in that shell."

"Yeah, he did, but he couldn't save his own ass, could he? Neither could I, and neither could you!" His fist slammed against the mattress. "I should've been teaching him how to shoot instead of riding his ass about being useless. I could've *made* him useful."

Realization suddenly flooded in. "You cared about him."

Python averted his gaze.

"You did, didn't you?" Diamond stepped closer. "Why pretend you hated him then?"

"Because I know what happens to pets, Diamond. They die." He hung his head. "They die, and there's nothing we can do to stop it. It's better not to get attached."

"These people aren't just useless pets or Domestics. They're people, and they've been through some shit and lived to come out the other side of it."

"Then they can take care of themselves. We can't save everyone, Diamond."

"Yeah, but you'd have us save no one. Just because we can't make the world right again, doesn't mean we should turn our back on it. We can't fix everything, but goddamn it, we can help these people, right here, right now."

A sniffling sound from the other side of the bed reminded Diamond that Hannah was still there, listening as she and Python decided their fate. Fat, wet tears streaked the girl's face.

"You'll help us, won't you, Mr. Snakes? We're friends. I took care of you."

Python's jaw tensed. Diamond held her breath, waiting for the explosion of anger to follow, but it didn't come. Instead, Python looked at Hannah and sighed, "I guess I owe you, little miss."

Hannah's face lit up with a shy grin.

Python turned from Hannah to Diamond and gave a single nod. "We'll try your way, but if I die, I'm going to haunt your ass."

"Deal."

PART THREE
THE BATTLE

According to Tracey and David, between two and three dozen ex-Corps frequented B8. They traveled in groups of five to ten when herding Domestics. Diamond hoped that meant they could pick off the soldiers in waves. If they all returned at once, it was almost certain the bunker would be overwhelmed.

Python had finally healed enough to attend the war room meetings. He sat now at the big table, shaking his head as he studied the map.

"We've set up traps along the two choke points leading up the ridge. We have explosives with remote detonation, all wired to my laptop," Glitch drew a line down the map along the explosives' path.

A hiss of static cut through the room, followed by a man's voice. *"Connor to Outpost Command. Do you read me?"*

Diamond looked at the control panel beneath the wall of monitors. A red light was blinking on a small transceiver. "Shit. I didn't consider radios." She looked over at David and Tracey. "Did you know?"

Tracey shook her head. "Domestics weren't allowed in here."

"Howell? Do you read me? Over."

Glitch glanced at the radio. "Think we can fool them?"

Python shook his head. "I doubt it. The best we can hope for is them thinking the equipment malfunctioned, or the guards are sleepin' on the job."

Sal walked over to inspect the monitors. "We don't have a visual yet. I don't know what sort of range these radios have. We're gonna need to get our defenses ready."

Diamond realized they were all looking at her, waiting for her to give the go-ahead. "We need eyes on the security cameras 24/7 from here on out. Glitch, keep your laptop close in case we need to use that remote detonator. Python, you take the first shift watching the monitors. Sal, take David and gather a small crew for reconnaissance. We need to find out how many of them are coming for us."

Tracey pushed back her chair and stood. "What about me?"

"I need you to make sure all the residents are outfitted. I need everyone prepared but not panicked."

"Damnit, Howell, come in!" the voice growled from the speaker.

"Johnson, do you read? Over."

When she fled, she'd taken the radio with her to listen in on communications. She hadn't considered that her superior officer would try to contact her directly.

"I know it was you who cut down the body, Johnson."

Her hand twitched. Part of her wanted to explain herself. To try and make him understand that she couldn't do it. She couldn't walk past the body of that little girl every day and convince herself what she was doing was right.

"You're a damn fine soldier, Johnson. If you surrender yourself now and report back to base, we'll go easy on you. You have my word."

Her finger pressed the button. It would be so easy to go back. She had a life in the Corps. She was respected. There was food, water and shelter. If she didn't go back, she'd be on the run forever.

But if she went back, could she live with the person she'd become?

"Damnit, Johnson, come in!"

She tossed her radio onto the ground and stomped it into silence.

Sal frowned at the transceiver. "How long do you think we have?"

"Not long enough," Python grunted, and pulled his chair over to begin his watch.

…

After hours of trying, the radio communications stopped. One by one, the cameras at the base of the ridge and in the valley below went dark. They still had eyes at the top of the hill, which meant the soldiers weren't willing to risk the climb until they knew what they were up against.

Sal returned, but the news was worse than they'd feared. Not only was there a full contingent of soldiers, but they had a large group of prisoners with them.

"We took an old goat path down to get a look. We didn't get close enough for an exact count." Sal ran a hand through her hair. "There were at least twenty armed men, and twice as many Domestics. They've set up on the eastern side, in range of Glitch's explosives. The Domestics are on the far side, between the soldiers and the main road. I couldn't see much more than that."

"Where's David?" Tracey asked, tossing nervous glances at the door.

Sal shook her head. "He wanted to split up, see if he could go around them in the other direction. We were supposed to meet at a rendezvous point, but he never showed."

"Probably captured then," Python growled. "Or dead."

Tracey's lips tightened into a frown. "Because your people left him out there."

"Listen, lady. We all have a job to do here," Python said. "It isn't our fault he got himself captured on a simple recon mission!"

Tracey crossed her arms over her chest and leaned against the wall, staring at Python through narrowed eyes.

The red light blinked, signaling the radio back to life. *"Attention Outpost Command. We understand the outpost has been infiltrated. Surrender, give up the intruders, and we won't hurt any Domestics inside, over."*

Diamond slammed her fist down on the table. "Shit."

"How do they know?" Glitch asked.

"David," Tracey replied. "They must have David."

Python scowled and picked up the radio. "This is Outpost Command, and you can go fuck yourself, over."

The room fell silent. Minutes ticked by that felt like a lifetime.

"Outpost Command, you have one hour to comply. Give up the intruders, or we start killing prisoners." There was a pause, and a scream. *"Tell 'em your name, honey."*

"Lorrie…" said a shaky voice through the crackling static.

A loud pop reverberated in the speaker. Diamond flinched.

"That one was to make it clear we aren't fucking around. You have one hour, over."

Glitch stared at the transceiver in disbelief. "What do we do now?"

Sal paced the room. "We can't turn ourselves in. They'll just kill us and put all the Domestics back in cages."

"Or kill 'em," Python added.

Glitch nodded. "More likely than not. Especially if David is talking. They'll know the Domestics helped us."

Tears streaked Tracey's cheeks. "We have to fight."

"Haven't you been payin' attention, sweetheart?" Python asked. "There's too many of 'em to fight."

"But we have the explosives," Tracey said. "We can blow them all to hell."

"What about the Domestics out there?" Diamond asked. "We'd kill them all."

"It's us or them," Python said, "and I vote for us."

"Never thought I'd say this," Tracey said, "but Python's right."

"What about David?" Diamond asked.

Tracey's voice was barely audible. "He isn't one of us anymore."

"No," Diamond said. "We don't have to resort to this. When we go out to face them in the field, Python can take the goat path down and get a better read on their position."

"Then what?" he asked.

"Get the Domestics as far from the blast area as you can."

...

Military tents stood in the dusty underbrush in the valley below B8. The returning soldiers had set up camp at the base of the hill, amidst a cover of cacti and dead shrubs, well within the blast radius of the explosives.

A voice carried across the distance. "You have five minutes. Surrender, or we execute another prisoner."

Diamond leaned against the corpse of a tree, peering into the valley below to survey the enemy lines. For a moment, she wondered what kind of tree it had been. Once, she'd at least known how to tell an oak from a maple, but years of blazing fires and droughts had set them on the path of the dinosaurs.

She wondered if there would still be trees in New Eden.

Diamond stepped out into view of the soldiers below. Beneath her clothes, she wore a bulletproof vest, but she knew that wouldn't stop a bullet to the head. "Are you Connor?"

"Yeah," said a large man with a ginger beard. "You the bitch squatting in our bunker?"

"I'm here to negotiate."

He chuckled and spat. "We aren't here to negotiate. You and your friends throw down your arms and surrender the outpost."

Diamond surveyed the area. Most of the soldiers were concentrated around the central tent. Their facial expressions ranged from bored to amused. These men weren't expecting combat.

"Here's our counter offer. Free the prisoners and leave. The outpost isn't yours anymore."

Connor stared at her for a long moment, then waved at one of his fellow soldiers. The man vanished, then returned pulling the body of a man so beaten he couldn't stand on his own. Connor grabbed the man's hair, jerking his head back.

It was David. His nose was busted, and one eye was swollen shut. Diamond cringed. Time slowed as Connor lifted his gun to David's temple.

A shot rang out.

It took a fraction of a second for her to realize it was Connor that fell.

She willed her body into motion, ducking and rolling out of the way. David had been positioned in front of Connor, which meant whoever shot him knew what they were doing.

Python.

Surprised and leaderless, chaos washed over the enemy camp. Soldiers scrambled in every direction like a swarm of angry wasps.

Diamond sprinted back to rejoin the company. "Negotiations failed," she wheezed.

Sal grinned at her. "We noticed."

As soldiers gathered at the path up the hill, Glitch popped from behind a tree to fire a burst of shots at them. "David's on the ground, but I can't tell if he's hit."

Diamond surveyed the group. "Python, take your people and fan out around them. The Domestics are under guard past their left flank. See if you can get them out of the blast radius so Glitch can play with his toys."

Python nodded and waved his group forward.

Diamond peered from behind a blackened tree trunk. The soldiers were ascending the hill in cautious packs, heads low and rifles at the ready. She searched their ranks to see who'd taken over for Connor.

A man with a bushy, gray beard stood behind the frontline, shouting orders. Diamond nodded to Sal.

Sal followed Diamond's gaze and returned the nod. She waved her contingent to follow. They crept along, keeping a slight distance behind Sal, trying to stay out of the soldiers' line-of-sight.

Glitch leaned with his back against Diamond's. She could feel his body tremble through the layers of gear. Glitch was tough, but he'd never been a soldier. He'd been barely a boy when the world went away.

"You okay?" she asked over her shoulder.

"Ready when you are, boss man." There was a shakiness in his voice she'd never heard before.

"Three...two...one."

The two stood simultaneously, and fired a volley of bullets at the approaching first wave.

...

Diamond had underestimated her enemy. Out of practice soldiers were still soldiers, and the people of B8 had never seen battle before. Some stepped up, but others remained frozen by fear and indecision. They were getting picked off one by one as the soldiers made their advance up the ridge. No matter how well they fought, defeat was a matter of time.

Sal pressed a bandage to the bloody hole in her shoulder. Her face was pale. She'd taken out the new leader, but another had stepped up just as quickly,. "It's not looking good, Di."

Diamond gave the signal to fall back to the next line of trenches, the last before the bunker. If Python didn't get back soon, all they could do was retreat inside. They would fight from room to room, killing as many soldiers as they could, but they'd all die in the end.

A crash through the underbrush startled her to action.

This is it. This is where we all die.

She lifted her gun, but her heart rose in her chest when she saw, not an enemy, but Python staring back at her.

"I took out the guards, but the Domestics were all chained up."

"Did you get them away?"

He didn't meet her gaze.

Diamond lowered her gun and exhaled. She swallowed the rising lump in her throat. "Then we're fucked. The explosives are useless. We've retreated too far, and the soldiers are too far out from the second blast area."

Tracey wiped her forehead, smearing dirt and sand across her face. "You have to blow it, or we're dead."

Diamond turned to face her ragged and beaten men. The first wave of soldiers had made their way to the blackened forest and the rest were right behind them. It wouldn't be long before they were overtaken. Tracey was right. If they set off the charges, it would kill the prisoners, but her people might survive.

She'd have to sacrifice the prisoners in order to live. If she gave the order, she'd be no better than her commanding officer when he'd ordered her to fire on civilians. Killing the many for the sake of the few.

Python grabbed her belt loop and pulled her against him, breaking her chain of thought. She was overcome by the taste of his lips against hers. Her body softened, pressing against him. Images flashed through her mind of a life that could be; a life in New Eden with food and friends. Without guns and war. Where each day was about more than survival. Where they could be happy.

Python pulled away, grinning like an idiot. "I've been waiting to do that since Sunnyvale."

Diamond struggled to find words. They were all dead in a matter of minutes, and there was a lot to say. "I'm sorry-"

He put a finger over her lips. "You were right. You can't save us all. Make sure Hannah finishes our book for me, would ya?"

She opened her mouth to ask what he meant, but he turned and lifted his gun.

"Hey, fuckers. Come and get me!"

He punctuated his yell with a blast of gunfire, and took off through the forest toward the right flank.

"Shit!" Diamond yelled. "Where are you going? Stop!"

If he heard her, he made no indication. He popped out from cover long enough to fire a few rounds and sling taunts at the soldiers. Diamond watched as the first-wave soldiers broke off and went after him.

"What is that crazy son of a bitch doing?" Tracey asked.

"He's leading them to the secondary site," Glitch replied. "The other explosives."

"God damn it, cover him!" Diamond shouted and stepped out, firing at the soldiers chasing Python.

The second wave had reached the top of the ridge and was advancing. Glitch grabbed Diamond by the shoulder. "Let him go. He's made his choice."

She turned to fire on the advancing soldiers. Her body took over, placing pressure on the trigger. Blood and dust mingled in the air as people from both sides fell. Her vision went red, and all she could feel was rage.

Seconds passed like minutes, but the sound of explosives shook Diamond back into reality. The ground trembled as she surveyed the battlefield. The enemy soldiers panicked, looking around as though they expected to be surrounded at any moment.

Diamond charged, screaming. The others leapt from the trenches and joined in her battle cry.

The remaining soldiers scrambled and pulled back, retreating down the hill. With the last of them dead or dispatched, Diamond started in the direction Python had led the others.

Glitch rested his hand on her shoulder. "Where you goin', boss man?"

"To find Python."

Glitch shook his head. "Di... He was in range when I set off the charges. There's no way he survived the blast."

Diamond felt pressure behind her eyes. "Why...?"

For a few seconds, she'd allowed herself to imagine what happiness might've felt like after all the fighting and running and hiding were done.

Glitch cleared his throat. "He knew it was the only way we'd have a chance."

Diamond's knees gave out beneath her, and she fell to the ground sobbing. Glitch held her as she wept.

PART FOUR
CARRY ON

Fifty-seven prisoners survived. Tracey took charge of bringing them into the bunker and giving them food and water.

The most difficult task for Diamond was facing Hannah. The girl had been fond of Python, and though she'd taken the news of his death stoically, when Diamond met her in the corridors, she saw red, puffy eyes and the ghosts of tears on the girl's cheeks. But even with Python gone, Hannah remained a regular in the infirmary.

For the sake of David and the other wounded, she started reading Hemingway's book from the beginning again.

The day after the battle, what remained of the council met in the war room. Sal, her left arm still in a sling, tapped the table nervously. "We were able to gather a little intel from one of the soldiers we captured."

Diamond nodded, but her heart wasn't in it. She was off somewhere with Python, Hemingway, and the little girl she'd cut down from the tree so many years ago.

"... was taken over by former soldiers, and it now serves as their base."

"Wait, what?" Diamond asked.

"New Eden," Sal repeated. "Former Corps soldiers attacked and took it over. It doesn't exist anymore."

Diamond went numb. They'd come so far, lost so many friends, and for what? If New Eden was gone...

"Assuming we can believe him, that is," Sal added, but from her expression, she doubted her own words.

"So, now what?" Glitch asked. "If New Eden's gone, where do we go?"

Diamond pushed back from her chair and stood. "We rest, we heal, and we train. Then, when we're strong enough, we march to New Eden and take it back."

Python had been right. She couldn't carry the world on her shoulders, but maybe they could all carry each other.

"We carry on," she said.

"We carry on!" the others cried out.

THE END.

Holley Cornetto was born and raised in Alabama, but now lives in New Jersey where she writes dark fantasy, horror, and weird fiction. To date, her writing appears in over a dozen magazines and anthologies. To indulge her love of books and stories, she became a librarian. She is also a writer, because the only thing better than being surrounded by stories is to create them herself. In 2021, she earned an MFA in fiction writing from Lindenwood University. She is a proud member of the Horror Writers Association.

https://twitter.com/HLCornetto
https://www.facebook.com/hlynn.cornetto.9/

SIN CHASER

BY S.O. GREEN

*For husband John, without whom
none of this would be possible.*

CHAPTER ONE
CRASH

The beast had to be at least a mile wide, tearing a swathe of destruction across the country as it belly-crawled coast-to-coast. Ness stared at the ruined fields and demolished buildings in its wake. Miles and miles of Kansas prairie, torn up to trenches and rubble.

At least i-70 was still intact, or as intact as anything could be after almost half a century and no maintenance. Heat-baked, fissured, littered with rusted wrecks and fallen signage. Chip steered their Hilux around the worst of it and powered over the rest, and Ness was just glad she had the easy job.

"You ever seen one this close before?" she asked, eyes flicking between the demon and the maps lying in her lap.

Chip adjusted his grip on the wheel of the truck. Ness caught his eye in the rear-view. He raked his fingers through his wiry, white beard. Not too many folks remembered the time before the Reaping, but Chip did. Made it worse that he was sweating.

"Saw Greed mow through New York City, back when it was more than just a graveyard. You could see people on the ground, like ants, slitting each other's throats for pocket change. Buildings collapsing, streets falling into the subway. Folks should have been running, but they were looting instead."

"How close did you get?"

"Not very. Saw the whole thing through a scope."

"Fuck..."

The true danger of the Big Seven. Not their size, not their casual decimation of anything that stood in their way, but the *aura* they gave off. Sowing their sin like seeds in their wake, inciting the darkest parts of human nature like a spark to dry grass.

The Leviathan might have been the kindest of the Seven. Get too close, and you'd succumb to the heaviest, most numbing sloth. Your muscles, your heart, your brain would atrophy in seconds. Even at that distance, Ness could feel her eyelids sagging, the overpowering urge to lay her head down on the dash and never lift it.

A billboard flitted past, flying the sunflower. 'Tiredness kills'.

Leviathan looked like a lizard—flat snout and dull, grey scales. Down below, it would have sat on a hot, flat rock somewhere to wait out eternity. On earth, it circled the globe tirelessly, another wheel spinning in the demonic war machine, purging the earth a city, a settlement, a soul at a time. It'd keep going until it reached the sea, slide into the Pacific somewhere along the California coast, emerge somewhere in Australia or Japan, killing as it went.

There was no pattern, no rhyme or reason to it. If you kept moving, kept an ear to the ground, you could avoid the Seven when they crawled or slithered or soared past. Some years, things were almost peaceful. Folks got to thinking about putting down roots. Always a mistake. They'd come back around, and they'd destroy everything you'd built. Nowhere was safe; nothing was sacred, and it could all change overnight.

Someone needed to warn people to get out of the way.

Ness lifted the ham radio handset. "Archangel, this is Sin Chaser Forty-Five. Be advised, we have Leviathan at the following coordinates and bearing..."

She rattled off her calculations, checked and double-checked. The only good thing about the Big Seven was that they seemed brainless. Easy to predict their movements. Leviathan would probably follow this course until she slipped beneath the waves. Plenty of time for everyone in between to move out of the way.

"Copy that, Forty-Five. God be with you."

"Yeah. Copy that."

Ness dropped the handset back on the dash. She'd learned her lesson about speaking her mind over the radio that time she'd cussed out their absentee father to a chorus of awkward silence. She hadn't thought much of it until Twenty-One hogtied her and tossed her off an overpass. She was just glad she shared a car with one of the few Faithful still tolerant of an atheist.

"You're doing God's work," he usually told her, "in your own way."

"There's a town coming up, few miles ahead," she said, overlaying her topographical map with the up-to-date settlement markers. "Sanctuary. Real original."

Most of the settlements on the map were labeled things like Sanctuary or Bastion or Haven. She wondered if it made them feel safer. Hell, if you believed in something strongly enough, didn't that make it true?

She tried to never compare the new settlements with the ones from the world before the Reaping. Seeing how many candles had been blown out made her drink.

"Are they safe?" Chip asked.

"Should be. So long as it stays on this course."

The radio crackled. Other cars sounded off. Reapers and road crews were carving up the remains of North America. Another of the Seven had crawled up out of the Atlantic, and there was a third heading south through Canada. It'd be a busy few months as the settlements in Ness's territory shifted and fluctuated, trying to keep clear of the chaos. There'd be losses, as usual.

The updates tailed off, and old gospel music spilled from the speakers. The broadcast from Archangel wasn't just news; it also carried an array of music from before the Reaping. Ness liked some of it more than others. She reached for the dial.

"Mind leaving it on?"

"Sure."

She pulled her hand back. For Chip, she could deal. And when the Shepherd started up, well, she'd play it by ear. Depended on what the sermon was today.

She watched Leviathan's hind leg lifting, so high it could have stepped over a building. The impact against the ground bounced the truck on its suspension. Rattling and creaking. Ness felt the vibration in her tired bones.

She cocked her head. Beyond the bulk of its massive body, she could just make out its titanic head, leaning past its left forelimb.

Cold sweat prickled down her back. "She's turning."

"Wha-?"

"Chip, she's fucking turning." She seized the radio handset again. "We need to warn Sanctuary. They're right in the-"

"Ness..."

Her gaze snapped to the rear-view, just in time to see Chip's eyes falling closed, his beard descending onto his chest.

Too close. We're too close.

She snatched for the steering wheel a second too late. Chip's hands fell away and the truck swerved hard.

The world flipped upside down.

...

"What is a Sin Chaser? I'll tell you what. They're the brave women and men, out on the frontline of a war we already lost, trying to keep us, the dregs of humanity, alive long enough that we might be able to rebuild. Should we be thankful to them, even if they are not of our flock? Surely. After all, are we not all at the mercy of the Big Seven, each and every day? But sometimes, Faithful, I can't help but ask myself, what must they be running from, if running towards the Big Seven sounds like the lesser of two evils?"

"Not right now, sister," Ness groaned, twisting the radio dial into silence.

She stared at the dusty asphalt through the shattered windscreen and realized the world was still the wrong way up. Above, her maps and charts were strewn across the ceiling of the cab. A crow sat in the open window, eyeballing her.

"Fuck off," she grunted, swiping at it. It shot skywards in a flurry of black feathers.

She popped her belt and landed on her shoulders, hard. With a growl, she kicked open the passenger-side door. It scraped on the concrete.

"Chip," she gasped, reaching for his blood-streaked face. "Chip, say something."

He dangled from his belt, expression serene behind his Santa Claus whiskers. His Circle hung from its chain, nestled in his beard instead of under his shirt. Slowly, pain creased his features and his blue eyes bloomed open.

"Gotta warn 'em..." he wheezed.

"I'd love to," Ness said, grabbing the handset and twirling the severed cable around one finger, "but we're off the air, old man."

"Gotta get to 'em..."

"Okay. Okay, I get it. Let me just..."

She reached for his belt. He grabbed at her hands, pushing them away until she stopped.

"What the fuck, Chip?"

"Leave me.... Slow you down..."

"I don't care."

"We both know...what happens...after... Stop...the Reapers..."

"How? How am I supposed to...?"

"You'll...figure it out..."

He pulled the Circle from around his neck with bloody fingers, pressed it into her palm. She cringed. A holy symbol didn't feel right in her hands, but how was she supposed to refuse the solemnity in his eyes.

"You're doing God's work," he whispered, "in your own way."

"Chip, I..."

"If the Reapers get there first, they'll... You *have* to go."

"I'll come back for you."

He shook his head, tucked his hands into his shirt to keep them from dangling. Just a little dignity. Red trickled through his hair and dripped from the bald patch on his crown. Ness tried to figure out where all the blood was coming from.

"Don't," he said, finally. "Won't be nothing worth coming back for."

She took a breath, false-started a sentence, and settled on, "God be with you."

He smiled, crimson-marbled teeth. His tears snagged in the blood in his eyebrows. "Copy that."

Ness crawled out of the wreckage, stopped just long enough to grab the tire iron that had fallen out of the trunk, and started the long hike towards Sanctuary.

CHAPTER TWO
AWAKE AND ALIVE

Sanctuary was dead.

Ness stood in what passed for the town square of the town with the hideously ironic name, tire iron in one hand, baseball cap emblazoned with a slogan that meant nothing to nobody anymore in the other. She chewed her lip, took a breath and pulled the cap over her fire-red hair, threading her ponytail out the back.

About one hundred people, all told. They'd lay down to sleep and hadn't got back up. A few folks were sprawled in the dirt outside the church—the biggest, grandest building in town—but most of them had died at prayer. She could see them through the doors, slumped in the aisle, kneeling with their heads bowed, leaning into each other in the pews. The little prefabs they called their homes had barely survived the tremors from Leviathan's passing.

It was on the horizon now, just a grey smudge. Ness wondered if it knew how many people it had killed.

The Big Seven didn't even stop to collect their own harvests.

The Reapers would come soon. They were scavengers. Fucking carrion feeders, and this was a meal they wouldn't pass up.

She needed to burn the bodies. All a hundred of them. As she saw it, she only had one option. Drag them all into the church and make it their pyre.

Doing God's work, in her own way.

She picked up one of the bundles that was easiest to carry and hurried into the church, trying not to step on anyone as she passed. She lay her burden down by the altar and mopped the sweat off her brow.

Just another dozen dead children still to go.

Something moved, inside the church. Ness twisted, eyes narrow, ears sharp, tire iron in hand.

"Someone there?"

She heard a gasp, a sob. She passed the end of the front pew and saw a girl—couldn't have been older than fourteen—kneeling beside a dead woman. She looked up, tan face emerging through a curtain of lustrous, black hair. Tears dripped off her chin and spotted her pristine, white church dress.

"Hands," Ness ordered, because pretty, little girls weren't always pretty, little girls, especially when they were alone in a dead town.

The girl did as she was asked, trembling with shock and grief and fear. She looked lost. Terrified. Ness realized the town hadn't prepared her to deal with something like this.

They called it Sanctuary for a reason. They never expected her to need to.

"Name."

"F-Faith," the girl whispered.

"You the only survivor?"

A sob caught in Faith's throat and she looked like she'd buckle. Instead, she kept her back straight and nodded.

"How?"

"I... I don't know."

"Can you stand? Walk? Carry?"

Another nod.

"Good. Then I need you to help me bring them all in here. We need to cremate them now, before the Reapers show."

"What's a Reaper?"

"You don't... Holy shit, girl, are you kidding?"

Faith shook her head. Outside, in the godless dark, an engine roared to a stop on the border of town. Ness heard laughter, jeering. Diesel-fed jackals looking for a corpse to strip.

"You're about to find out," Ness growled.

She slid back to the door, leaned hard against the wall, and glanced out. Three of them—two males, one female—dressed in hard-wearing leathers. Ink in the skin, faces full of shrapnel, hair both shaved and cultured in equal measure. Probably part of an old road crew, but the rot had set in. They were Reapers now, all sharp teeth and red eyes.

As she watched, the female straddled a woman in a summer dress, grabbed her by the shoulders and crushed their mouths together. She started sucking and sucking and sucking, until the dead woman's throat distended around something glowing so bright it lit up the veins in her neck. The Reaper pulled it into her mouth with a slurp, and the thing shone green in the line between them. Then she swallowed it.

Ness heard a gasp at her shoulder. Faith watched the whole thing, eyes wide and hands clamped over her mouth.

"Don't worry," Ness said, gesturing with the tire iron. "I'm not gonna let them get away with it."

The other Reapers stalked around the bodies, eyes lit with savage delight, probably wondering how many they could get away with before others arrived. And they *would* arrive. This was just the vanguard.

Ness still didn't know how the Reapers chose their meals. What were they looking for? Purity? Corruption? Conflict? Or was it just a free-for-all? Was a soul just a soul when you didn't have one of your own?

The closest walked up the steps to the church, lips peeling back in a shark-toothed leer as he glimpsed the extent of the feast ahead. Then he spotted Ness in the corner of his eye and his glee soured.

The tire iron smashed his temple, crushed his eye socket and burst his eye like an overripe grape. He pitched back. Ness grabbed his jacket and kicked his feet out, slamming him to the floor and hammering his face into the 'All Are Welcome' doormat until he stopped struggling.

By then, his friends had noticed.

The other male drew a pistol from a side holster. The bloody iron whirled across the space between them and flattened his nose. Before he could shake it off, Ness drop-kicked him in the chest and sent him sprawling.

She grabbed his arm and twisted, spiral-fracturing him from wrist to shoulder. He jammed the gun at her as she mounted him and she blocked it, thrust the barrel under his chin. She flicked the safety off.

"No, no, n-"

The top of his head popped like a bottle cap, spattering the ground behind him with black ichor. Before Ness could get to her feet, the female tackled her with a shrieking cackle and they tumbled in the dirt. The Reaper came out on top, straddling her, hammering fists into the side of her head. Ness covered up and the Reaper bit her on the arm, needle teeth piercing through the rough fabric of her drab army jacket.

Ness tried to throw it off, but it grabbed her by a fistful of hair and pulled her closer, their lips on a collision course.

"Let me taste you," the Reaper breathed. "Let me devour you."

"Hard pass," Ness grunted, sliding the hunting knife off the creature's belt and stabbing it through the underside of its jaw.

The blade pinned its mouth shut, and surprised it enough that Ness could flip it onto its back. She drew her leg back and toe-kicked the hilt of the knife. The point burst out the top of the Reaper's head and she stopped moving.

Ness pushed herself up, staggering from the tumble, and snatched the pistol from the dead man's hand. She ran to the woman the Reapers had violated, cold sweat chilling her back. She aimed the gun at her forward, just as she sat up with a scream and her teeth elongated and her eyes turned bloody red.

"No!" Faith yelled, and then the gun barked and the dead woman was dead again.

Silence reigned in Sanctuary. Ness tucked the gun into her waistband, grabbed the corpse by the ankles and started dragging it towards the church. It left a trail of black in the dirt behind it.

"What did you do?" Faith whispered, when she reached the door. "Wasn't she alive?"

Ness shook her head. "Not the way it works, kid. The Reapers take your soul, you're just another empty vessel for them to set up shop. She'd have preferred it this way. Trust me."

"They took her soul?"

"They can't take it into the ether with them. Every soul these three ever took, they're in the wind now. Hopefully they end up where they want to be."

Faith stared at the mess Ness had made outside the church. She gulped, then squared her shoulders.

"You said I needed to carry?"

"Yeah. I'd appreciate it. Then we can get moving."

"Moving?"

Ness nodded. "There'll be more Reapers coming. That's why we need to move quick."

"You want me to...come with you?"

"I need to get you to Archangel, let someone in charge know about you. Kid, you survived one of the Big Seven. Far as I know, that's never happened before."

She stared at Faith, at the wide-eyed alarm in her eyes, the vulnerable tremble in her lips. Odds were, she had no idea just how important she was.

"You could change everything."

CHAPTER THREE
AS YOU GO

"Isn't that what we're all looking for, Faithful? A place to call home? A place to call our own? I know, sometimes, things seem hopeless. Why, it seems like this maelstrom we're caught in is never going to end. But we're all part of the Struggle now, and what we build up will surely be laid low again. We must weather that destruction, together, and keep the Faith. Heaven above is our only place beyond the storm."*

"Yeesh," Ness grunted. "That lady is laying it on thick today."

Even on low volume, she could still hear the Shepherd preaching, but she needed the station on to know if the route was clear all the way to Archangel. Hell, she needed the station to know where Archangel *was* these days.

She'd taken a truck from Sanctuary with a full tank of gas. After dealing with the bodies, she hadn't been able to risk looking for food, water, weapons, so all she'd taken was the Reapers' pistol and knife.

Sanctuary probably didn't *have* weapons. Pacifists. Didn't even shoot varmints. They'd embraced the Struggle, big time. God only knew how they'd survived so long.

Before they mounted up, Ness took Chip's Circle from her pocket and pressed it into Faith's hand.

"This belonged to a friend of mine, but it don't feel right to me. Figure he'd want you to have it, since you're special."

"I'm not that special," Faith whispered, staring into the bonfire where her church used to be.

They'd ridden in silence since then, until Ness turned down the radio.

"I like her," Faith said.

"Who, the Shepherd?"

"She's nice. Lot of the folks back home said she helped them get through the day sometimes. Reminded them of what was important."

"The Struggle?"

The girl shook her head. "The Struggle's about getting to Heaven. That's not important. It's about being kind, no matter what else the world wants you to be."

"Not a good attitude for survival."

"Survival's not important either. Not really."

Ness scoffed. "We'll agree to disagree."

They fell back into silence, but Ness turned the volume dial up a couple notches, and smiled when Faith started humming along to old Christian rock ballads.

"Need to find some place to stop," Ness said eventually.

"Really? I thought you said we had enough gas for a day or two."

"We do, but I'm a little beat up and a little hungry."

"Oh," Faith said, glancing at the wound on Ness's arm like she didn't understand it. "Okay then."

There was a farmhouse ahead, lights on. Ness veered off the road and powered through the rough patch of dust that might have been a field once, until the topsoil stripped away. She came up on the house's dark side and parked. Problem with a place this quiet, Reapers and road crews could hear an engine a mile off.

She popped the door and stepped down, pistol at the ready. Faith saw it and shook her head.

"Don't," she said. "Please?"

Ness stared at her a moment, then nodded and slid the gun away under her jacket. Made more sense anyway. Less chance of being shot on sight if someone spotted her first.

She walked across the field, straddling the line between sneaking and remaining unthreateningly visible. Halfway to the house, a floodlight burst into life. She lifted her hands.

"Kiss the dirt," a man's voice ordered.

Ness nodded and obeyed. Reapers tended to shoot first and suck souls later—first degree ids, never satisfied unless something was blowing up. Could have been a road crew, but...

Set up in a farmhouse like this? Didn't seem likely.

She scanned the house as she lay down. Lights were on in the upper windows, but flickering. Candles. Dark shapes stood at the curtains. Watchmen? Or dress shop dummies, so's it seemed like a full house?

"Don't mean you no harm," Ness said, as the stranger approached. "But I'm kind of banged up and I've got a girl with me. Need some place to spend the night."

"And you were fixing to use *my* place?"

"If that's cool. I've got...a pistol I can trade."

Suddenly, she was regretting taking nothing from Sanctuary. Still, a trade was only important if this guy was a peaceable sort. Otherwise, he'd be more interested in the knife in her sleeve than the pistol.

"You Faithful?" he asked.

"The girl is."

"And she's travelling with you?"

"I'm her...guardian."

He stood over her, rifle aimed at her back. He studied her, then glanced over at the truck. Hopefully, Faith was staying out of sight for the moment.

Before Ness could slide the knife out of her jacket and find a place for it, he said, "Okay, on your feet. Bring the little lady inside."

...

"So it's just the two of you here?" Ness asked.

Harlon, her friend with the rifle, nodded. He stirred a cooking pot full of beans over a gas stove, the flicker of the hissing flame lighting in his greying beard. His wife, Marie—a fading blonde with sunken cheeks and a bright smile and work boots on under her dress—sat opposite Ness at the table, stitching the circular split in her forearm, while Faith watched. Ness had hung her jacket in the hall, like a real house guest.

"For a few years now, ever since our baby girl left for Archangel. Said she wanted to be closer to the Struggle."

"We're going to Archangel," Faith said, with a smile.

"Kid!" Ness snapped. Faith flinched.

"Don't be hard on her, Ness," Marie said, pushing the needle through a little more forcefully than before. "She's just a girl."

"No offence, but you don't know the shit I was doing when I was her age."

"And I'm sorry for that, but she's obviously come from a good home. Can't blame her for not being as suspicious as you."

"Maybe not, but I still need to keep her safe, and part of that is not telling complete strangers where we're headed. You seem nice enough, but plenty of people *seem* nice."

"Very true," Marie said. "Are you listening, Faith? Ness is giving good advice."

"Yes'm."

"Might have a proposition for you, if you're interested," Harlon said, setting a bowl of beans down in front of Ness, who started shoveling one-handed.

"Depends on the proposition," she said, full-mouthed. "We can't stay long."

He nodded. "You've got your reasons and I won't pry. But if you're heading to Archangel anyway, maybe you could deliver a letter for us. To our daughter. I can't offer you much in the way of payment, but I can point you some place you could find supplies."

Ness tried not to smirk. Folks like Harlon and Marie, she was pretty sure they'd give her the location anyway. Anything to help Faith, who they'd been smitten with from the start, reach her destination.

But she tried, wherever possible, not to be an asshole.

"Sure. I can't make any promises, but..."

"You should find her pretty easily when you get there," Marie said. "Most folk in Archangel know her."

"We'd love to help," Faith said, face all lit up.

Ness scooped beans into her mouth to hide a smile. "We sure would."

...

Ness slept on the floor in front of the bedroom door, while Faith took their daughter's old bed. They woke at dawn and ate coarse oatmeal with purified water. Marie had washed and mended Ness's jacket during the night.

Harlon gave them a map with the location of a good prospect marked on it. An old shopping mall, if Ness read it right. It had the potential to be a big haul, or a terrible dud. She'd approach it the same way she approached everything. Like a fucking landmine.

They departed with a wave and a tear from Faith. Marie remarked that it was like having their daughter back, just for a night, and she and her husband agreed that their baby girl could have grown up to be Ness quite easily.

Marie went inside to fix lunch. Harlon took his rifle and strolled around the farmhouse, thinking on the stranger and her ward, and their mission to get to Archangel, and how things happened all the time that he didn't understand, but which God still expected him to play a part in, so all he could do was try his best to do right.

He didn't see the car—the second parked on his land in two days—until it was too late. Then the knife was under his chin and the whisper was in his ear.

"Where did you send them?" it demanded.

"I'm not telling you a thing," Harlon said, breathing the scent of ash, "Reaper."

"Should I incentivize you? Perhaps your wife will be more inclined to tell me."

Harlon spat in the dirt. The knife shaved a quarter-inch of his beard.

"You don't know my wife," he growled. "She'll tell you, same as I will. Go back to the pit."

"That is unfortunate. But not altogether unexpected."

He felt the Reaper's muscles tense and twisted, bringing the rifle up. The shot rang out across the fields, scattering a hundred crows.

In the silence that followed, only one of them started the long walk back towards the farmhouse.

CHAPTER FOUR
SHADOWS

*"*What do you expect to find in the derelict places of this world? Food? Water? Or a sign from God that you were meant to survive another day? Salvage has become our way in this world, but beware the easy path, Faithful. Beware the harvest that was sown in the world before, because that harvest has already been Reaped. Why, you're just as likely to find death in those old haunts as anything to give life."*

The grey highway swallowed them up. Six lanes of open road and theirs was the only car. The only one driving at least. Plenty of jack-knifed trucks and burnt-out wrecks to swerve around. Urban obstacle course. The truck from Sanctuary had been well-maintained. It handled the jigsaw asphalt with aplomb.

The desolation could get heavy, which was why Ness was grateful for the literal break, when the road gave way to a field of sunflowers that'd transgressed its borders and overtaken the highway. They clipped through the overgrowth at speed, scattering yellow petals, and for a moment the truck cab was full of laughter. Not for the first time, Ness was reminded that Faith was new to all of this.

"Do you think we'll find everything we need at this place?" Faith asked, studying the map Ness had given her to navigate by.

"We should. These places used to have everything. Food, water, clothes. Speaking of which, we need to get you something to wear."

"What's wrong with what I'm wearing?"

"You look too much like a girl."

"I *am* a girl."

"Yeah, and that's the problem." Ness bit her tongue. She could feel her temper rising. She needed to tamp that shit down. It wasn't Faith's fault she didn't know better. "Some people do terrible things to girls."

"But that's not my fault, just because I'm a girl."

"No, kid. You're right. It ain't your fault. It's not any girl's fault when it happens, and in the best possible world, maybe it doesn't. But this ain't that world, and we need to be careful. I don't want you getting hurt, okay?"

Faith nodded, hesitant, and Ness wondered what the people in Sanctuary had told her about the world she lived in. Did she know about the Reaping? The Big Seven? She didn't have a clue about Reapers, and that alone was baffling.

How did someone go fourteen years in this world without ever seeing a single Reaper?

They drove on a little longer, and the only words that passed between them were directions. They rolled off the cracked asphalt tongue into the bowels of a ravaged suburb. A corroded sign dangling over the road welcomed them to Junction City. They circled north, heading for Harlon's cache, and avoiding the inner city. Faith stared at the crumbling buildings, threaded green with the promise of nature's second coming. Ness wondered if she was thinking about her own home, now a ruin.

"I'm sorry," she said. "About your folks."

"My birth momma died when I was born. She lived just long enough to name me. I was raised by the town. They...called me a miracle, on account of how I didn't have a daddy."

Ness nodded, but said nothing. She'd heard of a few miracle babies in her time. Usually, daddy was a Reaper, or someone well on their way to becoming one.

"You always live in Sanctuary?"

"Yeah, but... We moved around a lot at first. I remember...a lot of roads and things, when I was little. They said the place they settled down was better than where they started."

Ness chose not to point out they shouldn't have settled down at all. Not if they wanted to keep breathing.

"They always told me my momma was a good person. Close to an angel, they said. I...I kept asking why someone so good had to die so I could live."

"Some questions don't have an answer," Ness said. "Not a nice one anyway."

She chewed her tongue as she steered them through the demolished town. She thought over how much to share, how much of the story to tell. She decided, as she often did, to give unsolicited advice instead.

"Some people die and some people live, and it feels like it's all wrong. Way I figure it, all you can do is try to make the world as good a place as they'd have made it."

"Sounds like something the Shepherd would say."

Ness scowled. Faith laughed. Then her good humor tapered off and her eyes turned again to the tombstones of the old world all around.

"How does it get like this?"

"Neglect. All these places need maintenance, kid. Leaks, cracks, broken windows, fires. Not enough people to fill up all the houses and stop it so it...spirals. No one's lived here since the Reaping, I'll bet."

Such a waste. Water gone stagnant, food rotten, shelter crumbled and people dead. So much the new world could have used but...

Too static to survive the Big Seven. Too much that couldn't be moved quickly. Humanity had become a nomadic species, chased from one camp to another by the worst of supernatural disasters, carrying their lives in duffel bags and car trunks.

And then there were the Reapers, picking off the stragglers, the lost and lonely and vulnerable.

"I'm sorry," Faith said. "I don't know enough about this world."

Ness sniggered. "What, you think I do? Your guess is as good as mine, kid. I have a few more tricks up my sleeve, sure, but... The way you talk about survival, like it doesn't matter? I'd kill for an ounce of that grace."

"It's mostly tough talk. I don't want to die."

"No one does. No one who loves something anyway."

"What do you love?"

Ness pursed her lips. She cranked the dial on the radio. Faith didn't ask any more questions.

On the road ahead, the mall came into view, a shattered cathedral to the fallen religion of consumerism, glass smashed and steel rusted. Some-where, in those moss-speckled caves and silent tunnels marked by ancient obelisks proclaiming 'You Are Here', was the possibility of an easy ride the rest of the way to Archangel.

How many other people had taken that bait?

...

She parked the truck out of sight of the road, behind a decrepit billboard for consumer electronics bearing the logo of a company everyone now called 'The Apple of Forbidden Knowledge'. No one phoned anymore.

Ness advised Faith to stick close, but she didn't need to. The girl was glued to her hip, and every time she looked back she flashed a soft smile of encouragement.

The doors had been chained up decades ago. They stepped through an empty frame, boots crunching glass. Ness swept the flashlight Harlon had gifted them across the interior. Dust motes danced in the beam. Weeds between the tiles, ivy on the walls, stagnant ponds where fountains used to be, and a few dozen rusted shutters. Any one of them could have hidden a goldmine. Or a Reaper.

She tried to remember what the faded names above the stores meant. Some were useful—clothes, food, drink—others not so much. Once, she'd cracked open a unit in a place like this and found dozens and dozens of electronic appliances, each as heavy and water-damaged as the last—wash-ing machines, dryers, fridges.

Maybe people had felt safe enough owning those things, once upon a time, but imagining lugging even one of them around made her queasy. They were anchors now, nothing more, and they'd drag you all the way to the bottom.

"This one," Ness said, and used her tire iron to break the padlock off a unit with a picture of a mountain on its sign. "Get yourself a new look. I'll see if I can find us some food. Then we can go looking for gas."

"Will there be gas here?"

"Places like this used to have about a million visitors a day and just about all of them had cars, so yeah, some place would have been selling gas."

She yanked up the shutter and looked around the store's darkened interior. Racks of hard-wearing hiker's clothes, ski poles, boots and rucksacks. They even had a kiddie section. Perfect.

"Whatever you want, it's yours. Once you're ready, grab a bag and come find me."

Faith turned to marvel at the outfit choices and Ness caught her by the wrist.

"If anything happens, you scream bloody murder until I get there, understand?"

The girl gave a hesitant nod. Confident that she indeed understood, Ness snatched a rucksack from the rack and strode deeper into the mall, on the hunt for the kind of prey that came in cans.

She popped a couple more shutters, shuddering at the extravagant blooms of mold that had once been fresh food or badly sealed containers. The stagnant reek made her throat close in protest. One unit, signed as 'Nursery Days', turned out to be full of baby clothes and toys instead of seeds and gardening tools the way she expected. Part of her had hoped to find a flourishing orchard behind the steel.

She studied the shelves for a moment, wondering what an age-appropriate toy for a fourteen-year-old girl in the post-Reaping days looked like. She picked a plastic bracelet off a spinning stand. 'Faith' engraved on glittery, rainbow polyhedrons. She tucked it in her pocket and didn't even bother to look for her own name.

She had a good feeling about the fifth unit she cracked. The sign was camo-painted and covered in stars. Sure enough, when she dragged the shutter up, the place was full of military surplus—tents, sleeping bags, knives, crossbows. She'd age another year before she got through taking inventory of the place.

"Gonna need a bigger truck," she muttered, throwing down her rucksack and going straight for the MREs stacked in the back.

She crammed food and a couple of canteens into the bag, added sleeping bags for the inevitability of unconsciousness, and buckled a hunting knife to her thigh. She hadn't had a brand new blade in ever.

This was the conflict every wanderer of the Reaped world faced at one point or another. Travel light, or accrue stuff. Travel light? Accrue stuff?

Honestly, she could see the appeal of both.

No wonder materialism had been so popular.

She was browsing crossbows, trying to gauge the draw poundage that would give the best penetration of a Reaper's skull, when she heard footsteps out in the mall proper, echoing through the empty halls.

It wasn't Faith. Too heavy, too rhythmic. She was pretty sure that girl skipped everywhere. This was the sound of someone marching in solid soles.

Ness hadn't heard that gait in a long time. Not long enough. She snatched her rucksack and slung it over one shoulder on her way out the door, as cold fear raked its claws down her spine.

"Shit," she grunted, winding her way back to where she'd left Faith. "Shit, shit, shit…"

She was halfway to the store with the hiking gear when she turned a corner and almost collided with Faith. Her hand dipped for the pistol in her waistband before she could stop herself.

"Ready to go shopping!" Faith said brightly, holding up a rucksack that was optimistically as big as Ness's.

She'd changed into a thick, canvas jacket, a pair of cargo pants and hiking boots, and she'd snagged a baseball cap from somewhere that was just as meaningless as the one Ness wore. Her enthusiasm faltered when she saw the look in Ness's eyes, and turned to alarm when she dragged her by the wrist into the shadow of a door marked 'Employees Only'.

"What's going on?" she whispered.

"We're not alone."

"Reapers?"

Ness nodded. It was true; it just wasn't the half of it.

"But… You can fight Reapers. You did it before. It's…easy for you."

"Not this time. This time, we run. Take my hand and don't let go, and don't stop until we're back at the truck."

"We need supplies, don't we?"

"You know why the Big Seven destroyed the old world? Because people couldn't let go. They sat in their houses with all their shit around them until it was too late to run and then they died like fucking kings of ancient Egypt, with all their mountains of crap still piled up around them.

Sometimes, you have to let go."

Understanding slowly bloomed in Faith's expression. She nodded. Ness grabbed her hand until her knuckles went white and started running.

They burst back out into the corridor, pelting towards the broken window they'd climbed through, past the units filled with kaleidoscope growths of mold and the baby store and the hiker's paradise where Faith had dressed herself up like Ness's prettier little sister.

She heard the footsteps again, echoing behind her. They quickened in pace. Her heart leapt into her throat, panic rising with the tempo of her pulse.

They weren't going to make it.

"Vanessa!"

The voice filled the building to its rust-speckled rafters, not a shout but a command, and the terror almost paralyzed her.

"Go!" she ordered, shoving Faith ahead. "Don't look back!"

She spun, pistol drawn. Their stalker was a silhouette in the light filtering from the shattered panes above, striding inexorably after them, looming and muscled, the only color, the only detail, a pair of gleaming red eyes.

She fired. The shadow streaked to the side, vanishing through a side door. Ness bolted. She dropped into a baseball slide through the broken window, saw Faith leaning from the truck's passenger door, relief warring with terror in her expression.

She threw the rucksack—one, measly rucksack from the whole building—into the bed, wrenched the driver door open and dragged herself behind the wheel. She stamped the gas pedal and they roared away from the mall, a plume of dust billowing out behind them.

She didn't let up on the accelerator until the image of the building in their rear-view was nothing but a memory.

But wasn't that the point? Memories could always come back to haunt you.

CHAPTER FIVE
THE BEAUTIFUL

*"P*ay no mind to the words from the mouths of Reapers. They are the fading echoes of past lives. They may look like people you know. People you love. Heck, they may look like people. But these are not God's children any longer. They are but empty vessels, given over to house demons, and if they do not try to take your spirit through force, they will tempt you to break your spirit through sin. Then, you will become as empty and as wicked as they are. Keep the Faith. Embrace the Struggle."*

"I don't get it," Faith said, screwing down the radio volume. "What did you see? Why did you look so scared?"

Ness drummed her fingers on the steering wheel, fighting the temptation to crank the music back up and drive tight-lipped and angry until they reached Archangel.

It had to be a coincidence, him showing up again. Maybe it could have had something to do with the girl, her unique power, but he'd never cared about politics. No, this was all an unhappy accident. She was pretty sure of that.

"Everyone has a past," she said. "Sometimes, it catches up to you."

"And you're running away? That doesn't sound much like you."

Ness sniggered. "Thanks for the vote of confidence, kid. Nice outfit, by the way."

Faith checked the clothes she'd picked out at the mall and flushed. "Did I do okay? I don't know what people wear when they're on a road trip."

"Little different from your church clothes, huh?"

"Those weren't my church clothes; they were just my...clothes."

"You look just fine. Even if you are horning in on my racket."

She tugged at the peak of Faith's cap. She giggled and swatted her away. The laughter felt better than the uneasy tension that had dogged them all the way from the mall. Ness adjusted the wing mirror and gave one last, long look to make sure they weren't being followed, then resolved to leave the incident at the mall where it belonged: behind her.

"Got something for you," Ness said, fishing out the colorful bracelet from her jacket pocket.

"For me?" Faith inspected it, face lighting up. "It's got my name on it! How did you-?"

"I just found it in the mall. Figured you might like it. Guess Faith was a popular name even before the Reaping."

She watched the girl slip the bracelet on, still marveling at it, and hid a smile. She wished that moment could last forever, but they had new problems developing.

She tapped the fuel gauge. "Shit. We're redlining."

"Gas?"

"Yeah. Which leaves us with two options. Find gas or find a new ride with gas in it."

"I take it we won't make it if we try to walk the rest of the way to Archangel?"

She didn't want to make her feel bad, but Ness couldn't help but laugh. "Do you like having feet?"

Faith peered at the map Harlon had given them. It didn't just mark the mall, but a few other places too. Ness wondered if he'd scouted them all from the farmhouse, or if it was a relic from his own days as a wanderer. How accurate could it be?

"This could be a gas station, right?" the girl asked eventually, pointing at a marker on the road ahead.

Ness glanced at it. An arrow and a circle. The word 'Gas?'

"Great. I love question marks."

Even so, she was desperate enough to try.

They weaved through the rubble from a crumbled overpass, past a field of wrecks in the other lane, stuck waiting to escape Topeka, lying broken on the horizon. The drivers were still there, skeletal and weathered as their vehicles. A swathe wider than the interstate had been cut through the city center, the buildings shouldered aside like corn stalks. Ness wondered which of the Big Seven had flattened this place, what these people had felt crawling into their brains before they died.

She'd seen sights like this a few times before. The enormity of it hit you in the guts the first time, then it just made you feel tired and small and pointless. Finally, you just stopped looking.

Faith looked. She took in every morbid, grotesque detail—the bones and rags and rust and ash—like looking away would dishonor the dead who'd been given no cremation.

"Did the Reapers...?"

"Probably. I don't know much about the war. Before my time. But I heard it was anarchy. Big Seven destroying all the major cities, Reapers appearing everywhere, killing people, stealing souls. Whatever they use them for, some of them must be sitting pretty nowadays after places like this."

They rolled past the bone yard, but Faith's eyes followed it in the wing mirror for another mile. Then they reached the marker on Harlon's map.

It wasn't a gas station. It was a hotel—the kind of place that'd once had Michelin stars and charity galas, celebrity photo ops and fashion shows—and it still gleamed with all that luster, even in this grimy, gritty wasteland. Unbroken glass, uncrumbled stone, unplundered resources. Armed guards patrolling the grounds in sharp, black uniforms, gilded doors revolving idly, banners bearing an emblem of a narrow, green eye fluttering in the breeze. Ness stared, just as long and hard as Faith.

There were people in the lobby and in the windows. Languid movement, like predators at rest.

"We're not stopping here," Ness said.

"But we need gas, right?"

"Not this badly."

"Shouldn't we at least talk to them. I mean, they're human, aren't they? Like us?"

"Kid, a building like this, in a *world* like this? I don't know *what* these people are, but it ain't nothing like human."

She started up the truck. It was time to leave. But at the corner ahead, a jeep rolled out in front them, repurposed ex-military with more of the black-clad soldiers riding in it. The man riding shotgun pointed down, advising her to kill the engine.

Before Ness could throw the truck into reverse, either to find another route or get distance to ram them, another jeep blocked their path.

"Shit..."

Ness reached for her pistol. Half a dozen rifles locked on her and she lifted her hands back onto the wheel. Her new friend slid out of the vehicle ahead and sauntered up to her window. He stopped to kick the front tire on the way past, like he was a grease monkey about to tell her about tread depth.

"Can we help you, ladies?" he asked, leaning against the door.

"We were looking for gas, that's all," Ness said, because why not tell the truth? "Don't mean to pry. We were just about to move on, if you don't mind."

"And what brings you out this way?"

"Sin Chasers."

He arched an eyebrow. "The girl too?"

"She's my navigator."

"Well, you're not related. No resemblance. So you're, what, one orphan looking out for another?"

"That any of your business?"

Any good humor in his voice and in his eyes evaporated like spit off hot blacktop. "Everyone who comes this way is my business. This place isn't for just anyone. People who've seen us are a liability."

Ness considered her response. She settled on grabbing him by the collar and pulling him through the window. He swore, tried to fight her off, and she put her forge-fresh new blade under his chin so that he'd reconsider.

The guns stayed trained on her, but they wanted him alive more than they wanted her dead. Promising.

"Hold tight," she ordered, shooting a glance at Faith.

She wrenched the gear lever and stamped the gas, sawing the wheel around. The truck lurched, clipping the corner of the jeep in front, scraping sparks. Their passenger cried out, pulling his legs clear as they roared past. He grabbed for Faith so Ness banged his head off the dash.

The blockade gunned their engines, swinging around to give chase. Still no shots fired, so she figured she'd keep hold of her captive until they'd built up enough speed to make a clean break.

"Ness, look out!" Faith screamed.

She stood on the brake, because a pair of children had just run out into the road. Tires screeched and rubber burned. Ness's belt snapped tight around her ribcage. Faith let out a cry of pain and alarm. A moment later, a pair of military vehicles full of angry soldiers buffeted them with a one-two punch to the flanks. They shouted orders and dragged their kidnapped colleague out through the window.

Ness couldn't take her eyes off the kids. They were laughing, chasing, tossing a baseball between them like they hadn't just been run down. There were others, about a dozen in total, playing in the deserted street like it was a fenced backyard, not the doorstep of a blighted ruin. Their features were all subtly different, but there was sibling resemblance in them all.

On the verge, a woman in a flowing, white dress watched their games with an indulgent smile. Mom, because the resemblance was all hers. The soft, black hair like silk ribbons, the lean, willowy frame, the pale skin.

And the sparkle of those emerald eyes.

...

"You weren't even remotely tempted to steal from us?" Lailah asked.

Introductions had come after the soldiers had forced her and Faith out of their truck and frog-marched them back to the hotel, Lailah and her platoon of children following in their wake. Ness had broken a man's nose for clutching Faith's arm so tight she cried out and cable-ties had been threatened, but Lailah had insisted they weren't necessary. Not for 'guests'.

Ness wondered at her definition. Real guests didn't need to be invited in at gunpoint.

The guards had led them through the foyer, filled with gawking men and women in the finest suits and gowns the old world had been able to provide, patched and faded and frayed from forty years of constant wear.

They looked like guests at a dinner party that had gone on a few decades too long. Presumably, Lailah had been the one to invite them.

"I try not to be an asshole," Ness said, by way of explanation. "Stealing makes you an asshole, in case you didn't know."

Lailah chuckled. She trailed her fingers through the hair of the grinning girl sitting beside her in a way that made Ness deeply uncomfortable. She wore her children like jewels, adornments to caress and fondle for her own vanity. *I am mother*. Ness wondered what happened when she got bored.

Even in the eyeball-aching fluorescence of the opulent suite where she hosted them, Lailah's beauty was radiant. Her kids, even possessed of her features, couldn't compare. The blood of their fathers had left them subtly imperfect, and the sharp smiles and hunger in their vivid, green eyes did the rest.

Lailah reclined on her settee and folded one milk-white leg over the other.

"Are you Faithful?"

"What, just because I don't want to be an asshole? The two aren't mutually exclusive."

"No, I suppose you're right. But morality is a priority only for those who believe in a reward for their..." Her eyes twinkled and Ness couldn't tell if it was mirth or malice in those forest shades. "...struggle."

"The reward is being able to live with yourself."

"Eventually, one tires of living only with themselves, wouldn't you agree?"

Ness kept her silence, but she couldn't disagree. She'd promised herself, after what had happened, that she'd go it alone, keep everyone at arm's length. Less chance other people, good people, would get burned if they weren't in the line of fire.

She'd become a Sin Chaser for that reason, until the day Chip had found her lying under an overpass, gagged and bound, and taken her to a doctor he knew. They'd shared a car for months, years. Now she was driving a little girl cross-country and *actually* starting to like her.

So much for keeping them at arm's length.

Whatever Lailah was, she wasn't alone. She held out a delicate hand

and one of the men who formed her entourage placed a champagne flute between her fingers. She didn't even look over at him and Ness marked the tightness in his jaw. Her harem were all handsome and well-built, dressed in the kind of luxury threads that had died with the old world, but most of them bore all manner of mutilations—laceration, burns, even missing extremities. Punishments? Or just cries for her attention?

Lailah stared at Faith, curled up in an armchair reading a book the woman had presented her with, and trying not to notice the proximity of two of Lailah's boys, standing close at hand. *Paradise Lost* was printed on the cover in gold. The frown on Faith's face suggested she didn't know how to feel about it. Any of it.

"The girl is quite sweet," Lailah said, and it might have been a trick of the light, but Ness thought her eyes glowed a deeper green, just for a moment. "And there is something special about her, isn't there? I am sure she would fit right in here, among my children."

Ness caught herself before she could agree. Talking with Lailah was difficult, tiring. If she didn't focus, watch her words, she found herself agreeing with—and to—everything. The light of her smile dazzled.

"Who the hell are you?" she demanded, slowly and carefully. "Not the leader of some luckier-than-average group of survivors, that's for damn sure."

Lailah smirked and tucked a cigarette between her lips. She didn't offer one to Ness, like she could taste the withdrawal burning in the back of her throat. Like she wanted her to be jealous.

"You were going to Archangel, were you not?" she asked, tapping Harlon and Marie's letter to their daughter, lying on the low, glass table between them. "A long trip, with such an unrewarding destination. Is there nothing here that calls to you? Safety and security? The promise of fresh food, clean water, warm beds? The sense of belonging, family, a lover? Is there nothing we have that you want?"

"I just want to get the girl to Archangel."

"Why?"

"Her...family's there."

Faith glanced up from her book and Ness hoped she wasn't judging her for the lie. She couldn't tell Lailah the truth, that she was special, important. Or they might never get away.

"I *will* let you go, my dear," Lailah said, leaning back to let one of her men light her cigarette. She blew a smoke ring that hung above her head like a crooked, disintegrating halo. "But first, you must give me something that I want. Since you do not wish to be a thief, fair and equitable trade is the only reasonable solution."

Actually, given that they were prisoners who'd been taken against their will, the only reasonable solution was escape. And to set a few fires on their way out the door.

"You are a violent woman," Lailah noted, "and skilled. So I will make use of you. Fight for us. Entertain us, and you will have your freedom."

Ness scoffed. "You fight here?"

"Oh, have I intrigued you? Does that mean we have a deal?"

"Depends. Are you going to hold up your end?"

"I *always* honor a bargain," Lailah said, tone becoming grave. "Always."

It was hard to take the other woman at her word, but Ness didn't see that she had much of a choice. At the very least, she had to do something to keep from winding up in a ditch out back with a bullet in her head.

And a fight? In a place like this? How tough could it be?

CHAPTER SIX
MONSTER

They'd built a cage in the grand ballroom—chain-link and steel—and Lailah's residents sat at round tables covered in clean linen and champagne glasses. The atmosphere was cordially electric, a far cry from the fighting pits Ness had seen and competed in. No one was cussing or spitting or drinking straight from the bottle, but Ness was under no illusions. Each and every one of them wanted to see blood.

They'd given her a set of pristine road leathers to change into and an armored metal chest piece that no one in the wasteland would ever have worn. She wondered if this was how they thought people looked outside their hotel walls.

When she stepped out of her dressing room, Lailah was waiting for her, an enigmatic smirk curling the line of her lips. She reached under Ness's arms and tightened the straps on her armor. Stronger than she looked.

"Put on a good show for them, won't you?" she asked, and trailed a finger down the back of her neck as she walked past. "And for me."

She retired to a table of her own, surrounded by her sinister children and doting lovers, and Faith, who was dressed in an elegant frock that probably belonged to one of the ferals. She looked a lamb stumbled among the wolves. Ness shot her a meaningful glance. One fight and they were done. Gone.

A guard with a swollen eye and a vicious scowl showed her to the cage door. Ness flashed him a smile. No hard feelings. It seemed he didn't share the sentiment, because he took no small delight in locking her in.

Her opponent hadn't shown yet. She waited and wondered what kind of champion a place as soft as this could produce.

Then a door slammed somewhere in the bowels of the hotel and the genial conversation tapered off into an expectant hush. Ness heard overlapping footsteps, barked orders, the sound of a struggle.

The ballroom doors burst open. Four of Lailah's guards emerged, dragging a towering shape that had to duck to fit through the frame. They'd lassoed its neck with snare poles, the kind old world animal control would have used on rabid dogs, pulling it in all four points of the compass to keep it leashed. It twisted and bucked, snarling behind the muzzle buckled around its lower jaw, muscles bulging under its straitjacket. It threw its head back and howled, so loud it made the crystal chandeliers rattle. The audience gasped, then let out titters of nervous laughter.

Just glad they weren't the ones who had to fight it.

Ness looked to Faith, tried a grin and a thumb's up. The girl didn't look convinced.

Fair. Ness wasn't much convinced either.

The crimson sheen in the Beast's eyes could only mean it was a Reaper. She didn't know if it was too many souls or too few that turned them feral, but this one hadn't gotten the dosage right.

And she was going to be locked in a cage with it.

They dragged it to the door and her buddy from the road stepped forward to unlock it. The Beast twitched and grunted, eyes rolling and roving, feverish and insane. Some Reapers could pass for human in the right light, but this one? Not a fucking chance.

They wrenched the door open and shoved the Beast through. It stuck in the frame, shoulders too broad, and spat a garbled burst of noise. Then it kicked out, hit one of the guards square in the chest. The blunt force shattered ribs and sent him cannoning back into the guy with the keys. The others wrenched back on their snares, trying to keep it under control. The Beast burst into the cage, and two of the guards let go rather than be dragged inside. The third wasn't so lucky. He flew through the door and tumbled over on the marble floor, on the wrong side of the fence.

The guards outside did much as Ness expected. They slammed the door shut and locked it.

The Beast fixed its bloody eyes on her.

"Come and fucking get it, asshole," she spat.

It roared and charged. Ness had never stood in front of a freight train before, but she thought maybe this was what it felt like. She tucked and rolled at the last second, and the Beast slammed into the cage wall. The whole construction moved under its weight. Ness wondered how, exactly, Lailah wanted her to kill this thing.

Or maybe she didn't. After all, what happened if Ness died? Her residents were entertained and she got another daughter to add to her collection.

"Shit…"

It ran at her again. She slip-stepped and side-kicked, heel snapping the floating rib under its right arm. It grunted and staggered, so at least it felt pain. Then it rounded on her, eyes murderous, and she realized she'd made a mistake.

It kicked at her, bare foot bigger than her torso sailing past as she dodged. The force of the kick tossed her hair, it was so close. She pivoted and stamped through its knee. It was like trying to kick through rebar. It swung around and clubbed her with a massive shoulder, sending her tumbling.

She rolled to her feet, fists up. There was a murmur of appreciation from the audience. She could smell cigarette smoke, but it was a little early for pillow talk.

Three shots tore the air. Ness ducked, before she realized it was the guard who'd been locked in the cage with them. He'd drawn his gun and knife and were holding them cross-gripped. Unfortunately, three 9mm slugs in the torso hadn't done much more than piss it off.

It charged again. The guard had time to unload four more rounds and then the Beast kicked him into the cage wall. He fell, knife skidding away. One arm curled around his chest as he coughed, spattering the marble with a fresh coat of blood. The other raised his pistol, trying to aim as the Beast loomed over him. It lifted its foot and stamped his head into the floor. His skull fractured, a look of horror frozen on his compacted face.

Ness caught the knife under her boot, then flicked it into her hand with her toe. Impressive party trick, but not much help in this situation.

She was now the sole focus of the Beast's rage.

Lucky her.

It powered towards her, screaming behind its muzzle. She danced aside, grabbed hold of the straps on its back and hoisted herself onto its shoulder. She drove the knife down into the side of its neck, sawing at flesh and muscle, sinew and artery. Thick, black ichor gushed, staining her hands and the front of its asylum overcoat. It bucked under her, trying to throw her off so it could crush her underfoot. She heard fabric tearing, buckles straining, and prayed its jacket would hold up.

She kicked off its back, grabbing the top of the cage and clinging on. Her body swung against the fence, the steel frame hitting her like a body blow. She took a breath and scrambled up.

The Beast thrashed, seeking her out. When its eyes turned up and locked on her, it slammed its body into the cage over and over, trying to knock her down. Ness looked for something to use and saw the lighting rig hanging from above, covered in heavy spotlights. It was messy work, secured with rope and repurposed seatbelts, but no one looked behind the curtain around here.

She started sawing through the nearest rope, just as her opponent ripped its strait-jacket off with a roar. Its bare torso had hardened into a chitinous shell, and its gnarled arms ended in what were more knives than fingers. One swipe and it would turn Ness into red confetti.

This thing wasn't just feral. The demon had bedded down into the body so deep it had started to change it, twisting its physiology into the kind of nightmare you'd only have seen beneath the surface of the earth before the Reaping.

How long, exactly, had this thing been alive?

It leapt onto the cage, reaching the top in a single bound. Ness wobbled, trying not to lose her balance and split her skull on the unforgiving marble below. She sliced through a length of rope and another stretched belt as the monster began to drag itself up towards her.

It slashed at her. She pulled away, then kicked it in the face. It reeled back, giving her the opening she needed to cut one final tether. The rig collapsed, weight tearing it from the ceiling and turning it into a pendulum. It smashed the Beast off the top of the cage and sent it tumbling to the floor with a sick crunch. Then it tore through the other side of the cage, tearing fence and toppling struts. Residents scurried out of the way as it all began to tumble down.

Including the part Ness was standing on.

She rode the cage wall down, heart rising into her throat. She jumped at the last moment, hit one of the tables and skipped like a stone, rolling to the floor wrapped in the tablecloth.

"Bury me now," she groaned, then sat up and threw the premature shroud off.

The residents had retreated to the ballroom's far corners and the guards were approaching, rifles drawn. The lighting rig sparked and smoked, dangling from the last of its moorings. Under the wreckage of the collapsed cage, the Beast twitched.

Then it pushed itself up, shrugging off the tangle of chicken wire like it was nothing heavier than the linen Ness had been covered with. It staggered, head lolling. Its hateful eyes locked on Ness as she clambered to her feet and it launched into another charge.

"Ness!"

She turned at Faith's voice. The girl had broken from the safety of the room's outer reaches, carrying an old fire axe in her dainty hands. She tossed it and it clattered to the floor at Ness's feet. She kicked it into her grasp.

The Beast swung for where she'd been standing. She'd already dropped, chopping low, and took its leg off at the knee. It hopped, overbalancing, and dropping onto its hands. Before it could swipe at her, she lifted the axe and brought it down on the Reaper's bulging neck. She stamped on the side of its head, freeing the blade, and swung again.

And again and again and again.

And again.

The Beast hadn't moved in a few minutes by the time she stopped. She'd just been butchering it. Chopping dead meat. Its blood speckled her cheeks like pepper freckles and stuck her boots to the floor. Her breath came hard, ragged, seething with pain and anger, resentment and fear.

The only good Reaper...

"You wanted a fight!" she snarled, throwing down the axe in the pervading silence. "You got a fucking fight!"

The moment stretched. Then someone began to applaud. Lailah, striding forward to stand at Faith's shoulder, eyes flashing emerald and lips curled in a satisfied smirk. Her children were on her heels, joining in the congratulations like a host of grinning marionettes, copying her every move. Slowly, her residents followed suit. It was the most polite round of applause she'd ever received for murdering something.

Under the sound of her curdled victory, Ness hissed to Lailah, "Remember the deal."

The other woman just nodded. Ness stalked back to her dressing room, and tried not to see the quiet horror in Faith's eyes.

CHAPTER SEVEN
TRYING TIMES

She'd changed out of her costume and sponged herself off with water from the sink when Lailah swayed into the room. She couldn't have said what she expected, but she definitely *didn't* expect the other woman to drape around her shoulders and kiss her neck.

God help her, she could have fallen into that moment as it stretched into eternity. After all, they were alone now, weren't they? Privacy held promises.

Instead, she summoned the strength to push her off.

"What the fuck are you doing?" she snapped.

"Congratulating you on your hard-fought victory," Lailah said, not even remotely offended at her reaction. "I could feel their envy as you fought. Your skill, your power, your fearlessness. They watched as you dismantled that creature and wished they could do the same. They saw the defiance and the passion in your eyes and they *longed* to have that fire. The weak will always envy the strong."

Ness scoffed. She stared at the bruised and battered shape in the full-length mirror, clad only in its underwear. Old scars and ill-fitting skin. She'd ridden herself like a stolen car all her life and it showed. How could anyone be envious of her?

She pulled on her old shirt—she wanted nothing from Lailah, not even a new outfit—and reached for her pants. The other woman watched, eyes fierce.

"I almost want to keep you, but...as I said, I always honor my bargains."

"Great."

She snatched the truck keys out of Lailah's grasp when she presented them, and shrugged into her battered, old jacket.

"Are you sure you won't stay? We have everything you could ever wish for here. Safety from the Big Seven, running water, good food, drink, fine clothing. Company. I haven't had a woman to share myself with in quite some time. I promise I won't leave you to languish in the lower levels with the other servants. You could live in the penthouse with my family. You and Faith both. She would have so many brothers and sisters to play with and learn from."

Ness shook her head. No matter how tempting it might have been to find a safe place for Faith, leaving her with Lailah and her nightmare children was a bad idea. As for herself, this wasn't where she belonged. She needed to be out there, trying to make a difference.

The debt needed paying.

"A tricky Reaper's still a Reaper," she grunted.

Lailah laughed. "Is that what you think I am, dear?"

"Going to pretend you're not?"

"I am older than the Reaping. Older than the cities you scavenge from, and the country that was founded on this continent. I am older than civilization, older than Empires, older than tribes. I walked this earth before your kind began its first harvests, and long before you smothered it with concrete. Did you ever wonder why my symbol is an eye?"

"Can't say as I did."

"They called us Watchers. We were supposed to observe, gauge the balance of the human race. But we knew, when your kind raised its monuments on the backs of dead slaves, when they bent their knees to murderers and savages, when they hailed the great instead of the good, when they chose cruelty, we knew what the future would hold. Humans brought about the Reaping. Heaven is closed and Hell has arrived, and it is your fault. I am simply...profiting from it."

"Good for you," Ness spat, trying to ignore the way Lailah's tirade made her skin prickle. "Where's my fucking truck?"

Lailah chuckled. She cupped Ness's cheek, and just for a moment, Ness felt her lips tingling in anticipation. Then Lailah cut her with her fingernail.

Ness recoiled, fist clenching. Lailah was already withdrawing, turning to leave the room.

"Goodbye, Vanessa," she said, as the door fell closed behind her. "I hope I will see you again."

Ness wiped the blood off her cheek with her sleeve. "Not if I see you first."

...

"What is the emptiness that grows before the Reaper comes? What is the creeping void that appears within a person when they succumb to wickedness? It is the space where the love of God once was. Where love *once was. People who turn their back on each other, on the Struggle, become hollow within. And what is hollow in this world will be filled with darkness. Reject the Struggle, and invite the Reaper."*

They drove in silence until they were back on the highway. Faith, like Ness, had rejected all of Lailah's charity and changed into the outfit she'd taken from the mall. She clutched at Chip's Circle until her little fingers blanched.

Their hosts had filled the truck's tank while they were indisposed, but Ness considered that payment for services rendered.

She steered and stared at the black blood worn into the grooves on her hands. She hadn't been able to scrub it all off, but blood was like that. It didn't wash away so easy.

"Sorry you had to see that," she muttered.

"You don't need to apologize," Faith said, voice hoarse. Ness wondered if she'd been crying.

"No. I do. The place you grew up, it was nice. Not like that hotel was; I mean *really* nice. I thought I was doing the right thing, bringing you to Archangel, but... Maybe I was wrong. This world can be..."

"I'm not an idiot," the girl whispered. "I know what kind of world I'm living in. I know what people have to do to survive. But there's a difference between what you do and what Lailah's doing."

"Maybe."

"Some of those people at the hotel were slaves. They had collars on. They belonged to the residents. That's what Lailah does. She lets them stay with her, where it's safe, then she gets them what they want. *Whatever* they want. A trophy, a servant, a lover, a child..."

"We could go back," Ness said, "break them out."

"Where would they go? Their families and their settlements are the ones who sold them. The hotel's their home now." Faith sighed and sank low in her seat. "At least they're safe from the Big Seven and the Reapers."

Ness stared at the broken asphalt ahead, wrestling with all the platitudes that weren't going to make this right. Wasn't there something she could say? Just the right thing to make this all better? Wasn't that how it worked?

"That's how the world works, isn't it?" Faith asked. "Good people die. Evil people live together in luxury. They have slaves. And we're all just crops for the Reapers. God isn't here and the Big Seven won't stop until we're all dead. Why are we even going to Archangel? It's like Lailah said: Heaven is closed."

Ness stamped on the brake. The truck screeched to a halt. She reached over and took Faith's shoulder in one of those blood-stained hands.

"Listen to me, kid. I don't give a fuck about Lailah or Watchers or Heaven or the Big Seven. I give a fuck about you. About people like you. The *good* people. The ones who don't deserve any of this. Now, I'm taking you to Archangel because there's something special about you. Maybe someone there will know what's going on with you and how you can help, but if not, it doesn't matter. We'll keep going, right? You and me. We'll do what we can. Deal?"

Maybe there *was* blood on her hands. There always would be, because she'd never stop fighting to keep people like Faith safe. A soft smile bloomed on the girl's lips and Ness put the truck back in gear.

"I think I get it. Why the folks in your town never told you what it's like out here. They were trying to keep you safe. You were a ray of light to them, and that's worth trying to shield. They didn't see this coming, but...I'm here for you, like they were. Whatever happens, I'll protect you."

"You can't protect me from everything."

"I can try."

Faith nodded, hesitant. Her voice was a whisper when she said, "Thank you."

CHAPTER EIGHT
THE BEST IS YET TO COME

"And what is your interest in dear Vanessa?" Lailah asked, as one of her suitors filled her glass.

The man—for though a Reaper drove him, he was still very much a man—glared at her. He had declined every offering she had made, because he desired only one thing.

But what desire! A burning, desperate thing. A savage, unrelenting thing. A focused and fatal *need*. It took her breath away to feel it radiating from him.

"That is none of your concern," he said, and Lailah watched the way his fingers toyed with the wedding band on his left hand.

She smiled. "I must admit, I am...envious of your desire for her. She is very fortunate to be the focus of such ardent attention, though I'm sure she doesn't realize it."

He didn't answer. He was still waiting for the answer to his original question.

Where is she?

"I could never stand in the way of true love," Lailah conceded. "I can tell you exactly where to go, but I have a condition. The girl *must* reach Archangel. It is of the utmost importance. Do I make myself clear?"

The man nodded. He rose from his seat, a towering figure, all dark hair and angular features and blazing red eyes. Perhaps handsome once, in a stern way. Now, just frightening.

Vanessa was a lucky girl indeed.

"I will not interfere," he said. "She is the only thing that concerns me."

"In that case..." Lailah set her glass aside and smiled. "...it would be my pleasure to assist you."

...

"You think you know the rules, Faithful? Well, let me tell you something. Folks before the Reaping thought they knew the rules too. They thought they had it all figured—science, mathematics, physics, chemistry. They were slaves to their immutable quantum rules. Everything that is will always be. But those laws were not God's laws. They were observations of his world and his works, and they failed to appreciate that everything can change in a heartbeat. Like how a creature big as a city can just appear on an ordinary, August day, or how demons can whisper to us all, demanding the keys to the doors we use to keep them out. Never forget, Faithful. The Struggle has rules only so long as God says it does. Everything can change."

The truck didn't appreciate Ness's handbrake turn. It screamed as it swung out, and Faith clung to her seatbelt, expression panic-stricken. The next moment, they were roaring back the way they'd come.

"What's happening?" the girl asked.

"You see that cloud over there?" Ness asked, aiming a finger through the passenger-side window. "That's Archangel."

She watched Faith's features twisting with confusion and tried not to smile. Cute.

"It's moving!" she gasped. "You mean, the whole settlement *moves*?"

"Kind of has to," Ness said, with a shrug. "It's not like Lailah's enclave. If one of the Big Seven comes along, they have to get out of the way quick. That's why we need to listen to the radio, so we know where to find it."

Faith screwed up her face, trying to make sense of what she was seeing. "But that's not a road, is it?"

"Not exactly."

"Stop teasing me!"

Ness laughed and turned them onto the road that would intersect with Archangel. They'd stop soon. Then Faith would be able to see for herself what kind of place Archangel was.

Until then, Ness just wanted to see the wonder in her eyes, and enjoy the last leg of their long road.

She tried to ignore the nagging sense that something was going to go horribly wrong.

...

It had started out as a few box cars clustered in an old rail yard. Oil drum fires and flop mattresses, but it was shelter. It was home. Then the engineers had shown up, started tinkering with an old diesel locomotive. Pretty soon, the dream had become a reality.

They were living aboard a working train.

They'd added cars over the years, expanded, until they were a functioning town. They had merchants, an infirmary, a place of worship, even a radio station. They had law and order, and they had places for pilgrims to stay.

And, presumably, someone was in charge.

Ness parked the truck up outside the old freight station where Archangel eventually stopped. They weren't the first to arrive. Other vehicles were already there, ticking in the burning sun. This place had its dedicated satellites, vehicles that followed it everywhere like a swarm of steel flies.

She hadn't seen Archangel in years. Something was different about it. Might have been all the tall shapes in white jumpsuits standing around the platform, on the roof, in the dust around the tracks. Every single one wore black armor and—yeah, she wasn't mistaken—a sword strapped to their back.

"Don't see that every day," Ness muttered, as they stepped out.

The citizens were already rolling out their business on the platform, maintaining the cars and the tracks, dragging out the planters to catch the sun, praying thanks to God for this new slice of Heaven. The newcomers didn't join in. They kept their watch, like a platoon of monochrome statues. Ness started to itch.

Faith ambled behind her, clutching at the Circle around her neck pensively. Ness guessed nerves were starting to set in. She kept her pace leisurely, trying to tell herself it was for the girl's sake, that she just wanted her to have the chance to prepare properly.

She asked a couple of people who was in charge. The soldiers said nothing, wouldn't even look at her. Others pointed her to the car just behind the engine.

"You ready?" Ness asked.

Faith nodded and took her hand. "I guess."

"I'm right here with you, kid."

Most of the cars had their decorations—graffiti declarations of faith or murals of smiting angels and the rolling plains of a plentiful Heaven—but this one had been wrought from gold and silver like some kind of ancient burial casket. Its walls were carved with patterns that made Ness's head hurt when she tried to look at them, whorls and glyphs and spirals spinning into spirals.

She didn't think she'd ever seen anything like this in her life.

Faith clasped her hand tighter. They stepped up to the car. Ness lifted her fist to hammer on the door. Before she could, someone jumped down from above—Ness hadn't seen anyone on the roof—and stood in her way.

He was beautiful, hair thick and black and lustrous, skin burnished ochre. The blankness in his eyes was a void Ness thought she might fall into, and never hit the bottom. He wore the white suit and black armor of the newcomers suddenly infesting Archangel, but unlike the others he looked right at her. It was like someone taking a razor across her soul. His gaze settled on Faith.

She stared up at him, eyes wide. She looked terrified.

A smile formed on his lips. It looked alien on his pristine features, as much as the jewelry box car behind him. "Welcome, little sister," he said.

"And you are?" Ness asked.

"They have named me Elim. I would know your name also."

"It's Ness. And this is Faith."

"Yes, I know who she is," Elim said, still smiling. "The Father's wayward child, lost to us for fourteen years. Have you returned to embrace the Struggle, sister?"

He lowered himself to one knee so that he was on a level with Faith. Ness felt something tug at her sleeve and realized Faith had stepped behind her.

"Her home was wiped out by one of the Big Seven," Ness said. "She was the only one who survived. I thought...maybe someone here would know why, or they could find out."

"Then the transgressors have been punished for their crime. That is good to know. Thank you for these tidings, stranger. The Father will wish you to be rewarded. Every nephilim is precious to him and he only wished he could have come for her sooner."

"Wait, their *crime*?"

"They stole away one of his children while she was still in the womb, after her mother had been blessed with the duty of bearing her and bringing her into the world. If they had remained, her mother could have perished in the Father's purifying light. He would have shed a precious tear for her. Instead, she spurned his gift and fled to die in exile, carrying his beloved child with him. It was shameful."

Ness stared at him, trying to figure if she was reading this right. Elim's father—with a capital F, no less—had chosen Faith's mother to bear his child. Her dying in childbirth had all been part of the plan, it seemed. Only she'd gone on the run, rather than leave her little girl in the hands of whatever he was.

And now Ness had brought her back.

"Fuck me..."

"Rejoice, stranger!" Elim said. It sounded like an order. "Our sister is back with us, ready to take on her duty as part of the Struggle. We must begin her training straight away, to make up for lost time. She will take up arms against the Reapers, and when our numbers are great enough, when the Father commands the time is right, we will reveal ourselves to the world in all our glory. She will fight with us against the Sins and the other Watchers. This world will be ours."

"Watchers? You mean, like Lailah?"

Elim's expression twisted into vicious hate. Honestly, it looked more at home on his face than the smile. "Have you met the snake? That beast is not to be trusted, nor are the creatures she calls her children. What did you agree to in order to earn your freedom?"

"I didn't agree to shit. I killed a Reaper for her entertainment and that's it. She doesn't have anything on me."

Elim studied her. She felt seen. "Fine. Then you may leave."

"No!" Faith cried, and seized Ness's wrist. "I want her to stay. Don't make her go. Please!"

"Yeah, I'm not going anywhere," Ness agreed.

She wouldn't leave Faith with these psychopaths. They'd basically admitted to killing her mom—the least of their crimes—and now they wanted to turn the girl into a soldier against monsters the size of cities. The Father might have considered his kids precious, but that didn't mean he wouldn't use them up to own the world.

First chance she got, she was taking Faith back on the road.

Elim's expression was inscrutable, features slack and eyes hollow, just like before. Then the smile returned and Ness tamped down a shudder. "Of course you may stay. Any friend of our sister is a friend of ours. But I wish to introduce her to her other siblings, so I ask that you give us time. Perhaps go to worship with the other humans."

"I'm not really the worshipping kind," Ness said, and then remembered who she was talking to.

"No?" the nephilim asked, cocking his head. "Is it not our due? Will we not save you from those that prey upon you? The Father will not be pleased."

"Maybe he could come out of his box and rap with me a while. I might see his point of view."

Elim gave a soft laugh. "The Father does not deign to take human form. We are his voice, just as we are his hands. But, if you are going to stay here, perhaps you should think carefully about how you conduct yourself."

"Yeah, I'll do that," Ness muttered. And, *if* she'd had any intention of staying, maybe she would have. "Got an errand to run anyway, but I'll be back later."

"You promise?" Faith asked, eyes wet.

"Pinky swear and all that shit."

Ness ruffled her hair, squeezed her shoulder like she'd done back at the mall.

If anything happens, scream bloody murder.

She just needed the kid to be strong for an hour or two. Then they'd be out of there like a fucking bullet.

Nephilim—those white-clad warriors—glided from their positions around the station and crowded Faith as Ness made her way further along the platform. This whole place made her itch, but she couldn't leave without the girl. The moment her 'siblings' left her alone for even a second, they'd be so gone.

She unfolded the letter from Harlon and Marie. She hadn't bothered to check the name on the envelope—felt too much like tempting fate, before they reached Archangel—but now she finally read it.

"Well, I'll be damned."

The folks she asked pointed her to a car with a crook painted on it. It felt strange to have come so far and find herself on the doorstep of the closest thing their ravaged country had to a celebrity, one of the only people who was famous outside their own settlement, like the folks on the billboards and in the battered, old magazines they used for fuel.

Idly, Ness wondered if there were any of those folks left. Had any of them survived the Reaping? Or had they clung to their falling kingdoms, because they couldn't see a place for themselves in the world after?

The car was off the station. Everyone else had set up shop in the old buildings or on the platform proper. No one lingered at Archangel's back end. Ness lifted her fist to knock.

A powerful arm curled around her throat. Another trapped her head. She tried to fight the choke, adrenaline surging. She smelled the ash, the desolation, of a Reaper.

A Reaper she knew.

"How are you here?" she snarled, as her vision started to blacken.

"Have you not realized yet, Vanessa?" he asked. "You cannot escape from me. No matter where you run, no matter where you hide, you still belong to me."

"I wasn't running," she growled. "I was chasing."

Atop the train cars and the platform roof, she saw the nephilim still on guard, standing at rigid attention. Watching. Uncaring.

Her existence dimmed to a singularity of straining muscle and clenched teeth and fingernails piercing skin and growing darkness.

And then, just darkness.

CHAPTER NINE
WHAT YOU KEEP ALIVE

"God's love. Is that what we feel, when we sing to high Heaven above? Do we feel him in the warmth of a loving heart? And what about when we're sitting at the graveside, weeping into our hands? What about when we watch the life we knew burn down around us? Can we feel his love then? We are all in God's heart, but his is a heart of thorns. And that, Faithful, is the true essence of the Struggle."

One hand switched off the radio. The other pulled the bag off her head. Ness blinked in the greasy light of a concrete garage. Fluorescent paint and junk totems, tools and tires. The only car was a battered, old Ford, the one she assumed she'd been kidnapped in. Not much in the way of luxury, but it got the job done. His taste hadn't much changed.

This place had belonged to a road crew once. Judging by the bloodstains, it didn't belong to them anymore.

The Reaper settled on a metal folding chair. He'd lashed her to a battered, old office chair with thick, plastic cable ties. He sighed. Dark hair and dark eyes, just like she remembered from a lifetime ago. About Faith's lifetime, come to think of it. Only she recalled something softer than this. All the gentleness had vanished, leaving only hard angles and a promise of violence. The red flicker in his eyes and the sharpness of his teeth removed all doubt.

"Hello, Vanessa."

"Fuck you!"

Her voice sounded thick in her own ears, hoarse from where he'd half-strangled her. He took a breath, like he was trying to steady himself. Then he grabbed her around the throat so tight she choked.

"I have been patient. I have given you the opportunity to come back to me. Time and again you have spurned me. My patience has now run out."

"Boohoo," she spat, as his hand slipped from her neck. "Do Reapers get lonely too?"

"We are bound by a promise, Vanessa. Nothing you do can absolve you of that." He held up a steel band, the double of the one around his own finger. "I am still your husband."

"No," she growled, "you aren't. You're a fucking demon wearing the face of someone I loved more than anything else in this piece of shit world. He died and then you crawled inside him like a parasite, but you're not him. You're nothing like him."

"I remember what he remembers. The love you shared. The way your skin felt on his. The shape of your body in his hands. The taste of you on his tongue."

"Shut up!" Rage boiled up inside her, chasing away the cold fear stirring below her guts. "You think I give a fuck about your stolen memories? You're just a Reaper. Do you know how many of you I've killed?"

"Of course. I've been watching you, Vanessa. Following you. You know this. And it has all been leading to this moment."

He grabbed her left wrist, pinned it to the arm of her chair. He lifted the ring she'd worn once, years ago, and reached for her third finger. She curled it tight into a fist—so often her response—but he pried it free. She held it from him with every ounce of strength, hissing and spitting through clenched teeth.

The snap when it broke shot up her arm and hit her in the chest. She bit down on a scream.

He tried to force the ring back into its place, but her finger had already swollen too thick with bruising to accommodate it. Through the pain, Ness started laughing.

He seized her under her chin. She felt the bite of cold steel against her carotid, just under her left ear.

"There is another option," he told her. "Perhaps I should simply follow the course of expediency, empty you as a vessel for another like myself. A Reaper might choose to honor the promise that you have willfully forgotten."

All of Ness's bitter laugher, all of her anger, curdled with the sudden image of this thing wearing her husband's face sucking her soul out through her mouth, stripping her of everything that made her who she was, leaving her a sack of meat ready to be joyridden like a stolen truck by something that couldn't tell right from wrong, or love from obsession.

"You really think that'd work?" she asked, eyes narrowing dangerously. "You really think it'd give a fuck about you?"

He stepped away, stuck the knife point-down in a workbench with half an engine resting on it. He tapped the tools hanging from the racks—hooks and picks, wire strippers, heat guns and torque wrenches.

"I am sure I could exact some…influence over it, given time."

"Going to torture my dead body into loving you? Sounds like a plan."

"You have left me little choice, Vanessa."

Ness rolled her eyes. "I don't have time for this. I made a promise."

"To the girl?" He stepped closer, crimson eyes mocking. "Are you going to save her from her brothers and sisters?"

"Or die trying."

"I will not allow it."

"You don't get to decide that anymore!"

He lunged for her, and Ness couldn't tell if he was finally coming for her soul. She wondered what it would taste like as he dragged it over her tongue. Would she even be able to taste? Or would she already be dead?

She smashed her forehead into his chin and lurched back. Her chair toppled and the ties on her ankles burst from the impact. She kicked up as he tried to hold her down and caught him in the throat, sending him slamming back into the workbench. She rolled out of the chair, wrists still bound to it, and planted her feet. He grabbed the knife, but she rammed into him, pinning him to the wall with the wheels of her seat.

He slashed at her, expression livid, eyes murderous. She twisted and he hacked the cable tie off her left wrist. Pain lanced up her arm and blood streamed from where he'd cut the edge of her hand. She grabbed a panel beater off the wall and smashed him in the temple with it. Blood sprayed the concrete.

"You're not him!" she snarled, striking again, again, again. "You're a Reaper! You're just a *fucking Reaper!*"

And the only good Reaper...

His hand snapped out, seizing her by a fistful of hair. He slammed her against the Ford's driver door. Her head punched the glass out of the window. Blood ran out of her hairline, into her eyes. Literally seeing red. He swung a wrench at her and she blocked on reflex. She felt her radius shatter and the pain washed over, threatening to drag her under.

She cracked an uppercut off his jaw. He rocked back, gave her enough space to snatch a screwdriver from the board of tools. She stabbed for his heart. He caught her wrists, even as she kicked his feet out from under him. They went to the floor, her on top.

They fought, deadlocked, the point of the screwdriver poised over his heart. He glared up at her, but the mess she'd made of his face revealed only the Reaper that lurked behind it. The eyes, the teeth, the fury—none of it belonged to anything human.

"You're not him," she choked out, and drove the metal spike down between his ribs.

He kept struggling, kept trying to push her off, but she held the screwdriver in place. She twisted it, tearing him inside, until the blood soaked through his shirt and between her fingers and it would never wash off.

The fight went out of him all at once. The light and the rage died in his eyes. Drops of water spattered on his cheeks, cutting clear trails through the blood. Ness sat back and scrubbed her eyes with her sleeve.

"Fuck..."

She felt so tired, she could have lay down right there and slept forever, but she forced her head up. She'd made a promise.

She spotted the stack of jerry cans in the corner of the garage, the pile of oily rags, the heat gun on the wall.

She hadn't owed the Reaper shit.

But she owed the man he'd once been a cremation. And a final farewell.

CHAPTER TEN
MY SACRIFICE

Cut, bruised, broken and reeking of smoke, all of which she could deal with later, Ness floored the old Ford all the way to Archangel. The plume of dust she left behind was nothing compared to what she saw on the horizon.

The beasts had to be at least a mile wide, both of them, one a slithering, aqueous glob with a surplus of eyes and grasping tentacles, the other a lumbering quadruped made of nothing but claws and tooth-filled mouths, churning the dirt into its many throats with each step. They were moving slow but with unerring purpose, straight towards the train station and all the people that called that string of cars home.

And Faith. They were heading towards Faith.

The Big Seven never appeared so close together, but these two were on a collision course.

The news got worse when she tuned in to the Sin Chaser frequency. Frantic reports of Sins rising from the ocean or crawling down from the mountains, changing their course like nothing anyone had ever seen before, and their bearings were all taking them to the same place, like a noose tightening.

They were *all* heading to Archangel.

She hammered the wheel and begged the piece of junk she was driving to go faster. If she didn't get there soon, she'd miss the train, assuming the people of Archangel hadn't already realized they were fucked. No matter which track they took, no matter which direction they went, eventually they'd run too close to one of the Seven and they'd crash and burn. Maybe they'd murder each other on the tracks in the grip of wrath, or they'd rip chunks off themselves trying to fill bellies turned empty by the most over-powering gluttony. One way or another, the sin would kill them all.

Somehow, she arrived with time to spare. The people of Archangel were assembled on the platform. If they'd noticed the Seven bearing down on them, they weren't showing it. Instead, nephilim and humans faced off, something small caught between them.

"Oh shit…"

She fought her way up and pushed through the crowd. Worst fears confirmed. Faith was there, at the heart of it all.

"They're almost here," a woman told Elim. She had one side of her head buzzed to skin, the other combed over in a turquoise flick. She wore a leather jacket and a Circle around her neck, and Ness thought maybe if more Faithful looked like her she'd have considered religion sooner. "Two of them, with more on the way."

"Yes," Elim said grimly. "It would appear so."

"But this is what you've been training for, right?" the woman asked. "What you've been gathering weapons and armor for? What you've been building your forces for? That's why you came here. To protect us. Forty years, nothing, then you just show up and take control? It had to be for a reason."

"It is not our decision."

"We don't stand a chance against those things! People *died* so you could be born. Good people. Your father sacrificed those women to bring you into this world to fight the Sins. Right?"

Elim didn't respond to that. He was holding a crying Faith by her wrist so tight he'd bruised her. He snatched the Circle from around her neck and scrutinized it. It glittered in the light, all different colors. It hadn't done that when Chip had worn it.

"This is the beacon." He shook her, and most of the Faithful looked away in disgust. "You have allowed yourself to become tainted. You have become an agent of our enemies. I am disappointed in you, sister."

"Leave the kid alone!" Ness yelled, elbowing her way to the front row.

"You came back," Faith breathed, eyes lighting up, before the pain came back.

"Put her down. Now!"

"She allies with our hated foes and brings death to our doorsteps, and you would have me show mercy?" Elim boomed.

"Isn't that what angels do?"

"This...totem," he spat, "is a lure, bringing the Sins to our Father. Lailah has put her touch upon it. This was her intention all along. To use the Father's own child to destroy us. She knew we would accept her among us, and that we would only realize once it was already too late."

"But you're immune, right? Just like she is."

"Immune to the sin. But not to the destruction they will rain down once they reach here. You have seen these creatures only as forces of nature, inexorably moving across the surface of the Earth, but they will reveal their true purpose in battle against us and against the Father. There is only one course of action remaining."

In unison, the nephilim unfurled their wings. They burst from their backs in blooms of white light, feathers pristine, with wingspans that could have encompassed half a dozen people. Everyone stared, speechless. Even Ness.

For a moment, hope bloomed in her chest. They could take the icon, corrupted by Lailah, away and save every person in Archangel. Just as they had always been, every life on that platform was in their hands.

Elim dropped the Circle on the ground at Faith's feet.

"The Father has spoken," he told them. "The time is not right."

He soared skywards. The other nephilim followed.

In their wake, the golden carriage began to glow, dull red at first, rising to a blinding white. The heat and light beat the humans back like the sting of a roaring fire. Then the box erupted, and something radiant and inhuman, towering and impossible, rose to its feet in the ruins. It was vaguely humanoid, but sexless and golden-skinned. Ness didn't even come up to its knees.

It didn't look down at the ants around its feet. Instead, it loosed immense, golden wings from its back and rose into the atmosphere, following its fleeing children.

Leaving the humans to die.

What were a few more sacrifices for the glory of the Father?

In the silence that followed, the only sound was the seismic rumble of the approaching Sins. And Ness's angry breathing.

"You piece of shit," she muttered, and then the rage took over. "You absolute son of a bitch! Get the fuck back down here! Don't you run away from this! I'll find you, asshole! You hear me!"

She grabbed an empty bottle in her good hand and hurled it into the air. It fell well short of the diminishing flock that was their last hope. She stared after them—the Father, Elim, all of them—seething, then realized that everyone was staring at her.

She saw the dejection in their eyes. The defeat. They were all dead and they knew it. Worse, they knew their savior—the angel in their midst, whom they'd worshipped as a god—had turned his back on them.

Well, fuck him too.

"Stay here," Ness ordered, and snatched the icon from Faith's feet.

She jumped from the platform, the eyes of the Faithful following her, and ran for the truck they'd driven all the way from Sanctuary. She dragged herself behind the wheel and fumbled the key into the ignition, just as Faith jumped in beside her.

"Kid, get out!"

"We don't have time for this, Ness. Please, just go."

She wanted to put her foot down, wanted to refuse, but there were too many lives at stake. She threw the truck into reverse and wheeled around in the lot outside the station, steering one-handed, scattering dirt from a dozen tire tracks left by others peeling out at the first sign of danger.

"I'm immune, remember?" Faith was saying, as they bounced back onto the highway. "If the worst happens, I can keep driving. I can try to lead them away."

"I don't know what's going to happen if we get too close. I might claw my own eyes out and eat them."

"I won't let that happen."

Ness flicked a look at Faith in the rear-view, saw the steel in her eyes.

"Why'd you do it, kid? Why'd you agree to work for Lailah?"

"She said she'd kill you if I didn't," Faith whispered.

"So much for always honoring her agreements. Bitch."

"I didn't know, Ness. She just wanted me to go to Archangel. That was all she said. I figured it wasn't a problem, since we were going there anyway. If I'd known, I wouldn't have-"

"I know, kid. I know."

Faith's eyes fell to the corrupted Circle Ness had tossed in the ashtray. "I knew it belonged to your friend. I begged her to give it back to me. I should have figured it out, the way she smiled…"

"Don't beat yourself up. She's a tricky fucking Reaper, no matter what she says."

Ness flicked a look in the rear-view. The Sins had changed bearing quicker than she'd ever seen before. It was hard to tell which end was their front, but she was pretty sure they were both pointing in their direction. Moving away from Archangel.

"Don't know if I'll have the chance to say this later, so listen up. There are people in this world who're only in it to get what they think they deserve. People like Elim and his fucking murder-daddy, people like Lailah and her enclave. Doesn't matter if you're human or a Reaper or an angel, being a piece of shit is universal. It's what you *do* that decides if you're one of the good ones. Sin Chasers, we're not angels and we don't have even half the shit nephilim do, but we get by. And the only way we do that is by helping each other, working together, doing right every chance we get. You could be one of the good ones, kid. Better than your daddy, because he made one big mistake when he looked at this world. He assumed it was all about him."

"I'm not going to be like him, Ness. I'm not going to be like any of them."

"I know."

She reached over and squeezed Faith's shoulder.

The horizon, previously clear, suddenly clouded with something rising in the distance. A flat, grey snout and a long, reptilian body with immense, trunk-like legs.

Leviathan.

"No way."

"Is there…a way around?"

Ness shook her head. "The other two are on our ass. Won't stand a chance. And, contrary to the image I give off, I'd rather die peacefully in my sleep."

"I don't want you to die at all."

"You're sweet."

They were running out of road. Pretty soon, they'd be within Leviathan's sphere of influence. Already, she could feel the pull of sloth, dragging her into a deep, warm darkness. Her head nodded forward and she had to fight to keep her eyes open.

Were they far enough away yet? Had the folks in Archangel managed to get the train moving, as far from the closing circle as they could? What would the Sins do once they'd reached that point and found no angel to destroy?

"Whatever happens, you get as far away from this fucking thing as possible," Ness grunted, lifting up the icon. Her arm felt impossibly heavy and her voice sounded slurred in her ears. The truck shook as it veered onto the verge and she corrected the wheel sharply.

Not long now...

Then Faith snatched the Circle from her hand. She snagged the chain in her numb fingers, caught in a tug of war.

"Kid..." she warned.

"Ness, this is my fault. Let me fix it. Please."

"Kid, don't."

"I can save you. I can save everyone. I told you, I'm not going to be like them, but I'm still a nephilim. I know what to do. Please, just trust me."

Ness opened her mouth to ask just what the hell she thought she was doing, and then Faith's jacket bulged out at the shoulders. She shrugged it off with a pained gasp, and Ness watched magnificent, white wings tearing out of her tee.

They filled the truck cab, glorious and blood-stained. Faith looked back at her, features tight with pain and regret. Ness felt a sick feeling welling up in her guts that she was too tired to properly reckon with.

"I'll take them far away," Faith whispered, finally wresting the Circle from Ness's failing grip. "To the middle of the ocean. The bottom of the sea. Maybe no one will ever see them again. I could save the world. That'd be good, right? That'd make you proud of me?"

"Faith..."

"I want to be one of the good ones. Like you."

She shot out of the window, wings billowing, lofting her into the dismal sky above. She flapped awkwardly, like a fledgling learning to fly. Then, with one powerful beat of her wings, she soared, just like her siblings had.

It was the last thing Ness saw before the truck flipped.

CHAPTER ELEVEN
ONE STEP BEHIND

Two truck crashes in one week. Yeah, when she came around, she felt it. Every bruised bone, every friction rash on her skin, every bloody laceration.

This time, she wasn't still in the truck. She was in some kind of infirmary, white sheets boil-washed to within an inch of their lives and plastic sheets dangling, the sound of beeping medical devices and the acrid tang of disinfectant. They'd strapped a brace around her busted forearm and she felt the tight pull of stitches in her hairline.

A woman sat by the bed, the one from the platform who'd confronted Elim. Ness felt a pulse of immediate kinship.

She was clutching a familiar, folded letter in her hands.

"Anita Shepherd?" Ness asked, voice scratchy from disuse.

Only daughter of Harlon and Marie Shepherd. Also known as *the* Shepherd.

"Looks like I owe you one," the Shepherd said. "I mean, apart from saving me, my settlement and everyone in it."

"It wasn't me. It was Faith."

"The prodigal daughter. Yeah, we saw from the station. Some of the others found you, after the dust had settled. They brought you in, patched you up. I thought I should come pay my respects, since you're the reason we're all still breathing."

"I just did-"

"-what an angel and a horde of nephilim feared to do. Seriously, modesty's not a sin, but maybe it should be."

"Someone did the same for me once. I'm just trying to balance the scales."

Except now, someone else had done it for her. How was she ever going to tip this back in the other direction?

"Well, good news for you, looks like you get to take another shot at it. Any idea what you'll do with your new lease of life?"

"I was a Sin Chaser," Ness said, pushing herself up and wriggling to the edge of the bed. "Still am."

"That right? Which car?"

"Forty-five."

The Shepherd nodded. "With Chip, right?" She cracked a smile at the surprise on Ness's face. "I remember them all. All the Chasers, all the places that go dark. Someone has to. It's all part of the Struggle."

"You really believe in all that?"

"The Struggle is real."

"Yeah, Elim thought so too."

"Elim and his family were struggling for themselves," the Shepherd said. "That's not the Struggle I know. This was never about him and his father. Archangel was Archangel before they showed up, and it will be now that they're gone. We all embrace the Struggle. So do you. Call it what you like, call it 'balancing the scales' if it suits, it's all the same. You do the right thing, no matter what. And you yield to the truth that it's not about the destination; it's about the path, and the people you help along the way."

Ness chuckled. "Good spin. You'll make a Faithful out of me yet."

"Each to their own, Forty-Five. I ain't looking for converts. Just trying to give some good advice."

Ness nodded and pushed herself up. She'd never really been the type to take good advice. She pulled on pants, grabbed her jacket and liberated herself from the gown they'd dressed her in. The Shepherd didn't try to stop her. When Ness reached the door, she tossed her a set of keys.

"To replace the one you totaled, saving our asses."

Ness offered her a salute, and stepped out onto the platform. The infirmary was in a train car too, with a big, red cross painted on the side.

She walked to the lot out back of the station. Folks nodded as she passed. Not the grudging respect for the migratory Sin Chaser that she was used to. Real respect, both for what she'd done and what she'd lost.

She found the truck—a Hilux, same model as the one Chip had driven—versatile and dependable. She slid behind the wheel and sat, staring down the highway, to the last place she'd seen Faith.

Then she cranked the engine and adjusted the radio. Wherever the Sins were going, that was where she'd find her girl.

Maybe she was still a Sin Chaser, but she was chasing something more important now.

Faith.

"Carry on, Faithful. Carry on, my people. Whether you embrace the Struggle or not, so long as you fight for the right, you may find Heaven waiting at the end of your road. So carry on. This world can be cruel, but it can be kinder than you know."

THE END.

Simone Oldman Green (they/them) is a genre-fluid writer and editor living in the Kingdom of Fife with husband, John. Author of over 70 published works with imprints including Dragon Soul Press, Black Hare Press and Eerie River Publishing. They also won 3rd Place in the British Fantasy Society's Short Story Contest 2018. Writer, vegan, martial artist, gamer, occasionally a terrible person (but only to fictional people). They keep a holiday home at the end of the world, because it's a nice place to visit, but you wouldn't want to live there.

More from Eerie River

Eerie River Publishing, is a small independant publishing house that is devoted to releasing quality dark fiction books and anthologies.

Stay up to date with all our new releases and upcoming giveaways, by following us on Facebook, Twitter, Instagram and YouTube. Sign up for our monthly newsletter and receive a free ebook Darkness Reclaimed, as our thank you gift.

https://mailchi.mp/71e45b6d5880/welcomebook

Interested in becoming a Patreon member?
Patreon membership gives you exclusive sneak peeks at upcoming books, early chapter releases, covers art as well as free ebooks and discounts on paperbacks.

https://www.patreon.com/EerieRiverPub

**ALSO AVAILABLE FROM
EERIE RIVER PUBLISHING**

NOVELS & NOVELLA'S
Sentinel
In Solitude's Shadow
Dead Man Walking
The Devil Walks in Blood
Storming Area 51

ANTHOLOGIES
Don't Look: 12 Stories of Bite Sized Horror
It Calls From The Forest: Volume I
It Calls From The Forest: Volume II
It Calls From The Sky
It Calls From The Sea
Darkness Reclaimed
Midnight Shadow: Volume I
With Blood and Ash
With Bone and Iron
Forgotten Ones: Drabbles of Myth and Legend
Dark Magic: Dark Fantasy Drabbles

COMING SOON
It Calls From the Doors
It Calls From the Veil
The Void
A Sword Named Sorrow
Miracle Growth
Blood Hex
Last Stop on 13

www.EerieRiverPublishing.com

SENTINEL
DREW STARLING

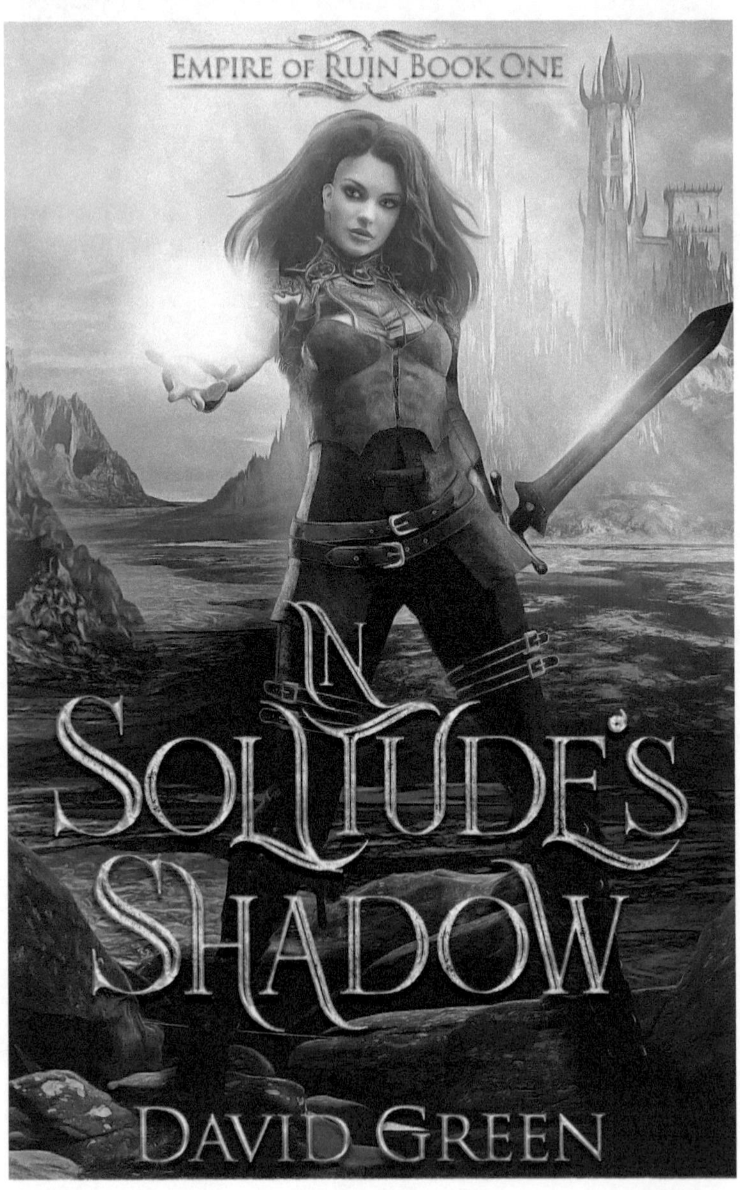

EMPIRE OF RUIN BOOK ONE
IN SOLITUDE'S SHADOW
DAVID GREEN

AN EERIE RIVER PUBLISHING ANTHOLOGY
IT CALLS FROM
THE DOORS
EDITED BY LYNDSEY SMITH & M. RIVER

AN EERIE RIVER PUBLISHING ANTHOLOGY
IT CALLS
FROM
THE SEA
AN EERIE RIVER PUBLISHING ANTHOLOGY